TRUCK DANCE

TRUCK DANCE

A NOVEL BY **OLIVE HERSHEY**

HARPER & ROW, PUBLISHERS, New York

1817

Cambridge, Philadelphia, San Francisco

London, Mexico City, São Paulo, Singapore, Sydney

FIRST EDITION

Designed by Ruth Bornschlegel

Library of Congress Cataloging-in-Publication Data

Hershey, Olive.
  Truck dance.

  I. Title.
PS3558.E768T78   1989   813'.54   87-46146
ISBN 0-06-015937-5

---

89 90 91 92 93 AC/HC 10 9 8 7 6 5 4 3 2 1

To the last cowboys

I wish to thank the MacDowell Colony and the Edward Albee foundation for their support while I was writing this book. Also the writing faculty of the Creative Writing Program at the University of Houston. Many generous individuals answered my written queries and telephone calls. They cannot be named here, but I am indebted to them all—truck drivers, mechanics, Border Patrol and INS officers, Mardi Gras captains, Zydeco fiddlers, folklorists and parade riders. Without the help of a young lady trucker who gave permission for me to ride with her for four days, I should never have gotten any part of what it feels like to drive a truck, the loneliness and speed, the drudgery and the freedom.

PART ONE

1

WILMA DIDN'T FIND OUT Vernon had taken the money until the first time she asked him to put his combines down on a note for a truck.

"It's a filthy crowd, those truckers," he said, "no place for a woman."

"It's better than fixing fries," she said. For eight weeks she'd been working at a truck stop and reading the ads in *Trucker's News*.

He moved a couple of inches closer to her on the porch swing and patted her shoulder. When he touched her she got up fast and stood facing him, a tall woman, robust, with heavy reddish hair. Without her weight the ends of the swing fishtailed crazily, and the chains clanked.

She took him with her to the bank to draw out her part of their savings, $4,500, all she had left of the money she'd made at the hunting and fishing club before they were married. On the way into town he sat next to the open window of her Chevy talking fast and waving his hands as if trying to keep flies out of his face.

"It makes me feel lowdown, sugar, your not having more faith in me than that." He'd get a job, he told her again, take care of her like he always had. She gazed steadily at his face, still boyish at fifty.

"You might have a little faith in *me*," was all she said. It was three months since they'd lost their land. They were barely getting by on Wilma's salary, Vernon spending the days moving aging parts from one tractor to another.

When the teller checked the balance and told her there was only $800 left, she swayed a little on the blue-and-gold fleur-de-lis carpet, trying to listen while Vernon told her he'd used the money to buy a crawfish farm.

"It's over in Lissie," he said. "I got a flat-bottomed skiff and a motor thrown in. You got to have a boat to kick around the ditches in."

His voice came through a kind of buzz in her ears, and the pattern in the rug turned to stars swimming in a green sea. She waited until they stood outside the bank. At the top of seventeen granite steps she made a fist and threw all of herself into his middle. There was a lot of give there. He drew his breath in sharply and closed his eyes and kept them closed while several of their neighbors went through the revolving door a couple of times to see what would happen next. It was a clear December day. Cardinals and mockingbirds were flashing and hooting from all the high telephone wires in town.

And he had the nerve, after that, to tell her he forgave her.

"Now, that fist you stuck in my gut, that was all right. I can understand it. I wish you hadn't hurt me that way, in front of that gang of people at the bank, but mad as you were I couldn't hold it against you."

"That's big of you," she said. They were sitting in the kitchen watching *Dynasty*. Every now and then she stomped across the linoleum and yanked open a drawer so all the silver clanked.

"Want to go to a ball game?" he asked.

"With you?" she said.

She didn't talk to him all through dinner, just slammed the plates down, peas flying into the air, gravy spattering. Everything seemed to happen in slow motion. They lifted their forks to their lips like zombies.

After dinner he went straight into the living room with the paper. This was unusual; most nights he took the hawk from its metal stand, stroked its feathers, and fed it table scraps. Switching on the lamp next to the couch, he started reading the paper, holding it up to cover his face. Wilma stood in front of the sink a long time, scrubbing the iron frying pan, wiping it dry, rubbing it with a paper towel dipped in bacon grease until it shone like a piece of coal. She peeked at him once in a while, the visor on his cap pulled low, his hands on the newspaper so peaceful that she picked up a Pyrex bowl full of mustard greens and, instead of putting it into the refrigerator, let it slip through her fingers and fall to the floor.

"What's the matter, you need help?" he called.

"You want to help *me*?" she yelled. When had he ever helped her do anything?

She hit the door frame with her hip as she squeezed out the back way and walked across the yard to the tin shed where he kept his combines and wagons. Holding the long blade of the butcher knife inside her sweater sleeve, she stepped into dark so heavy it was hard to breathe. A few long minutes passed before the faint outlines of the machines sharpened. The one closest to her, the Case combine, had tires that cost two hundred apiece, with rubber thicker than elephant's hide and four-inch treads. Raising her right hand she brought the knife down hard on the left front. The blade buckled, the knife flipped out of her hand.

"Fuck," Wilma said, for the first time in her life.

She didn't bother to look for the knife but continued along the side of the combine until she felt the small metal ladder. Pulling herself up hand over hand, she dropped into the seat, panting. Quickly she turned the key all the way right, switched the lights on and off to make sure, and climbed back down the ladder, leaving the power on. When she walked in the front door, Vernon was still sitting on the couch grazing on the newspaper. He never even asked her why his batteries were dead the next day, or why she was growing quieter and quieter until almost the only words that passed between them were "Good morning" and "Sleep tight" and what she needed from the store.

2

CHRISTMAS WEEK ROLLED IN on the back of a howling blue norther that made the frame house shake. When the thermometer on the porch hit twenty-eight Vernon brought the ferrets and coyotes into the kitchen and lined up their steel cages in front of Wilma's pie cupboard. Listening while she asked him why they couldn't stay in the shed with the dogs, and how could she cook with that stink anyhow, he stomped out the back door in his waders without an answer. At dinnertime he'd come back with a couple of snow geese slung over his shoulder. It was big of the new owners, letting him hunt the fields they'd bought from him six months before. Hunting gave him a place to go and kept him out of the vodka-and-Coke awhile.

There was no shopping money this year. When Clint, their sixteen-year-old, asked for an eighty-pound hunting bow, Vernon leaned up against the fireplace with his hands in his pockets.

"Ask me for a new Trans Am, why don'tcha, or a Cessna? Ask me for a John Deere 360," he said in a voice without a single dream left.

"Let's forget about presents," Wilma said. She was

sitting in the blue velvet armchair with her lap full of Vernon's rusty old socks. She'd throw the rags away, darn whatever had enough fabric to survive another couple of washings. All Vernon's socks were royal blue so she never had to match pairs. "I can't think of a thing I want anyhow," she said.

This was a lie if there ever was one. To begin with she wanted the farm back and Jody, her oldest son, driving Vernon's combines, Vernon with his blue eyes clear again and his old laugh that made the world home. She wanted to be size twelve again, striding across the rice fields with her old twenty-gauge, stepping down into the sunken blind with Vernon while pintails wheeled overhead, and it seemed she could never miss.

Vernon bent over and poked at the logs, sending little spark showers up the chimney. He stood up, then, and started pulling on his camouflage jacket.

"Where you going this time of night?" Wilma asked. It was the one evening she had off work till Christmas Eve. There was a long awkward pause.

"Over to the library, see can I help Ruby get ready for a book fair she's havin' for the kids." Vernon had that lowdown sorry look on his face that meant he was up to something, but she didn't press it.

When he went out the door Clint stood up and switched on Ted Koppel. Some interview was going on. A Contra general or a power lifter.

"I hope Jody'll come home Christmas," she said, to nobody in particular. She hadn't seen her oldest in a couple of months, not since he'd made foreman of a drilling crew. He was living in Goliad with a girlfriend named Cindy and two coon hounds.

"Maybe Daddy'll feel better," Clint said. Jody's leaving home had been hardest on Vernon, after all. Maybe he was on his own guilt trip. But nobody felt as guilty as Wilma because she'd made the kid leave when she finally couldn't stomach his dope or his meanness another night, him hunkered down smack in the middle of her house like a poison toad.

Then she couldn't breathe; his anger sucked all the goodness out of the air. Now, sitting in that chair, Wilma got the same heavy feeling in her chest and had to work at breathing. Taking the air in smooth and deep, she didn't permit herself to exhale out loud. Still Clint watched her from the floor like a forest-fire lookout until she had to get up to fix a dish of ice cream.

"If I can't afford Christmas I can still eat," she muttered, and walked out to the kitchen. The coyotes curled their lips, showing perfect teeth, and the two golden ferrets paced behind the bars. The animals snarled as she scooted their cages away from the cupboard doors and brought out age-blackened cake pans and pie plates. Sliding her hand onto the top of the ferret cage, she started to move it back into place when she felt a quick rip and saw blood flowing from the ham of her hand.

It didn't hurt all that much, so she couldn't tell what made her eyes fill fast and her stomach knot up so she crouched on the floor, hugging her knees and rocking till she could collect herself. She had a whirly feeling in her head just then, for some reason remembering herself as a stocky girl alone in the cedar woods behind her papa's house. It was four o'clock. She knew where she was. But for a moment the shadows made the world so strange she thought she was lost in another country. Harsh cries from wild turkeys came out of the shadows, and suddenly there were bandits hiding in the trees.

When Wilma was small her papa used to cut one of the cedars for their Christmas tree, driving it home in a wagon drawn by two mules, with Wilma and her brothers making mole tunnels through the fragrant branches.

Returning, they found the house full of ginger smells, the kitchen table covered with gingerbread people and ducks and chickens with holes at the top for ribbon to hang from the tree. Wilma's mother, skinny and quick as a girl, flew about the house, stringing up cedar boughs and red bows and bits of yaupon with waxy red berries. At Christmas it was always cold; the fire was never out. Her mother had made sauerbraten and a spiced round so heavy they made the table sag. There were turkey, cranberries in copper molds shaped like fishes and a centerpiece of red and green apples, tiny cornstalk dolls and a felt Father Christmas. Thick beeswax candles set in tall glass candlesticks flanked the centerpiece, and almonds and pecans and walnuts were dropped among the silver forks and bone-handled knives and old pewter goblets from Germany.

On her knees on the kitchen floor Wilma wondered whatever happened to those goblets. Maybe Mack or Jeff, one of her brothers, had them; she hadn't spent the holiday with her parents for a couple of years but didn't remember seeing the tall goblets then. She wondered if she could get it together in time to fix a real Christmas. In spite of her boast she was exhausted, didn't have enough spunk to start a piecrust, not at nine o'clock in the evening with Vernon gone and guilt standing on her chest like a dog.

Wilma guessed she'd started losing it sometime in the late seventies. Maybe during the hurricane year when they had to mortgage the farm. That April Vernon took her out on the prairie road to see the caracara. He stopped the truck a hundred yards shy of the clump of dead *bois d'arc* trees, put his arm around her shoulder, and pointed through the windshield.

"Mexican eagles," he said. He got out of the truck and started walking toward the trees. Wilma squinted, holding her hand up.

"How'd they get here?" she asked. The birds rarely came this far north.

"Whisper," he told her. "They're nesting."

When six pairs of black and white wings started flapping, Wilma thought she was seeing things. On wings seven feet across, the eagles rolled heavily out of the trees like giant cartoon kites. Flapping awkwardly, as if their wings were too cumbersome for flight, they drifted into a Cherokee rose hedge on the other side of the road.

"They're like vultures," she said, "those red naked heads. Will they stay?"

"Maybe," Vernon told her, "if nobody messes with 'em."

In May the eagles had eggs, and rains flooded the young rice so farmers didn't have to buy water. By June there were two chicks, the rice standing three feet high, slim and green in brown water. On August 19 Hurricane Alma flattened the crop in three counties, and when Wilma and Vernon drove through the mud to survey the damage they found the eagle tree empty, two of the branches torn away by eighty-mile winds.

That summer Vernon took out a second mortgage on the farm and started carrying a pint bottle of vodka under the pickup seat. Wilma dreamed she got a job, but when she suggested it he said no.

"I can take care of us, sugar," he said, but she didn't like the way his eyes skittered away when she asked him about the new note.

After that she started dreaming she was an old lady. She still lived in the house, but Vernon wasn't there.

11

Nobody lived in town anymore, no black people, no whites, no dogs. She dreamed she walked alone along the shoulder carrying a gunny sack. When she saw a can or a bottle or a half loaf of bread, she'd bend down and pick it up and drop it in the sack.

About that time Jody started shooting speed and life got to looking lopsided. The kid was only fifteen, but tall, brawny. Fully developed. He was too big for the little hallway of their bungalow; he'd have to turn sideways to pass her on the way to the bathroom. Then he started bringing those little girls home, creeping onto the porch at night so she woke and stayed awake, listening to the cries of some animal dying. The next morning the girl would stumble out of Jody's room, eyes in pools of mascara, hair like a rat nested there. Wilma got Vernon to talk to Jody, tell him there was such a thing as manners. Fifteen. He'd have to do it in cars like everyone else.

"I've studied the law," he said. "You got to keep me here until I'm eighteen. No matter what I do." He was leaning up against the kitchen doorway, a good six inches above her.

"Wrong. You got to go by my rules," Wilma said, hearing her mother's voice in the car years ago, her mother insisting on rules for living.

"It makes everything so much easier," her mother said, turning her eyes from the road so they bored into Wilma's. "You don't ever have to think."

Wilma considered this for a few minutes. She was twelve at the time.

"I'd rather think," she said. Her mother stepped hard on the gas.

"Who lets you make the rules?" Her son was chewing a wad of tobacco.

"God," she said.

12

Jody hawked and spit into an orange juice can in his right hand. His front teeth were stained brown. She wanted to stroke his blond hair from the back, moving the hair the wrong way, then brushing it flat, but he was so tall now she couldn't reach it.

"Why do I have to do what you say? You're just a fat old woman," he said.

She never could tell what made him so mad, his anger filling the rooms like gas. She heard the door slam in the afternoons, the heavy fall of his boots. He never spoke, just slammed past her into his room. Then she'd hear the bed creak and his boots fall, and she'd ask if he wanted anything. After a while she stopped asking and went out to chop weeds in the garden. The land had dried and cracked in the heat. When she swung the hoe it hit the earth and recoiled, the sound of impact a resonant humming of struck stone. Small clods flew into the air and over her back, and sweat ran off her face onto the ground.

When she found out he was dealing she went to the law. At juvenile probation they gave her two choices: turn him in and have him prosecuted as a juvenile or keep him till he was no longer a minor. She consulted a Houston psychiatrist, a man in his sixties.

"These things take time," he said. "When can you bring him in?"

"He's too big to carry," she said.

This doctor might help, she told her son. She was sitting on the end of his bed watching as he did slow, steady bench presses. Two hundred and seventy-five pounds, little drops of sweat hanging in the down over his upper lip.

"Fuck that, Mama. Okay with me if you want to hang out with shrinks," he gasped. "I'm not goin'."

That night she locked the door to his room from the outside to keep him from meeting his connection. At four she woke to the sound of glass breaking and found the window in his room looking like an iced-over pond some fool had stepped in.

"I'm scared of him," she told her husband, as she crawled back under the covers, and Vernon couldn't see it.

"He's nothing but a big kid with runaway hormones, sugar. You're overreacting." He had spent a lot of time with the kid when he was small, teaching him to hunt, letting him sit in his lap, his little hands grabbing the steering wheel of the combine. No wonder Jody was always the favorite; he looked so much like Vernon in snapshots taken when he was a child she couldn't always tell the difference. And maybe that was why Vernon never yelled at Jody when he started sneaking into their bedroom at night, stealing pocket change off the chest of drawers.

"It's no more'n the price of a comic book, Wilma," he told her. "Let the boy have some fun."

"It won't be fun in a little while," she told him, and rolled over.

Clint, her youngest, adored and feared Jody. He never knew when his big brother would ask him into the room to read girly magazines or trip him with his big boot and laugh a mean laugh. That was when she lost control, when he'd bully the little one. Then she threw something heavy at him, an iron skillet or a casserole, hard and hurtful.

Once when he was high on speed and whipped to an angel-food froth about something, she backed him into a corner of his room. Now she couldn't remember what the argument was about, probably a waterpipe she'd found, or a joint. She was probably yelling at him, too, his long bare feet sliding backward away from her when he stepped on the axe blade leaned up against the corner. When Wilma

14

heard him yell and looked down and saw the white heel of his foot dangling like stew meat, she had to grab the back of a chair so she wouldn't fall.

"Get me to a doctor," Jody yelled, and all she could think of to scream back at him, God help her, was "Is that my job?"

She stood it until he was seventeen and started a fight in the school parking lot with thirteen Chicano students. He telephoned her at one in the afternoon, his voice shaky.

"Can you come get me?" He was at a convenience store near the school, his face bloody from a cut over his eyebrow, knuckles raw and bleeding. But he took long, swaggering steps from the pay phone to her car, keeping his face stiff all the way home. She knew not to ask him anything, and he stayed quiet until they pulled into the driveway. Then he said, "I got to borrow the car."

"What for?"

"I got to get the bastards," he said. "I know where they live."

A wild animal was living in her house. Hers. And she wasn't safe.

"You have to get your mind off this," Vernon said, reaching for her shoulder in the dark. She had heard bare feet slipping down the hall, and was swinging her own feet over the side of the bed, picking up a sweater from the floor.

"Let him alone," Vernon said.

"He's taking my car," she said and made it out the front door and down the steps faster than she had in years. She stood beside the gravel driveway as the red taillights came toward her, the white, scared face of her boy looming at her in the rear-view mirror. Raising her arms over her head she yelled "Stop" as loud as she could, but the car kept backing toward her until it came alongside and hesitated. Jody rolled the window down a couple of inches. She grabbed the door handle.

"Get outa the way," he said.

"You stop that car and get out right now," she said.

"I have to go," he said, his voice low and gritty. "Turn a loose."

"Don't come back," she said. "Don't ever." But she still held on to the door. When the car began to move she had to release her fingers, standing in that exact spot, her bare feet on the wet gravel, with her arms folded across her chest until the front wheel ran over her toes.

When the bank took the farm six years later, she thought she'd lose her mind or shoot somebody. The bank had informed them by letter: the land would be sold at public auction, and they would have two weeks to move the combines and trucks out of the rice fields and into the shed next to the house.

"We may as well sell them off, too," she said. Vernon was quiet for so long she thought he hadn't heard her. They were sitting at the kitchen table watching the Mac-Neil-Lehrer report about a Pennsylvania farm family that had sold out and moved to Philadelphia.

"I can still farm somebody else's land," Vernon told her finally. "But I need my machines. Damned combines are ten years old anyhow, won't bring nothing." He stared at his plate.

She reached across the table and touched the gray forelock falling over his forehead where the skin was white from the billed cap he always wore. Lifting his hair a little, she combed it back from his face, letting her fingers run across the top of his head and scratch down the back the way he liked.

"I never thought I'd have to go through something like this," he said.

They were calm right up to the day of the sale. She made a pot of coffee for the neighbors who came not to buy but to watch the passing of another piece of history out of their hands. It was hard not to hate her neighbors, all of them acting like they were at a funeral not knowing what to say to the bereaved. Wilma dragged out the kitchen table with a piece of gingham-printed oilcloth on it and the coffee carafe and a few cups. Damned if she'd throw a party. Devel and Jeanette brought over a couple of links of sausage they'd made, and Zeno gave her a pumpkin. As if they couldn't afford groceries. As if they'd taken Chapter Eleven. Ruby Taliaferro, the librarian, came on foot, carrying a black umbrella as long as she was. Under her arm she'd tucked a stenographer's notebook with a yellow pencil stuck through the rings. She walked up to Wilma and set a straw bag down on the table.

"Wilma, honey," she said, "this is a crime." All her little raspberry ringlets shook with sympathy.

"Nice of you to come, Ruby," Wilma said. "What's in the bag? Life preservers?" Ruby had a weekly gossip column in the paper published in the county seat, thirteen miles away. The column was called "Little Egypt Notes," and Ruby didn't have to work too hard on the stories since she got most of her dirt from the party line.

She waggled her finger at Wilma. "Now, honey, don't you be bitter. This'll make you stronger in the long run." Her eyes narrowed, and she stretched her skinny neck high. "How do you feel?" she asked.

"Not for publication," Wilma said. Across the lawn Jayran Tucker and Eloise Dittmar and seven kids were spreading a picnic on a torn blanket. "I should've made lemonade," Wilma said. "Hell, I should've blown up balloons and tied 'em in those trees."

She wasn't sure what she felt, watching Vernon lean his back against the mesquite tree, keeping his eyes closed while the two bankers shuffled papers and asked the crowd to pipe down.

She'd known right away who those boys were even before they opened their mouths. They'd slid out of a late-model Olds at eight that morning. Young guys in vests, carrying patent-leather briefcases full of Monopoly money. They might've been loan sharks, with their neat mustaches and shiny moccasins and blow-dry haircuts from the unisex haircut store in town. When they got out of the car, she'd been sitting on the back porch watching Vernon clean the ferret cage.

"Hahr yew, Mister Hemshoff," one of them said. He looked familiar. "I'm Brett Halsell from Security. This here's Benjie Towner." Vernon grunted and looked up, but went right ahead spraying water inside the cage so the small glistening turds ran out onto the St. Augustine grass. After a moment he stood up, still holding the hose in one hand and the cage in another. The air was filled with a powerful stink.

"These weasels of yours make some pretty rank pets," Benjie said, nodding at the makeshift cage Vernon had made for the ferrets out of a couple of old window screens and a whiskey carton.

"Whatja do with 'em?" Brett asked, combing his mustache with his fingers.

"Hunt," Vernon said. He took his time walking over to the two animals, opening the enclosure and taking one in his hand. Its long sleek body lay along his forearm, and the tail dropped down toward the ground. The animal's reddish eye rolled crazily. It bared its fangs at the bankers.

18

"Here," Vernon offered, holding out his arm toward Benjie, "want to hold 'im?"

Benjie backed off and put his hand up. "Hell no. I'd rather go to bed with a rabid coon," he said. "What does it hunt?"

"Rabbits, snakes," Vernon began.

"And old split-T quarterbacks," Wilma yelled from where she sat on the steps. She placed him now. Halsell used to play football with Jody. He had the sense to look embarrassed.

"How are you, Miz Hemshoff?" he said.

"I'd be doing a lot better if your outfit would pick on somebody else." She'd like to knit him a nice ferret muffler.

"I'm just as sorry as you are, Miz Hemshoff," he said.

"The heck you say." She put her hands on her knees and pushed herself up slowly until she stood on the top step. "Do me one little favor, will you, son?" she said, letting the door slam behind her. "Don't try to be our buddy, okay?"

She couldn't stand out there listening to it all go. Although she hadn't hunted geese in Vernon's fields for years, she knew that a younger part of herself, sharper-eyed and quicker, would go when the fields did, and she'd never get any of it back. That was how she always thought of the farm—gold-dusty in the hot harvest time or wind-whipped blue in hunting season. Wilma sat on her couch, the scooped-out place in her stomach growing larger, and peeked through the venetian blinds at Vernon, with his eyes closed, his back against the tree. As always his face didn't show much. He looked lost, that was all.

He wasn't exactly a lazy man. He might have been the last farmer to get his seed planted in the spring and his second crop cut in September, but he always got it done. It wasn't his way to drive a crew hard. If one of the black men who worked for him got held up drinking beer or rolling his best girl around, Vernon never said much about it. She heard him kidding the fellow a little and threatening to dock him a dollar or two on his pay, which he never did. He'd remind his boys of their wives' birthdays and child-support payments coming due. Quite a few times he'd had to get up in the middle of the night and drive into Bonus to post bail. Wilma used to get on him about not making them pay him back.

"How's Coy gonna pay me back if he's broke, sugar?" he'd say.

"He's spending it all on some girl," she argued.

"I'll bet he's giving it to the church," Vernon said, and he winked. Then he'd drive off down the road to play pool or skittles with Coy.

She didn't understand why Vernon liked hanging out at the black honky-tonk bar called the Farmer's Hall or why he wanted her to go with him to the black Pentecostal church.

"You have a church," she'd told him, as he opened the pickup door for her. They were members of the Church of the Heavenly Rest. It was the only Episcopal church in town, and all the big-time farmers and ranchers belonged.

"I ought to bring that long-faced Reverend Druse over and teach him how to put a little more zip into those anthems over there." Vernon was sweating heavily in his blue seersucker suit, but he looked cheerful.

It was stuffy in the brick church, and the kids were noisy, but she had to admit there was a lot of bounce there. The small organ near the altar was playing "Golden Slippers," and the sixteen-member choir was singing and swaying, warming up in the hall, while wasp-legged girls in bouffant skirts ran up and down the aisles. Their hair, plaited in little tails fastened with colored plastic barettes, flew out from their heads, and their big eyes threw sparks. When the first strapping girl singer came two-stepping into the room Wilma couldn't help smiling and tapping her foot and admiring the six whiskered deacons in pinstripes marching behind the choir.

She looked over at Vernon and saw his eyes filled with tears.

"What's the matter?" she whispered, holding onto his arm.

"They're full of love," he said.

Though she was always a talker, she was seldom able to tell him she loved him. When he brought her a bunch of Indian paintbrush in a bottle all she could show him was a slow smile. He must have known how she felt from the platters of dumplings and wiener schnitzel she served him, the breads of complicated shapes with twisted loaves and sprinkles of sugar frosting. Into his fields she brought brown paper sacks full of deep-fried chicken and biscuits and celery sticks wrapped in waxed paper. In the long afternoons she'd sit beside him on the combine lumbering over the levees, watching the big marsh hawks hover low over the cut grain, hunting field mice. They didn't talk much; the grinding of the machine was too loud.

Looking out the window at Vernon she knew suddenly it was rage she felt, and this surprised her so much she doubled over and hugged her stomach. The sky above the mesquite tree was gunmetal gray, a north wind whipping the hair of the women around. People were getting into their cars, the bankers stuffing papers into their brief-cases. When Smut, her white cat, strolled across the yard toward the few neighbors still gathered under the tree,

21

Jayran Tucker ran over and swooped her up in her arms, and Wilma heard her call to her mother,

"Who's gonna get the cat, Mama?"

Wilma stood up slowly so the black spots wouldn't flood her eyes. Her movement stirred the animals in their cages, the mother coyote taking long strides to the end of the three-foot enclosure, wheeling and pacing back. The pups, curled into puffballs in one corner, never moved their flattened foxy ears. She looked at her watch. Nine-thirty. Time enough to crack pecans for a pie and start the crust she'd bake tomorrow with the seven loaves of whole-wheat bread she made every week, no matter what.

Walking back into the living room she picked up the basket of small native pecans she'd gathered from the three young trees in the yard. Clint, sprawled on the couch, his sneakers dangling over the edge, was reading a copy of *Sports Illustrated* spread open on the rug and watching *Firing Line*.

"Help crack some pecans?" she asked, and he got up slowly and followed her out to the kitchen. She hadn't had a good talk with her son since she'd started working nights.

She reached into a drawer and pulled out two nut-crackers and a couple of picks. The small nuts were harder to crack than the big soft-shell varieties, but their flavor was strong and sweet. They sat opposite each other on stools pulled up to the old-fashioned kitchen table with a slab of marble on top for rolling pastry dough.

"How's Chemistry?" she asked, squeezing two nuts against each other in her palm until the shells gave way.

"Eighty-five on a test last week," Clint said. "Had to study most of the night." The ceiling lamp flooded his blond hair with light, but his face was in shadow. He had to work harder than Jody had to earn Bs and Cs, lost two front teeth making JV football, but he went ahead and tried.

"You tell your daddy the good news?"

"Not yet," Clint said, lining up four perfect pecan halves on the marble.

"Why not?" Vernon should spend more time with this kid.

"He's not around much" was all the boy would say.

"You like your job all right?" he asked her, looking for the first time into her face as if he wanted to know.

"It's just a five-buck-an-hour job," she said, "nothing special." But it kept her out of the little house stuffed with animals and rusty traps and Vernon's unexplained absences. Wilma didn't tell her son about the early-morning runs after quitting time and about the trucker who was teaching her to drive.

3

As she ran out the door on the way to work one night later, Wilma found Vernon asleep in a chair with his lap full of old decoys. He'd been hunting geese every morning to cut down on grocery bills, and in October she'd starting cooking at a truck stop in El Campo, where the gravel and livestock haulers stopped for breakfast at five. She worked eleven at night to seven, which gave her an excuse to stay up all night and snooze all day if she felt like it. It was a place where she didn't need to share the air with anyone she knew. Gray-faced drivers swaggered in like scared showoff baby boys and huddled over coffee, keeping their faces down, mostly, unless a woman came in. She could be seventeen or seventy; it didn't matter what she looked like. Any old time of night a woman might push through the double glass doors, and those men's heads would snap up and swivel around, their eyes running all over her like fingers stroking a perfect peach.

Most of the stuff she dished out to truckers she'd be ashamed to serve Vernon's dogs. Truck-stop food looked like it'd come out of computers; photosynthesis was never involved. This food had no point of origin except the can, the sack, the plastic tub or the clear plastic wrapper, nothing in common with a New York dairy cow, Minnesota wheat, or Oregon apples. These eggs had never been fertile, had never even touched a chicken. They sprang, peeled and boiled, from incubators, vending machines, service companies. The chickens had never touched the ground with their yellow scabrous feet.

It had been six in the morning sometime in November when she met Gary. He was sandy-haired and pale-eyed, about forty-five, with a chin that meant business and a twelve-hour beard. All the way in from the door to the counter she watched him, glad she was wearing Vernon's big shirt buttoned to the chin because this one would spot the pulse quickening at her throat. Like all of them he looked her over hard. Usually she just put her eyes out of focus so she wouldn't feel the men staring, but this time was different. She wished she'd had a second to run back to the Ladies to brush her hair. Instead she stood behind the counter, her big hands dangling, and grinned like a damned fool. He picked up a menu, pulled off his cap, and ordered chili.

"It's not the best," she said, "if you want my opinion." She smoothed the front of her uniform and waited for him to pick something else while she took a good look. He had a long face with a generous nose and a full-lipped mouth. He might have been a farmer, his hands and arms big enough to toss square hay bales onto a trailer, stack them five deep. It surprised her how much she missed the farm.

"I'll have the gumbo," he said, showing deep dimples. "Gary Perdle. Kansas City. You look too nice to sling hash."

She got a little gruff. "My oil wells all dried up. How about you? You always been driving these rigs?" *Listen to me, talking like a truck-stop waitress,* she thought, watching his blue eyes flatten and retreat under her gaze.

"Ever since I quit teaching high school history," he said. "You'd love it, driving a truck."

She'd never considered it, but now she was hearing the words. She needed to talk to Sarah about it. Sarah was twenty-two and looked thirty-seven. Been raped twice and had to have an abortion both times. Every morning at five she came in to help with griddle cakes and fried eggs during rush hour. Now she was leaning across the counter, one bra strap slipping down her skinny brown arm. A tall trucker with a ponytail had his big hand over her little one.

"Hadn't thought about driving," Wilma said. "I'd have to pass a test."

"Two, in fact. Texas and DOT."

"What's DOT?"

"Department of Transportation. They run the scales, hand out fines, big trouble if they catch you with an illegal load," he said. "You'd love it. Give you a chance to slip out from under, get something going for yourself. Know what I mean?" He leaned over and nudged her shoulder.

"What do I have to do to get you to teach me to drive?" she said.

Gary tipped his head toward the lot. "You could lie down with me in the bunk out there and let me tickle you with a feather duster."

"Dream on," she said.

She backed away from the counter and stood with her arms folded, wanting to telephone Vernon. A part of her wanted to cuss him out; she couldn't stand the way he smelled anymore. The other part wanted to curl up in his armpit.

"You got a lot going for yourself on the road?"

"I try to keep warm at night," Gary said.

"How does your wife feel about that?" He had shown her a snapshot of Corinne, a skinny blonde in spit curls and jogging shorts.

"Tell you what. I'm a fair-minded man," he said. "When I get home I keep my mouth shut. No questions, and she don't ask me."

"I get it," she said. "A coffee break." She'd always tried to keep sex under the covers where it belonged.

"A truck's the loneliest place in the world," Gary said. He reached across the counter and took her hand. "Want to go sit in the cab with me awhile?"

"Come on," she said, rolling her eyes. His line made her sad, but she went anyway.

There was a high pitch to his head as they walked across the parking lot past rows of Kenworths, Peterbilts, Freightliners, Macks and GMCs lined up like cars in a drive-in movie. And his walk turned her on, proud as a rodeo cowboy's when he knows a crowd is watching. When he snaked his arm around her waist and did a few dance steps she slapped at him and said, "Let go. I'm too old for this." He didn't listen, but tightened his arm and swung her over his shoulder.

"Put me down, idiot." She couldn't help laughing. "Somebody'll see."

"Don't worry," he told her. "I'll just tell them you're my poor old crippled mother."

"Are you interested in the guy?" Sarah asked later. She plucked a long gray hair of Wilma's and quickly pulled it out.

"Mostly I'm interested in learning to drive," she said.

"How come? He'll be all over you."

"Maybe I could get someplace," Wilma said vaguely.

"Then why worry?" Sarah removed a big zircon ring from her ring finger and placed it on Wilma's left hand. "Worry is bad for the face."

"What's this for?"

"If you want to look like you aren't interested, put it on and pretend Vernon gave it to you. If you want to look like you are, you can wear it on the other hand. And for God's sake take your wedding ring off." This girl knew a lot. All of them seemed to know a lot these days.

"But I can't," she said. "It's stuck. I haven't been able to get it off for years."

"You said it, I didn't," Sarah said.

Around two in the morning she started checking her watch like she did every Tuesday, and at two-fifteen she walked around the counter past the little tinfoil Christmas tree and into the Ladies, pulled out her hairbrush and took the rubber band from her long hair. Leaning over from the waist, she brushed a hundred strokes, letting the blood run into her cheeks so she wouldn't look dead when he walked in. With a new lip brush she drew an outline around her full mouth and filled it in. Then she walked back behind the counter and started frying the gray sausage that didn't have much of a bite but he liked anyway. At four he pulled his brown longnose into the lot, blinked his headlights twice at her through the window. One nice thing about Gary, he'd notice the lipstick like he'd noticed everything about her. It didn't take him an hour to find out she was sensitive about her size and vain about her thick, coppery hair. Right away he'd discovered she was scared of numbers; she didn't like the dials on the dash because she thought she couldn't understand them.

After three cups of coffee his face lost its pallor, and he looked closer to par. He walked her across the lot, and they sat in his cab watching the pearly light spread over the trucks.

"These numbers here," he said, pointing to the dials and gauges on the dash, "you have to keep track of. Big time. Your brake pressure, oil pressure, fuel in your two tanks, weight over front and rear axles. You're taking this patient's pulse. How's his ticker? The juice in his pipes?" He saved ten thousand a year fixing his own truck.

In spite of herself Wilma was grinning, sitting pretty in one of the big rigs, starting to learn the ropes. Gary's was one of the best-looking trucks on the road, too, never without a double coat of hard-shine wax, chrome that blazed under the suns of thirteen states. It was a Kenworth with chrome twin stacks, double chrome headlights, guide rods with shiny chrome dolphins on them, and twin air horns mounted on top of the cab. A truck built so far off the ground she had to strain for a long, embarrassing minute to hoist herself into the seat.

"I'm too old for this," she told him.

"What does that make me?" he said, sliding her into the seat behind the wheel. Leaning forward, she reached for the jar of jellybeans on the dashboard. Gary switched on the Cobra. There was a screen of static; then a young girl's voice.

"Hey, longnose in party row. Got a copy?"

The man's voice came back right away, didn't even sound sleepy.

"Hi there, hon. What's on your dirty mind? Want to ride up the road with me a ways?"

When Gary told her the girl was a hooker, Wilma was shocked. "They circle these stops like Comanches," he said. "Sweetheart, would you believe? There are probably thirty-five commercial beavers working this joint while we're sitting here talking."

She checked the lot for prowling beavers. Sure enough, there were six or seven civilian cars with lights off. "Can't the cops do anything?" Wilma said. The girl sounded like a baby.

"Whereat you goin'?" the voice went on.

"T-town."

"I was hoping you'd say New York," the girl said. She sounded skinny and scared.

"I don't hardly get up to Big Town. I heard they're some mean old women up there, so I stick to southern comfort. After Tulsa I'm headed up Chicago way. Ain't that far enough? They tell me I'm good-lookin'."

"Hey, big guy," the girl said, "I'm crazy to lay in your lap no matter where you're goin', but my momma's sick. Could die any time, and ain't even seen this baby yet."

"I don't believe this," Wilma said.

Gary plugged in the cord to a heating coil set in a white china cup.

"Like a Sunday parlor," Wilma said. *Any minute he'll be putting a lace doily under the cup.*

"Maybe we could cut a deal," the man on the CB said.

Wilma grabbed the receiver. "Didn't you hear the lady, son? I believe she just told you no," she said, but nobody listened.

"All I got's a box of Pampers. What you askin'?"

Wilma fumbled for the door handle. She had to find this girl, wash her mouth with soap, keep her from ruining her life.

"Wait a minute," Gary said, putting a hand on her shoulder.

"Money's not the objective," the voice said. "If you got the time and the right moves, hon, I got all the money we're gonna need."

"You ain't dreamed about the moves I got." The girl's

tough voice wasn't smart enough or worldly enough to be using the come-on words. In the silence that followed she heard a high, reedy whine rise to a double-edged whistle. Nobody answered. Gary switched it off, keeping his head turned so he could watch Wilma's response. The grin on his face was down-and-dirty.

"It's better than NPR," he said.

Wilma needed to speak to this girl; she wasn't sure why. "Go home," she wanted to tell her. "Call your folks. They'll forgive you." She was hitching all over the country with a baby and couldn't be more than fifteen. Where was her mother? Gary had a daughter, a follower of Rajneesh, he hadn't seen in three years. No matter how many times she'd forgiven her Jody she finally had to kick him out for good.

Gary gave her ponytail a yank. "Okay, how many gears?" he said.

"Fifteen," she said, "and reverse."

"What's this?" he pointed to a blue clock face just right of the ignition key.

"That's measuring the air," she said. "Hot air." She grinned. "Air-ride supply to the airbag."

He reached up and flicked her under the chin. "Start her up," he said, and she pushed on the starter and listened to what the big Cummins engine would say. It wobbled a little, then roared like a caged lion. The vibration shook the cab. She wanted a big animal like this.

"Now when you're driving in rainy weather there's a little valve called a proportionate front-wheel eliminating valve that'll let out fifty percent of the air in the front brakes. It's a feature you want to look for when you go shopping. It'll keep you alive a hundred times a year," he said.

Front-wheel eliminating valve? Had he mentioned that one before or had she dreamed it? Twin screw axle, gooseneck, horse light, lowboy, feather-hauler, forty-foot flat, redwood tree, reefer, rag top, pony wheel, possum belly. She had to stop him after every sentence, ask him to explain. A man who knew something she didn't turned her on, and she never stopped trying to pick his brain like Samson's girlfriend.

"Hey, girl, tell me one thing," Gary said. "After I teach you all I know, who you gonna work for?"

"Whoever'll give me the best deal," she said. "I'll go to work for just about anybody, long as he doesn't mess with me." She'd tucked her ponytail into a knot at the back of her head and sounded so prissy he laughed.

The girl on the CB, the one with the baby, showed up two days after Christmas, only Wilma didn't know she was the one till she opened her mouth. It was a Thursday the girl came in, a little after four in the morning, carrying the baby in a sling that held its body close against her chest. She was thin and black-eyed, with hair as black as a grackle's wing. When she sat down at the counter she threw Wilma a challenging look, hot pouty lips and narrow eyes. It was weird seeing a child like that: tight black jeans and a low-cut T-shirt, with that baby pressed between her padded tits. She wished for the millionth time she had a daughter.

"You doin' all right?" Wilma asked, pushing a water glass across the counter.

"Bitchin'," the kid said, and Wilma placed her right away. "Okay if I wash up?" She spoke as if she were accustomed to being tossed out of restrooms.

"Sure, go ahead," Wilma said. "I'll hold the baby." The girl pulled the sling over her head and handed the bundle across the counter. The baby's eyes were shut, the five eyelashes on each lid as delicate as frost lace, under the lids the palest veins.

32

When the girl came back she'd freshened her lipstick and eyeliner, but she couldn't do anything about the black pools under her eyes. She slid onto a stool and asked for a Dr. Pepper.

"On your way somewhere?"

"New York."

"You have folks up that way?"

"My old man," the girl said.

"You got a husband? You aren't old enough, honey," Wilma said.

"I'm seventeen," she said.

A lot of them weren't old enough for a lot of things. She was pretty, though, slight and pale, with those velvet eyes and black hair. All her life Wilma wanted to look like that. Fragile, with toothpick arms and legs. "I'd like to see New York," she said. "Never got out of Texas."

"Too bad," the girl said. She pronounced it "bay-ud."

"Tell me about it. Buildings? Bridges?"

"Buildings like the Grand Canyon. A trillion of lights." The girl was staring vaguely at the wall behind the counter.

"How many bridges they got in New York? They'd have to have a bunch to connect them to the rest of the state."

"Uh huh, quite a few," the kid said, running her index finger along the handle of a fork.

"How'd you wind up way down here?" Wilma asked. She couldn't get the girl to look her straight in the face.

"I got an aunt in Lone Star." The girl looked at her as if she'd forgotten the name of her best friend and was trying to retrieve it. "She's got a nice place, my aunt," she added softly. She patted the baby's head as if it were a puppy or a kitten. The baby was dressed in a soiled cotton pajama set that had pink bunnies on a white background covered with coffee stains.

Wilma pulled back the blanket so she could see the baby's face better. "Sweet little thing," she said, winking at the girl, "and with all that black hair it looks just like a spider monkey." The girl looked impassively at Wilma. *If this was the girl's baby,* Wilma thought, *she'd eat a pacifier.*

"Okay, where'd you get the baby?" Wilma asked.

"Same way ever'body gets 'em," the girl said. Her arms tightened around the bundle, and she checked the exits. The baby began making tiny bleating sounds.

"Sometimes she won't quit that for an hour," the girl told Wilma. "I keep stuffing things in her mouth, every last thing I can think of, and she don't want it."

"Sometimes what babies want is to cry," Wilma said. "Okay, let's have the real story." She leaned toward the girl with her big red hands on the counter. "We have to call this kid's people before they run off to work."

The girl looked down at the sleeping face and touched the baby's eyebrows and the pink ear like a plant deep underground.

"She's mine," the girl said in a thin voice.

Wilma tried to remember if she ever wanted a baby of her own when she was seventeen. She thought she remembered that what she wanted was a horse.

"She's precious," Wilma said. "Why'd you take off with her?"

"I was sitting home watching *Miami Vice*. Daddy came in from the sugar plant mad because there was nothing for supper."

"You cook for him?" Wilma said.

"Sometimes I fix cheese grits, and he won't even eat it. He just lays on the couch and sucks on those beers till he passes out."

34

"What's your name, honey?"

"Oralee Sweet. I was named after my mama," the girl said.

"Where is she?"

"As far underground as she can get," Oralee said, starting to chew on her thumbnail.

"You got anybody living with you besides your daddy?"

"Nobody. Mattie comes in twice a week and cooks a big pot of greens and a pan of cornbread and sweeps out. The rest of the time it's just him and me." She was starting to fade out, her voice getting weaker and her eyes getting big and full. Wilma could picture the house in Lone Star where Oralee lived, full of roaches and beer bottles. The old man probably felt her up, on top of everything.

"Why'd you run off?"

"Don't tell on me."

"So who'm I gonna tell?"

"Welfare. Preachers. Police. Whoever hell asks." She was snipping off the ends of her words now.

"He wanted me to . . ." She let her voice trail off.

Wilma waited. The girl stared down at the baby in her arms. She started humming a few bars of a song Wilma didn't recognize. Probably from some rock album. Iron Maiden or The Police.

"He wanted me to—uh . . . Oh, shit." She was blushing.

"Do something you didn't want to?" Wilma volunteered.

Oralee let out a sound, half laugh, half snort. "He made me let him suck my tits," she said, and covered her mouth.

Wilma didn't answer.

"Perverts," the girl said. "We're both perverts, right?"

"I wouldn't go that far," Wilma said. "The Girl Scouts wouldn't get it."

Oralee ran her fingers through her hair to get it to stand up. It was already up. "I never told anybody before," she said defiantly.

"Well, I don't blame you," Wilma said.

"They'd put me in jail, or the psycho ward, you mean."

"You didn't do anything wrong, honey," Wilma said. "He looking for you?"

"If he's not too drunk. Don't tell me I gotta go back."

"You don't have to go back," Wilma said.

"How'd you get this kid, anyway?" Wilma was beginning to feel like some kind of caseworker, and she'd never know if the kid were telling the truth.

"My boyfriend," Oralee spoke in a near-whisper, keeping her eyes low. "Papa beat up on him when he found out, so he wouldn't hang out with me anymore."

"You miss him?"

"Yeah, we miss him, but now there's two of us, we're cool." When the girl gave the baby a little bounce in her arms, and her face lit up like New York, Wilma knew it was having the baby that mattered most to Oralee, holding her next to her skinny chest.

"What's her name?" Wilma asked.

"Car."

"Car?"

" 'Cause she's a travelin' lady."

"What're you hanging around a truck stop with a baby for?" Wilma asked. It didn't look good.

"I gotta thing for truckdrivers," Oralee told her. "You oughta know."

Twice a week, when he had a couple of days between runs, she was spending eight hours at work and another two in the truck with Gary. This time of year he was hauling Valley fruit out of Pharr, running to Chicago and back in four days. Though he usually got a loadback, frozen meat or eggs, she wondered how he could afford to hang around El Campo losing money, but she was enjoying herself too much to ask questions. After six weeks of lessons, he'd told her she was ready to hit the road, and on a cool, bright morning she sat behind the wheel, letting her brake leg up slow, easing the truck onto the two-lane. They drove a couple of hours, blasting through El Campo, Edna, Nada, Lissie, and Newgulf. As she drove, she rolled down the window, stealing a look at the furrows in blackland fields spinning backward like wagon spokes in cowboy flicks. Her big dangle earrings swung in the wind and she leaned out the window and cut loose with a long high-pitched holler.

"It's good-looking country," she yelled at Gary.

"Downshift, dammit," he said, "and watch your curves."

Her subconscious mind had been slowly piecing together a plan about seeing more of the country.

"Drive with me awhile, get some experience," he said. "It's a bitch breaking into this business without it. They'll give you hell about being overweight, too."

"The only people who object to my size," she said, puffing up a little, "are intellectual midgets. Thanks anyway."

She didn't know who she'd go to work for, but she'd think of something. There were thousands of oil service trucks hauling drilling equipment for flushing and fracturing wells, well-logging trucks with electrons that could penetrate hundreds of feet below the earth's surface to sniff out oil and gas. On nights she wasn't at work these trucks woke her, and she got up, threw on her old purple robe, and walked outside. Fifteen flatbeds lined up across from her house, lights glowing hot, then dying in the dark. As she stood in the tall grass beside the road they started moving, the heavy gear chained to their beds creaking and groaning, brakes hissing and squealing. She watched them turn down a dirt road on their way to one of the gas leases. Hauling those machines would be a kick; she'd learn every back road in the state.

Or she might sign on with a bedbugger company moving household furniture. She could see herself walking into a small house where a young couple might be moving to New York or California and a shiny new career. Some of the moves wouldn't be steps up—the carpenters and mechanics and their kids from Detroit or Chicago who'd come to Texas because they figured the Southwest was still full of oil and jobs were having to go back to their sooty cities empty-handed. That was sad. But whether they were bound for glory or a slow death by boredom, she'd get them where they needed to go. She liked that idea. Meanwhile she needed practice.

"Pull over here," Gary told her. They were just passing through a tiny town called Danevang.

"What're we doing?" she said.

"See that dirt road across the way? That old pump shop? Pull in there, and we'll go over backing and parking." It was a one-lane road with high weeds on the shoulder.

"You copy that sign on the far side?" She looked across the road at a sign that said THREE SISTERS CAFÉ.

"I want your nose parallel with the S in SISTERS and your tail sitting smack on the sixth fence post back. Got it?" he said.

He was leaning slightly toward her, his arm on the back of the seat. She looked out her side window, then stuck her head over his way to look in the rearview mirror. She should've known better. He swooped into her face, kissing her so hard their teeth scraped together, and he locked his arm around her waist.

"This is stupid," she said, putting both hands on his chest and pushing him away. But it was impossible to get angry at a good-looking man who couldn't keep his hands off her. Turning her back to him, she watched the mirror on her side as she moved the stick into reverse, releasing the clutch half an inch at a time. It took her only two minutes to align the truck and the trailer with the THREE SISTERS sign across the road.

A low-slung woman came out of the house on the other side of the road, crossed her arms and stood gazing at the truck. She wore a black velvet vest embroidered with flowers, a black skirt and wooden clogs. She smiled and waved and called out something.

"Can't hear you," Wilma called back.

"Why don't you all come in for a cup of coffee?" the woman yelled. Her fuzzy blond hair shook.

"We might as well," she said to Gary. "How'd I do?"

"I've seen worse," he said. "Wilma, sweet thing, you must be worn to a fringe. Want to take a little nap in back?"

"Maybe another day," she said. She knew exactly how far she was willing to go with this. On the other hand, she kept having these ripply snorts of energy. When he touched her she felt like melted chocolate. She didn't want to run him off until she could pass her test and get her license. Tossing her head so her hair fell around her shoulders, she turned her face to him and closed her eyes.

"Wilma, girl," he said. "I'm afraid you're a big tease."

They were finishing their second cup of coffee when Vernon opened the door. She set her cup down and stared

39

at him as if she didn't know him. She almost didn't, he looked so awful. Day-old beard and red eyes, clothes stinking and rumpled.

"I stopped at Harvin's and asked the girl there," he said. "She told me the truck to hunt for."

"What's wrong?" she said.

"I knew you were cookin', Wilma," Vernon said, his voice low. "I guess I didn't figure you had something like this on the front burner."

"Driving lessons, son. I just been teaching Wilma downshifting." Gary looked like he'd just been caught in a honky-tonk bar with an eleven-year-old cheerleader.

All the way from Danevang to Little Egypt she kept wishing Vernon would say something. But she didn't feel like initiating the conversation, so she sat with her hands in her lap, staring out at the signs flowing past. Mahalek's Grocery, Biseida's Pump and Tool, Krenek's Barbecue. This part of the state was filled with people with short upper lips everybody called Bohemians. They came from Denmark, Czechoslovakia, Yugoslavia, Poland. When she was first married Vernon took her to dance in little country joints where bohunk bands dressed in knickers and vests and funny velvet hats played oompah music.

"Vernon," she said finally. Turning his head, he stared at her. She couldn't tell what he thought or felt.

"Well," he said after a minute, "who's that?"

"Gary," she said. "He comes in a couple of times a week and we talk."

"Yeah?"

"That's all," she said. "Besides teaching me to drive."

"He married?"

"Yeah."

"If I see you with him again, I'll kill him," Vernon said.

4

JUST BEFORE MIDNIGHT on New Year's Eve she spotted Vernon's truck parked on a bridge over a levee in one of the fields he used to farm. He couldn't get it through his head this land was gone; he kept driving out to check on it. Wilma wouldn't have driven out the muddy road herself if it hadn't been for a chance remark overheard at the party Calvin Merriweather gave every year.

At a quarter to twelve the wood floor was rocking from the weight of dancing feet when she went out to the kitchen looking for her husband.

"Seen Vernon?" she asked Devel Edwards, who was standing by the stove stirring a cast-iron pot full of black-eyed peas.

"I think he already gone," Devel said, vaguely.

She grabbed her jean jacket from a hook by the back door.

"Where you goin' in such a hurry?" Devel held her arm.

"I need to find him," she said, her head woozy from three beers.

"Stay awhile," Devel said. "If you do find 'im you gonna wish you didn't."

She never asked Devel who Vernon was with.

When she turned off on the dirt road, she rolled her window down so she could hear wind moving across the prairie and sniff the brackish water in the ditches. Things didn't smell or taste much anymore, maybe because of all this weight she'd put on, and because of Jody and Vernon and the money worries. But tonight she felt the damp northerly breeze blowing off the surface of the shallow ponds, and it went right through her, leaching down into her bones.

Not knowing why she did it, she switched her head-lights off and drove slowly down the rutted road toward Vernon's taillights. The Chevy labored through the mud. The lights were off in Vernon's truck, but she could hear the radio so he must have the windows down. Some cow-boy who sounded like Hank Williams, Jr., was singing, "I bought the shoes that are walkin' out on me."

When she heard a woman's laugh over the music, Wilma stopped the car fifty feet from the truck, got out and started walking in her old birdshooter boots, which made deep slurping sounds in the mud. She could see the white blur of Vernon's license plate and the bumper sticker that said I PAUSE FOR PAWS.

She saw him and Ruby before they saw her. Silhou-etted against the constellations, they were stretched out in the truck bed, wrapped in one of her quilts. They had a couple of six-packs in there with them, and Toby, Vernon's pointer. When he heard her footsteps, Toby made a clean hurdle over the side of the truck and trotted up to her.

"Get back, Toby, get back," she whispered. The dog jumped up and placed his forepaws on the front of her jacket. He whined, and she whacked him on the nose. Though Wilma was well within earshot she kept having a fantasy that she might turn around and walk back to her car and nobody would notice. She had none of the wronged wife white-bra outrage of soap-opera heroines. Her husband had a girlfriend older than she was with wiry hair and skin like crumpled waxed paper. Ruby Taliaferro didn't have a thing on Wilma except seven years and a mouthful of teeth she would never let you forget.

Wilma had never considered herself a jealous woman, but that was because for twenty years she and Vernon fit together tight as two walnut halves. But now that she was working she hardly saw him, and when she did she'd catch him staring into space with a sad, dreamy expression. He liked to switch on country stations and listen to sappy ballads like "Blue Eyes Crying in the Rain" or "Please Release Me, Let Me Go." Library books like *What Color Is Your Parachute?* and *The Power of Positive Thinking* lay around the house. Whatever Vernon was doing his powerful thinking about, it wasn't her.

Wilma had been so busy learning to drive she hadn't paid much attention to Vernon's flirtation with Ruby. She was working nights so she didn't have to know where he spent his long evenings, and she slept half the day in their bed, which held only a faint smell of him now, as if the sign and the scent of him were fading from her life one week's washing at a time.

Since the dog was dancing around and whining, Wilma took the direct approach. She walked up to the truck whistling "A Fine Romance" under her breath loud enough to alert Vernon.

"Who's that?" Vernon said.

"Nobody but just your fat old wife of twenty years." There was the sound of boots scraping on metal.

"Hi, sugar," Vernon said. He threw one leg over the side of the truck. It was too dark to make out his face. Ruby was silent for once.

"Chilly for a picnic," Wilma said and jammed her hands into the pockets of her jeans.

"Aren't you getting chilly yourself, trucking around in this mud?" he said, after a long pause. He had her off-center for only a second. She reached out and put a hand on his shoulder.

"I thought you might want to celebrate New Year's, honey," she said. "Drink a toast, call up a bobcat?"

A light cough rose from the truck. "Vernon," Ruby said, "it's time to go home."

"Oh, don't let me interrupt anything," Wilma said.

"What'd you come out here for, then?" Vernon said. "I'm celebrating New Year's my way." She turned around without saying anything and started walking back down the road toward her car. The dog whined, then trotted after. Vernon whistled for him a couple of times, but the dog kept following Wilma. Finally he yelled, "You bring my dog back!"

"You're lower than a polecat, Vernon," she called back over her shoulder.

Whenever he took her two brothers into the dark cedar grove behind their stone house to stalk wild turkeys, Wilma's father never allowed her to go. He knew his twelve-year-old wanted to hunt because she always hung around, weekend afternoons, watching him and the boys clean their guns and put mink oil on their boots. Sitting in a rocker on the back porch, she kept a pair of binoculars trained on the skimpy trees behind the house.

"There," she whispered, pointing at the tall birds strolling in the shadows. Once in a while she picked up one of the heavy shotguns and held it to her shoulder. Her father decided not to notice. Herman Fritz wasn't mean; he just never thought a woman ought to be shooting a gun.

She didn't learn much more about hunting before she took a job at a fish and game club at nineteen and flirted with Vernon Hemshoff until he took her out in a duck blind. Girls who looked like Wilma never got much flirting practice at junior college, where the beauties had silky hair swinging in half-moon arcs across their cheeks, and long perfect legs. Miss America material, better than the Rockettes. Leggier, toothier, more chesty. Wilma was okay in the chest. Her teeth were fine, too. But she was five feet eleven inches tall, and she didn't have the right legs.

In the tenth grade she had attended her first school dance; the only boy who spoke to her stared for a long moment at her arms and asked if she lifted weights. His chin just reached the tips of her nipples. She scowled and left the dance floor, then telephoned her mother to come and get her out of there. Among the companies that sponsored the Miss America pageant that year were one that made pastry flours and cake mixes and another that made deodorant.

At five in the morning Vernon stuck his head through the door of the game club's kitchen, where Wilma was already sweating over the blackened stove. It was hunting season so she had walked downstairs at four and put the twelve-cup tin coffeepot on the gas burner. Vernon didn't have much to say that early in the morning, just grinned at her and gave her the University of Texas "Hook 'em Horns" sign before heading out to the boathouse to clean out the skiffs. At five-thirty six hunters came in, their long bootlaces clicking on the oak floor, and drank thick black coffee with biscuits before stepping into the skiffs with the guides. For the next three hours Wilma worked on breakfast. Oatmeal in a double boiler, pancakes made of fine rice flour and a couple dozen yard eggs beaten thick and orange with a rotary beater. She fired up a pan of bacon and warmed toast made with salt-rising bread and crisp feathery biscuits split and oozing butter. At nine she brewed twenty-four more cups of coffee, one ear cocked for Vernon and the other guides stamping their boots on the front steps. The guests walked in and sat at the long table, their fingers blue from the cold, bragging about their long shots and their doubles. Vernon caught her eye and winked. Only the guides knew about the easy shots they'd missed. In front of every place setting on the long table was a tall blue pitcher of milk and a pink grapefruit half with a cherry in the center. For an hour Wilma and her two helpers passed in and out of the swinging door to the kitchen carrying platters of eggs and pancakes, biscuits and bacon.

"I'll have some more of those biscuits, Wilma," one of the men said. "I'm gettin' lighter with every bite, they're so spiritual."

"Wilma's biscuits are a religious experience, no doubt about it," said the Admiral, who was president of the club. Wilma passed the biscuits. While standing between the two men she felt a hand come to rest lightly on her hip and whipped her head around fast.

" 'Scuse me," the Admiral said, his smile filled with mischief. A few of the men were always trying to get fresh, reaching out as she walked by with a tray and brushing her bottom or the backs of her knees. Wilma lowered her eyes and walked quickly around the table and out into the kitchen.

The three women passed food for an hour and a half while the men ate and drank coffee and told stories about wood ducks landing in the decoys and the pair of pintails someone had bagged with a clean double shot, and about the alligators and nutria gobbling up the game. The next time Wilma had to pass the Admiral she sucked in her stomach and looked him square in the face as she slipped by so he'd know she had her eyes open. It would be sweet to spill a pot of hot coffee into his lap. As this thought walked through her mind she caught Vernon looking at her across the table. He had a loose, easy smile on his face, but his eyes were taking inventory. There was no way of knowing if he'd seen the caress or what he thought about it. Wilma needed a girlfriend in the worst way. She wanted to tell Delia and Dara about the Admiral, but it wasn't cricket, complaining to black women about white men's foolishness. So she reined herself in and slammed the trays down on the drainboard.

Since her arrival at the club three months before, the shooting guides who worked there had been politely distant, pulling off their caps when they came into the drafty old house, saying "Hidy, Wilma," then ignoring her, going on with their talk. All except Vernon. He was the only one who rattled her cage; something in his sleepy-eyed grin teased and challenged her. Something friendly and disarming, and sly. The sly part was as attractive as the friendly part. Wilma wondered what he could be hiding behind that smile, but she didn't worry about it because he was teaching her to shoot.

The first time Wilma had met Vernon she thought he was a smartass. She was carrying a stack of cotton blankets up the outside stairs when he slammed the door of his truck and whistled at her legs. Her short plaid skirt just grazed her knee caps, and even before he opened his mouth she felt his eyes on her. Vernon wore a cap that said Purina and a short-sleeved T-shirt with the Budweiser logo. He had blond eyebrows and round blue eyes, and her mother would have said he looked like a man who didn't know the meaning of rejection.

"Want to take a boat ride, ma'am?" She whirled around, dropping a blanket.

"No, but I wouldn't mind learning to shoot," she said.

"High time, too," he said. He had a boy's face, though she knew he was thirty, at least.

The following Thursday at six he steered the boat toward a blind on the east side of the lake, where nobody shot much because alligators had cleaned out most of the game. She stayed as still as she could, straining her eyes to see the blind through the fog. She could barely make out its outline ahead and to the left. Against the lightening sky it looked like a castle with jagged pieces of shale along the roof.

Pulling the canvas decoys out of the sack, Vernon stood up and threw them out one by one into the water on the north side of the blind. The boat scarcely moved. The decoys settled themselves and bobbed realistically on the lightly rippled water; Vernon cut the motor and poled the boat in between the thick reed walls.

"Load your gun," he said to Wilma, who was hanging on to the side of the boat. He had shown her how to lay her right cheek against the fine-grained walnut stock of his Ithaca and sight along the cool blue barrel.

"I'll just watch you awhile," she said, her breath coming a little quick in her throat.

"Oh, no you don't," he said, and handed her the gun. Then he leaned back against the gunwale, his feet resting on a thwart, hands clasped behind his head.

Opening the chamber, she shoved two shells in, closed the barrel, and pushed the pill-sized button that put the gun on safety. It felt heavy in her hands, and she had to crouch to see over the tops of the cattails wired around the bamboo frame of the blind.

"What am I doing here at the crack of dawn freezing

my feet and breaking my back?" she said in mock resentment. She turned her head to look at him all stretched out like a millionaire on a beach.

When the first flight of six mallards stalled in midair and turned toward the decoys she got panicky and whispered, "When do I shoot?" and waited with her barrel ready, the steel sticking to her fingers in the cold until Vernon said, "Now." Then she stood and aimed, lining up the bead on the end of the gun barrel with the blur of the moving bird, swinging the gun so the bird was just under the bead and then a little more so she led it by two inches and pulled the trigger twice. The duck splashed heavily into the water in the middle of the decoys.

Wilma leaned over the side of the boat, staring at the duck floating like a small drifting ship, its head hanging down under the water. She saw the gray, brown, and green feathers above the surface, just a few drops of water on the backfolded wings. When she reached for it the duck's body was dead weight, the feathers mostly dry. Except for the head. The mallard's green head was water-blackened, the eyelids half closed.

"I guess I got 'im," she said.

In two months Wilma got over being squeamish. She got so she could shoot doubles like picking up twosies in a jacks game. Vernon began taking her out on the lake or through the fields so often that she had to ask her two girl helpers at the club to take on more housekeeping duties. Before daylight he'd knock on her door, hand her a mug of coffee and tell her to hurry, they were going out to walk his traps. She'd shiver in the dark room, pull on corduroy pants and lace-up work boots and a wool shirt, and they'd tramp through rice fields and pecan bottoms, their breath rising like wisps of camp smoke into the nippy air. When they'd find the rusted traps he'd hidden in ditches, he'd show her how to place the meat inside the mean steel jaws, and how to pry them open to release the coyote or raccoon without injuring its paw.

She had a natural style, an easy rhythmic way of bringing the gun up fast to her shoulder and swinging with the moving target. It seemed like dancing, and she wasn't afraid of the gun's recoil; in the excitement she scarcely felt the sharp kick in her shoulder and was always surprised after peeling off her shirt at night to find plum-colored bruises above her right breast. In March, when she got so she was hitting eighty-five or ninety percent of the targets, Vernon said it was time she got her own gun, so they drove into Houston to Oshman's Sporting Goods.

He looked for a stock that would nestle sweet and tight in her shoulder and told her the side-by-side barrel suited her style better than over-and-under. Wilma leaned against the wooden counter trying eight or ten different shotguns. Now and then she asked him what he thought. Was the Remington twenty the one to buy or the Browning twelve for a hundred more? All the men she saw come into the club shot twelve-gauges with a longer reach.

"You're a big girl now, Wilma," he told her. "Get the one that feels right to you." It sounded rough, the way he said it, and she wondered if he were a little put off when she decided on the twelve.

After bird season closed, he took her into pastures with a hand trap and a box of clay pigeons and threw eighty or a hundred at a session. The clay disks were harder to hit than a live bird; it was impossible to predict which way he would throw them. He stood behind her, his arm cocked back, and when she was ready she'd yell, "Pull." Vernon would whip his wrist, releasing the yellow disk overhead. She'd raise the gun quickly to her shoulder, try to get a fix on it fast, follow it, lead it, and shoot. The first seven times she tried, she missed, but Vernon told her to keep after it.

"Why are you doing this?" she asked him, glancing at him sideways. He was spending all his time with her. If she looked at him straight, she'd have to know he liked her wide shoulders and big hands, the thick red hair she pinned back with combs. She was afraid of handsome men. His eyes were steady on hers, more curious than anything, as if he wanted to know all her secrets.

"I need a buddy to go with, don't I?" Vernon said, putting an arm around her shoulder, but from the way his rough fingers closed on her arm she knew it wasn't a buddy he wanted.

When he stared down into her face, she got a little flustered, and for the first time began wishing she were pretty. Wilma wasn't bad-looking, a tall striking girl, her clear freckled skin reflecting light, with a faint flush along the cheekbones. But Vernon was the type who had seventeen girlfriends, all of them cute. She'd rather be his buddy, if she had to choose.

"Okay," she said, because playing with Vernon was a hoot. She'd always known men had a better time. When she was ten she had twisted her right arm fiercely in its socket, trying to kiss her elbow and turn into a boy.

"You're not scared of trying things, are you?" he said. He thought she was brave, but that wasn't it. When she was with him she just felt like there wasn't anything she couldn't do.

When Wilma got so she could hit seventeen out of twenty clay pigeons, Vernon decided she should enter the club's pigeon shoot the first weekend in May. There was plenty of conversation about Wilma's entry; she was the first female employee ever to enter the contest.

"Are they mad?" she asked Vernon, the day of the shoot.

"Why should they be?"

"Because I'm a girl and I work for them," she said.

"Forget it," he said. "Have a drink."

They walked into the crowd under a buff-colored tent borrowed from a local undertaker. A couple of Mexicans dressed in white jackets were crushing ice and pounding fresh mint for juleps. They handed Vernon three jiggers of straight bourbon, crushed mint and a teaspoon of sugar in a silver tumbler filled with packed crushed ice and passed more juleps among women in flowered shirtwaists and men in plaid jackets and white buck shoes. Under a canopy of live oaks four mariachis were playing "Cu Cu Cu Ru Cu" and already starting to sweat in their brocade shirts.

A brunette wearing dark glasses walked up to Wilma carrying her shotgun in one hand and a drink in the other.

"I just wanted to get a look at what the competition was wearing," she said, smiling faintly as she looked around the tent, and glanced down at the razor crease in her lavender silk racehorse legs. Small diamond elephants twinkled in her earlobes.

Wilma had heard the Admiral at the Calcutta after dinner the night before, insisting his girlfriend sleep in his room. This went against club practice of accommodating wives and other female guests in the upstairs dormitory.

"This way everybody gets a good night's sleep before the shoot," Wilma had offered.

The brunette drew a long red fingernail along her right eyebrow. "Oh, do you shoot?" she asked Wilma.

"A little," Wilma said.

The guests had gathered in the crowded living room

after dinner, working on Martell and cigars. Someone switched on the old standup Victrola, and a few couples started dancing before the Calcutta. Four men sat at the card table in chairs with antler backs, building stacks of red, blue and white chips. Looking down from the high plaster walls were a pronghorn antelope, a twelve-point whitetail buck, a bobcat, a ring-tailed cat and an enormous javelina boar with two-inch tusks. Against the wall stood a glass-fronted bookcase containing ledgers that went back to 1898. The books showed the kills taken each day, who shot and with which guide. It was pretty clear who the best guides were and the most consistent shots.

Wilma came in from the kitchen just as the Admiral stood up on a table and called for the bidding to start.

"Our first shooter is Landin Wilson from Newgulf," he said. The fringe on his buckskin jacket danced lightly. "People, this is a grand sportsman. You know it and I know it. Won the shoot last year."

Vernon was sitting on the Victorian loveseat next to the brunette. Wilma came over and squeezed between them.

"What's she think she's doin'?" the brunette complained.

"Just gettin' settled, honey," Wilma said.

"Do I have a hundred for Landin?" the Admiral said reproachfully. The Admiral himself couldn't shoot his way out of a Wheaties box.

"I used to shoot skeet when I was married to my first husband," the brunette said.

"Was that before you started running up those magnificent bar tabs?" asked an elderly man with a Mark Twain mustache, sitting at a table nearby.

"Oh, shut up, Ernie," the brunette said. "This was way before your time."

"Five hundred dollars on Landin Wilson," yelled a plump blonde dressed in hunting khaki.

"Raise you a hundred," said a heavy-set man across the room from the blonde.

"Goddammit, Clay, can't you let me have my way about anything?" The blonde stood up, pounded the table in front of her with her fist, wobbled and nearly fell. She grabbed the back of her chair.

"Why do we allow these women in here, anyway?" Clay complained to the crowd at large.

"I swear," the plump woman said, and sat down.

"Ladies and gentlemen," the Admiral said, "our next contestant's a man who came into the world with one eye closed. Who'll start the bidding on Vernon Hemshoff?" Vernon stood up and walked over to stand next to the Admiral, his hands clasped behind his back. Several hands went up right away, including the brunette's.

"Eight hundred dollars," she said. Her red lipstick was smeared. After three minutes of heavy bidding, she bought Vernon for seventeen hundred.

Wilma was drinking a Jax beer and feeling okay. She was proud of Vernon, and if she'd had the money she'd have bet on him herself.

"I feel like the grand champion steer at the Fort Worth stock show," Vernon said, sitting down again on the couch.

"You're no steer, honey," the brunette said, leaning across Wilma to plant a big kiss on Vernon's cheek. She was wearing a green silk cowboy shirt and a suede skirt that barely grazed the tops of her knees and white cowboy boots with three-inch heels. On her right hand sat a six-carat marquise diamond and around her left wrist hung a collection of seven rubber bands.

"She needs a cane to carry that ring," Wilma said to Vernon in a stage whisper. Then she turned to the woman.

"You might've bet on Vernon, but you don't own him."

Vernon looked at her in amazement. She wished she hadn't spoken. The brunette was just a rich playgirl swishing around. Wilma didn't own him either. Once or twice he had taken her dancing, and later he'd mussed her up and kissed her a little, but nothing serious.

"What the hell is the matter with you, Wilma?" Vernon said.

"Beg pardon?" the brunette said, trying to focus.

"Get lost," Wilma said, shoving the woman's shoulder. The brunette clutched the arm of the couch as if it were the railing of a storm-tossed ship.

Vernon looked at Wilma. "Simmer down," he said.

Wilma got up from the couch. "I think I'm going to throw up," she said, and went to bed.

"Most of us aren't so worried about our clothes at Coon Lake," Wilma said to the woman, who was standing in the striped shade of the tent. It was eleven the following morning.

"Where did you learn to shoot?" the brunette asked, flashing a smile like one of the Andrews sisters.

"I'm a dark horse," Wilma said. "Just a beginner. Vernon taught me." She nodded her head in his direction.

"Then you're no beginner, hon," the woman said, giving Vernon a wet smile.

"What kind of work do you do?" Wilma asked, not knowing why the question came up.

The brunette flicked her hair over her shoulder.

"Hell, honey," she said. "All I learned after Smith was how to give good dinner parties and take care of a man."

Stepping between the two women, Vernon took Wilma's arm and steered her over to the boathouse, where the Mexican handlers in high-crowned hats and white wrinkled shirts and trousers squatted in the shade near six wire cages. Inside the cages the pigeons moved nervously, making soothing ripply moans.

"I'm sorry for the birds," Vernon told her. "They manhandle 'em so bad."

"How?" Wilma asked. Some of the birds did seem droopy from the heat.

"You watch Paco over there." He pointed to a short stocky man with a thick pirate's mustache. "He'll pluck their tail feathers to make 'em fly crooked. Massage 'em to gentle 'em down, pump 'em up to excite 'em." Then he gave her a serious look.

"How about it, sugar? Feel like a winner?"

"Why not?" she said, with more confidence than she felt. Though the guides were sometimes contestants in these affairs, she felt funny.

She took a hard look at Vernon as he finished the last of the bourbon. He had paid the $75 for her entry fee.

"You look like last week's newspapers. Where were you last night?" It was stupid to worry about him; he had his own life.

"Cut it out, Wilma," he said. He grinned and ruffled her hair. "Listen up," he said, all business. "I need to go over some things. That Mexican's the best *columbaire* in Texas. He can make a bird fly straight or zig or zag or shoot for the moon. It's all according to how he releases it. And there ain't a way in the world you can second guess 'im. So you better be on your toes."

She nodded, but didn't feel like a contender.

Wilma stood watching the mother-of-pearl pigeons waddle back and forth in their cages. Their rainbow colors changed in the light and shade filtering between the wooden slats. Wilma could handle clay pigeons, but these birds were something else. Two eleven-year-old Mexican boys stood next to the cages, their heavy bangs nearly hiding their dark eyes.

"Who eats them?" she asked. Her papa and brothers always ate whatever they shot.

"The wetbacks eat 'em," a voice behind her said. "Wetbacks'll eat anything."

"Uh oh," Vernon said, making a face. "Somebody's got me covered." The brunette had sneaked up behind him and placed her hands over his eyes. She'd hidden her own eyes behind a pair of sunglasses with pink plastic frames shaped like bats' wings.

"I'm your fairy godmother," she whispered. She was holding him as close as she could, purple fingernails like tiny knife blades over his face.

"I'm ready to grant you three wishes, love. All you gotta do is pulverize a couple of little old pigeons."

Vernon reached around behind him and removed her hands. His complexion was a deep rose.

The woman wound one arm around his waist, cocking her head sideways while she put her near hand on his shoulder. From three feet away Wilma could smell her perfume. She hated herself for feeling jealous but wasn't able to keep quiet.

"Go back to the mansion, honey chile," she said.

The brunette looked at Wilma with the gun in her hands and made her eyes big. Vernon was staring at Wilma as if she were wearing a tutu.

"Lordy," the woman said. "Don't want to make Mama mad." She took a couple of short steps backward.

Wilma held her gun lightly, counting the wrinkles in the woman's neck. There were little beads of face powder in the creases. In the deeper fold between her freckled breasts lay a blue enameled javelina on a gold chain.

Wilma turned and walked to a grassy clearing east of

the tent, where a gang of tall elderly men dressed in fancy shooting jackets stood together. As she approached they stopped laughing. One of them removed his straw Stetson and bowed deeply from the waist. In the crook of his arm he held a Merkel twelve, the prettiest gun she'd ever seen, with hunting scenes engraved on the barrel and a shiny gold number 1 next to the trigger, which meant it was one of a custom pair.

"Good lord, Wilma, are you shooting?" he asked.

"Well, I was thinking I might get in a little target practice," she said softly.

"Well, don't you go getting cute and showing the rest of us up," the man said.

Wilma winked her dimples at him.

"I'm just a plain old girl, Mr. Sartwelle," she said.

The sun was hot on her shoulder as Wilma finally took her place in front of the *columbaire*. She turned around and smiled at him.

"*Que vaya bien,*" Paco told her. May it go well.

"*Mil gracias,*" she said. She was terrified.

One of the little boys bent down, removed a white bird and a gray one from the cage and gave them to a handler, who walked over and presented them to Paco. Around the *columbaire* a gray carpet of pigeon feathers had spread over the grass. Once in a while a puff of breeze lifted one of the feathers so it rose, transparent as a wisp of cobweb, then drifted to the ground. Paco examined the two birds and chose the white one. He turned his heavy-set body away from her, plucking several tail feathers and letting them fall to the ground. He folded the pigeon's wings back so the dorsal sides met like a paper airplane's, then cupped his hands around the bird as if in prayer.

"*Listo?*" he asked. "Ready?"

"Como no?" Wilma grinned. "Pull."

She watched him twist his torso like a discus thrower, holding the bird behind his right hip. She faced forward, looking over the sun-washed clearing. When the handler spun his body and uncurled his right arm she was ready, swinging gun to shoulder clean and quick, following the bird's confused, terrified flight, passing, leading it and firing. After her shot the bird seemed to hang for a moment in the air, like a tiny parachute toy shot from a popgun. The crowd exploded into hooting and clapping because she'd been so neat.

Wilma felt good and relaxed when the Admiral came over and removed his hat. He held out his hand.

"Pretty shooting, young lady," he said. "We're all real proud. But I hope this doesn't mean you'll quit making the biscuits."

"If you hadn't given me this job, I'da never learned in the first place," Wilma said. "If I win this darned thing, are you gonna make me a member?"

"Shoot, Wilma," the old man said, "you know good and well the club charter doesn't let us take in ladies."

"What makes you think I'm a lady, Admiral?" she said.

She was amazed at the careless shooting in the second round. Kyra Lee Hubbard, said to be the best woman shot in West Texas, couldn't hit a dirigible at fifty yards. And quite a few of the other contestants missed their shots, too. Some birds were only winged and kept on flying, flapping loosely across the clearing and lighting in trees. By the end of the second round only five of the original twenty-five contestants were left: Dan Ferguson, Chilton Tyler, the Admiral, Vernon and herself.

The Admiral, first up in the third round, switched to French 75s and ruined his chances; he got his shot off even before the Mexican threw the bird. Ferguson, favored to win the match, never shot because of a jammed gun, and Chilton missed clean. So now there were only Wilma and Vernon; he'd drawn the short straw and would have to shoot first.

The seven or eight pigeons left were hot and sleepy, hardly moving when the handler reached into the cage. Wilma had noticed him roughing up the birds in the last round, stroking their feathers the wrong way to waken them. She was beginning to feel the heat, too; her feet had mules standing on them.

Right before he was to shoot, Vernon walked over to her and whispered something she didn't catch.

"What?" she said, frowning.

When he bent closer she got a blast of bourbon. "Paco's been pulling out feathers on the left wing. Your bird's gonna turn sharp right; be ready."

She took a step away. "Forget it," she said. Who needed his help?

"Trust me," he said.

"Vernon, you ready?" called the Admiral.

"Yo," Vernon said, stepping out of the shade onto a little patch the contestants' boots had worn bare. His face was purple, and his white cowboy shirt clung to his shoulder blades. Wilma stood next to the Admiral at the front of the crowd. She waved and called out, "Good luck, buddy." Vernon didn't acknowledge her. He held his neck and shoulders stiff, cradling his shotgun in the crook of his arm, and leaned over to say a few words to the *columbaire*. The Mexican kneeled on the ground, making love to the birds.

"Pajarito dulcito," he said, lifting the bird's beak to his lips.

"Que vuela derecho," Vernon said. "Make him fly straight."

Wilma reached into her back pocket, pulled out a rag and wiped excess oil from her gun barrel. She checked the two chambers, then looked along the periphery of the crowd where the brunette spoke with three club officers, her face flushed and animated. She held red roses, as if Vernon were a thoroughbred she might win in a claiming race. Wilma snorted.

"Pull," Vernon said, and the Mexican unleashed his right arm, releasing the bird. It rose straight up, then took off toward the trees. When it was seventy-five yards away Vernon dropped it. The shot was difficult because of the speed of the bird's flight and the angle of ascent. She'd never seen him shoot better.

"Pretty," she told him, grabbing his arm, but he wasn't smiling.

As she stepped into the clearing she felt drops of sweat trickle between her breasts. Paco's boys held out two birds. One was a buff color, the other blue-gray. When the birds' eyes moved it was as if a speck of gravel had disturbed the surface of a tiny rose-colored pool. The buff one, make it the buff one, she muttered to herself. It was her crazy idea that the pale bird would appear larger against the sky. Paco took the gray bird in his hands and asked if she was ready.

"*Como no?* Pull," she said, and Paco swung in a circle, the hand holding the bird whirling at the end of his big arm. He threw it so hard his cap flew off. The bird flapped and somersaulted, a toy airplane out of control, then recovered, climbing the air. She'd gotten on it as soon as he let go, anticipated its turn to the right, not starting her swing yet but ready for it. So, when the bird took off toward the treeline to her left, she was one split second behind, enough so she only winged it. She could see it flinch when a piece of shot hit it, but by then it was out of range, dropping into the trees.

Afterward Vernon came up and put his arm around her.

"Rotten luck," he said.

The following winter Vernon didn't ask her to hunt. Whenever she suggested it, he agreed to go along, but insisted on carrying both guns and all the decoys, and made her take his hand when she stepped into the boat. On these mornings Wilma shot her limit, and Vernon wanted to quit before he'd killed his ten ducks.

"Let's get coffee," he'd say, rubbing his hands.

When Wilma asked him to take her to the deer stand he'd built in the pecan bottom, Vernon told her he was partners in that blind with another guide and it wouldn't be fair to bring in another gun.

"I'd rather take you to the picture show," he said. "Go buy you a new dress and let's go dancing."

He took her to the Blue Goose, the open-air dance hall, where two fiddlers and a guitar picker sat at the base of a huge live oak tree passing a bottle of Jack Daniels around. Thirty or forty people were two-stepping around the cement floor when Wilma and Vernon stood up. Wilma wore a green Mexican skirt with sequins and a white peasant blouse that did right by her full bust and plump shoulders. She wore her thick russet hair pulled back from her face with two heavy mother-of-pearl combs, and when Vernon put his hands on her waist and spun her around, the combs slipped from her hair and her skirt stood out like a fan so everyone saw the quick, sinuous movements of her legs and feet. Then everybody else quit dancing to watch Wilma break free of Vernon's hand, moving in a lonely solo that brought the place alive. He didn't offer to dance with her then, not wanting to dull the glitter she shed on everything: cement tables, sweating fiddlers, matrons in flowered dresses and lean, creased men in jeans so starched they could stand alone.

Wilma was flattered by Vernon's sudden romantic turn, but she missed his cussing at her when she let an easy shot get by and yelling at her to wade into the lake and pick up the decoys. Instead he brought her small square boxes tied with ribbon, with nests of cotton inside and a string of imitation pearls from Kress's, a pair of dangly earrings and a gold heart pendant on a chain. Wilma put them on and stared at her reflection in the small oval mirror over her vanity, lifting the hair off her shoulders to see the ornaments better.

"Don't you want to be buddies anymore?" she asked.

"Can I be your buddy and still neck with you?" he said, teasing. But when he held her tight against his chest and kissed her, she knew what he was asking for wasn't companionship, or even a good time.

"You don't want a tomboy girlfriend, do you?" she said one night. He'd been asking her to pin her heavy hair on top of her head.

"You don't look anything like a tomboy to me," he said seriously, touching one of her earrings. "And it's not a girlfriend I want."

She had never given marriage much thought, except when her feet hurt or when some redneck leaned out of a truck window and yelled something ugly. Usually she wouldn't let these people bother her. Only now and then she felt she needed protection.

Most of her friends at home were already slow wives. Some were pregnant. She did have one friend who was different—tall, rangy Rosemary, with faded blue eyes and cornsilk hair she wore in two ponytails like little horns. Rosemary stayed skinny helping her husband farm two hundred acres of cotton and maize. Whenever the subject of men came up Wilma tried to explain what she wanted.

"I want to learn to do something as well as a man. Take care of myself."

Rosemary laughed. "Nothing special, doing what your old man does. It's just nasty, dirty, hot hard work."

Rosemary moved fast. She could change a tractor tire and plow a furrow straight to the turnrow. Wilma wanted to ask her if she'd slept with Don before they got married, but they didn't have conversations like that in their little town after eleventh grade, when they finally got broken in to French kissing.

"You keep those boys' hands off your privates," Wilma's mother had told her when she was thirteen and they'd come sniffing around. "You're a well-developed big old girl, and all they're after at this age is pussy. You'll ruin your life."

Wilma had never heard her mother use language like that before, but she believed every word she said. But, in spite of the warning, she necked furiously on the living-room couch with one slim, black-haired boy named Steve until her mother called from upstairs, and hauled her into the bedroom. Her mother was terrified of boys.

She sat in front of an old-fashioned dressing table with a mirror behind it. The back of her head was reflected in the mirror, along with twenty-five tiny perfume bottles.

"Don't let me catch you down there on the couch again. Tomorrow he won't respect you."

Wilma could tell from her mother's tone: she wouldn't respect her either. Her mother looked at her with suffering Jesus eyes that grew huge, their light blending with the rainbow reflections of the perfume bottles so Wilma felt confused. Then she didn't see anything for a few minutes after that because she fainted and fell down on the floor. Her mother had to call the doctor. Wilma had never fainted before, and she never fainted afterward. Her mother said it was from growing too fast.

Going to bed with Vernon for the first time terrified Wilma so much she cried. Vernon stopped and turned on the light.

"What's wrong?" he said. "I hurt you?"

"No," she said, sniffling. She didn't want to meet his eyes. "I'm worried about tomorrow."

"Why, for God's sake?"

"You'll be disgusted. Won't talk to me. I'll shrivel up."

"Hush your mouth, monkey," he said, and buried his face in her soft stomach. She didn't tell him it would ruin her life.

In May and June she set out tomatoes on the north side of the club building and sprayed for pests. Rosemary had a baby. The plants flourished. Vernon took her into Houston to look at china. He talked about fixing up an old bungalow near the lake. Wilma dreamed of riding a horse through a field of high grass, her long hair streaming. She woke in the night, sweating, short of breath, feeling the mane of the dream horse whipping her face. It was quail season when he proposed. They were sitting on the porch in the twilight on a weekday when there weren't any guests.

"I want to get married," Vernon said, "if you'll put up with me." He tugged at the bill of his cap.

That was the way it was, then. If you went to bed, you got married. She had known him over a year.

"Yes," she said. She felt as if she were made of wood.

Standing, Wilma put her arms around Vernon's neck and kissed him. Then she walked to the corner of the porch and picked up her shotgun. She unzipped the canvas case, removed the gun and started wiping it with an oiled rag.

"Need to keep the rust off," she said.

She held the gun lightly, enjoying the weight of it, and the balance, the cold smell of the gun oil. She felt like she was driving through an old neighborhood she had lived in once and hadn't seen in years.

When her papa placed her hand in Vernon's on their wedding day she could see tears in his eyes. After the ceremony he danced with her to the wheezy polka band that sweated under the mesquite trees in the front yard, Wilma holding up her heavy train in one hand and smiling like Miss America Bride, twenty years old, her green eyes shining agates, her skin pearled with tiny beads of sweat.

"Honor your husband, *liebchen*," he told her. "Never tell him no." She wasn't so sure this was good advice. She wasn't even sure she should be married. She didn't feel old enough, and Vernon looked solemn and stuffy in his blue suit.

She had never felt closer to her father than when he picked up her left hand with the ring on it and held it to his lips at the end of the dance. Then he told her one more thing: "Don't sell the farm."

A few weeks before their wedding Vernon's daddy had handed him the deed to part of the farm he'd inherited from his own father, whose father before him had won it in a dice game at Andersonville Prison. Wilma rode and drove and walked with Vernon over every inch of it. A long slice of Caney Creek land with the Colorado River lapping the southern tip, the eight hundred acres ran north two miles out on the prairie. That was where the best fishing holes were, where water ran cold out of deep ditches and purple horse mint stood tall on spiky fragrant stems. She followed him into river bottoms so thick a hundred deer could hide in the dappled shade, and a million garden spiders bounced on their webs between the trees. Every time she walked through one of the webs and felt the spider crawling down her back she yelped and bent over, shaking her head like a wet dog. Vernon laid her down on a sand spit next to the muddy river, reached his arm across her shoulder, and pulled a long strand of her hair, pulled it gently but steadily so she had to turn on her side to face him.

"What's going on?" she said.

"Comanche raid," he said, and covered her mouth with his. He tasted like grape gum, and his stocky body smelled of the salt on his skin and the sun-dried shirt he wore. She moved away, opening her eyes, shy from looking at him so close. He had a good face, round, with a generous nose and deeply dented chin. His blue eyes had brown spots in them. He was a man who smiled easily on the world and took his comfort as it came. He stroked her breasts until the nipples stood up like raisins, the cracked skin of his fingers scraping her body like a cat's tongue. She dug her heels into the wet sand, keeping her eyes on the thunderheads behind his shoulder.

5

SHE DIDN'T ROLL OVER when Vernon slipped out of bed at seven on New Year's Day. Whatever he had in mind he sure was creeping around, hardly making any noise, a few splashes in the bathroom, heavy whuffing as he leaned over to pull on his boots. Then he slid out the bedroom door, and she could stop holding her breath. Opening her eyes, she examined the wallpaper daisies in the thin light. On the wall between the living room and their bedroom the paper had begun to pull away a little, leaving a slack spot, a pouch big enough for a cat to climb into. Big enough to hide the bundle of bills, $167 she'd been salting away out of the truck-stop money.

When she heard Vernon's truck backing out of the drive, she left the bed, pulled on her robe and started brushing her long red hair on the way to the kitchen. Striking a match, she held it over one of the eight burners and put a kettle of water on to boil. The ferrets in the cage on the opposite wall uncurled their long bodies and started snarling at each other. Wilma reached up to the third shelf of the cupboard and took down the flour canister. Measuring by the handful, she sifted flour and salt together into a large earthenware bowl, added cooking oil and dark honey and a couple of yeast packets, mixing everything with her hands. When the dough was thick and rubbery she punched it down with her fists a few times, covered the bowl with a cotton towel and set it inside the oven to rise.

She opened the screen door, walked down the cement steps and stood in her winter garden, hugging her bathrobe around her. The sky stretched vacant and blue, a few geese honking overhead so high she couldn't see them. On the road that was higher than the fields on either side she noticed a tank truck heading out toward land Vernon used to farm. Behind the house the last hundred acres the bank didn't get had a small fenced cemetery plot in the middle where Vernon's granddaddy and great-granddaddy were buried, and her acre of vegetable garden.

Wilma had chopped weeds in this dirt for twenty years. Vernon told her he'd pay someone to do it, but it gave her a place away from the little house stuffed with boys and their feet, Vernon's ferrets and coyotes. Even with Jody gone she couldn't breathe in the house, and when no one could hear she often talked to herself.

"A place of my own, a small place. Quiet." Some days, while mopping the kitchen floor or driving to and from work, she caught herself saying, "I want to go home." *I'm crazy,* she thought.

There wasn't much in the garden: a few wrinkled eggplants, winter lettuce, onions. Dry pods in the magnolia tree in the middle of the plot had dropped their red seeds in the rows like hard candy. Picking up a hoe leaning against the house, Wilma began chopping at the Johnson grass. After a minute she stopped, feeling her strength leaking down into the soil. She smelled the sun on the earth, but it did her no good, only filled her with the scary news that she was at the edge of all she'd known about living on her piece of ground.

"No point crying about it now," she said and walked back into the house to pack.

She was ready to close her old leather grip with the stickers from Hot Springs, Arkansas, still on it from her honeymoon, when Clint walked in.

"Why's everybody up so early?"

"I'm going to work," she said.

Clint rubbed the corner of his right eye with his finger. His football jersey barely covered the curve of his butt.

"You got to work New Year's? Bummer," he said. He looked at the suitcase. "Taking a trip?"

She shook her head, looking at him standing in a shaft of sunlight slanting through the bedroom window. His hair was the color of dandelion heads, the fuzz golden over his upper lip. "Taking a walk," she said.

When he was too little still for school he padded around the house behind her barefoot, carrying his tin pail and a washrag while she mopped floors and gathered up dirty laundry. Together they carried a wicker basket full of Vernon's filthy jeans out onto the porch, and Clint sat up on the edge of the round GE washer poking the trousers down with a dish mop and stuffing in shirts with proud pearl snaps that clicked against the enamel tank and had to be pulled carefully through the wringer so they wouldn't dissolve like aspirins.

For his fifth birthday she'd stopped by the highway where a Mexican was selling spotted goats, and bought one for seventeen dollars, along with a crude wooden cart with rickety red wheels and a cheap red leather harness decorated with silver studs. After Vernon left in the morning, taking Jody off to school, she harnessed the goat, whose name was John Lennon, set Clint on the driver's seat and led the whole contraption out into the driveway.

"Pretend you're the wagon-train boss," she said. "Hold the reins in two hands and show him who's in charge." Clint held the reins in tiny red hands, his chin at a determined angle. The goat immediately trotted off into the ditch and began chewing a bull nettle. Instead of kicking the goat, as Jody would have done at that age, Clint giggled and yelped.

"We gonna be late to Dodge City, Mama," he said, shaking his white head like a baby goat himself. She could've eaten him up.

"Divorce," he said now. "You're not coming back."

"I don't know. Not for a while."

"Not coming back for a while, or not getting a divorce?"

"Not for a while," she said.

When he was ten she went with him out into the rice fields to net crawdads. This was when Jody used to stay late after school for football practice, only he sat out most of the games because of grades. For months Clint kept the crawdads in a big aerated fish tank on the kitchen table. This made breakfast more confused and cramped. The day the crawdads were missing Jody came downstairs with a gloat in his eye and said, "Mama, could you fix us some gumbo for supper?"

Clint folded his arms over his chest and shook the forelock out of his face. "You find out about Ruby?" he said.

"Why couldn't he fall for some girl?" she said.

"It happens all the time, this stuff," he said. "You don't have to let it get to you."

But she couldn't help it. Everything she'd ever had to fight against had gotten to her, every dream she'd ever turned loose.

No matter how much she'd wanted Clint to play Varsity he only made second string. Before there was Little League in town she stood in back of their house throwing a football to him till her shoulder screamed. He never asked her to do this; but he'd run into the house after school, letting the door slam, and yell for her: "One, two, seven, fifteen, fifty-seven . . ." By the time she'd run into the living room he was leaning down, shooting the ball at her through the V of his legs. *"Hike,* Mama," he yelled, as the pointed end of the ball smashed into her chest. In all the years of Little League, Peewee and Junior High football, Wilma never missed a game. When Vernon came with her, the two of them huddled in the open stands, ducking their heads under a blanket to pass a pint bottle of Wild Turkey, Vernon jumping to his feet and nearly knocking her over when Clint threw a block or caught a pass.

"Come here, honey," Wilma said. "You know your mama loves you to death."

Her youngest son had closed his face.

"You're not my mama," he said. Then he turned and walked out of the room, his pale hair sticking up like Dagwood's. *He must have slept on it funny; I'll buy him some hair tonic in town. You can't keep people happy forever.*

6

AFTER NEW YEAR'S everything changed. Wilma was running the road with Gary, getting in a few hours' driving practice on the interstate where she didn't have to shift. After a sixteen-hour run and seven beers, Gary usually ate a steak and fell into a trackless sleep. This left Wilma plenty of time to telephone Vernon collect and tell him she was sorry she called him a skunk when she found him and Ruby in back of his truck. But she didn't do it.

There was too much to find out about, for one thing, how to detour around highway weigh stations when a load was due and Gary was short on sleep and long on road time. In spite of federal rules requiring drivers to rest after ten hours, shippers squeezed their schedules so every last trucker on the road was breaking the law or going broke trying to play it straight. Gary showed her how to shift cargo over the wheels to make a load sit right, how to drop illegal weight if there was no way to avoid the scales, doubling back later and dragging part of the load out of a farm-to-market ditch a few miles from the interstate. He had to fudge times in the log book so DOT inspectors wouldn't slap on a fine.

"Christ," Gary said the night a uniformed inspector pulled out a flashlight at one in the morning and insisted he show every scrap of documentation he carried. "Between their frigging road taxes and licenses and their asinine rules this pissant government'd nickel and dime me off the road if I didn't lie like a punk with his pockets full of coke."

Her first day out Gary had a load of dry goods headed for Roanoke, but there was no rush so they went south through Louisiana on Interstate 10, dipping down to Morgan City, cruising through New Orleans, Mobile, and Jacksonville, Florida, where they got a motel room with two double beds. She'd insisted on sleeping separate, and Gary had grudgingly agreed. While he was tucking the truck in, Wilma turned down both beds so there'd be no confusion. By the time he opened the door she had crept into her bed, the blankets pulled to her ears. In the morning she was embarrassed about changing clothes and using the bathroom, so she made him go to the coffeeshop while she showered. She was hot in her jeans when she walked out the door into the parking lot. It was eighty-eight, the sun bouncing off the dagger leaves of the palms.

"I want to go to the beach," she said. "I need a bathing suit." The coffeeshop was full of retirees wearing flower prints.

"Let's go shopping," he said, and he snooped around the store as if he went shopping with women every day of his life. She bought a one-piece suit with red and purple flowers on it, the legs cut high, the fabric hugging her bust and hips and nipping in her waist. Looking at herself in the boutique mirror she didn't exactly approve. Mae West. Whatever happened to her? Healthy was beautiful, nowadays, and *Vogue* models had muscles, but compared to Wilma they were twigs. Wisps.

They strolled a long way down the beach, Gary in boots and jeans, Wilma wearing the new bathing suit under her pants. Only a few beachcombers were out so she didn't feel awkward pulling her clothes off and dropping them into a pile on the sloping sand. At the water's edge she stood watching the sea, still as a meadow, deep green with a frill of foam that lapped at her bare feet. Feeling him looking at her in the bathing suit, Wilma took a breath and sucked in her stomach until she saw stars. Then she relaxed and sat down in the water. The hell with it. He came up beside her, his pants rolled to mid-calf, his feet under the water the color of bleached shells.

"There's marlin out there," he said. "Wish we had a boat."

"A boat with one of those little sails on it," she said, "and a year to learn to drive it." She stood up so she could look as far as the horizon.

"I wish I had a year to sit here looking at you standing in the sun," he said. He put one hand behind her back, pulled her quickly against his T-shirt and put his mouth on hers. Her breasts were mashed so tightly against him they nearly popped out of the bathing suit. She pushed him back, but the kiss was okay.

From Jacksonville they headed north on 95 past Cumberland Island National Seashore, Fort Sumter, and the Francis Marion National Forest. For days they dawdled on two-lane Highway 17, passing through Valona, Shellman Bluff, and Halfmoon Landing, sometimes looking across waving seagrass to slow barges and cruisers on the Intracoastal Canal. Between Savannah and Charleston the grass was so high it nearly cut off the view to the flat black water beyond. Often they stopped at white frame houses where they ate cracked crab for fifty cents apiece and talked with black people who spoke the thick accent of the Gullah slaves Gary said were their great-grandfathers.

He told her Swamp Fox stories from the Civil War, and they told each other stories about buying a boat and settling down on Daufuskie Island, making a living netting the big blue crabs. The campground at Hunting Island had a broad beach empty except for a pickup with a family of migrant workers, and Wilma talked Gary into renting one of the beachfront cabins so they could spend a couple of days watching the big shrimpers spread their butterfly nets. Wilma could have stayed there a month, but there wasn't time. In a week they got as far as Kill Devil Hill, where the Wright brothers launched their glider, then jogged west, hooking through Raleigh, and she was breathless with the speed they'd been traveling, the excitement of all she had seen.

For three weeks they took short runs, one or two days through five southern coastal states and inland as far as Columbus, Atlanta, Charlotte and Roanoke. This time of year they didn't want to mess with mountains, and there was enough frozen meat, dry goods and a few fresh vegetables hopscotching state lines to keep them in fuel and motel money. Then in early February they got a load of peppers going from Mobile to Houston. Three days they had to kill in Mobile before they got word about those peppers. It finally came over the computer at the truck stop, and they didn't have much choice. The pay was better than they'd been getting, though it wasn't as good as the gold-mine deals that came only once in three months when somebody wanted heavy equipment or lethal chemicals hauled a thousand miles in a day and a half. There was money in hot-dogging, but those runs were killers. At least this time Gary'd had a little rest, pulling out of Mobile at midnight, hitting Hammond around two. At five-thirty she waked him and by seven-thirty they were nearing Baton Rouge and the bridge, and his eyes didn't want to stay open. He gulped another cup of coffee and pressed on through thickening traffic.

"Look in my overnight, will you, and hand me a couple of those blue ones. The bottle with the red screw cap," he said. She turned around and unzipped his flight bag, fishing around in the bottom of it where he kept maybe twenty bottles of uppers, downers and Lord knows what. She hated what the stuff did to him, his voice grazing the lip of hysteria, his words pouring out in a chemical babble. She wished she'd had more practice so she could drive while he slept. He only let her take the wheel on the flat, lonely stretches of the interstate, never through towns where she'd have to shift.

"Lay off this stuff. Let me take her instead," she said, handing him the bottle.

"No can do," he said. "Too much traffic this week, and if there's a pileup on the bridge you'll wear your arm out. Stop and start for an hour. No thank you, pretty."

He took out the bottle, unscrewed the cap and rolled three white capsules into his palm, licking them up into his mouth. He switched on the radio to a Lafayette station. They were playing a kind of Cajun two-step with a cute roll to it: Buckwheat Zydeco, Rocking Dopsie, Clifton Chenier.

"Let's hotfoot it down country, baby. Hear some of this friendly music." His grin was looking lit-up and loose already, and he started whomping his foot down next to the clutch, keeping time to the corny accordion. He wouldn't stop now for another eight or ten hours. She just smiled at him and didn't say anything, wishing he didn't have to rip himself up.

It was Monday before Fat Tuesday. Highways were choked with fun seekers all juiced-up and full of desire, turning the road into a crazy mix of honky-tonk and high school gym. The night before, at the Ragin' Cajun truck stop in Metairie, she and Gary did their share of partying. Sixty-five rigs were lined up on party row at the back of the lot, commercial beavers crawling between the rigs, everybody drinking and smoking every kind of weed, popping uppers and downers like raisins and snuggling up close. That night Wilma got to see her first lady truckdriver fight. A twenty-five-year-old owner-operator who called herself Lady Madonna took offense when a hooker mistook her for another commercial and told her to clear out.

"You come on back here to party row and repeat that, girl," Madonna said, and took off all her bracelets and earrings, rolled up the sleeves of her cowboy shirt, and put on some extra eyeliner. Her boyfriend was making book on the outcome, and when the hooker nosed around the last row in a late-model Camaro, stepping out of the car dressed in high-heeled boots and red velvet pants and a purple satin halter, everybody knew she had too much skin showing to be a fighter. She was taller than Madonna by three inches and outweighed her by thirty pounds, but this didn't bother the blonde any. She faced the hooker with her hands on her narrow hips, gave her long hair a toss and smirked.

"Now, what did you call me, whore?" she said.

"Bitch," the woman said. She had one foot slightly in front of the other as if she were posing for *People.*

"Well, you gotta chance to prance right out of here without paying no blood money. All you gotta do is take it back."

"Make me, baby," said the other woman, folding her arms over her chest and tapping her toe.

"Looking at you, girl, I can't figure out why anyone would want to."

Wilma and Gary were leaning against the tailgate of a

big reefer unit across from the two women. "Somebody's gonna get hurt," Wilma said, shaking her ponytail.

"Honor's everything on the road," Gary said. "Shh."

Lady Madonna started taking short, bouncy steps on the balls of her sneakers until she was a foot from the satin halter. She slammed the other woman's mouth with her little white fist.

"Now what was that you called me, whore?" The blonde had her face close to her opponent, who was cradling her jaw with both hands.

"Madonna," the girl said. "Lady Madonna."

"That's better," the blonde said, turning and walking back to her truck.

"One of 'em knocked on my door at six one spring morning," Gary said, "looking like Miss Teenaged America. Asked me did I want some. I said if it was Girl Scout cookies I didn't need any, I was trying to trim down, and you know that girl said—and she used these very words—'This little snack's no-cal, cowboy.' I told her to clear out before I gave her a boot in the tail." He shook his head. "What's happening to young America is plain scary."

"I wonder where that girl is," she said.

"Who?"

"Oralee Sweet, the punk rocker with the baby," she said. "I miss her."

She missed every damned thing she ever lost, everything that changed. The puppies that got run over or ran away and Vernon's dirty socks and his caps lying all over her table and the smell of ferrets. Oh, Lord, and she missed her piano lessons and Ben and Virginia and Ruby Taliaferro and Cornelia, Jody and Clint, those boys she'd have to whip up on and nag and throw out of the house when it felt like grown men shouldn't live in the same house with their mother.

Everybody was running away from her, everybody and everything she cared about, and they were getting so old it was pitiful. Vernon had breasts now, though he didn't have to wear an undershirt yet. And while she hadn't let herself go completely, her face was starting to look like somebody lay down and slept in it. Her papa wandered out of the house if you didn't watch him. He called Senator Tower every other week, but couldn't hear unless you climbed into his right ear. Maybe like they say, when you got old God fixed it so you didn't see or hear well, so you didn't mind when they cut everything off for good.

All day Gary kept popping the pills that gave him a staring wall-eyed look, slept heavily and woke in a sweat, hugging her hard against him. He wasn't her lover; that wasn't part of the deal. But there were plenty of nights since she came on board that he turned to her and she opened her arms to him. And it wasn't just for his comfort she hugged him; the highway was surely one of the coldest spots in this windy world. For a long time he didn't talk much about his wife, and Wilma didn't tell him about Vernon losing the farm and stealing her savings.

Even with all that Dexedrine in him she could tell Gary was pushing it to make Houston before suppertime. The two lanes approaching the Mississippi bridge at Baton Rouge were clogged with pickups and station wagons filled with families on the way to Mardi Gras parades in small towns: Basile, Church Point, Eunice, Mamou. When traffic slowed to ten miles an hour nobody seemed to mind except Gary.

Beautiful country girls were still sleeping in cars all around them, their hair rolled. Horses dozed in their trailers. Fathers at the wheel sipped coffee out of mugs and complained to backseat children, who stuck their long, restless feet through the window and danced to the radio.

The mothers leaned their heads against back rests and slept with their mouths open.

"Jesus," Gary said, stamping his foot on the floor, "we'll be here till Easter. Don't nobody in this state have any business today?"

"Nope. You're the only trucker in Louisiana trying to be serious the day before Fat Tuesday. Don't blow a gasket." Wilma switched on the CB. A man's voice came on black and slow and dreamy as Steen's cane syrup.

"You people crawling down this road this morning, is you heard the true story about Moses in the bullrushes?"

A second voice came on.

"No, son, but I heard one about Jesus in the cathouse. You see, friend, Jesus was walking downtown one day and he got a hard on just thinking about sweet Mary Magdalene, and he says to himself, now it's time for a little poontang, got to cool off these Tabasco *cojones* quick."

"Will you zip your scummy lip, my man, or do I have to jam you off the air?" That was the first voice.

"Nigger, place your zinger in your ear, you hear?" The Cajun voice was high and wheedling.

A thick voice came on, even higher.

"Beaver mechanic; need a beaver mechanic. Where all you for-rent baby dolls? Where you at, sweetheart?"

Wilma looked at her watch. It was eight-fifteen.

"Lord," she said. Gary's eyes were slitted down and his jaw clamped. His hands gripped the wheel as if it were a lifeboat railing, and he didn't seem to know she was in the cab.

Traffic halted. Cars and pickups and flatbeds and RVs started honking. There were a lot of different flavors of horns. Drivers were walking up and down the center line carrying cups of ice.

When she saw the back of Gary's shirt turning a violent Mediterranean blue she rubbed the back of his neck, his shoulders knotted like roots. As her hand first touched him he jumped as if he'd been burned. After a few minutes the truck nosed its way onto the bridge and across the railing she saw brown muddy water whipped to a chop. A camper full of blond kids slammed on its brakes, and Gary barely stopped in time.

"I need that radio," he said shortly. She switched it back on. The static was a steady stream of white noise with an occasional streak of blue in it, some machine scream she could never identify. The boys in the truck in front were shooting the bird at them. The voice that came on was telling a story about himself and two girls in a truck-stop motel.

"One had little red pirate boots on and short hair cut to a point in back, and the other'n was tall and big with long, long hair she switched into her face. Beautiful."

"Man, you got all the luck. The only wear this hooter's getting is rubbing upside my fly. These young gals is mean."

"Jesus, how come they never talk about anything different?" Wilma asked.

"Keeps 'em awake," Gary said.

"One of them little gals dripped honey all over me from a plastic bear and licked off every bit with her pointy tongue."

"Tell me a story," Wilma said. "Make it original."

"How about the time the firemen came to the house. Corinne was yelling; we were having a party in bed, and the granny lady next door had her windows open. She thought somebody was butchering a pig in there so she called the police and the fire department and the SPCA. The firemen got there first. We were so busy we didn't notice a thing till I heard voices, took a look out the window, and there's a guy in a yellow slicker carrying an axe and hanging onto a ladder alongside our house. He took that axe and smashed the glass to smithereens and was halfway through the window when he saw us."

Wilma laughed, but she felt pretty blue. She couldn't remember the last time Vernon made love to her. When she was young and proud she loved to straddle him, her hair swinging over her shoulders. She'd hold his hands in hers, stretch her arms wide and let her eyes run along her ribs and down her belly and flanks to where they fit together.

"We're pretty," she'd say. Then she'd be shy, having said that, and try to lie down and hide her breasts. Now she didn't like to reveal her body at all, she'd gotten so big. Was it the last time in bed with Vernon she'd cut the light out and hidden under the covers?

The kids in the truck ahead of them were wrestling around on the floor of the camper. It looked like six or seven, all around twelve. Maybe a Boy Scout troop. They had reached the midpoint of the bridge. Gary's hands on the wheel shook a little, and sweat dripped from his chin.

"Want something from the cooler?" she asked. His color was bad. "I got 7-Up and grapefruit juice."

"Reach back in that bag and pour some of that bottle into a cup for me, and put a splash of 7-Up in it. We got ice?" he said.

She did as he asked, though she didn't want him to have it, not after all the booze the night before and the speed. He didn't even give the ice cubes time to cool the drink down. One of the kids in front of them stuck his tiny white ass out over the tailgate of the camper and pulled down his jeans. The rest of them hung their noses out the back waiting for a reaction. Cars and trucks hooted.

"Christ almighty," Gary yelled, and gave them a blast from the horn mounted on top of the cab. The kids thought the horn was terrific. Two more dropped their pants and sat on the tailgate. She would've laughed if Gary hadn't been so mad. He slammed on his brakes and came to a stop a couple of inches from the pickup's Louisiana license plate. The boys dove into the cab.

"Cool it," she said, grabbing his forearm. It felt like the skin of a fever patient's. The pickup was pulling farther ahead. Gary put a hand over his eyes.

"Look at me," she said. His pupils were dilated, his left eye twitching at the outside corner. "You're strung out. Let me drive."

"You're dreaming," he said. He stepped on the accelerator, shifting into first, and looked out over the barrier on his side of the bridge at the mean little waves he said he saw sometimes in his dreams. The radio was quiet.

"You want real radio?" she asked. "Cowboy ballads, preachers, punk lyrics, talk shows?" He didn't hear her. His foot beat on the floor next to the clutch. She turned the Cajun station back on.

"You folks from around Mamou, now come tomorrow mornin', you shake out them covers and saddle up. Paint that old pony's toenails pretty, and come on out to the courthouse. That's where we gonna be at six in the mornin', and you all be there, or be square."

"Want to watch a parade?" she asked him, staring out the windshield at two black horses' butts with green blankets on. Gary didn't answer. Again they slowed to a halt, the engine shuddering so the whole truck shook. When she turned to look at him, Gary was cheek down on the wheel, his hands dangling at his sides. His head was turned away from her toward the window so she had to crawl out of her seat and lean over to see his face. His eyes were open. She shook him a couple of times without raising a whisker-twitch. Behind her people were sitting on their horns.

She took his wrist and felt his pulse. Jumping like a cricket. Fifty-five years old. Could be angina. Embolism. She'd seen it on *General Hospital*. They had to get someplace with a doctor. She couldn't drive this truck. Had to. Horns yammering behind her. Boy Scouts miles away. She put an arm around Gary and tried to pull his body toward her so she could lock her hands across his chest, but he weighed one-eighty, and the leverage was wrong. So she squeezed back into the bunk behind the cab, reaching over and locking her arms that same way, and hauled him like a log, putting the long muscles in her back into it. It took several minutes to work his torso sideways through the space between the seats. The hair around her face was dripping. She had to climb over him into the driver's seat and turned the ignition. The first time she let out the clutch the truck leaped forward, hiccoughed and died.

"Mama," she said, moving the stick around to find neutral. She tried again, and this time the engine sounded right, so she put it into first and started moving. The truck wouldn't go any faster than fifteen miles an hour. That was okay with her. She wasn't in any hurry to deal with the other side of the river. This bridge was all right. At least she was moving. Fifteen miles an hour in first, the choppy river below, half of Baton Rouge behind her. She hadn't looked at the map lately to see what lay ahead; she didn't even know what road she ought to take out of town. Where was the hospital? How would she get the truck out of first? Trucks behind her honked. She'd have to move it into third or fourth. She'd studied that diagram he gave her enough times so she should have it memorized, but without him her mind was a white sheet flapping on a clothesline. Wilma took a deep breath, swallowed and went on driving.

7

THE FOG SWIRLED LOW OVER Louisiana. The pink zinc lights on the freeway had halos around them, and the lights in city skyscrapers behind her dimmed and brightened, dimmed and brightened as if on rheostats. Each time Wilma looked in the rear view she had the sensation of being in a boat caught in a whirlpool because the street lamps kept moving. Three A.M., the four lanes almost empty, thank God. She had to keep the truck at thirty if she wanted to read the exit signs. From the hospital she'd want to keep heading west on the loop past Broussard, Aldine and Bayou Current, until they neared the Mississippi bridge and started looking for the ramp for Interstate 10.

The intern had given her directions she copied on the back of a matchbook in the waiting room while they pumped Gary's stomach. After three hours they wheeled him through the double doors looking half dead. His skin was a frog-belly white tinged blue by his beard. When he woke in the waiting room outside Emergency there wasn't any question about where he was heading.

"Get me out of this joint," he whispered. "I don't want

the company to find out." His eyes swept up and down the corridor.

"You're nuts," she told him. "We've got to report this. They'll think you were hijacked or hit on the head."

His eyes were wild. "I guess it don't matter to you if I lose this job, lose this truck. Wind up sitting in a Barcalounger watching Merv Griffin." His voice still had road static in it.

"Spies tell the company everything. They'll put a boot in my butt and it'll be all over." Wilma had heard him rave about the informers who'd report him for carrying extra weight, going too fast. He was always on the lookout. He probably needed to dry out awhile.

He grabbed her hand and squeezed.

"You get me out of here and back in that truck," he said, and passed out again.

It wasn't easy: the doctors on duty wanted to keep him under surveillance, run a few tests over the next couple of days. There was reason to think he might have had a light stroke.

"But it's his life," Wilma said, "and he wants to clear out."

She planted her feet in the middle of the hall.

When they slid him into the bunk behind the driver's seat, he didn't come to, so she waved goodbye to the orderly, one hand already fishing in the pockets of her jeans for the matchbook with the street names and exit numbers on it.

It was a hot night. The fog settled over the road, making it slick as owl shit. She'd have to handle the brakes like a toe dancer. Passing a sign that read Denham Springs and another that said Livingston, she checked the matchbook and frowned. They weren't on the list. In another quarter mile she reached 12 East. The bridge was west, she was sure of it. She looked into the rear view hoping to see where the city was, but the fog hid everything except jumpy neon signs from low-rent dives along the access road. She must have gotten turned upside down and backward. Hell and damn. The road made a wide-banked turn, and her stomach flipped. A long white Lincoln passed her going seventy-five, two women in the front seat. Heading home from a party, maybe. She tried to remember the last party she'd been to. Then she tried to remember the names the intern had told her came before Broussard. A blue exit sign loomed ahead: Westminster, Sherwood Forest ¼ mile. She turned off.

The visibility was so bad she could barely make out the red light at the intersection at the end of the ramp. Switching on her wipers, she groaned. The blades were spreading a pale brown scum across her windshield. Acid rain? Pollution? She tried the washer button. Nothing. The longer the wiper blades moved over the glass, the worse it got, until she finally had to pull the truck over to the curb and set the brakes. Her hands sweating and shaky, she sat for several minutes listening to the engine rumble. It gave her a good at-home feeling, that rumble, like she used to get sitting in the seat of one of Vernon's combines. Lord, would Gary ever snap out of it? When she thought of how she'd needled him, begged him to let her drive, she had to laugh. She'd driven all she wanted to drive as long as she lived.

At the light she hung a left and another and then she was headed back down the ramp in the right direction, past signs for Westminster and Wickland Terrace showing her their backsides now, and picking up the sign for 10 West, breathing easier. To take the edge off her fear she switched on the CB.

"Whaaaooow, chil'ren, ain't we aaawal awaaaaaaaake yeyut? Sheeeeeyut. Bleyus yo' sweeeeeeeeeeeeeeeeeeeeeeeetaaaaaaaaaasss Aaaaaayayum." The man's voice was shrill, and he was running it through an echo box that squeezed the sound like Play-doh into stars and moons and tulips. It was the strangest human voice Wilma had ever heard. She couldn't even be sure that it was human. She picked up the mouthpiece.

"Headed westbound on 12, come back?"

"Little laaaaaaayudeeee? This here's Raccoon Grand-daddy at 4589 headed east, come on."

She wished she hadn't raised this one, but right now anything was better than quiet.

"You got a route to Church Point, son?"

"Yes ma'am," he said. "A-a-a-a-a-a-a-a-t's where I come from. Best boudin in the bayous." His stutter came out of a strange machine. She got a vision of a robot, sitting behind the wheel of a Kenworth.

"Y-y-y-y-y-y-y-y-y-y-you take 10 to La. 13, shoot up through Carencro to Sunset. At Sunset take 93 to Church Point. W-w-w-w-w-w-w-w-w-w-hat you haulin' down that way?"

"Peppers," she said. That was when it hit her. What the sky-blue hell was she doing driving forty miles out of their way to some puny crossroads town no bigger than Little Egypt? Gary had a coonass Korean War buddy down there who ran a motel. He'd told her before he went under the anesthetic: they could lay low there till he had a chance to build himself up before driving on to Houston.

"What about the green peppers?" Wilma had asked him. He waved a big hand in a vague, weak sort of way.

"They'll keep," he said. "Long as you keep the reefer running. I'll call the dispatcher in the morning."

"Why don't you let me drive this thing to town?" she said. "You could take it the last quarter mile, do the paperwork like you always do."

He shook his head and frowned.

"I ain't ready to face 'em," he said. And then he grinned and looked more like himself. "I got no stomach for it," he said, rubbing his hand over his belly and making a grimace. She was so relieved to see him making a joke she bent down and kissed him.

"Hang on," she said, and they wheeled him out to the OR.

While they were pumping Gary's stomach she tried calling Vernon. When he answered she could almost smell the booze.

"That you, Vernon?"

"Yo. Who's this?"

"Who else calls at four in the morning?"

"Hi, Will," he said, his voice paper-thin.

"You all right?"

"What do you think? Sure I'm all right."

She wished he'd ask her something. "How's the ferrets, how's the coyote, how's Ruby?" she said.

There was a pause. "Everybody's just fine, sugar," he said.

"What have you been doing?"

"Huntin' a few geese. Butchering hogs. Starting on the income tax. They sent me something called Notice of Levy, means the bastards are gonna try to squeeze my bank account, ain't that a ticket?"

She turned around to look at the clock in the hospital office. Four-thirty-five. A couple of orderlies were wheeling Gary down the hall.

"Got to go, Vernon," she said into the receiver. "I got to get down the road fifty miles before I quit."

"Where are you anyhow?" Vernon's voice sounded washed-out and far away.

"Louisiana," she said.

"Drive careful," he told her. "Look out for polecats on the road."

"Vernon?" she said. "You take care. You can't beat the government anymore than you can beat the bank." She'd already hung up before she remembered she hadn't asked him about the boys.

She missed Vernon like she missed the tomboy part of herself that had hunted and trapped with him, done everything with him she could for twenty years until she found out about the money and sat down. She couldn't remember the last time she'd gone with him at night, but it must have been hot still because the bugs were bad. He had stopped four miles north on the rice-field road, turned the lights off and reached in back for his Sears sleeping bag.

"Shhh," he said, coming around and opening her door. They spread the bag on a grassy patch next to the road so she could lie on her back and he could tell her the names of constellations his father taught him when he was a boy.

"The one almost straight up. That's Orion, and over to his left and a little below is the Queen, Cassiopeia. Orion's her partner, or he ought to be." Vernon told Wilma he imagined Orion bringing game, gazelles and unicorns, and laying them at Cassiopeia's feet.

She slapped a mosquito on her right arm.

"When are we going to get to see the bobcat?"

She knew he didn't hunt the animals that came up silver in the headlights. He just liked to watch their slow approaching shapes and listen for the quick yip of a dog or a higher-pitched bark of a coyote, and often a long ululation, especially when the moon was full. She heard the throb of big pumps moving water across his rice and the high hum of seventeen million mosquitoes.

"Hear that, honey, that little high-pitched yell?" he said.

"What?"

"That's a rabbit, and it means the bobcat's hunting within a quarter mile of us." He felt connected to things in a way she never had, to the Bears Major and Minor and Scorpio who never stings.

In twenty minutes she couldn't see five feet ahead of the truck. She picked up the CB mouthpiece.

"Raccoon Granddaddy, you still out there?"

"Yaaaayauh," he said. "W-w-w-w-where you at, gal?"

"Coming up on Broussard. You crossing this bridge up here?"

"Naw, I got to cut off and make a delivery at Blanchard. You remember what I told you? When you get there you be sure and look up Blaise Broussard over at the Squeeze Inn Club. You have any problem, tell him I sent you."

"Thanks, buddy," she said. "Much obliged."

"Adieu to yew too," he said, and clicked off, his voice resonating as if in a cave.

She wished she'd asked him to give her a highway marker number so she could keep a little map of where he was in her mind. She wouldn't know if there was traffic on the road now; nothing was visible either side of the four lanes to the bridge. Only peach-colored lights bending sinuous necks over the road like herons, and the silver barriers on the shoulders, and now the lights glowing on the scaffolding above the bridge furry through the fog. All around the horizon a heavy black band. As she came closer four sets of brake lights formed a train of red eyes retreating ahead of her into fog like smoke from a strange cold fire burning in Louisiana.

The fog shut out her map of Little Egypt, where Devel Edwards and Jeanette butchered six hogs every year and sold the hot sausage that was their livelihood. She thought of the eight hundred acres that were Vernon's and were gone now, except for the cemetery patch where his great-grandparents were buried. The land was gone, and her oldest boy had moved. Clint was the last little cub to leave, and she couldn't call up in her mind an image of Clint, just now, couldn't even remember the color of his eyes. The fog was closing out everything. Approaching the Mississippi bridge for the second time, she was glad there were one or two other trucks on the road, crossing the river ahead of her.

8

SHE FOUND A THREE-STORY frame house lifting brick chimneys over a grove of live oaks. Driving down the circular drive she leaned out the truck window, took a long look at the white pillars and peeling paint, the cane-seat rockers, the blue nude statues on the porch. This had to be the place. There was nothing like it in southwestern Louisiana. Wilma had never seen a man who looked anything like Pudge Thibodeaux, either. He moved like an astronaut encased in hard plastic and screwed down tight. He'd been a boxer in the Army, Gary had told her, and could lick his weight in gila monsters. Skipping down the seven porch steps in tight jeans and a turtleneck, he seemed bigger than five foot seven. By the time she had her door open, he was standing next to her on the gravel, pumping her arm and standing tall, uptight as a general.

"It's Gary? Where's the rascal at?"

"Lying down," she said. "Like I told you, he hasn't been feeling real well."

Pudge jogged in place and threw a couple of punches. His eyes bugged out.

"Here, let's get him out of there and up to the house,"

he said. "Grab his feet." She climbed into the cubby from the other side and picked up Gary's feet. He moaned a little when she touched him but didn't wake up.

"How long he been like this?" Pudge asked. "He's not a thing like himself."

"He just came out of Emergency," she said.

They had a time maneuvering him out of the cab and tried to be gentle carrying him up the front steps of the house. They turned into the living room where they laid him on an old sofa with claw feet.

"Kid's let hisself run down." Pudge gazed at his friend. "We'll stuff him into a sweatsuit, trim him down."

"I'd rather give your one-eyed grandmother a blow job," Gary said, in a firm voice. He swung his boots off the arm rest and onto the floor. Pushing up with his arms, he heaved himself erect and stood in front of the couch, straight but not so steady.

Pudge reached out and grabbed Gary's right arm with the tattoo of Daisy Duck on it.

"At ease, fellah. Don't go blasting around."

Gary threw off his hand. When he spoke his voice sounded mean. Ready to get down.

"Since when do I take orders from you, punk?"

"Got a beer or something?" Wilma said, squeezing herself between the two of them and putting her arm around Gary's waist.

"How about breakfast?" Pudge said. "I do grits and eggs better than Georgie. Come on out to the kitchen."

"Who's Georgie?" she asked.

"My wife," Pudge told her. He waved at an Egyptian statue in the dining room. "Georgie's an artist. She copied those sculptures from a magazine. Beautiful, huh?"

Sitting on stools pulled up to a long table covered with plastic lace, they ate scrambled eggs and boudin. Wilma had never eaten boudin before. It tasted like something buried underground and spoiled. She'd read someplace how Eskimos liked to eat fish they'd left in a hole in the ground for two weeks.

"You doin' any more fightin'?" Pudge asked Gary.

"Do I look like I been fighting?" Gary rubbed his belly and grinned. "The most calories I burn all day's from chewing," he said.

She kept watching Gary's face, wondering if he was going to be all right now. In the morning they ought to clear out. Already the load was a day late, and they hadn't put a call in to the company dispatcher. He'd think Gary was bushwhacked somewhere, or drunk.

"Say, big gal, did you know this boyfriend of yours was the heavyweight champ at Fort Sam? He used to lay 'em down like dominoes." In his black sweater and wool plaid shirt Pudge had the taut look of a jockey. His hair was combed precisely over his high, retreating forehead in seventeen strands.

This was the first time she'd heard about Gary's being a fighter. Also it was the first time anyone had called him her boyfriend, and it made her skittish.

"Guess I better look out." She grinned.

Gary wasn't smiling back. There was a pinched look about him; otherwise his expression was blank. She had no way of telling from his face what was happening in his head. Maybe he didn't want her for a girlfriend.

"Tell me about it," she said.

"Later," he said. "I'm a whipped puppy."

The room Pudge led them to was on the second floor, directly above the front porch. It didn't have much in it besides an old iron bed, the headboard fashioned in fantastic shapes, hearts and flowers and in the center a cupid with purple wings.

Pudge opened the double doors leading to the balcony. A hot breeze blew in from the Gulf, rattling the leaves outside. Gary lay down and kicked his boots onto the floor without even turning the covers back. She walked out onto the balcony, leaning on the railing to inhale the humid air. It was good to stand somewhere fixed.

"Don't get excited if you hear a bunch of drunks carrying on downstairs later on," Pudge said. "I'll throw 'em a chicken, and they'll dance around and raise hell awhile and go on into town. You take a rest now." He was gone, slipping out the door like smoke.

When she woke five hours later she could hear music in the distance, a funky accordion with guitars and a bass voice laughing. It wasn't the music that woke her, but Gary's arm sneaking up behind her and curling around her waist. She tried not to stiffen. If she pretended to be asleep, maybe he'd forget it. His hand slipped up under her right breast, twirling the nipple between two fingers. She ought to ask him what the hell he thought he was doing, but she didn't want to make a big deal out of it. In a minute she felt his other hand on her leg. She was a married woman; still some part of her didn't want to acknowledge his hands. Twenty-five years earlier she had felt this same embarrassment while her boyfriend Steve was halfway through unbuttoning her blouse, and she thought maybe if she stayed put he'd lose interest or go away. Gary's hands didn't disappear, but they didn't feel like a stranger's. His fingers ran along her thigh to her hip, then drifted toward her crotch.

She climbed off the bed slowly. Each separate bedspring spoke, but not too loud. Lifting one of the slats in the blinds she looked down the drive below, where a man stood wearing a black mask, a purple cape and a black hat. At the entrance to the driveway fifty yards behind him stood a group of eight horsemen in masks and costumes, the riders spurring their mounts so they pranced on the gravel. On the road beyond the driveway more horses and riders were jostling each other, milling around a beer wagon and a truck carrying musicians. The melody had a little jive in it, something like a country two-step with a whiff of the blues. Two riders wearing tall conical witches' hats were standing in their saddles twirling invisible partners in slow foxtrots.

When she turned back to face the bed, he was sitting up against the headboard, cleaning his nails with a pocketknife.

"Check out the weird party downstairs," she said.

"Not very friendly, are you, this evening?" he said.

"I'm beat," she said. What did he expect?

"I was figuring you might be good for something," he said.

She ran a brush through her hair, watching her reflection in the mirror. "That wasn't part of the deal," she said. His face behind hers in the glass looked puffy.

"You're too old to be cheerleader, Wilma," he said.

"I never made cheerleader. What makes you think you know so damned much about me?" she yelled.

She couldn't tell from the way he was looking at her what he thought or what shape he was in. His voice wasn't angry. Just kind of tired.

"I know a prick tease when I see one, and you are definitely it."

She opened the door and left the room. She wasn't anything he said she was. Heading down the corridor to the stairwell, she hung over the bannisters to listen. Pudge was at the screen door, saying something to the riders, and then he rushed out onto the porch. Wilma trotted down the steps until she was halfway to the front hall, sat on a step and peeked through the door at the riders on their small, scruffy ponies. They seemed more and more like a gang of bandits.

Out in the yard a lot of people were dancing, a werewolf cheek to cheek with a big-breasted woman in a T-shirt, a harlequin doing the foxtrot with a gray-haired witch. The dancers were circled by a stream of horses and riders moving counter-clockwise as if stirred by a giant invisible spoon. The masked faces swirled past like merry-go-round animals, grim and terrible. The north wind was blowing silk capes and pantaloons, pennants and ribbons tied into the horses' manes, the litter pinned to the costume of the trash-can man who wore over his head a rubber garbage can with a cut-out peek hole. Out on the driveway the trash-can man danced all by himself, shaking small gourd rattles in his hands. His oversized head bobbed crazily, and scraps of paper pinned to his trousers and sleeves flapped and fluttered.

"Hey, François, what you think you doin'?" Pudge yelled at the leader. "What for you bring this bunch of rascals to the house? Jiving my guests outa they beds?"

The man in the cape removed his hat, releasing a hank of black curls, and bowed. Wilma had never seen a man bow before. His cape swirled like a bullfighter's as he brushed the gravel with his hat. When he started talking his voice was like a chant. The other riders started singing. They, too, had taken off their hats but left the tight rubber masks that weren't quite masks with their lifelike hair and lips. After several moments she realized why she couldn't understand the words to the song; they were French. But she caught enough to figure out the singers were asking Pudge to give them some ingredient for a gumbo they were making. This wasn't a thing like trick-or-treat, she thought, and then she remembered Gary had told her in these Louisiana prairie towns it was traditional to beg on Fat Tuesday.

Walking out onto the porch she stood next to a pillar, trying to resemble one of Georgie's blue statues of naked nude girls with their hair in buns. She knew before she started she'd be conspicuous, but she didn't expect the riders to yell at her like they did.

"Hey, Pudge, where you pick up that big mamoo?"

The man who spoke had a high, silly voice. It took her a minute to find him in the crowd sitting on his horse with his chin tucked into his chest. She didn't know how anyone who knew the man could recognize him in the mask, which had a shock of red, spiky hair attached to the scalp. Not unless a neighbor could spot his white long underwear, all he wore except for a pair of old jockey briefs pulled over the bottoms. These were no ordinary Halloween costumes; they disguised the riders completely, even down to cotton gloves that would hide a giveaway wedding ring. There were plenty of clowns in the crowd, faces painted half red, half white, with furry eyebrows and red stripes along the cheeks, but nowhere a conventional round clown's nose. These masks were more sinister than that.

The man in long johns noticed her watching him, raked his horse's sides, and smacked it on the hindquarters with the reins. Leaning low out of the saddle and pointing a gloved finger at her, he trotted up toward the porch. "Mardi Gras hostage," he called out, still pointing. His voice strained, as if he were trying to alter it.

She thought he must be kidding while she watched him trotting toward her, the horse's hooves shaking the wooden porch and its nostrils pink and flaring, white mane tossing, the rubber face hanging at its shoulder like a Comanche shield. It was time to move, with the horse's grassy breath blowing in her hair, but she was unable to budge, frozen there until the man leaned down to grab her and swung her up into the saddle in front of him. He smelled like a still. She wiggled and kicked, and the horse pranced, but the man had hands like Vernon's traps. Great God, when would it happen? When would she finally get too big and too mean for some pissant to grab her and carry her away?

"Let go of me," she yelled. This was stupid. She hadn't ridden a horse in years and didn't want to fall off this one.

The rider responded by tightening his arms around her waist. The horse's mane was braided in little tails fastened with green yarn, and small plastic skeletons were tied into the braids.

"Don't worry, ma'am," he said into her ear. "It ain't a thing in the world but Mardi Gras. We gon have us big-time fun. Ef you don't mine." He cocked his head so he could see her expression. She tried to look disapproving, but in spite of herself she was starting to feel the little lift she always felt when she got some attention from a man.

"C'mon. We movin' own," he yelled.

"Hold it," Pudge said. He was jogging alongside the trotting horses, snatching at Wilma's Nikes. "Wait just a minute now. Out back I got me a yardful of chickens. You can have ever' last one. Just give me this old gal back."

"Who you think you calling an old gal?" She kicked viciously at Pudge, grazing his nose. Pudge headed off in the direction of some sheds behind his house, and the man in long johns joined the other horsemen, who continued through the yard, under live oaks hung with moss swinging in the wind. They trotted past a wheelless 1962 Mustang with its engine hung up on a singletree, seven sets of bedsprings and a couple of ruined bathtubs with a trail of rust under the spigots.

As they rode the men started singing the Mardi Gras

song again, trotting out onto the wide blond prairie beyond the yard, where a few white cows were grazing. It
was strange feeling this relaxed, sitting on a horse in front
of a drunk, following a bunch of crazies into a field. Behind
her the man was singing hoarsely, the rhythm of the song
keeping time with the beat of the horse's hooves.

Capitaine, capitaine,
voyage ton "flag,"
Allons se mettre dessus le chemin.
Capitaine, capitaine,
voyage ton 'flag,'
Allons aller chez l'autre voisin.

As if in response to some signal she couldn't see, the
captain turned around in his saddle and yelled, "Suds,"
and a tall man in a cowboy shirt with red fringe on the
arms threw him a can of Lite.

"Billy Lee Stringer?" the leader called out. "Where's
Billy Lee at?"

The man behind her said, "Here he is," and the leader
waited while they caught up with him.

"Now you the one won it last year, son, so you stay
back today, you hear me?"

"Yessir," Billy Lee said.

"What you gon do with that woman?"

"Pat her a little, and pinch her and squeeze her," Billy
Lee said. "Ef she'll let me."

"Says who?" Wilma said.

"Be a nice boy, now," the captain said.

"I'll be a Boy Scout, babycakes."

The leader waved his Confederate flag and rode off
toward the middle of the field. She wondered whether they
might be planning to carry her clear to another town, but
they stopped and turned their horses around to face back

toward the house. Pretty soon Pudge appeared, carrying a white Leghorn by both feet. The chicken twisted and flapped trying to get loose, raising its head up with its beak open, pecking at Pudge's fingers, but Pudge slapped it down with his free hand. She was pretty glad to see old Pudge. He walked up and leaned against the horse she was on, looking up into Billy Lee's face.

"I reckon you better let this old gal loose while they running."

"She be all right where she is, Pudge," the man said. "Turn the bird a loose."

Pudge smiled, shrugged and walked to the center of the horsemen. "Your boys ready?" he asked the leader. The horses were stomping, jogging in place, tossing their plaited manes.

"I want to get down," Wilma said, starting to feel weak in the knees.

"No ma'am," Billy Lee said, and he gripped her tighter around the waist.

The others dismounted, bending to tie their shoelaces and roll up the bottoms of their jeans. They were joking and jabbing ribs, breathing alcohol into one another's faces. A big man in a skeleton suit and Frankenstein mask carried a four-year-old in a clown outfit. He held the kid's hand out to the side and waltzed a few steps to the wheezy bandwagon music.

"I'm lettin' 'er loose," Pudge said, kneeling down with the chicken between his hands, its neck stretched high and skinny and scared. The riders stood in a circle around him, yelling and jiving, and maybe they didn't even hear Pudge because one or two were sitting on their heels when the chicken went hopping over little hanks of grass toward the line of trees. Six men trailed the bird, their legs flying out from under them, bodies leaning so far forward they looked like they were falling headfirst into the turf.

From fifty yards away now the yelps and hee-haws of the runners drifted backward on the nippy air. Billy Lee Stringer yipped and yelled. A stiff wind blew the runners' hair back, whipping their trousers around, flapping their collars and coattails so they looked like a basket of laundry ballooning across the prairie. She was forgetting about being a hostage and starting to get into this. Billy Lee was giving her little squeezes and bouncing around in the saddle, swearing in French.

The sky was filled with blackbirds. As they passed overhead they made a sound like a wind outside a train, and through the whoosh came Gary's voice calling out to her to wait.

Even at a distance of two hundred yards she could tell his eyes were wrong, his face too red, knee action too high, his fists clenched hard and white against the resisting air. The minute he woke up he must've dived back into that flight bag and taken more pills. Watching him narrow the distance between them she felt a chill because he was flying blind, not seeing her or Billy Lee or the red devil or Pudge, looking past all of them into his private story.

Before he reached them Billy Lee swung his legs over the saddle and slipped to the ground. He patted her knee.

"Take care of Sally," he said, placing the reins in her hands. "I'm no good at sittin'." Then he took off after the others. For a short-legged man, he could travel.

When Gary stopped next to the mare's shoulder he grabbed her mane for a second, and gave Wilma a wall-eyed look that plainly said he felt ditched. Then he turned around and looked out toward the line of trees, holding his hand up to shade his eyes. Bright splashes of color were flying every which way as the bird made desperate dashes for safety. "Where'd they go to?" he said, then took off running like the devil was hung in his short hairs.

Wilma squeezed Sally between her knees and rode off toward the runners. The leader's horse was in her way. He removed his hat, but kept his mask in place as she slowed to a stop before him.

"You got to talk to him, ma'am," the leader said, looking serious. "Tell him to sit down, watch all he wants, but leave that bird alone. He just making a circus, your old man."

"But he's not my old man," she said.

"Is he got anybody else?"

She looked around for Pudge, his old buddy. He was hopping around on his bowlegs taking Polaroid snapshots of the scene. She looked at her watch. The chase had been going on for ten minutes. Leaning forward in the saddle she whispered "Giddap," and bounced around as the horse broke into a canter. Between the horse's ears she saw Gary, twenty-five yards in the lead, his pants legs heavy with caked mud pulling the rest of his trousers low so his white ass shone like two moonstones.

"Gary," she yelled. "Come on back."

He stopped in his tracks, turning to face her, his legs wide apart. The others moved past him a little way, their eyes focused on next year, but he showed no sign he'd noticed.

"Come on home, boy. We're too old to be ripping across this field with a bunch of kids."

"Chicken," he said. His skin had a high, waxy shine, and his eyes were huge and skittering all over.

"Never mind," she said, and took his hand.

"If it ain't Miss Ice Capades," he muttered, shaking her off. He'd never been rough with her before. Then in a moment he was running again, leaping high, shouldering his way through the other runners until he was in the lead. He made two unsuccessful dives after the chicken, lying full length on the ground for a couple of seconds after each landing, as if he'd passed out. She thought she wouldn't be able to stand it, waiting for him to gather himself to his feet, focus all his energy into a last lunge after the bird. He stood up, ran a ways, dove at the chicken. It let out a shriek and released a handful of feathers into the air. He scrabbled to his feet, holding the bird high over his head in both hands, taking long proud strides toward Wilma. The Cajuns made a long infantry line behind him, Billy Lee walking abreast of Gary and taking hold of his arm.

"Hold on, son," he said.

Gary stopped walking. "What's your name?"

"Billy Lee Stringer. And that 'ere's my chicken." He was using his own deep voice now. His long underwear was soaked with sweat and mud, and the grinning mask made him look like some crazy actor.

"You wrong, buddy. Yours must still be running around in that field somewhere. This chicken belongs to old Gary. Had it for years."

Billy Lee was still holding onto Gary's arm when Pudge walked up to the two of them and slung an arm around their shoulders. "Now if you boys'll think back a while you'll recall that's my chicken."

Billy Lee giggled. "His chicken. He says it's his chicken." He looked at Gary, pointing his finger. Gary's face was blank. Without any sign, he drew his arm back and hit Billy Lee an uppercut to the jaw, so sharp he went down fast. Gary stood looking down at him, the chicken still dangling from his hand. Now and then it let out an exhausted squawk. The riders had made a circle around the two men.

"Sheet, boy," Pudge said. "If you ever thought you could run, better do it now."

But Gary stayed put. After a minute or two Billy Lee

106

reared himself up off the ground, holding his jaw. He snatched the bird out of Gary's fist, ducked outside the circle and stood spraddle-legged, maybe twenty feet away from them. He looked a lot less lively than the chicken.

"Le Gran Mardi Gras," he yelled, holding the bird aloft. It flapped its white wings a couple of times, then hung loose in the last of the sun, which was lighting up the red hair on Billy Lee's rubber scalp. Then, while everybody watched, he reached high with his other hand, took hold of the bird's head, and with a quick twist severed it from the neck. Blood spattered his mask, running down his hand and wrist and forearm, spotting the white underwear.

She felt a hand on her shoulder. The trash-can man bowed low, reaching for her hand. Through the square cutout of the brown rubber she saw a wide mouth with a thick black mustache above it.

"Dance?" he said, and didn't wait for an answer. His arm around her waist was strong and weightless, his legs against her own pliant as ropes, but knowing where to run. She didn't have time to feel self-conscious before the wheezy, tinny music filled her with champagne bubbles. He danced her away from Gary and Pudge and the others, out to the front yard, where sunlight was starting to hit the pink camellia bushes, making them glow like Christmas angels against the brown grass. She closed her eyes and let herself spin.

"You like this la-la music?" he said.

"It's like the two-step," she said, knowing that was wrong because there was something more limber and light about it, like traveling-carnival tunes.

When they danced over a cattle guard she felt no alarm. Leading her to a black horse with a green saddle blanket, the trash-can man removed his arm from her waist and reached under the camouflage jumpsuit he wore, pulled out a mask and handed it to her. The mask was a woman's face with curly red hair and a headdress of turquoise blue feathers.

"You want me to wear this?"

"You want to ride Mardi Gras, *n'est-ce pas?*"

"I thought women couldn't do it. I thought it was a traditional male thing." She wished she could see his eyes.

"Who you think'll find out you're a woman? You'll look like a big man dressed like a woman dressed like a bird of paradise."

She looked down at her heavy legs in the tight jeans, at the Reebok workout shoes on her size-eight feet. She wasn't a thing like a bird of paradise, but she pulled the rubber mask over her head anyway.

Inside it smelled like a combination of sweat and old rubber tires. It was hotter than hell. Out of the eye slits she saw the trash-can man laughing through his peephole. He put his arms around her and squeezed till she thought she'd pee in her pants.

"What're we gonna do now?" she said, her voice sounding deep and hollow. "What is a bunch of grown men doing in this foolishness, anyhow?"

"Don't you know, *chère?* The child's the father of the man," the trash-can man said. "We're gonna play."

When she got back to the house it was dark. Georgie was in the kitchen working on a tinned ham with a can opener. She wiped her little hands on a towel and extended one to Wilma.

"Glad y'all got back all right," she said, shaking her perm like a black lamb and showing good teeth. Her grip was firm.

Wilma looked at Gary. He was walking around the kitchen, opening all the cupboard doors.

"I was too fast for 'em," he said. His eyes showed a lot of white. "Think I'll go upstairs awhile before supper," he said, like he was telling them he was going to take a shower and put on a tie.

"Stay here and I'll fix you a cool one," she said, putting a hand on his arm. "I'll rub your shoulders."

He shrugged off her hand.

"Be down in two shakes," he said, and walked out of the room. She counted the cracks in the old green linoleum. Pudge coughed.

A large piece of furniture turned over upstairs. Glass shivered. Everybody got up from the table.

"Sit down," Wilma said.

When she opened the door to their room she thought someone had broken in and ransacked the place. A chest of drawers was on its face beside the bathroom door. Their two bags were emptied out all over the floor, and the sheets peeled away from the mattress ticking. The mattress itself was rolled up at one end, as if someone had been trying to hide a body. The flight bag was open on the bed, brown medicine bottles spilling Gary's pills over the sheets like pieces in a children's game.

"Where you?" she said, keeping her voice low. What could she expect of a man who'd taken hundreds of milligrams of Dexedrine in eight hours? When Jody was into this stuff she'd learned caution. If she caught him with the dope, or yelled at him about it, he broke a plate or ripped off her purse or tore up the truck. He never did hit her. A few times he came too close, his distorted pupils inches from her own, his breath hot on her cheeks. When he wasn't out raising hell he pressed a hundred and fifty pounds, lying flat on his back on the narrow bench that took up most of his room. While he stood looking down at her and hollering, she closed her eyes, hoping to click off his anger like TV.

"I gotta get on the road," Gary said from the bathroom, and stepped out holding one red sock in one hand and a razor in the other. She couldn't get him to focus on her. Standing in the middle of the torn-up room, she racked her brain for something to say.

"You wanted to lay back for a couple of days," she said.

"I just talked to Corinne. My boy's in trouble. They need me home."

She walked around the room picking up pieces of clothing, stuffing them into her bag, not knowing whether to believe him or not. She found his second red sock under the bed with the Grateful Dead T-shirt he wore to sleep in. Her mind was already working ahead to the price of a motel room near Kansas City. In her purse she had exactly forty-three dollars left out of what she had taken from behind the wallpaper. She might get a lot of reading done in that room.

"What d'you think you're doing?" he said. He had zipped his bag and pulled his tweed cap over his eyes. There was a lot of Robert Redford about that cap.

"What's it look like? I'm getting it together," she said. "We're leaving, aren't we?"

"Who said anything about 'we'?"

"I don't get it," she said.

"All good things must end, puddin'," he said. "And you're at the end of this road." He walked toward her with this sorry smirk on his face. When he was a quarter inch away he put his arms around her as if nothing had happened, as if they were old friends who'd just run into each other in a grocery store. Maybe there had never been much between them after all, just the driving lessons, and the girl with the baby on the CB, a few kisses, a lot of need. Now he was leaving as if she hadn't listened to his troubles all the way from Houston to Hatteras and back, hadn't saved his ass on the Mississippi bridge.

"Life's too complicated," she said, her face in his shirt. When he bent to kiss her, she laid her forearms against his chest and leaned hard.

"What's wrong?" he said. "You aren't gonna give me a good old truckdriver's smooch before I go?" He tilted her chin up, placed his lips firmly on hers and started pushing with his tongue.

The trouble with Gary was he was this great kisser. Maybe the best she'd ever had. He was also leaving her on foot by the side of the road.

"Get away from me," she said, and shoved harder with her arms, but his hands on either side of her face only held her more firmly. His own eyes were closed so his lashes curled up toward the ceiling. His body smelled salty from his running, and his mouth tasted brown and funky from the Camels he smoked. With one hand she reached around behind him and grabbed a hank of his hair. She gave it a couple of good hard jerks until he took a few steps backward, still holding her so she was forced to walk with him.

"Wanta dance?" he said, pulling her right hand stiffly out to the side. She picked up one of her feet and slammed it down on his boot, but since she was wearing jogging shoes it didn't have the effect she wanted. He started to turn the two of them in tight circles in the space between the bed and the balcony. She wasn't mad enough yet to fight him with all her strength.

"I don't," she said.

Gary was dancing her toward the double doors to the balcony. The oak leaves were dark against the sky, and scraps of music floated downwind from the town. She thought of low ceilings and tables with brown beer bottles on them and a small band playing.

"You'll be all right, sport," he said. "I can leave you

some cash." He nuzzled her cheek, and tried to kiss her.

"Quit that," she told him. What made him think she was his good sport, anyway? She was sick of him. He didn't seem to hear her, just kept his cheek next to hers, turning his face now and then to kiss her again. She took a step backward. He still held her around the waist.

"Baby," he said, "want to fuck?" He'd never used the word before.

"You're crazy," she said, turning away.

"Don't play games. You know you want it," he said. His eyes flickered like blue gas flames.

"No," she said. For the first time she was frightened of him. She wrenched out of his grasp and should have kept going, but she stopped next to the doors to the balcony, holding both hands across her mouth.

"Tease," he said. "Slut." Stepping forward he slapped her cheek. She kept backing away from him, through the doors onto the narrow balcony with the waist-high railing around it.

"Leave me alone," she said.

"Who do you think you are? Miss Texas?" He had his hands on her shoulders, shaking her so her head flopped back and forth.

She never thought she was anything so special. Just a girl with big muscles who used to be able to shoot pintails at fifty yards.

His shoulders canceled the light from the room, and his eyes were looking into some place she never wanted to go. Bending quickly from the waist, she grabbed his legs, heaved herself upright and flipped his feet up and over the railing. He fell onto the gravel below.

"Sorry bitch," he yelled. It was only fifteen feet down.

She tossed his flight bag over the railing, walked back inside and shut the door.

112

9

THE MUSIC WAS LIGHT like the man was, with a steady rock-and-roll underside and some serious blues. Sorrow underlay the romp of it, and a funky my-woman's-took-off-and-I-don't-give-a-damn defiance. The songs weren't about girls; they were about grown women. Maybe that was why this wasn't the usual twenties and thirties crowd. Half the couples on the floor were over fifty, and two or three pairs of middle-aged women danced with each other, smiling like sphinxes. These dancers had seen enough of this world to know if a woman's old man started talking about turning the damper down she had better look out because another woman was doing more than his cooking for him. This wasn't any punch-out punk tune, either, about dope and fast-food sex. It mourned the gritty hard times that come when a man and his woman get to feeling lonesome and ornery and before they know it restlessness or something else pulls them apart. In spite of the blues this music had the kind of wacky spirit that made Wilma think she could dance through anything. She heard it in her bones.

Wilma had run into the trash-can man again at the

Squeeze In Club in Church Point a few hours after she left Pudge and Georgie's. He was sitting at the end of the bar smoking a skinny cigar that matched his mustache, only she didn't know it was him at first without the trash can. A Zydeco band was playing onstage, and the audience turned their faces toward the lead singer as if he were a small sun that would warm them.

The minute she stepped inside the bar she felt like a trespasser. Nobody looked anything like a truckdriver, and she was the only white woman in the place.

"You wan' dance?" The trash-can man was tugging at her sleeve. He wore a straw hat pulled low, and when he opened his mouth she instantly recognized him.

"Maybe," she said. It was impossible not to smile back at him, with his eyes full of devilment.

"You just out of practice. I can show you some of that Zydeco dance, *pas problème. Regardez.*" He pointed to the middle of the dancing crowd where a frail elderly man was guiding his partner in a strange slow step. He held his upper body straight and kept his fedora tilted over his face. There wasn't a speck of frivolity in the man, except for his knees. And the knees had seen some long slogging through cane and cypress swamps; they'd stiffened and become brittle, like old tires. But on the dance floor everything melted, knees, shanks and ankles, as if bone turned to liquid silver in the hands of the music.

"He's beautiful," she said. The stout woman he danced with had the right knee action, but hobbled a little in her high heels.

"He don't look no better 'n you're gonna look," he said, watching her steadily, with appreciation. She never could resist a man who appreciated her, so she walked out on the dance floor with him.

The minute she walked into his arms she knew him by

his lightness. He wasn't a young man, forty-five, maybe fifty, but slim and limber. He held her at a decent distance from himself and inclined his upper body toward hers, his left elbow held out to the side like they do at country square dances. His face was turned slightly away from hers as he moved her between the other couples, and his expression wasn't sad but concentrated. All his energy and attention seemed to move down through his neck and chest and arms to the wooden floor. She stole quick looks at his legs and feet, noticing they moved with a slide, not a step, and his knees swiveled right and left, making circles in the smoky air. His hips swung so slightly you'd have to measure to be sure they swung at all, and his eyes were closed a lot of the time so his movements might be part of a dream about the strong sweet music.

"Dance with me *dix minutes*," he said. "When the time's up, I check out, leave you *toute seule,* if that's what you want. If you like it we keep on. I guarantee." His name was Sylvestre Blaise Broussard, he said, but everybody called him Blaise. Wilma thought she remembered the name from somewhere but couldn't pin it down.

The band was playing *"Zydeco Est Pas Sale,"* the accordion player pumping the old Monarch and flapping his elbows like crazy. He had on a pair of railroad overalls size 48, and his round face shone with drunkenness, sweat and joy. He had two guitar players backing him, one of them a white boy with a long ponytail slung down his back.

"You from around here?" she asked, panting a little.

"Born in East Texas. Piney woods," he said. "Mama was from Mamou. You catching on fast. You like it all right, yes?" His eyes were a couple of inches from her own, not real dark brown as she'd thought at first, but a mixture of wood smoke and caramel. His skin was pale.

"Yes," she said, and smiled, still concentrating. She was off balance, off the beat, outweighing him by thirty pounds. People were looking at them funny because she was so big, and her clothes were wrong. None of the other women wore pants. She tried to suck in her stomach and relax and flow with the music, but this required a coordination she had lost years ago.

But in spite of her self-consciousness she flirted with Blaise like a seventeen-year-old at a sock hop. She watched herself laughing too loud, showing her dimples, swinging her hips too wide. Once she caught herself turning her face to the right so her good side was in profile against the wall. Seeing her reflection in one of the mirror windows, she thought, *What is to be done with a forty-year-old face?*

"Are you married?" she asked.

"Ain't ever'body?"

"Yes, but I'm separated," she said.

"Sorry 'bout that. Families be made for hanging on to and hanging out with. Pretty much till the end come round."

"I don't mean divorce," she said.

"Whachoumean then?"

"Arrangements."

"I seen some. They ain't real marriages."

Now she felt hot and defensive. She thought about calling Vernon. She hadn't seen her husband in thirty-two days.

"Sometimes you can't live with 'em," she said.

"And you know what I say to that trash? Listen, if you tired of weeding your garden, quit farming and try something else for a while. You going good now."

Her stomach hadn't stopped hurting, and she couldn't get the picture of Vernon out of her head, the way he had

116

looked when she asked him if the thing with Ruby was serious.

"Nothing half as serious as meeting a trucker every Tuesday for a month," Vernon said. His small mouth had a stubborn turndown to it, and he wouldn't meet her eye.

She'd forgotten to watch her feet, concentrating on the sad lively music and the quick slide and shuffle, the voices and whispers and Blaise's talk. She wasn't tripping over his feet now, and she wasn't feeling like any minute she might fall down. He was holding her light and steady, turning her across the floor, and she was starting to think she might be dancing.

"Maybe you stay awhile in town?"

She had to get home, she told him, figure out how to buy her own truck. Gary had told her you could buy a rig, tractor only, used, for fifty thousand. That meant five thousand down. If she wanted to haul interstate she'd have to get permits; that might set her back a couple of grand. Where would she get it? Once it had seemed like a piece of cake, riding high next to Gary, when she could do damned near anything. Where was he now? On the way home to Kansas City? Wrapped around a median pole, the paint inside the cab bubbling in the flames?

She hadn't done right by Gary, maybe. She hadn't done right to run out on Vernon. For better or worse she'd married him. For loan and foreclosure, big harvests and Chapter Eleven. But not to be ripped off.

"I got too much to do," she said. "What do you do for a living?"

"See that red Kenworth across the street? You see that? *Magnifique. Chérie,* what I do for a living is, I travel all 'roun this country. I deliver ever'thing. Onions, scallions, cabbage, scotch."

"Like what you do?"

"Man be crazy not to."

"Where you headed after tonight?"

"Over Beaumont way. Houston. Stopping to see the family."

"Your wife and kids over there?" Had he said he had children?

"I got me three sweet girl, living in Pasadena." His wife was named Beatrice, his daughters Jeanne, Pauline and Marianne.

"You got room in that truck for me?" she said. "I can drive."

He pulled on his thick mustache and looked at her.

"Bien sur, I got room. In a couple of hours we be ready. Then we drive into the sun. Get the spirit warm." He winked.

On the first leg he let her drive, heading south on 13 through Pine Prairie and Vidrine until they saw a sign on the roadside for Interstate 10. By this time Blaise had gotten well into a discussion of love.

"R'garde," he was saying. "This is the way I sees it. One most signif'cant thing in this world is love. That be it, what keep the man's hand on his plough and his feet in the stirrups. Keep his hand up under his woman's skirt. Trouble is, not too many people knows how to do it; the chil'rens grow up in ignorance." He looked over her way. *"Comprenez?"*

She drove on about a mile before answering.

"How do children learn it if the parents don't teach 'em?" She bet he knew about loving a woman.

"I'll tell you what I learned and how I learned it 'cause it was simple. I never learned a thing about love from the peoples I was with, who was empty as gourds and mean besides. Mama died when I was a baby, and I never knew

118

my daddy. For six years I stayed with my aunt and uncle, and after that I lived in the woods eating on pecans and berries and a little wild cane. Then I went to live with folks a few days and chopped cotton along with their chil'rens. They'd commence looking at me strange in a day or so when the cornbread got low, and I pick up my knife and my extra set of britches and *allons*. They was some kindness in those people, but I don't know as I'd call it love. The most things I learned to love was berries on the fences dripping juice, and roasting ears in July.

"It be just a step from lovin' things to lovin' people. I'm so crazy 'bout my boys, peoples say I'm cuckoo. I'll go 'round Nacogdoches way, pick 'em up, take 'em out to Toledo Bend and fish. They crazy 'bout sleeping on the groun', cooking up a mess of bass for dinner."

He hadn't said anything about having three boys. She knew he hadn't.

"How many children do you have, anyway?"

"Thirteen I know about," he said. "I ain't been home in a good while."

"Which home you talking about? You got more than your share." It had to hit her in the head before she knew he was a bigamist.

"*Vraiment*. But I got more than two pretty little women, *chérie*. I got five. Count 'em." He looked like he'd just told her he'd won the pot on *Wheel of Fortune*.

"You keep all those women happy?" she said.

"*J'espère*," he said, showering light from his perfect teeth. After a moment he got serious.

"*C'est le travail.*"

"What do you mean?"

"My job. Keeping the womens happy. Keepin' 'em loved."

"Your wives, you mean?"

"Ever'one I can touch." He leaned over and kissed her lightly on the lips.

She'd heard plenty of talk about love. Especially from born-again Christians wanting to kiss you and hug you and capture you for Jesus. She wanted a love that didn't make you a fool or a saint.

"How do you figure that's your job?" she said. "I thought it was God's."

"Lissen, *chérie*. Already God's job is way too big. He can't keep the whole world warm. It's a *beaucoup* of people down here, and ain't you heard yet? Ever' last one of us is a motherless child."

10

WHEN THEY PASSED a highway sign that read WELCOME TO TEXAS her stomach turned over. They were blasting down Highway 10, ninety miles east of Houston, rice fields and pine woods and the Trinity River shining in the sun like a vein of mica.

"Whachou gon do when you get home?" he asked.

"Clean house. Talk to the bank, I guess. Figure how to buy my own rig." Her mind was making tight circles around the five or six thousand dollars she figured she'd need, and as the circles got smaller the amount looked bigger.

"Maybe it's better to work for a company. Get some experience."

"I want to drive for a moving company." She liked the idea of people changing jobs, towns, buying fancier chairs. The prettiest trucks were Wild Goose's, royal blue with the yellow honker on the side.

"It ain't a bad job. But they won't hire you, I guarantee."

"How come? They won't hire women?"

"They not crazy about 'em. But, mainly, you got to

have experience. How much time you spent in a truck? Couple of weeks?" He was right. Plus she'd have to study the rule books, take a test, pay for the license.

He shot a hard look at her. "How long since you talk to your old man?"

She couldn't remember the last time she'd called home. Ten days ago, maybe, when her road still looked clear, and Gary's eyes, and Gary wasn't hitting the speed yet. If she was going to buy her own truck Vernon would have to help her. He could borrow something on the combines he still owned. Could they take a mortgage on the house? There had to be a way. She didn't want to face her friends, not knowing what Vernon had told them. Maybe they thought she was visiting her papa and mama. Or on a vacation somewhere. A fight-your-cellulite health spa? Or maybe he had told them the truth, which was that she'd run off New Year's Day. If they knew the whole story they might refuse to speak to her.

"Blaise," she said, "when you go home, how do you decide which one?"

"No problem." He winked at her. Even after driving all night he looked fresh. Full of the devil. "I pull out my map, phone the one that be's the closest. See where the wind lay. If she sound mean, *voilà,* I call the nex' one."

"Do they get along?" It would be like wearing a different mask with each woman. Or maybe he stayed the same, changed his name. How did they know where to send his IRS refund?

"You think I tell 'em? Could be I'm crazy, *pas* stupid."

Would Vernon tell her the truth if she asked him about Ruby?

No matter how mad she was at him, she longed for the sight of the bridge across the ditch in front of her house, for the deep cerise of her azaleas, for the sag in her king-sized bed. They passed a sign in front of a bridge that said LOST AND OLD RIVERS.

" 'Scuse me for gettin' personal," he said.

"Don't, then. Skip it."

"I just wanted to ask is you been gone long?"

"A month," she said. It seemed like four years.

"You been with another man?"

She whipped her head around.

"Not like you think. I was helping him drive."

He smiled like he didn't need her to tell him how to think about things.

"I had to take the wheel the first time in the middle of a bridge in Baton Rouge," she told him, as if this would explain everything. He swung the wheel to avoid a dead possum hugging the yellow line.

He nodded. "Sleep with him?"

"Snuggled. No big deal."

"For you, maybe. How 'bout for him?"

She'd never thought very hard about it. What did she mean to Gary? A scrap of conversation in a New Wave world. Prick tease, he'd called her.

When she didn't answer he drove on, turning his head now and then to look at her. She was careful to keep her face toward the side window, where the fields sliding past looked like Vernon's, pinky-gray soil harrowed to a fine powder, heaped-up levees rising a couple of feet above ground level. In the sky to the east the white stacks of refineries, trails of greasy smoke, a few cartwheeling gulls. Was Gary right? Was she a tease? She had some flirt in her, always, and what was so bad about that? He might have thought she'd be easy, but she was a married woman, after all, and he had a wife and kids in Kansas. His freckles were the color of clover honey, and his eyelashes curled tight, like a baby's. She loved the way he kissed.

Blaise smiled. "Want me to tell you what a man think? How he think?"

She nodded.

"He don't think with his head no way. He think with his hands and his feet and his mouth. His whole body. That be his mind. And whichever way his feet want to go and his hands want to touch, that what he be thinking." She could buy this.

How could she go home? She hadn't been gone long enough.

"How was it on the road? Had you some laughs?"

She wanted to tell somebody about the light-headed feeling of rushing through too much time and space to worry about anything much. The way it was on good days when every stupid sign beside the freeway made her laugh. A country beauty parlor with the motto "We curl up and dye for you." Pink letters on four weathered planks reading "Parsley's Fried Chicken: Pure Prize Pullets." The creeks and roadside ditches were full of coffee-colored water. East Texas never cared much about tidiness, but there was always stuff to look at: old cars without their wheels, rusting in little islands of black-eyed susans, scrub white pine and mimosa and a shredded armadillo hide like a blown-out tire on the shoulder. On bad days the junk turned uglier, turned to the bones of the rotten world gone cold and dead for her and hopeless. Waking up in the cubby, hearing the rush of wind along the truck body, she'd feel a throbbing in her jaw, the pain running up her neck into the muscles below her scalp, and she'd remember the caved-in face of the hired man, born on the place, who worked for her father until a sore tooth put him in the hospital. In two weeks he came home with a hole in the side of his face, through which she could see all the tender parts of palate and throat. It was cancer. She had it on both sides of the family. Her oldest brother, Mack, used to tell her, "There's not a one of us is gonna get out of this thing alive."

Turning to face Blaise she said shortly, "Some of it was a hoot, all right. But it ain't all New Year's Eve."

"I got for you a big surprise, *madame*. You read *Trucker's News?*" When she said she didn't he told her about the Highway Hero of the Year. "Them truckers write letters, tell stories about they friends picking up frozen hitchhikers, pulling drivers outa trucks when they on fire. Could be they'll win a thousand dollars, maybe more. That way you get your truck, how 'bout it?"

He was nuts.

"You believe in the tooth fairy, too?" she asked, and punched him in the arm.

"I write the letter," he said and grinned. "But you got to spell."

Three different times she made Blaise stop so she could telephone Vernon, but each time he was out. Must be having a beer with some of his old crew, maybe with Ruby. Thinking of Ruby jazzed up her pulse considerably, but it wasn't anger she felt but a sordid panic. She kept her head by counting to a thousand while sitting next to Blaise and pretending to be asleep. In calmer moments she sometimes felt relieved that Vernon had Ruby now, so she didn't have to feel guilty. At least he had a warm place and somebody to feed him.

But where in hell was he? It was Saturday afternoon. No reason to expect him to be home. Or Clint either, for that matter. No reason for them to expect her to be calling in. Did she think they'd put a lantern in the window? She missed Rosemary, who used to come over in the mornings and drink coffee and watch *General Hospital* with her.

Rosemary and Don kept a roadhouse now called the Pink Pony that got a lot of play on weekends from local farmers and oil-field workers. It was a good place for beer and pinball and skittles, nothing fancy. It had a Wurlitzer jukebox with blues and rock from the fifties and sixties.

At the last wide turn before the town she stuck her head out the window, watching, listening for the dusk sounds: cattle lowing, shambling single file toward the fence; the angry shrieks of a low-flying marsh hawk after a rabbit; the chitter and hum of juice through the wires. She embraced these sounds like old stuffed animals found in a trunk. Little Egypt was smaller than she remembered. The neighboring fields were empty and green, the green brassy-gold and still warm though the sun was down.

"This a one-swallow town," Blaise said, shifting down into second.

"What's that mean?" she said, feeling defensive.

"Means you get a chance to take one good swallow of Pearl and, boom, you're out of the city limits." He smiled to show he meant no offense.

When they came out of that wide turn she saw the Madison sisters' Bluebonnet Café. Hattie Mae and Edna Mae Madison lived together in a trailer house in back of the one-story wooden structure. On the bar's cheap commercial sign with movable magnetic letters the message was always the same: BIG BIRTHDAY PARTY. BEER. DANCING. SATURDAY NIGHT. ALL NIGHT. COME ON IN. Wilma never did know whose birthday, or when the actual date of it was.

They passed several houses before the crossroads, all of them dark. It was lunchtime. Where was everybody?

"Where you get out?" Blaise said. She pointed to the gray bungalow ahead on the right, and he braked to a stop. She sat there silent for two or three minutes, staring at the house. The gutter was hanging off the west corner of the front porch, and one of the dogs must have jumped through the screen and torn a big flap in it. Vernon had covered her azaleas like she'd asked him to but had forgotten to remove the bedsheets when the temperature started to climb. Now they hung on the plants like sad forgotten laundry.

"This is it," she said, reaching into the cubby behind her for the duffel. "I'm much obliged for the ride down." Smiling at Blaise she stuck out her hand.

He shook his head and wagged a finger. "You'll never stay warm that way," he said, and leaned over and put his arms around her and stuck his mouth up close to her ear. "Just keep on smilin', girl," he whispered, "and give him to the Lord."

"Give who?" she said.

"Your old man, who else? The one who be all time on your mind so you can't see nothing else. If you give him to the Lord you can start lookin' around, start drivin' your truck. Be good now." He stuck the tip of his tongue in her ear, then pulled back and laughed so he showed all his silver.

She opened the door, stuck her foot in the ladder and stretched the other leg to the ground.

"You know where you can find me, *chère*. Bye-bye." He'd given her one of his business cards. "Sylvestre B. Broussard," it read, "A Man for All Seasons."

She stood there watching the Kenworth round the curve, then walked up the brick steppingstones leading to her porch. A hand-lettered sign was tacked to the door:

HOG KILLING
February 8
1:00 P.M.
EDWARDS PLANTATION

She opened the door to the house gingerly, not wanting anything wild to fly out, and set her duffel on the floor.

"Vernon?" she called, but there was no answer.

It was only a quarter-mile walk to Devel and Jeanette Edwards's place behind a thicket of huisache trees. Through the wood smoke hanging over the clearing in back of their house Wilma could make out Devel's '58 Ford Fairlane settling to its fenders in mud and a couple of tin-roofed sheds leaning toward each other like dancing partners. Everything she saw had the scuffed, comfortable look of broken-in boots. Three wood fires were burning where men in overalls and knitted caps sat in metal chairs watching liquid bubble in iron kettles. In the center of the yard someone had parked an old Dodge flatbed, Jeanette standing on top in her long skirt, pushing a string mop with long strokes. Devel walked across the yard carrying a six-foot length of chain.

She was fifty yards from the house when she first saw the stranger. Standing next to one of the kettles was a blond woman wearing a see-through plastic raincoat with a pink tailored suit underneath, holding a pen and clipboard.

"Isn't it dreadfully hard, living like this?" she asked in a loud voice.

"Like what?" Devel said. He caught sight of Wilma. "Where you been, girl?" he shouted across the barbed-wire fence.

The pink woman wouldn't even look at Wilma, as she climbed over the fence, but she took a long snooty survey of the yard and the cabin, its chimney pulling away from the north wall so the wind had an easy passage. The house stood on four eighteen-inch cement blocks, the crawl space below filled with the kind of junk that collects in forgotten corners: automobile tires, rolls of barbed wire, a purple banana-peel bike, an old slot machine with three lemons showing.

"It's pretty muddy," Vernon said, walking up behind Wilma and working hard at not noticing she was there. He turned to the pink woman. "Next time you come out here better wear boots," he said.

"This is rather a perilous assignment," she said, with a faint smile. "Already this morning I was attacked by two wild dogs when I walked up to somebody's door. Then my back wheels got stuck in the mud and I had to honk till they'd pull me out. Is there a ladies' room somewhere?"

Vernon looked at Wilma briefly, and nodded.

"Hi, honey," she said.

"I got one at my house, but it ain't fit for comp'ny," he said.

Wilma was staring at Vernon as if she'd never seen him before. He looked okay.

"Who are you, anyway?" she asked the pink woman.

"Lydia Pursley, State Welfare."

"What brings you all the way out here?"

"Our office got a call." Her clipped words hit the chilly air like toenails on a bathroom floor. "They sent me down to check on you people's diet. The Governor's Commission on Aging."

Wilma stared at her. Ugliest woman she'd ever seen. "What's the Governor care about our diet?" Vernon asked.

"These satellite towns, you see, Mr. Hemshoff, are too far out for Meals on Wheels. Our office is under constant pressure: Gray Panthers, Health Department, Housing Department. Fanatics going on about old people falling through porches, eating dog food, burning up in gas fires."

"Nobody around here eats dog food, ma'am," Vernon said, mildly. "Let's mosey over to this pen and have a look at the sausage," he said. He made his arm into a loop for Lydia to slip her own through.

The fence was made of chicken wire and scraps of tin. Devel and two other men stood looking over the top of it. Inside were three black Hampshire hogs, each with a thin collar of white around its neck. The hogs must have weighed three hundred pounds apiece.

"Beauties," Wilma said, leaning against a fence post.

Vernon had moved Lydia ten yards further down the fence line, but her voice carried. "What do they eat?" Wilma wondered why Vernon was hanging around her.

"Slops," Vernon told her.

"Garbage?" she said. "What about disease?"

"Yes, ma'am," Vernon said, patient as a mule. "Don't you worry. They put enough bird pepper in that meat to clean it out good."

"I see," the woman said. "How do you decide when to kill the pigs? Do they have to be a certain weight?"

Hearing the woman's question, Jeanette walked up jangling her bracelets. She looked like the back end of an eighteen wheeler, with huge arms that stood out from her sides, and swelling hips. She could pick a Canada goose clean in twenty minutes, hot wire any Detroit engine in seven and make a voodoo doll and cast a spell in an hour. If a man had another woman she could make him give her up, and cure rheumatism, gout, whooping cough and the d.t.'s, too. She put her hands on her hips and pushed between Vernon and Lydia.

"We always kill pigs by the sign," she said.

"What sign?"

"The moon," Jeanette said. "If it be too small, the meat's too rank, but don't wait too long."

"Why not?"

"That meat'll spoil," Jeanette frowned. "Where you from?"

"Des Moines."

130

"Well, then," Jeanette said, sailing off to inspect the fires.

"How many people live here?" Lydia was bored by the pigs.

"Just Jeanette and Devel," Vernon told her, "and their two boys." He pointed to a couple of tall men standing at the other end of the enclosure. "Coy and Phil."

"Boys?" Lydia said and whinnied through her nose. "Pretty big boys to still be at home."

"Wives kicked 'em out, ain't they?" Devel said. "Ain't we got to move over for fam'ly?"

Ugly as she was, there was something pathetic about the woman, looking around at the crowd of people as if they were the Sunday funnies.

A tall man with a full fluffy beard walked over to the fence and pointed a .22 rifle at one of the pigs. When he pulled the trigger the animal lay over with a moan and kicked its legs until someone cut its jugular. In a moment its eyes were opaque, all fires out. The welfare woman swayed slightly and grabbed Vernon's arm. He put his arm around her. "Poor piggly-wiggly," he said. "He's gone in."

"Is it over?" she said. She was hiding her face in his jacket.

"You sure you're cut out for this kind of rough work?" Wilma called out.

Lydia lifted her head from Vernon's shoulder, fluffed her hair with one hand. "I started my training in 1965 in the worst slums in Chicago."

Wilma couldn't figure the woman out. Why would she decide to work in a slum? Now and then she'd do something almost human.

It was two when they started butchering. Vernon, the pink woman and fifteen of Devel's neighbors stood around the flatbed truck working on the carcasses with cleavers and long knives. The welfare woman watched everybody work as if she were a *National Geographic* reporter at a tribal barbecue. Hands glistened with animal fat. Mongrel dogs nosed around under the flatbed for scraps. Bits of blood and tallow flew through the air, and a tape on top of the truck cab played B. B. King.

The ground underfoot was littered with brown bottles by the middle of the afternoon, when Miss Cornelia Caldwell rolled her wooden-backed wheelchair across the yard. Miss Cornelia was ninety-three. She'd lived alone since Haze, her third husband, was killed by a hard drive into right field in the 1942 Gulf Coast World Series. She must have been a beauty then, Wilma thought. Now she had the careful, brittle look of ancient parchment. Her eyes were black and sharp, and her hair was going. She rolled across the yard to join Wilma and two other women stooped over holding long pigs' intestines over the grass. Wilma was flushing the contents out with boiling water from a pail when Vernon walked up and introduced Lydia to Miss Cornelia. The old woman nodded.

"Mr. Caldwell, he used to make this sausage," Cornelia said. "He used casings like these to stuff it in." She peered sharply at the hogs' entrails as if she might divine something there.

"How old are you?" Lydia asked her.

"Old enough so the preacher passes me the bread and wine," she giggled.

"You live by yourself? Aren't you afraid of falling and breaking a hip?"

"Ain't no kind of falling scares me except falling in love." Cornelia grinned.

"That's a good one," Vernon said.

When a small boy came up to greet the old woman,

Lydia started to perk up and dig around. Cornelia held out her little stick arms toward the child, then reached into her apron pocket for a Sugar Daddy. "You come on by this evening, precious," she said, "and I'll fix you some hamhocks and beans, and we'll watch *Dynasty*."

The welfare woman raised her eyebrows and looked at the kid hard.

"Ain't he a jim dandy?" Cornelia said.

"Whose child is he?" the woman said. She was looking hard at all the scratches and mosquito bites on his arms and legs. "What's your name, son?" she asked, smiling down at him.

"Zenie Ray Harrison." He stuck a grubby hand into his mouth.

"You're named after your daddy, I'll bet," she said.

"Don't have nayun," answered the child, sticking his index finger into his right ear and looking away toward the house, where Jeanette was carrying out a machine that looked like an old airplane engine with a funnel attachment.

"What's that?" Lydia asked as Jeanette approached.

"Grinder. Want to give me a hand?" She put the machine down on a piece of plywood set on two sawhorses. Three bowls were on the table, one with chunks of hog meat in it, the other two containing sage and chili peppers. Devel plugged in the grinder, dropped pieces of side meat into the top, along with a handful of sage and pepper. He held his palm flat over the top, as the machine's whir deepened to a throaty grumble and long strings of meat poured out of the grid around its funnel. A fine haze of red pepper filled the air.

"Quick, somebody, hand me one of them skins," Jeanette said. Lydia reached into a paper bag, pulling out a translucent casing.

"That's the ticket," Jeanette said. She pulled the casing over the funnel, securing it with a rubber band. As the casing swelled and lengthened, Jeanette ran her hand along its slick sides, squeezed it and tied it with string at six-inch intervals until the whole casing was filled. Then she removed the rubber band and set the links aside. Her hands shone like a wet inner tube.

"It's fun, You try," Jeanette said. Lydia began fastening a new skin onto the funnel. Her fingers moved clumsily at first, but she soon got the rubber band around the funnel and left her hand resting on the casing. It swelled; the loose skin tightened. Lydia's white fingers curled around the sausage as it extended itself to nearly two feet. She stood there watching the link grow until Jeanette noticed and yelled.

"Hey, sister, ain't nobody can handle anything that long." She cut the motor on the grinder and giggled, showing her gold tooth with the star cut out. Everybody around the table laughed.

Lydia blushed.

"This one look like your old man, no?" Jeanette said, pointing to the giant sausage. Her other hand gripped the handle of an iron skillet on a hot plate. Lydia turned to Jeanette, still blushing. "Would you introduce me to Zenie Ray Harrison's parents?" she asked.

Jeanette's eyes wandered over the sixteen faces standing around the table. "Don't see 'em right this minute," she said. She turned the sausage patty with a spatula. The grayish meat hissed in the black skillet, its edges starting to crisp and curl.

"Well, I have a thing or two to say to them," Lydia said. "Leaving a baby like that to walk around this yard all by himself." Jeanette raised her eyebrows. "All these knives. Tubs of hot fat everywhere." Jeanette slipped the spatula under the cooked patty and lifted it out of the skillet. She placed it on a piece of white bread, set another piece of bread on top and handed the sandwich to Lydia with a napkin underneath.

"See did we get the seasoning right," she said, watching as Lydia took a bite and choked a little from the pepper.

"Delicious," she said.

"I'll give you a mess to take home," Jeanette said.

"About this child," Lydia began again. "Who's the mother and father?"

Jeanette shook her head.

"He ain't got nayun," she said.

"But where did he come from?" Lydia's voice rose. Jeanette took another handful of sausage from the mixing bowl and slapped it between her pink palms. She pressed her full lips together, avoiding Lydia's eyes. It took her a few minutes to get the sausage patty flattened out in the pan. Then she stared squarely into the welfare woman's face.

"Now, miss, I want you to listen to a thing might do you some good. If your business is driving round the country asking questions, you need to figure out what kinds of questions ain't nobody's business but the peoples you talking to. Dig?"

Lydia held on. "I'm here to tell you it's the business of the State of Texas to take care of everybody who can't take care of themselves, and it's my job to find out what's going on."

"Last time I heard from the State of Texas they were cutting my food stamps," Jeanette said.

Lydia came on like a fast freight. "We're acting on recommendations from the Governor's Commission on Aging," she continued. "The Governor's earmarked funds for this . . ."

"I don't care if the state is loaded or broke, Miss," Jeanette interrupted. Still holding the spatula in her right hand, she shaded her eyes with her left against the late-afternoon sun.

"We're doing all right out here," she said firmly. "We takes care of our own."

11

SHE WAS GLAD she'd worn her silver-and-fake-ruby dangle earrings that chilly February morning, and remembered to rub green on her eyelids, because the salesmen at Truck City tripped over each other scrambling out of their fake leather chairs when she stepped in. There were five of them sprawled in a circle in front of a blond wood console watching *Superheroes,* a kids' program about a wonder-world where everyone could fly.

"And what can Mark Lowry do for you today, pretty lady?" said the one who reached her first. He was the youngest in the bunch, a slender blond man wearing a western shirt and jeans.

"I want to buy a truck," she said.

"We got 'em here. What kind you need?"

She looked vaguely around the showroom, gazing through the picture windows at rows of trucks lined up outside.

"A big one," she said. "Eighteen-wheeler." When she saw disbelief on his face she said, "You got a brown Kenworth?"

He had Kenworths in every color of the rainbow, he told her, also Macks and GMCs and Peterbilts.

"What else?" How many kinds of trucks were there, anyway?

"International Harvester, Volvo, Mercedes, Ford, Freightliner."

"Do you carry all kinds of engines? Cummins?" That was the only engine she knew about. Gary had said it was the best.

"Sure, lady. We got Cummins and Caterpillar and Detroit. Imports, too, if you go in for the exotics." They were still standing in the middle of the empty showroom. The truck business didn't look terrific. She hadn't even heard a phone ring yet.

"Do you have trailers, too?" she asked.

The young salesman stared at her as if she'd forgotten an important item of clothing. He put his hands on his hips.

"Lady, we got everything here. Why do you think they call us Texas Truck City? We got box trailers, reefers, drop bottoms. Then we have rag tops and dump trucks, tippers and hopper bodies, side dumpers. Tankers we got, and bull racks and possum bellies and single-drops and convertibles and lowboys and goosenecks. Mind if I ask you something?"

"Shoot," she said.

"Are you buying a truck or doing a research paper?"

"I'm a bona fide buyer," she said. "But right now I'm in the research stage." She was in the stalling stage. What made her think she could negotiate this deal by herself? She squared her shoulders and sucked in her stomach. Moistening her lips she enunciated carefully. "I'm a comparison shopper."

"For your husband," the kid said. He had it now.

138

"No," she said. "My sister's driving. I'm going into business with her, but she's the one with experience. She's worked for Wild Goose for three years." Wilma crossed her fingers way down in her pockets. She wished she had a sister who could drive. She wished she had a sister, period.

"You ever drive a truck?"

"I've spent a month in one," she said.

"Hitching?"

"Driving." She stared him down with steady green eyes.

He grinned and ran a hand through his sandy shoulder-length hair. "You're too cute. Most of those gals look like they could juggle lug wrenches."

"You and I both know I'm not cute," she said, giving him the benefit of one of her frowns. Then she paused for a split second. "Precious, maybe," she said, and grinned.

He had the good sense to examine his boots.

"Can we go outside and sit in a truck?"

"Sure," he said. He took two sets of keys off a desk and held the door open for her. "Go ahead and take a look at the blue and green models near the fence. An '81 Freightliner and a '79 Kenworth, real clean."

Outside the spring light felt sharp as a knife blade. In the paved yard trucks stood at attention like parade horses. Without their trailers they looked naked, even obscene, the axles grease-coated, the fifth wheel a dirty joke. She walked a few steps to the green Kenworth with the long nose, turned the key in the lock on the door, took hold of the chrome grab handle and hoisted herself into the seat.

She stared at the dashboard a long time. Nothing looked familiar. Fifteen small round dials, six toggle switches to something, several gauges from one to a hundred and twenty. One to a hundred and twenty what? PSI.

She'd forgotten PSI. Two of the dials rated temperature in degrees Fahrenheit 50 to 200. How would she know the right level if she couldn't tell what it measured? Lights front, rear and running, shift stick, a diagram on the knob showing five forward positions and reverse. What was the little button on the shift knob? How did these gears work? Were there five or ten forward gears? Who could tell? Her breath came faster and she glanced nervously out the side window toward the door to the office. She'd have to ask Mark to come out here and tell her what everything meant. But she'd already told him she knew how to drive. God bless. Foot. Those footing lies always did make you look like a worse fool. What if he came out and asked her to take the truck around the block? What if she hit the highway median going fifty?

She sat in the green truck for thirty minutes, memorizing the numbers on the gauges, though how this would be helpful she couldn't say. Once she turned the ignition key to the right, pushed a button, and was startled by a loud humming. Stepping on the brake pedal, she produced the whoosh and screech of a braking train. She was surprised how uncomfortable she was in this truck. There was no air-cushion suspension in the seats, and the dashboard, intimidating as it was, looked primitive compared to the cockpit-style front seat of Gary's '85 Kenworth. For a while she lay down on the stained mattress in the sleeper and studied the fake leather ceiling. She tried pulling down the drop cloth so she shut out all the light from the cab. Where were the goose-down pillows? The Sony TV and the stereo speakers? Why did she think she could do this alone? Why didn't Mark send her out to look at new models? She must have "Used Truck" written all over her.

She climbed back into the front seat and saw that Mark had opened the driver's door. "How'd you like it?" he said.

"Fine," she said. "The tires look pretty good."

"They're only a few months old," he said. "Any questions?"

"What's PSI?" she said.

"Mind if I get in on the other side? This might take a few minutes."

He told her everything she might need to know without her having to ask: tachometer, speedometer, temperature gauges for engine oil, transmission oil, even truck exhaust.

"That there's the pyrometer," he said. Wilma frowned. "It tells you how hot the exhaust is comin' out of your turbo-charger. Normally it'll be around 900 to 1000. At 1300 you'll start hearing something knocking around, like you've got a rod going, and then look out, lady."

"Why, what's it mean?" Wilma said.

"Means you're meltin' down your pistons, chunks of 'em rattlin' around in there, that's all," Mark said. When he finished they walked across the yard to a beautiful silver-gray '86 Kenworth W900 with more chrome per square inch on it than a Harley-Davidson. As she opened its door the new-leather aroma hit her like a whiff of ether.

" 'Scuse the stink. They spray all these interiors with some new-boot perfume in an aerosol can." Hoisting herself into the front seat Wilma felt like a rock climber on a cliff. She put her hand on the gear shift.

"Hold on, please, ma'am," Mark Lowry said. "If you don't mind I'd like to describe some of what you see before you get to moving it around." He wiped her fingerprints off the steering wheel with a chamois. She folded her hands in her lap.

"Since that's where you started, let's talk about gears. This is the shifting stick, as you can see." He grabbed it with the chamois. "The little nipple on top of the handle's called the air shifter. That pushes you from low to high."

"Low to high what?" she said. Her head was buzzing. He looked at her strangely.

"Range, ma'am. You go one two three four five and then you go one through five in high. That's just extra speed." He paused, watching her face for clues. She tried to make her expression intent, but succeeded only in looking desperate.

"Try thinking about it this way," he said. "It's about trading torque for horsepower."

"What is?" She wanted to go home.

"Moving from low to high range," Mark said. "Remember what you learned once in elementary school . . ."

"I don't remember a blessed thing from elementary school," Wilma said. "What's torque, anyway?"

"They never told you you can pull a locomotive with a lawnmower engine if you gear it low enough? That's torque. Now put your foot on the clutch and move it into first. Just jam it all the way forward. That's it." He showed her five forward speeds, then five in overdrive.

"Don't forget Granny Low. That's the one when you're stuck in a ditch hub-high in gumbo." They practiced reverse gears and talked about speed. The new Kenworth had thirteen gears in all, and if she had to find any of them again she'd have to have a map. It was harder than fitting oysters into a slot machine.

"Just remember that one in the middle's Mexican overdrive. Neutral. You got to be sure you get that clutch hammer down all the way. You don't want 'em to call you a gear bonger. This here that you're standing on is a Spicer Angle Spring Super Duty with a Ceramic Coaxial Dampened Hub. How'd you decide to start driving a truck anyways?"

She answered, off guard. "My sister and I are both divorced." Sweet Jesus, the lies were pouring out of her like sweat in September.

"Where are you getting your financing?"

She didn't have that figured out yet, she told him, so he went back to showing her the gas and oil gauges, the air-pressure gauge for the brakes, the lever to shift the fifth wheel, changing the distribution of the load over the axles.

"Why do you need that?" she asked.

"That's one of the things the inspectors'll hang you on." She nodded, remembering there was something about where the weight was, and you had to have it right or they'd give you a ticket.

"You got kids?" Mark asked her. When she said yes, he asked their ages, and how many were still at home. She didn't want to think about her kids. She'd talked to Jody on his birthday a month earlier and found out he was still living with his girlfriend and working the rigs.

"Where you calling from, Mama?" he'd asked.

"Scott, Louisiana," she told him.

"What're you doin' way over there?"

"Learning to drive a truck," she said. "I'm going into business."

"With Daddy?"

"Not this time," she said. He wanted to know how long she'd been gone, and when she told him he laughed and said he guessed she deserved some time off after all these years. His laugh had a cold underside to it. She hated to scare him. They'd already had their bad times. As usual, when she hung up the phone she had felt guilty.

"Have you even thought about your financing?" Mark asked.

"I asked at my bank at home, and they turned me down," she said.

"Vernon would have to come in here and sign that note with you, Wilma. That's not my decision. It's bank policy." And this had come from Clarence Ustynik, whose son had played high school football with Jody.

It was just that she didn't have a credit rating of her own, no matter all those times she'd cosigned on Vernon's notes.

"How do I get one, a credit rating?" Borrow a lot of money, they said; pay it back fast.

And who would lend it? Maybe one of the finance companies. Maybe the Farm Bureau or the Federal Land Bank. Was she a veteran? Did she own any real property? What was real property? A piano? A diamond ring? A twenty-gauge shotgun nobody had fired for years? The house. She owned half the house she and Vernon had lived in for twenty years. Her name was on the title.

"We'll finance it for you," Mark Lowry said, interrupting her thoughts. "That's what we're here for. 'Course our interest is a little higher than the bank's."

"How much?"

"Eighteen percent," he said.

"How much?"

"Forty-seven five," he said, "without the extras."

She didn't even want to know what the extras were. "How much down?" she said. She had exactly seventy-five dollars left from her truck-stop savings.

"We can probably work something out around ten, twelve thousand," he told her.

She stared at the hairs on her arms, at her boots on the brown carpeting, at the purple shadows on the faded blue of her jeans. It might just as well have been twelve billion.

"You haven't got twelve thousand?" he asked her after a minute or two.

Her voice was muffled. "I haven't got five hundred." She felt like a criminal.

"Hell's teeth, ma'am," he said, "I've seen days I couldn't raise five dollars. I left Dime Box when I was fifteen, went to work on a ranch and got thrown the first six times I climbed on a horse." He'd worked cattle and cooked and chopped wood, got oil-field roustabout jobs when he'd filled out some, and learned enough surveying to apprentice himself to a title company that went bust.

"I always wanted to break horses for a living," he said, "but nobody was raising horses anymore, and I couldn't get enough work so I came to town." He'd learned a lot about trucks in this job. Driving was a hard, dirty way to make a living. Owner-operators had it tough. "But don't let me slow you down. If that's what you got your heart set on, go ahead and try it. There's always some way to raise the money."

She was staying with Rosemary, a good friend, now heavy into Pentecostal thinking. For a week she'd been working on Wilma, trying to talk her into going to a counselor with Vernon to save her marriage.

"Save it for what?" Wilma said. "I'm not interested in rotting in place for the next twenty years while my husband flirts with another woman and puts away a pint of vodka every afternoon. I go over it and over it, honey, and I can't see anything in it for me."

"You owe it to him, Wilma. After all these years."

After twenty years she owed it to herself to do something different, she said.

Rosemary said she was crazy. Out on that highway

was every kind of degenerate. "You know those rest stops? They tell me the hookers are out on 59 and 10 in platoons, just working those big rigs for all they're worth. Some of 'em aren't seventeen. Some of 'em aren't even women."

"Well, I don't guess a hooker would think of a whole lot to say to me," she said. "Don't worry about it." She wondered again where Oralee was, and the baby named Car.

"Vernon's looking peaked," Rosemary said.

"Vernon's surviving. I didn't see any holes in his socks."

"Man doth not live by bread alone," Rosemary said.

"He doesn't look cold, either," Wilma said, winking to show it didn't hurt.

"Wilma, come to church with me Sunday. It'll help you to give. To forgive. If you can't think of another reason, do it for Clint."

Until then she'd had herself under a tight rein, but at the mention of her baby an awful looseness hit her in the gut. Ten minutes after Rosemary left for church she telephoned the house, but when Clint answered he said he didn't want to see her.

It was the eighth morning she'd been in town without seeing her own husband, her kid. She finally decided and dialed her number again.

"I'm at Rosemary's, Clint, and I'd like to see you and Daddy." There was a five-second pause at the other end, then a loud screech from a new kind of bird.

"What's that?" she asked.

"Falcon," Clint said. "Come on over."

The azaleas and redbud were starting to bloom in front of the house. Someone had tacked the screen back on the front porch, and the grass was cut. Her son sat on the top cement step, throwing sticks for a Labrador puppy. His blond hair fell over his shirt collar. She wondered if he was taking flak for it in school. She felt awkward stepping up the walk, standing in front of him with her empty arms.

"Hi, honey," she said, and smiled. He rubbed the puppy's ears and cocked his head up at her.

"Hi, Mama. How's it goin'?"

"Great," she said. "I'm shopping for a truck to drive. How's Chemistry?"

"Passing," he said. "I'm not Wernher von Braun."

"Where's your daddy?" Vernon's pickup was sitting in the drive, the back end full of empty Coke cans and vodka bottles.

"Out in back with his bird," Clint said. "You fixin' to stay around awhile?"

"That depends," she said, uncertain what it depended on. "I need to talk to Daddy." She leaned over and rumpled the kid's hair. "You forget where the barbershop is?"

As Wilma walked around the north corner of the house the bird on Vernon's hand beat its wings so loudly she jumped and let out a little squeal. She hadn't had a real conversation with her husband since she left the house New Year's Day.

"What's that?" she asked.

"Shhhh," Vernon said. "You'll scare her." As he stroked the bird's head and back feathers with his big rough hand Wilma could almost feel his fingers in her hair. He looked thinner.

It was a peregrine falcon, he told her. A whole tiny world was reflected in the bird's eyes.

"Can I talk to you?" she said after a minute or two standing in her backyard in the ten-o'clock sunlight.

"I'm listening," he said. He hadn't even looked at her.

"Honey, are you doing okay?"

"Is that what you wanted to talk about?"

"I just wanted to see my family," she said. "It's been over a month."

"You don't have to tell me how long it's been. We're all right."

"Vernon, I need fifteen thousand dollars," she said. Why should he care what she needed? "It's for a truck." Something in her wished he would yell at her, walk up to her and slap her hard across the cheek. Another part remembered he'd taken all the money she ever had in the world and blown it on a piece of prairie.

"What do you want from me, Wilma?" he said, wearily. She had never noticed the hollows just below his cheekbones. "That sweathog Welfare woman sicked her Health people on me." Reaching into his hip pocket he pulled out a letter and handed it to her. It had the state seal with the Texas star printed at the top. She tried to read the seventeen lines.

"It didn't take her a week to do it," Vernon said. "I found that Rat Patrol letter tacked to my door yesterday, says if I don't wash some dishes and put out rat poison they're gonna close me down. Even tried to tell me my ferrets were vermin. The nerve."

She didn't know how to respond. "I told you those weasels smelled terrible," she said.

"Sorry I can't do anything for you."

"I didn't really expect anything," she said. She couldn't think of any more to say to him. Turning quickly she walked back around to the front of the house. Clint was gone. The Taylor house across the road had begun to lean to the west, its white paint peeling. Looking east toward the crossroads she noticed the old Texaco sign in front of the general store had rusted so that the star wasn't red anymore but the same muddy russet as the two aging gas pumps.

She didn't remember the town looking like this when she left a month ago, but the decline, she knew, hadn't come quickly. It was the steady drop in oil and gas prices that did it, the slow slide of rice, cotton, corn and maize, the only crops anybody had ever tried to raise here. Walter Carrington's boy, Bo, had put in a peach orchard five years earlier, but, because of freezes, droughts and a rare local beetle, he'd never picked a decent peach from one of those baby trees.

Wilma walked across the front yard, opened the white gate and crossed the bridge over the ditch to the road. All the way to Rosemary's she held her head high, face front, and didn't let herself cry until she got inside, shut the front door and crashed.

As long as she didn't rattle around too much at two in the morning it was all right with Rosemary. Wilma could sleep on the living-room couch, get up, throw her two paper routes and get home just after everybody left the house. She had called the daily Houston paper after hearing how much Rosemary's oldest boy was making throwing five hundred *Chronicles* daily and Sunday. Try to get an inner-city route, the kid told her, easier to get around, more papers per square mile. She earned twelve hundred a month for six hours' work daily, slept nine to one A.M.; drank five cups of black coffee and cleaned the house, then drove to the truck stop for a six-hour shift. The roar of the old Hoover reminded her of her mama, blotted out the hard, hurtful garbage in her brain. If she thought too much about something it never worked out.

Having Wilma there to help with the mountains of laundry gave Rosemary a chance to join the Altar Guild and begin attending Bible-study class. Wilma wished she had waited until she'd bought a truck and left Little Egypt because Rosemary was giving her even more grief about a wife's place in the world.

"You're meant to be a helpmeet for Vernon, his joy in the morning," she said.

"I helped him in the field and in the house," she said. "I helped in good times and in the hour of famine." God, she was even starting to sound like Rosemary.

" 'His word shall be thy law,' the Lord said." Rosemary had stopped wearing lipstick. She was letting her hair grow, wrapping it in pink plastic curlers to sleep in. This was the 1980s, for God's sake.

"Rosemary, you sound like a Phyllis Schlafly Total Woman clone. What the hell happened to your brain?"

"He's broke, Wilma. This whole town's broke. He needs you," Rosemary said. She was mixing her famous chocolate macaroon cake for the church bake sale and had flour up to her elbows.

"I don't see why I should stay and let my own walls fall in just because that's what's happening to the rest of the town," Wilma said.

No matter how gritty her eyes were from lack of sleep, she'd be excited starting each paper run. It was a game she played with herself and time. She had an hour between leaving home and picking up the papers at the *Chronicle* warehouse at Shepherd and Richmond by three. There'd always be thirteen other carriers jammed in there rolling the sections into cylinders and slipping on the plastic sleeve and rubber band protecting the day's news. They sat at a long table filling their sacks as they finished wrapping. Somebody was always late, and there was nervous bickering about who would be able to take over a route if he didn't show. Wilma kept her mouth shut and listened to the fussing. She usually finished wrapping her five hundred papers in two hours, hauled the sack out to the Chevrolet and dumped it in the driver's seat. Then with the window rolled down she'd drive east on West Alabama, where there were still a few families and old couples who read the terrible local papers.

The best part was the drive through empty streets—West Main, Hazard, Branard, Portsmouth—cats gliding across sidewalks, trash cans stationed at curbs. Passing the old brick houses, she began looking for the windows of early risers, one light where a student was cramming, an old man brewing coffee, a mother warming bottled formula in a pan on top of a small gas range. Babies were complaining in their cribs. Husbands rolled over, groaned in their sleep. She liked to imagine this as she leaned toward the open window, drew back her muscular arm and, cocking her wrist, threw the paper as far as she could. If it slammed against the door they'd know it was there, maybe hurry downstairs in their socks to let the cat out and bend down and pick up the paper.

Once in a while someone would wave at her as she stepped on the gas and drove on to the next delivery. Often she had an impulse to stop the car, get out and run up to the bright doorway and tell the person there, young or old, "Whatever you do, don't run away. It's better here than you think." And at the same time she kept dreaming about the road stretching out beneath her, running east to the rising sun and the Gulf and the Atlantic, west to the moon dropping behind the Balcones Fault, the Sangre de Cristo Mountains, the Palisades. With the new day rising behind her she'd drive back to Little Egypt, the radio playing cowboy songs. She was listening to country and western music for the first time in her life. The lyrics were mushy but hit hard. "Next time you walk out my heart's door, you won't be welcome anymore."

*　　*　　*

Her father must have died in his sleep while she was throwing papers. When she walked up the porch steps, her shoulders warm from the nine o'clock sun, she found a note in Rosemary's handwriting tacked to the screen door. "Call home," it said. At the bottom Rosemary had scrawled, "I'm at the Altar Guild if you need me."

She didn't get scared until she began dialing her number. When Vernon answered his voice sounded hollow, as if he were talking from a mobile phone.

"What's going on?" she said.

"Your mama called here twice trying to get hold of you. It's your papa—" He couldn't finish the sentence. While her breath jerked she was getting an image of the back of her father's neck. When she was five and six she loved to ride around in the back seat of his Chevy. "That's a Jersey cow," he'd tell her, pointing to the fields going past. Holstein, Hereford, Beefmaster, Aberdeen Angus, Charolais, Black Angus, Brahman, Santa Gertrudis. She memorized the names of every breed and traced with her finger the deep creases on the back of his neck.

"What's wrong?" she said.

"He had another attack last night."

"Can I take the pickup?" she said, unzipping her jeans, running a comb through her hair. "The Chevy won't make it."

She'd have to call the paper, arrange for a leave. Her mother couldn't stand up to nursing for more than a couple of days. The last time he came home from the hospital he'd only been there three days before he'd asked her mother to crawl in bed with him and she'd thrown a boot at his head. To be certain of hearing him when he woke, Wilma slept in the same room. He wasn't having much pain; just that the fear would jump him sometimes in the dark. The other thing bothering him was Wilma working in a truck stop.

"Wilma," Vernon was saying, "it's different this time."

"You don't have to explain. Mama can fill me in when I get there. I'll come over and pack a couple of skirts." Papa didn't like seeing her in jeans. She hung up and ran out the door, ran all the way to the house. He was sitting on the front porch, holding the screen door open and looking like he'd eaten something godawful.

When she had her foot on the bottom step he came forward and grabbed her by the shoulders. "Sugar, he's dead," he said gruffly, still holding on tight. She stared and stared, but his eyes never looked away from hers.

"Who?" she said finally.

"Your papa. He died last night. Died right after the second attack, thank God."

There was something huge lodged in her throat. "Goddammit," she said. "What was the big hurry?" She didn't get to tell him about the truck, about the Mississippi bridge and Mardi Gras and the Cajun dancing.

"You be a brave girl, now," he used to tell her when she'd fall off a fence or skin her knee. Her papa had nothing against girls; they just didn't interest him much. He might've taught her to hunt and fish, she thought, if he'd been raised differently. She guessed he was proud of her accomplishments; he came to most of the tense piano recitals, and after the last one he took her to Schlimmer's Drugstore for a banana split. He must have loved her, he worried about her enough. "Hang on to your own money," he told her once before Vernon lost the farm.

"How's Mama?" she said. She was probably already going through her father's papers.

"Okay," Vernon said. "She wasn't crying." When she

was a girl, her mother tried to temper Wilma's emotional swings. Whenever she banged her hands down on the piano keys during a practice session, her mother would cluck, *"Liebchen, liebchen,* don't be so angry. It's a waste. So inefficient."

"Do you want me to come?" Vernon asked. Though he'd let his hands drop from her shoulders she still felt held.

"You want to?" What was better than his hand on her shoulder? His eyes looking into her shifty heart?

He didn't trust her in his truck, he said, and her papa meant something to him, too, after all.

It was generous, she appreciated it, and that was pretty much all she said on the way to Stonewall. Near Johnson City the hills were windy and brown, here and there a single paintbrush, and long lovegrass blowing like copper wires. It was Palm Sunday. In a couple of weeks bluebonnets would cover the meadows beside the road.

Her mother met them on the porch. Her gray hair was still curled after a permanent, her fine skin smooth, with a light dusting of powder. She stood leaning against one of the short pillars that held up the porch roof, looking as if she were holding open house. Wilma wished she would cry, collapse in her arms, sniffle, but she kissed Wilma lightly on the cheek, and patted Vernon's shoulders. "I've got coffee made. Come on into the kitchen," she said.

They sat at the white-tiled counter drinking coffee hot and black and talking about the weather until Wilma said she wanted to see her papa.

"He's in his bed," her mother said, wiping her lips with a napkin.

When her mother had moved him out of the heavy Victorian double bed they'd slept in for years, Wilma had felt some sad and final bond had broken between them. It was his snoring, her mother explained. He still addressed his wife as "Emma, sweetheart," and kissed the back of her neck, but after the bed switch there were more starch and more ruffles in her blouses and more spray in her hair. And every time he'd kiss her she'd shrink away into herself a little more.

When Wilma stepped through the doorway into his bedroom she didn't expect him to be so small. He lay face up under a sheet, his hawk nose making a little white pyramid, his arms and legs lined up straight, as if someone had gotten him ready for inspection. Gently she pulled the cover down from his face and stood next to the bed, watching him for several minutes. She watched while the Seth Thomas clock on the mantel in the living room chimed twice and a rooster in the yard crowed. Water was running in the kitchen, and a murmur of voices floated through the four downstairs rooms. She waited for him to cough or move. Her grandfather in a cutaway and grandmother in a black silk dress smiled down from an oval frame on the wall next to the bed. In a long christening dress her father stared solemnly at the world from his mother's arms. Was he ever not serious? He joked now and then, she recalled, but rarely laughed except when someone told a Texas Aggie joke. He belonged to a German singing society in town, and he might have laughed there, but, since women weren't allowed in the domino parlor where the meetings were held, she'd never know.

When she came back into the living room her mother was seated in front of the old secretary turning a stack of typed pages. "Where's Vernon?" Wilma asked.

"He's feeding the dogs for me," her mother said, handing her the papers. "Take a look at this. A will takes a while to be probated, so I thought you'd want to know what you can count on." Her mother spoke with great distinctness, as if she were speaking to someone slightly deaf.

Her eye ran down the pages past her father's bequests to her mother and brothers. After their mother's death her brothers would inherit the farm. Wilma felt a pang. No big blow, just a twinge. Mack and Jeff would have a piece of Papa's land. Now that Vernon had lost his farm she'd probably never own an acre. Okay, she was traveling light now. Her brothers did know more about running a farm, though she'd always hoped they'd run it together. When she was eight the three of them had taken Mack's pocketknife into the hay barn, made small cuts in their index fingers and touched them together so the blood smeared. They would teach her to shoot. When she got down to the cash bequests she'd already resigned herself: her papa hadn't left her anything. But there it was on the fifth page. Ten thousand dollars. His life insurance policy. Hers. It didn't even bother her that it was the same amount he split between the Lutheran Church and the Sons of Bismarck.

The preacher started into the "ashes to ashes" part. Her mother was sitting in a chair with her father's hat on her knees, and when the four undertaker's men stepped up to lower the casket into the grave, her mother rose to her feet. She watched the casket drop slowly down the sides of the grave, which was lined with green canvas so it wouldn't look so much like a hole in the ground. The casket had cost seventeen hundred dollars and was supposed to be made of walnut, but it looked too smooth, like molded fiberglass. The undertaker's men picked up their shovels and peeled back the green plastic sheet from the pile of black earth next to the grave. Wilma's mother removed a fifty-dollar bill from the wallet. Turning the hat over so you could see the green band darkened with sweat and the name Texas Hatters on the inside of the crown, she tucked the folded bill inside the hatband. Then she stood gazing down for a moment into the hole that didn't look like a grave. She closed her eyes and tossed the hat so it fell on top of the casket. When she opened them again she didn't look lost. Her eyes were clear and dry.

"He's got everything he needs," she said.

PART TWO

12

THEY WERE HALFWAY BETWEEN San Angelo and El Paso when she saw the two Mexican women on the shoulder and started shifting down. West Texas stretched ahead of her like a scorched sheet in the July sun.

"What're you doin'?" Oralee said, shifting the baby to her left arm.

"Those girls're fagged out. We've got room," Wilma said. The women wore cotton dresses and jogging shoes and carried paper shopping bags so heavy their shoulders sagged.

"Goddamn. Can't you quit?"

"Quit what?"

"Pickin' up strays," Oralee said, giving Wilma a disgusted look.

"Well, I could," Wilma said, "but then I might never run into another one like you." Three weeks earlier she had found Oralee and the baby at a Denton truck stop. Oralee and the truckdriver she was with were practicing fly fishing between the booths, and when the girl saw Wilma she dropped the fly rod and the trucker, picked up Car and jumped into Wilma's lap like she was the original mother possum. Now the cab was pretty full. On the floor under Oralee's feet Wilma's Lab puppy, a brother to Clint's dog, whined and rooted around.

When they pulled off the road the Mexicans stopped walking and stood on the shoulder, their eyes watchful. As Wilma dropped down from the step, Bear wriggled off the seat into her arms, and she set him on the grass. The two women backed off, their eyes never leaving the dog.

"*No se preocupen,*" Wilma said, smiling. Bear was swarming all around the women, tail wagging his body so hard he bent in half-circles.

"*Adónde van?*"

"El Paso, *señora,*" the older woman said. She hesitated.

"*Quieren* ride?"

"*Mil gracias, sí,*" the woman said.

Wilma knew just enough Spanish to ask where they were coming from. San Antonio, they told her. Looking for jobs as maids. Hotel work was okay, *más o menos,* but they didn't give you a room. In Alamo Heights they thought they had found small servants' quarters over the garage, but Salvadorans had gotten there first. The woman made a face when she said Salvadoran. They hated going back home.

Wilma opened the door to the sleeper and showed the women how to grab the rail and pull themselves up. They were small and wiry with delicate hands. The younger of them wore a locket around her neck with a picture of Michael Jackson on it. They smiled nervously as Wilma climbed in and closed the door.

"Sure, I'll bet they live in El Paso," Oralee sneered from the passenger seat. "I'll bet they still got river mud under their toenails."

Wilma said she didn't see the point in making jokes

about other people's misery. Oralee just raised her jet eyebrows and stuck a bottle in the baby's mouth.

"Want me to drive?" Oralee said. Wilma could scarcely hear the question over the roar of the engine. After five months in the truck she still hadn't gotten used to the noise and the vibration that churned her insides. If Oralee took over she'd curl in the cubby with the baby inside her arm, and wake feeling like bread kneaded and beaten down. Usually she slept fitfully, dreamed of standing in front of Truck City without enough money to buy the truck. It was worse when she dreamed about Vernon forgetting his heart medicine, having an attack, dying alone on the kitchen floor while the coyote paced in its cage.

The day she had walked into Truck City with the cash, Mark Lowry had waltzed her around the terrazzo floor till she had the whirlies. She had decided on the green Kenworth because she liked its lines, and she could handle five gears and overdrive. Also, it had a good radio. Wilma was feeling pretty damned good as she slapped down her papa's money and took the key.

"Take it easy, Wilma," Mark had told her. "Don't try to make all your miles at once. Who you gonna sign with?" he asked. She didn't know. All she could say at the moment was she was an independent who planned on breaking into the moving business. Pulling out of the chainlink fence onto the feeder, she switched to a country station, and the first song she got was "Honkeytonk Angel." She decided to name the truck Jessie Louise after her grandmother.

"I can make it to Van Horn okay," she told Oralee. "You want to snooze or tell me a story?"

"This one doesn't look like sleeping," Oralee said, over Car's shoulder. The baby was working on Oralee's ear, trying to make a pretzel out of it. "Whatcha wanta hear?"

"Tell me that one again about the onion field," she said.

"Oh, that guy. Hillbilly. Nicest rear I ever saw, and red hair. Picked us up in Dallas, told me he needed a second driver. What he didn't tell me was we had ten hours to the Valley and ten more in a stinking mudhole of a field, waiting for a bunch of wetbacks to load the truck with onions. I'm tellin' you, that whole field smelled like onion soup. We got through it by getting higher than Mount Rushmore on the best *sinsemilla* in Dallas. We're laying there in the cubby, and he's getting kinda fresh, nothing serious, when along comes this prick of a foreman telling us we got the wrong onions.

"He wanted the *mojados* to dump the little bitty onions we already had on board and fill us with the large economy size. Another four hours. He's Loonytunes. I take a big breath, lean out the window, and yell in my best Spanish, '*Federales,*' and those Mexicans scatter. We try to haul ass out of the field, but we're hub deep in mud. Need forklifts to get out. Get into a motel in Crystal City, back the truck into a space in front of the manager's apartment and park. Next morning hillbilly gives me the keys while he's shaving, tells me to fire up the truck. I'm sleepy. Haven't got my contact lenses in. Turn the key and crunch, wham, I've backed the truck into the side of the manager's office. Hillbilly runs out covered with shaving cream, and we scream outa there, and lucky, too, 'cause there's the outline of the rear end of the fuckin' trailer printed on the motel wall."

She could listen to Oralee for hours. She must be better than speed. When she picked her up Wilma was amazed how much the girl had learned. Since October she'd hitched rides with cattle truckers, fruit and vegetable haulers,

long-distance freight drivers and hazardous-chemical ka-
mikazes. There wasn't a state in the West or Southwest she
hadn't been in, or a state of mind, either.

"Worst thing about trucking is body grit," Oralee said.
"There ain't enough truck stops with showers. So I'm with
this sweet old booger driving a Volvo hauling a trailer full
of baseball gear. I meet him in Amarillo.

" 'I'm on my way to Scottsdale,' he tells me. 'I carry
stuff for the New York Yankees. Wanta learn somethin'
about baseball?'

" 'What you got on board?' I ask him, and he says
fifty-seven gloves, a hundred and thirty bats.

" 'You know the way to Arizona?' he asks me, and I say
no, but I read maps okay. 'I got fifty-seven gloves, a hundred and thirty bats and a couple hundred bags of clay,' he
tells me.

" 'What's the clay for?' I wonder, and he says it's for
patting down around the pitcher's mound and home plate.

" 'Arizona's got sand, no clay,' he says. This is a fine old
guy, about seventy-five. What a trip, I think. What a trip.
The Yankees. It turns out this sweet old guy's a speed
freak. He doesn't need food, sleep, showers. Also he never
stops talking about his heroes—Babe Ruth, Whitey Ford.
He wants me to know every friggin' piece of equipment
he's ever hauled. Whitey Ford's sailboat hadda go to Florida, and Mike Kekich's motorcycle. When he was a kid it
cost maybe four bits to go to the ball game. So he's in the
middle of tellin' me these stories, and we're going across
the state line at Clovis, where there's this big mo-fo truck
stop with the laundromats and the showers and all, so I
holler so loud he has to stop. Ouch, you quit that."

She peeled the baby's fist from her nose.

"I paid for a towel and a shower stall for a buck-fifty,
and carried my clean clothes and makeup kit down a hall

with numbers on the doors like a motel. Then a weirdo came out of one of those showers. Big droopy tits and a towel wrapped around the waist, and greasy wet hair hanging down. Also, she's got whiskers.

" 'This one's dirty,' she says, in a bass voice. 'There's some confusion here,' I say, and pick up my heels and hightail it back to the manager.

" 'Listen,' I tell him, 'there's a man in here. Probably dresses like a woman,' and you know what that creep says? He says, 'Lady, first you dames want us to build you showers. We build showers. You want us to clean up our language. So we sweeten up our language. You get every damned thing you ever asked for, including a license and a truck, but we got no guarantee against confusion.' " Oralee laid her curly head back against the seat and laughed, a deep, satisfying sound. Wilma wished again she had Oralee's smooth pale cheeks and inky eyelashes.

"Did you get your shower?" she asked.

"Three days later in Yuma. That truck was beginning to smell like a rendering plant, I swear to God."

From behind them in the cubby one of the women spoke in faltering English.

"A man, *esmell muy malo.*" It was the Mexican woman, grinning out of the dark cubby like a little mink in a cave. "He make the whole house estink."

"Tiene marido?" Wilma asked. Did she have a husband?

"Sí, divorciado," the woman said, rubbing her hands together as if she were brushing off dirt. Life was easier in some ways, some ways harder. He had a green card.

"Tenemos tanto miedo," she told Wilma. "There is no safe place to work." Her name was Marianela; her friend's name was Corazón. Before the hotel job they'd worked as

166

pressers in a laundry. When a woman ran into the room and yelled *"Imigración"* one morning, Marianela grabbed Corazón by the arm and dragged her into a cardboard crate. She had a mother in Juarez who kept her two children, and a father with Parkinson's disease.

"Were you born in Mexico?" Wilma asked her. "Tell me about Mexico." Oralee had told her she wouldn't take Car back to New York until she'd taken her to Mexico. "She shouldn't come all this way and not visit a foreign country," she said. "It's educational."

"No soy de Mexico," the woman told Wilma, frowning. *"No más."* Her dark eyes were angry. "I left my country. I don't never go back." Wilma heard the words "always" and "never" from every drifter she picked up.

They were approaching Van Horn. A few minutes later, past the dusty town with seven storefronts, Wilma knew she would have to pass through a Border Patrol station. Did she hide the two women in the cubby or let them out on the road? They could detour around the checkpoint if they waited till nightfall. This much responsibility scared her.

"Tenemos La Migra," she told them. "What do you want?"

The older woman said to stop. Wilma opened the door to the driver's side and got out. Marianela slipped down the side of the truck and stood on the road. Her white tennis socks had little blue pom-poms on them.

"Cuidado," Marianela told her. Take care. Reaching into her sack she pulled out a piece of pastry, hard and dry, and thrust it into Wilma's hand.

"Para buena suerte," she said, for good luck. *"Adiós."*

"Mucho gusto," Wilma said. *"Mil gracias."*

"Bye y'all," Oralee said. "Car says bye-bye." She waved

the baby's fat hand at the women as the truck pulled back on the road.

Wilma passed through Van Horn seven minutes later, and pulled in next to a small cement-block building two miles further on. An officer in olive green walked around the nose of the truck and wrote something down on a clipboard. After a minute he climbed up and stuck his head in the window. He wore kidney-shaped glasses so dark she couldn't see his eyes.

"Papers, please, ma'am," he said. He spoke with a slight accent, perfectly polite, but all bone and gristle.

She reached into the leather briefcase between the seat and the engine, pulled out the log and the bill of lading and handed them to him.

"Permits?" She gave him the Bingo Card, which had the permits for every state she went through. While he looked them over she had time to notice he had dark skin and hair, with a sprinkle of gray in the sideburns.

"Have you been to all these places? New Mexico, California, Arizona?"

What was he fishing for? "Sure," she said. "You ought to try it."

This cooled him off. "Are you a United States citizen?"

"Sure," she said.

"Any agricultural products aboard?"

"Just this dog," she said, pointing to Bear. It turned out he loved dogs, so he made them get out of the cab and stand there for ten minutes while he talked about training dummies and guns and fussed over the Lab. Wilma was glad she didn't have to worry about the women from El Paso.

"How long have *you* been driving a truck?" he asked Oralee, looking at her intently. She gave the officer a look suggesting he was a lowdown gigolo. "Ever since I hitched my first ride," she said. "How long you been running in your own people?"

The man's face darkened under his tan. The badge on his pocket said GARCÍA. "Come with me, please," he said, his voice tight.

They followed him into the office, Oralee dragging her flip-flops over the dusty cement. Inside were two plain oak desks and on the wall behind them a large map of the border counties. Different-colored pins were stuck in clusters along the snaky black line representing the river. A section of the room had been partitioned off with hurricane fencing painted green. Inside the enclosure eighteen young men sat on benches. One or two looked up when the women walked in, but then went back to staring at the floor.

"How long have they been here?" Wilma asked.

"We drive them back over every eight hours," García said. "I brought you in here so you would understand there are too many."

"All they want is a better deal," she said.

He stood a little taller. "I was born an American citizen. My father and mother had to wait seven years for papers."

"How far is it to the border?" Oralee said. "I want to go to the border."

"It's forty-seven miles from where you're standing," García told her. "And you're the only one in this room who wants to go."

At the terminal in El Paso they had to wait for the dispatcher to call in about their next load. At eleven there were only six or seven truckers marking time in the coffeeshop booths or leaning against the Coke machine outside, cracking dirty jokes. Oralee knew more jokes than seventeen men. Mostly raunchy but short.

"What's the best thing comes out of a penis?" Oralee asked.

Wilma never had answers to any of these questions.

"Wrinkles," Oralee said, doubling over. The baby was sitting in her car seat on the floor playing with a rubber flashlight. Oralee bent over and tickled her stomach, and the baby gurgled and crowed. Wilma couldn't remember if she'd had this much fun with her own babies.

"Girl, you ought to be ashamed," Wilma said. Oralee had a five-pound rubber barbell in each hand. She lifted her arms slowly out from her body without bending her elbows. After fifteen of these lifts her face was flushed, and her blue eyes had a stressed, glazed look.

"Oralee, why don't you straighten up and fly right?" Wilma said. "Take that child back where she belongs. A truck's no place to raise a kid." Oralee said she didn't know why not.

"I'll take her back after she sees Mexico," she said.

"Think I should call Vernon?"

"You just called him last week to ask him to send in his quarterly IRS. You asked him then if he was taking his medicine. He ain't sending you flowers, is he? Or paying back the money he stole? Quit worrying about him. Where'd you say our load started from?"

"San Miguel Allende," Wilma told her. "We can pick it up from the other driver soon as he gets here."

Gary was right. Waiting around was the worst part. Waiting for the dispatchers to call, for the load to come in, for the inspectors to run down the bill of lading, for the owners to decide which wall they wanted the piano on, and the matching wing chairs and the elephant's-foot umbrella stand.

She was waiting now for her first international load. "They'll have to come through Customs first," she said. "They might have to switch trailers or something. It might be hours before we see 'em."

By the time the van finally pulled in it was close to five A.M. The driver jumped down and handed her the two-page bill of lading, listing all the furniture in the trailer. She looked it over briefly, noting several large painted chests and a piano. She'd need at least two men to unload her in Houston tomorrow night.

After they switched trailers Oralee went to the john while Wilma paid for two coffees in the restaurant and picked up a couple of toothpicks. On the way out she glanced at a wall phone and decided against it. Walking around behind the van she checked to see the seal was secure. Once inside the cab she turned the key and began checking gauges. Brake pressure, oil pressure, fuel, battery—everything looked good. She switched on the small rotary fan on the passenger side and checked the supply of ice in the Igloo under the seat. Four Granny Smith apples and a pound of feta cheese lay on top of six cans of grapefruit juice. Turning halfway around she opened the five-gallon metal can and reached inside. Plenty of Purina for the dog curled in a tight crescent on the bunk.

Aside from making her truck payments, Bear was the single biggest problem Wilma had. A six-month-old Lab with more energy than a pound of uranium, he was limber, lean and so enthusiastic that he'd knocked down one of the ICC inspectors at a weigh station. The man was over fifty and overweight, and he hadn't expected to be hit in the chest with fifty-five pounds of young dog. Wilma bought a pair of Nike trainers and took Bear on three-mile runs along the shoulder or around city blocks, whenever there was a break or a layover. It was a terrific way to pass the time and tone up. As the dog's legs lengthened and he started growing into his feet, big as an adult mountain lion's paws, Wilma wasn't sure she'd be tough enough to keep up with him.

She wasn't sure Oralee wouldn't turn out to be more than she'd bargained for as well, especially with a kidnapped baby on her hip. The girl sure had to be a tough one. After her mama died she'd had to dodge her old man whenever he got into the sauce, which was most evenings. He came home from the steel mill already half lit and either tore into her or crashed under the newspapers. The little girl spent a lot of time entertaining herself. She was eleven when she became convinced that everything in the world depended on sex. It was after a pajama party that she got turned on and started writing twelve-year-old pornography. An older girl who'd taken the pseudonym Love Bucket and wrote stories for *True Confessions* used these parties as a proving ground. Seven or eight twelve-year-olds in shortie nightgowns, their cheeks painted with pink pimple medicine, sat on a shag rug, hushed and breathless. Finally Love Bucket launched into her reading, the usual *True Confessions* material.

"You know," Oralee told Wilma, " 'I Was Ruined in the Park,' stuff like that. I got pretty interested in those stories. I got real turned on, right? There's nothing in my house like this. My father wouldn't allow *Hawaii* because of the sex scenes."

After the steamy readings at the pajama parties she'd come home and start rewriting what she had heard. "I'd be all keyed up and start redoing Love Bucket's story. You know, I think I was gettin' off, writing that stuff."

"What was in your book?" Wilma asked. She'd never thought of writing a dirty book.

172

"Most of it I don't remember. I had people screwing upside down, eating shit. Some of the stuff I put in there I don't even know if it's physically possible."

When her father found the book in her bureau drawer, he slapped her face.

"Have you heard the word 'lewd' very much in conversation?"

No, she hadn't, Wilma said.

"Well, I got 'lewd' for half an hour. Also I got grounded. I never thought about anyone reading this book because it was like I was writing it to the Devil, know what I mean? Daddy took me to church and made me throw all my Stones albums into the bonfire."

Watching Oralee push open the restaurant door with Car still asleep on her shoulder, Wilma felt the difference in their ages.

"Wilma, did you have sex before you were married?" Oralee asked, settling into the seat.

"It was God," Wilma told her. "God was Love and it was the easiest thing in the world to lay down as long as you could say it was love."

They were on their way back from El Paso, five miles west of Van Horn at six when she first heard it—the faint sound of a baby crying behind her in the van. She turned to see if Oralee had noticed it, but she had her head up against the windowsill and Car asleep on her knees. The bleating was so weak she could scarcely catch it over the engine's roar. She rolled her window up so the wind wouldn't swallow the noise and cocked her head around so her ear was toward the back wall of the cab. *Maybe I'm getting some inner-ear thing,* she thought. But the cry grew louder as she drove on, backing it down to sixty, fifty-five, forty and finally pulling off the road into a little park with a fiberglass sun roof painted aquamarine and a couple of concrete picnic benches.

She rolled down her window and listened. A thin cry, and now she heard other sounds: a sharp metallic ring, a hot hissing like a trout fillet makes when you first set it down in Crisco. Wilma opened the door and got out. Bear followed her over to the shelter and sat at her feet as she rested her fanny against one of the benches.

"Oralee," she called out. "Wake up. I need you out here."

"Christ," Oralee said, climbing down with the baby on her shoulder. She was rearranging the diaper under the baby's head when the cry from the van came again, louder this time, with lots of vibrato. Oralee's eyes were wide open, her eyebrows scrambling up her hairline. "We got us another baby?"

"Let's find out," Wilma said, pulling out her Buck knife and walking to the rear door of the van. Bear stood on his hind legs with his forepaws on the bumper as if he were looking at a rib roast. Oralee balanced Car on one hip bone, shading her eyes against the morning light bouncing off the chrome. Wilma cut the tin seal with the knife, stepped down from the bumper and opened the door.

Smoke billowed into her face, burning her eyes. Mesquite smoke. At least it wasn't the furniture. She squinted, trying to find the baby, but all she could make out was a four-legged thing standing on top of a drop-leaf table halfway to the back wall of the van. It shook its wedge-shaped head, stamped a front foot and made a sound so much like a baby's cry that Wilma let out a little shriek herself. The animal bleated once again and vaulted from the table onto a red leather wing chair closer to the door. When it lowered its spotted haunches into the chair, Wilma saw it was

174

a nanny goat with a deep udder. As the goat folded its forelegs under its body, nestling into the chair, a man and a woman crawled out from under the table. They walked to the doorway, the man carrying a girl of three, the woman a smoking tin bucket.

"*Buenas días,*" said the man. He wore jeans and a denim jacket with a Mexican eagle embroidered on the back. The man smiled, but the woman just stared at Wilma with eyes hard as river stones.

Wilma fished for some Spanish, but for some reason all she could think of was the words for "Shut the window." They looked at her blankly.

"*De dónde son ustedes?*" she tried again.

They were from San Miguel, the man said. They had worked for two years for the Simmonses, the people who owned the furniture.

"*Y adónde van?*" she asked.

"*No importa,*" the man said. It didn't matter to the stowaways which *gringo* city they wound up in, as long as they stayed with the *familia.*

Wilma motioned to them to step down from the van. They moved stiffly, cautiously, the mother setting the tin bucket down next to the picnic table and poking at the burning branches inside it with a stick. She reached into the fire with blackened fingers, pulling out a yam covered with ashes and quickly dropping it onto the ground. She pointed to it and smiled shyly at Wilma.

"*No gracias,*" Wilma said, pointing to the little girl. The child sat on top of the table, her thumb in her mouth. Her hair fell over her eyes in a blue-black bang, and she swung her tiny leather huaraches back and forth. The mother waited a few moments for the yam to cool, then broke it in half, handing one piece to the child. The little girl threw back her head and laughed, her hand squeezing the yam so the insides oozed between her fat fingers. Then she opened her mouth and stuck her whole fist inside.

The sun rose higher, glancing off the soaring roof of the aquamarine shelter. The wind had risen a little, and it was pleasant hearing the wings of small canyon wrens rustling in the brush across the fence behind them. They'd stop in Van Horn, eat some breakfast. Later she'd get through the Border Patrol checkpoint on the other side of town. She'd kid around with García, and he'd let her through. García didn't look mean but she'd hate to tangle with most Immigration officers. From the stories she heard they were throwbacks, like the horned toad or the Texas Rangers. Maybe they had to be mean to do their job.

"I can tell you're figuring on taking that bunch home, putting them to work, getting 'em food stamps. I know you." Oralee was lying on the concrete bench, doing situps with her arms folded across her T-shirt that had HANK'S GYM printed on it.

"Just think about this, willya," she said. "If you get caught with these dudes you'll lose your license, they'll slap a fine on you. If it were my call I'd tell 'em to start walking. Or try to thumb a ride." She slid easily into the cobra position, her head thrown back, the veins in her arms swelling and pulsing.

"I don't get it, Wilma. You had me all convinced you were hot to start a new life, have your own thing for the first time. After we put our heads together at the truck stop I said to myself, 'Now that's a real live grown woman, and I need to spend some time with a lady like that.' Now, here you go, deciding to be Mother Teresa to the wetback millions, risking your freedom and your future, your whole beautiful trip."

Wilma didn't know how to put it into words. "Try to

put yourself in those people's shoes. What if it was you and me? What if we were that poor and that scared and nobody'd help us? And with a kid?"

Oralee kept staring at her knees. "People like that, they're used to it. They're refugees."

Wilma was quiet. Finally she said, "They're desperate. You'd never leave your home and your friends if you weren't desperate."

Oralee sat up quickly. There was no pity in her black black eyes. She'd been there.

"Everybody down there is desperate," she said.

13

GARCÍA MUST HAVE SMELLED something wrong the minute she pulled into the driveway beside the quonset hut. He was waving her over behind the office to a parking place marked UNLOAD.

"Here we go," Oralee said. "I always wanted to spend a year in a border jail." She laid her head against the back of the seat and closed her eyes.

They had decided to try to hide the family in the largest piece of furniture in the load, but Wilma could see there wasn't room for all three when she raised the mahogany lid on the baby grand. It took some doing to persuade the mother to flatten her back against the strings and hold the baby still in the crook of her arm. They would be as uncomfortable in there as they would be hiding under a load of bricks.

"*Bueno,*" Wilma said. "Thank God they're skinny." She smiled at the husband. He didn't smile back. Lifting the lid, she explained to the mother the need for quiet. She would prop the lid a crack for ventilation, but the baby must not cry. The mother shifted her weight across the strings, making a fine trembly sound. Wilma's heart fell five feet.

"Espero que derma," she said. She hoped the baby would sleep. She wondered if the couple would be any better off working in Houston or Dallas than in Mexico. On Saturdays they'd be picking through pyramids of oranges and mangos at Fiesta, circumnavigating the enormous store as if it were the village *paseo.* At the door of the market they could buy Madonna rings for fifteen cents and imitation Rolex watches for $18.95. The cowboy and rooster piñatas were cheap there, only $3.95, and fajitas over the counter were fifty cents. But it wasn't going to be so easy living in the new Texas. Oil prices were down. Jobs were scarce, even at $3 an hour. If they were able to hide from La Migra for a few years, so what? In a year or two they would own a TV set and a table and chairs. Some curtains. In a few years the mother would have two more children. This was as sure as arithmetic.

"What'll we do with that goat?" Oralee said.

"Let it eat Fritos till it conks out. Then, when we get to the checkpoint if the baby cries we'll pull the goat out, and those boys can get all worked up over livestock crossing the border."

She watched García on his way out to the truck. His hand brushed the butt of the .357 magnum in its black holster. They wouldn't think of looking in back, she thought. They'd never notice the wire seal was broken. He touched the front of his brown felt hat.

"Sorry, *señora,* but we have orders to check everyone from the border. It's the Camargo killers they're after." A U.S. drug-enforcement agent had been found murdered near Monterrey, small pieces of him stuffed into a plastic bag.

"You want us to get down?" Wilma asked him, and he looked embarrassed.

"With your permission," he said.

She slung the strap of her leather purse over her shoulder, snapped Bear's leash to his choke collar and opened the door. García held her lightly by the elbow. It had been so long since anyone had laid a hand on her to assist that she got a dumb tear in her eye. As she dropped to the ground a couple of old Diet Coke cans rolled out from under the seat, along with Bear's heartworm pills and three pieces of red and blue gum from a pinball machine. Oralee pretended to sleep.

A second man came around the corner of the office, a star pinned to his blue vest. "Deputy Sheriff," it said, and Wilma's pulse jumped. In towns like Van Horn local law-enforcement officials hung around Border Patrol installations like gulls behind shrimpers, waiting for action. The deputy had a tight-skinned look. His shirt buttons strained over his belly; his face and hands were nicely crisped.

He walked up next to García and pushed back his hat brim, staring at Wilma as if he'd never seen a woman with a puppy on a leash before.

"Well, good evenin', grandma, how you doin'?" he said, extending a huge club hand. A silver name plate on his pocket read "Roscoe Britt." García looked at Britt, surprised. "Just wanted to take a look at her papers," Britt explained.

She handed him her license and her Bingo Card. Britt squinted at the license like a jeweler looking for a flaw, turned the license over to read the signature on the back and returned it to her. He removed his glasses. His eyes were blue and cold.

"You're a fine big woman," he said. "Why ain't you home with your old man 'steada rattling around on the road trying to get killed?"

"I guess I'm out here for the same reason you are,

180

Sheriff," she said, keeping her voice sweet. "I got a job to do."

"You wear glasses, ma'am?"

"Contacts," she said. She was slightly nearsighted and vain enough not to like the way she looked in glasses.

Britt walked up so close she could smell the peppers he'd eaten with his eggs. His eyes bore in, giving her no place to look.

"I sure cain't see anything, hon. You'd better take one of 'em out so I can see you're wearing your perscription."

"Come on," she said.

"You rather have a ticket?"

She pinched her right lens between thumb and finger and showed it to Britt. Then she spit on it and put it back into her eye. When the grit from her hand began making her eye burn, she got that racy heart that meant she was angry.

While Britt was talking, García reached for the grab rail, lifting himself quickly into the front seat. He searched underneath, removing a rawhide bone of Bear's and a black satin bra size 36D. Turning around, he pushed aside the Naugahyde dropcloth in front of the cubby, removed his dark glasses and crawled in.

Wilma groaned. She thought she heard a faint bleat, then definite sounds of a scuffle: limbs thrashing around, a sharp crack and a yelp of pain.

"*Madre*," García said, breathlessly, and then, "*Diablo*," as he slowly backed out of the cubby and climbed down the side of the truck.

He stood before her, the black-and-white goat in his arms.

"What in the name of God is this?" The goat was lying on its back in his arms like a baby in a christening dress. Britt walked closer to the truck. The nanny goat nibbled at the silver name plate on García's shirt collar. She had a small, wet patent-leather nose and blue-aggie eyes.

"It's a pet," Wilma said, avoiding his eyes.

"Last time you came here—yesterday, no?—you had the dog but I never saw this before," he said. There might have been a slight tremor in his cheek, as if he were suppressing a smile.

"She must've been asleep, in back," Wilma told him, keeping a straight face.

"Oh, lady," Britt said, shaking his head, the smile spreading across his face like a broken yoke, "how do we know you haven't got a herd of javelinas in that van?" He was only halfway kidding.

"If I do, I'd hate to see the furniture by now," she said. "What would I be doing with a bunch of Mexican hogs, anyway? I'm no coyote." Anyone who tried that had to be crazy, even for five hundred a head. Too much surveillance above ground and below. Close to the river Immigration agents were using dogs, helicopters and buried electronic sensors to sniff them out. They had computers that tracked blips on the screen as they came across the river, so sensitive they could distinguish between a man and a deer.

She'd nearly convinced them she was harmless when Oralee yawned and stretched in the front seat, and climbed out of the truck. Standing next to the long green front end she looked like a cheesecake ad for trucks and waxes and chrome accessories. In the morning sun her black eyes glittered, and her hair and the tiny, fake diamond studs in her ears. Oralee was still lean as a spirit, but with the workouts she'd earned herself some new curvy quadriceps and calves. Her long tanned legs swooped out of her tight black cutoff jeans.

The deputy stared. Oralee pretended she didn't notice

his eyes running all over her legs. He rubbed his ear, hitched up his pants, looked at his boots. Crickets buzzed in the dusty grass at the edge of the cement slab, and a little breeze lifted a strand of Oralee's hair from her neck. There was a long, interesting silence.

"Would you come over here, little lady?" Britt said, pointing to Oralee.

"What for?" she said. She was standing spraddle-legged, one hand on her hip.

"Just get on over here, and I'll tell you," he said.

She took her time, swinging her tiny hips in the cut-offs, whose fringe just brushed the curve of her butt. Britt didn't miss a ripple.

"That your kid?" he said, looking at her sharply. Car was hanging from a blue sling on Oralee's chest.

"Sure," Oralee said, tilting her chin up a notch.

"She don't look a thing like you. Where's her daddy at?"

"A long ways from here," the girl said, "just where he ought to be."

Britt walked up a few steps closer.

"*Cuidado, hombre,*" García said. "Let it go."

But Oralee couldn't.

She put a hand up. "Hold it right there," she said. "You're steppin' in my grass patch."

"Just trying to see a resemblance." His face was so close to Oralee's he could lick her with his tongue. "You always this mean?"

"No sir. Just when I run across a nasty scumbag that sticks his nose up my crotch."

Wilma had never in her life heard a woman talk like Oralee. Britt probably hadn't either.

"That's all I needed, little darlin', those kind words," he said. "I guess I'll have to examine the cargo." He walked around to the back of the van and observed the broken seal. "García, come over here, willya. I just noticed something funny."

"Waitaminute," Oralee said, buzzing after him like a yellow jacket. Searing white sunlight touched the delicate gold chain around her neck. "This is federal government business, and what in hell are you doin' messin' around in it anyway, creep?"

Britt turned to Wilma. "This your bouncer?"

"I'd like to bounce your sweet ass," Oralee said, a grin on her face as wide as the Trans Pecos. "We got us a king-sized Sealy in that there van with 'Britt' written on it."

Wilma walked over, gave her a look and punched her arm, but there was no stopping her. When she looked around for García he was walking toward a clump of cactus with the goat in his arms. Britt was opening the double doors, heaving himself up onto the floor, picking his way through carved Spanish chests and wrought-iron lamps and mahogany tables to the back of the dark van. He wasn't going to miss getting a look at every last thing they had.

"Wait for me," Oralee called. "I'll give you a hand." Britt's knees rapped against a five-drawer mahogany highboy with brass pulls. He picked up a small rocking chair and set it aside out of his way. While Wilma watched from the ground, Oralee vaulted onto the van in a panther's spring. She started hoisting pillows and small rolled rugs over her head and tossing them into corners.

Britt glared at her. "If you don't cut that out and get down from there, Thunder Thighs, I'll ticket you for interfering with an officer."

Wilma wished García would come back and stop her before it was too late. She guessed Oralee had had a chip on her shoulder all her life, and no wonder. Whenever a guy stared at her in a truck stop, Oralee refused to lower her voice or her eyes; she'd keep right on talking and stare him down until he looked away and pretended to read the local news on the paper doily. *She ought to have a steady boyfriend*, Wilma thought; it would tone her down.

When a second deputy walked out the back door of the office and saw Oralee and Britt fighting in the van it must have looked like some kind of rodeo. Britt had grabbed a big hank of Oralee's hair as she wrapped her skinny arms around his waist trying to squeeze the air out of his belly. The deputy walked up beside Wilma and stood watching with his hands on his hips. He was young and blond with a nice cowboy build.

"What's her story? A lady wrestler in her off time?" he said.

"This ain't no woman, Corey," Britt yelled. "Look at the peach fuzz on her lip. She's probably hung like a grandfather clock."

Wilma never got a chance to collar Oralee or holler for help before the girl picked up a heavy brass lamp and crowned Britt with it. Bear whined and pulled on the leash, baring his teeth. Britt sagged slowly to the floor, his fall broken by a bundle of Oaxacan rugs. In a minute or two he rose again, his hat off, arms spinning like a windmill. He grabbed Oralee's wrists, pinning her between the grand piano and a twenty-one-inch console TV. The girl twisted under him like a muscular fish and bit him on the shoulder.

"Cuffs, Corey," he yelled, and the younger officer handed him a pair of black metal handcuffs. "Get 'em on that other gal," he said. "Quick, before she runs off." He slapped Oralee hard across the cheek.

When Wilma saw Britt hit Oralee she felt a swarm of

bees fill her head. She'd seen violence before but never up close. Vernon hadn't ever hit her, and no one had ever laid a threatening hand on her. She was afraid of being caught and stopped now, just as she was shifting into high. Full and heavy with anger, she felt her legs grow weak. She couldn't hold this weight, but instead of falling she counted the steps the man had to take to reach the edge of the van, measured the distance he had to drop from the van to the ground and how much of her weight she could throw into her right foot.

When he was so close she could count the pores in his nose, she punted into his groin. His face pulled a neat trick. Five different expressions passed over it, all kin to astonishment, shame and rage. But he was young and recovered quickly enough to catch her running around the near corner of the building, Bear pulling the leash hard ahead of her, ears laid back and tail flying. Corey tackled her from behind, slamming her down on the pavement so her elbows and forearms skidded along the asphalt, peeling away a long strip of her shirt and a thin layer of skin on the underside of her arms. The pain made her nauseated. She tried to kick, but he was a brick blanket over her legs. The last thing she saw before she closed her eyes was García running toward them carrying the goat.

When Roscoe Britt walked into the jail lobby it was nearly six in the evening. Three stuffed pronghorns stared impassively at the seven women sleeping against the wall. On the opposite side of the room two men sat cross-legged on the floor, one in a straw hat with the brim pulled low might have been asleep or dead or planning a revolution. The other, only a kid, was still turning the pages of a comic book entitled *Los Desesperados de la Guerra*. Britt stood in the middle of the lobby slapping the side of his gabardine pants with a rolled-up copy of *Playboy*.

"Okay, everybody *arriba*. Time for beddy-bye, ladies," he said, motioning to Wilma and Oralee and the others to get up and follow him through a wooden door with a smoked-glass window. Behind the door stretched a long hall painted pea-green and smelling like a hundred dirty toilets.

"You can't keep us here," Wilma said. "We haven't been booked. You're holding us without bail."

Britt whipped around and stuck his big pig's nose into her face. "How wrong you are, sister. It's down in the book. Bail's five hundred apiece and the soonest you can pay up and get out is tomorrow morning when the judge comes in." He sneered, showing teeth as yellow as old field corn. "This bunch of *putas* is in your party," he said, nodding at the other women. "Looks like you'll fit right in."

He opened the gate to the big cell. Wilma and Oralee went in first, and the others followed. As she passed the sheriff's deputy a woman wearing a purple sweatshirt lowered her eyes and spat on the toe of Britt's hand-tooled leather boot. He raised his hand as she went by, but let it drop.

There wasn't a lot of talk in the twelve-by-fourteen tank. At first the five *latinas* huddled together in one corner, and Wilma and Oralee stood in the other. Oralee had Car bedded down in the plastic car seat. She'd placed the seat in the corner farthest from the rusted open toilet, which had a black seat but no cover and a terrible, far-reaching odor.

When the light in the cell was put out, leaving the walls striped with shadows from the bulb in the hall, the women on the other side of the cell began murmuring softly to one another and folding their skirts around their knees. One of the younger women brushed her hair with a pink plastic brush, speaking quickly in a low voice. Wilma strained to hear, but the flow of words was too much like drops of water running together.

"Grandmother," said the woman wearing the purple sweatshirt and tennis shoes, "if you like, we have food." Speaking to an old woman who had moved to sit apart from the others, she fished in the pocket of her long skirt and brought out a small jar of peanut butter. When the *abuelita* said nothing in reply, the first woman passed the jar to the woman next to her. When the jar reached the old woman she looked at it a moment, then at the others, as if for permission, and finally unscrewed the top, trailing a brown finger along the smooth surface of the butter. She stuck her finger into her mouth.

"Do we have a piece of bread?" the woman in sneakers asked the others. The prettiest of the two younger ones untied a scarf and brought out two hard rolls. She broke them into five pieces. Then she looked across the room at Wilma and Oralee, and tore each piece again so there were ten, each the size of a small beaten biscuit.

The women arranged the jar and the bread in the center of the scarf. The sweatshirted woman nodded at Wilma and smiled.

"I am Marta," she said.

Wilma smiled back. "They want us to come to their picnic," she said to Oralee, who was just finishing the last of Car's bacon-and-egg dinner.

"We shouldn't take their food," Oralee said. "Who knows when they'll get another meal?"

"We won't eat much," Wilma said. She walked across the floor and kneeled, then sat cross-legged at the edge of the scarf, white with small Indian figures embroidered on the cotton. She looked around at these women, so shy their eyes only brushed hers for an instant, then hid behind heavy lashes. Why were they in a local jail if they were aliens? What was the charge? Prostitution? For twenty minutes no one spoke.

When Wilma asked in halting Spanish where they came from, Marta told the story of their long walk from Chalatenango in El Salvador through Guatemala into Mexico. Mostly at night they traveled, hiding in fields and jungle during the day, from the *Escuadrón de Muerte* and government soldiers that were the same thing and then from the *Federales* in Mexico, who were willing to betray them for a few hundred pesos. In Mexico City they paid a coyote the equivalent of five hundred American dollars to take them across the border. The coyote had a truck, he told them, but the truck was in the town near the big river they would have to cross on foot. He would buy them tickets for the local buses. He would buy them food, find them a place to sleep. But he didn't tell them they would travel with so many strangers, that some of the strangers were *criminales,* and the coyote, too, would steal from them.

Marta's voice trailed away to something between a hiss and a whisper. She shook her head. The pretty ones would have to fight the coyote and lose. If they had husbands to protect them, or brothers, they could lose their men, too. Marta nodded at the youngest woman and blew quickly through her lips, as if blowing a dandelion head.

The girl had lost a brother in the jungle somewhere in Chiapas. It was a night with a full moon. The coyote pulled a knife from his boot as Miguel tried to release her from his arm, the moonlight glittering on the long blade. From the beginning of the trip the coyote had eyes for the girl, Marta said. No matter what old sack she put on to conceal herself, she shone in the fields and forests like a Christmas angel. It was possible the brother followed them still, keeping himself hidden. Sometimes in the night, if they slept in the open, the girl would creep away from the others into the darkness and call his name, Miguel, in the shadows so softly no one could hear.

Her own husband was missing, Marta said. They had disappeared him two years ago. He picked coffee for a living, as most of them did, never involving himself in the politics. That was for people in cities, he always told her.

"In the village, we try to know only a little," she said. "We give soup to the soldiers one day, the next day tortillas to the FLMN, the guerillas. Every week the children find sacks filled with *orejas y lenguas,*" ears and tongues.

After her husband was gone, Marta took the children every night to sleep in the fields. In the morning they returned. Finally she and some friends decided to leave. They took all the money they could raise from relatives and friends, packed small bundles and fled.

They had left the coyote after he beat up the old woman for lagging behind. He already had their money, so he was indifferent when the five refused to get into the tanker truck with the other forty-five. It was ninety-seven degrees at nine in the morning, and the coyote had no water. "Okay," he said, "go back to San Salvador. They'll put you on the plane, send you to El Playón." This was the name of a rock pile outside San Salvador where bodies of the disappeared often showed up. The dead lay on their backs, their faces peeled and the pelvic bones gleaming above excavations where genitals used to be. She had seen this place, Marta said.

14

IN THE MIDDLE OF THE NIGHT Wilma woke to the sound of her own crying. Her jacket on the cement floor was sweat-soaked, smelling strongly of Bear and the goat. A hand reached out of the darkness to her right and rested lightly on her shoulder.

"You okay?" Oralee asked.

Wilma's head throbbed, as if she'd been running. In her dream she was in Chalatenango with the Salvadorans. They were walking along a narrow path lined on both sides by tall trees with broad, flat leaves. Marta was walking behind her, telling her about a custom in her country of tying rags and garbage in the trees if they did not bear fruit. "It is so the tree will be *vergonzozo*, ashamed," she said. The things hanging in the trees beside the path looked like garbage, but they were human skin and hair. Then, as she walked along, unable to turn her eyes away, she began to see faces in the leaves.

"I want to talk to Vernon," she said. "I haven't talked to him for two weeks. I'm forgetting what he looks like." She sniffled, propping her head on one elbow, and began to realize where she was. She'd been in better places. In jail with seven El Salvadoran women and Oralee in a small West Texas town where the local cops were bored and mean. Wilma looked at her Swatch. She was due in Houston in less than seventeen hours. If she didn't show up on time the Wild Goose dispatcher would start getting calls. They'd fire her after five months on the job; she'd have to go creeping back to Vernon like an unwed mother.

"You could split and go home tomorrow," Oralee said. "Anytime you feel like it you can go home. Vernon would love it."

"It's been five months. My clothes are way too big. I don't know where home is. Not where I left it, is all I know." The back of her shirt was wet; she'd started sweating again. Also her mouth hurt. The back molar on the right side had started ringing like a gong.

Oralee took a brush out of her pocket and began brushing Wilma's hair, giving it long, firm strokes from the scalp. Wilma rested on her elbows, her head hanging back, letting her neck and shoulders go.

"Know what they say about truckers?" Oralee whispered. "How they gotta be like land turtles? Carry it all with 'em: bed, fridge, microwave and Betamax—everything on top. And whatever don't move with 'em they can't afford to bother with, right? They can't afford to slow down. KnowwhatImean, Will? It's in the contract."

Wilma really started to cry then, big gushy tears, and for what? For the pain in the hole in her chest where she used to keep all the good stuff she'd run away from? Traveling light was okay for Oralee, who looked like a Conan the Barbarian drawing, okay if you were eighteen, with all the energy in the world and great glutes. Hell, all she had was a plain round face, red hair and pretty fair teeth. And a truck, she reminded herself. Don't forget the truck.

So Oralee held her. All that jittery jailhouse night she

lay on her side and opened her skinny, strong arms and wrapped Wilma up. She rocked her like a fretful baby, kissed the tears on her cheeks, kissed her lips and ran her fingers through her hair. Gradually Wilma's sobs came shallow and slow as the panic drained away, leaving her dry and peaceful on Oralee's bony breast.

When Wilma woke again at five their bodies were still braided tightly together. There was a clanking of somebody rattling pots in a kitchen, and when Wilma lifted her head from her arm she saw Britt and Corey standing by the open cell door staring at her. It wasn't breakfast she was smelling but smoke from Corey's cigar. How long had they been watching?

Corey blushed and cleared his throat and shuffled his feet on the concrete floor.

"Pete and me, we're just country boys, ma'am. We never saw nothing like that before." Britt spoke in a wheedling tone with a thick undercoating of nastiness. "Pete and me, we reckon we can arrange it for you gals to head on down the road before the judge gets here, if you'll do us one little bitty favor."

Wilma poked Oralee in the ribs and sat up rubbing her eyes. She buttoned the top button of her red-and-black-checked flannel shirt and shook her hair over her face in a heavy rain of ringlets. When she was excited about anything her cheeks began to flare up, and now she was blazing.

"You mind repeating what you just said?" Wilma asked.

Britt put his hat in front of his face and conducted a quick conference with his partner.

"You never heard secrets are rude?" Oralee said, groggily.

"You see, ma'am, we're just a coupla dudes who's never seen two women . . ."

"Never seen two women what?" Wilma said, finally starting to get a whiff of what he was driving at.

"What I mean to say is, we never watched two women . . . together."

Wilma had never seen a grown man look so lowdown and pitiful. She didn't know whether to get mad or laugh, but she did know she was embarrassed. It made her sick, him standing there watching. She might have started cussing if she hadn't heard boots echoing in the hall and seen the dark brim of García's hat over Britt's shoulder.

"You gentlemen busy?" he said, and right away Britt started shoving papers at her through the bars. Forms outlining the charges. Wilma skimmed the words "disorderly conduct" and "resisting arrest." When she looked up a moment later García's long brown eyes were steady on hers. She nodded.

"Why, sure I'm busy, Mario, but don't I always have time for my brothers in La Migra?" Relations between law-enforcement agencies were ticklish at times.

"When it's convenient, then I would like *un momento.*"

"We were just leavin'," Britt said smoothly. "Don't say I never gave you warning," he hissed through the bars, then turned and led the way back down the hall.

"We're in for it," Oralee said.

When she stood in front of Elroy P. Thatcher and heard the charges read against Oralee and herself, Wilma thought it must have been someone else who'd called the officers filthy names, bitten and clawed and kicked them in the privates. Already the memory of that roadside scuffle was dimming in her mind like childbirth and other embarrassments. Some valve in her mind was closing against the drone of the D.A.'s voice, the ugly yellow light coming through the cracked window shades on the right wall, the judge's face, florid and avuncular, already starting to tip forward onto his chest. Beside her on the prisoner's bench Oralee had closed her eyes, her breath coming in regular soft rumbles like a cat's purring. She couldn't see how Oralee could sleep through this.

"Did willfully inflict bodily harm to the person of Officer Roscoe Britt . . ." Wilma could catch only a few isolated words in the dense lawyerly language of the bailiff, who had a square Steve Canyon jaw and a flat-top haircut.

"Hold on," the judge said, his chin snapping up from its resting place on his chest. "They were carrying weapons? What kinda guns?"

"No guns, Your Honor," the bailiff said.

"They were unarmed?"

"Yes, Your Honor."

"Then what the hell kind of damage could they do?"

"She kicked him in the groin, sir."

The judge gave Wilma a serious look. "Did you kick him?"

She nodded. Why wouldn't he ask her why? Then she could tell him it was Britt's hand on Oralee's neck in the truck. There would be some sense to it.

The district attorney was sweating heavily; the back of his jacket hung on to his shoulder blades when he stood up, and big juicy drops glistened on his forehead.

"These two ladies," he was saying, and his voice drew a nasty black line under the word "ladies," "these ladies clearly interfered with deputies Britt and Corey. Now, Your Honor, these officers have a clean record, not a hint of misconduct. So I'm asking you to look at these ladies here and decide if they had any good reason, any just cause to act like they did. If you will bear with me the State of Texas will show that Wilhelmina Hemshoff and Oralee Sweet did resist these officers in attempts to perform their duties and did use filthy, disgusting language and finally did physically assault these officers and committed these acts purely out of devilment, with no provocation whatsoever." The D.A. paused, blowing like a fat man who'd run two hundred yards.

The judge blew his nose, then waved his hand. "Go on," he said.

"And that's not all," the D.A. said. "These gentlemen behaved themselves with admirable restraint in a situation where they were under what you'd call psychological assault."

"Say what you mean, Davies," the judge said.

"I mean these ladies have some pretty unusual tastes."

"Tastes for what?" the judge said. "Out with it. I usually understand American all right."

Davies glanced at Wilma and Oralee, then looked quickly away. "They're lovers, Your Honor."

"Who?" the judge said. "Who and so what?"

"The defendants. They were observed in the cell last night, hugging and kissing on each other." Having described this scene, the district attorney stared at the floor, as if he couldn't ever face any other human being again.

Wilma squeezed Oralee's arm, but the girl was already wide awake. Her eyebrows had disappeared into her hairline. "Dirty mule-fucking cocksuckers," she said between her teeth.

"*Con permiso,* Your Honor." Wilma turned all the way around in her seat, saw García in the rear of the courtroom, as tall as Sam Houston.

"What's up, Mario? This isn't exactly your jurisdiction," the judge said.

"I saw what happened."

"And?"

"These ladies had provocation."

196

"What kind?"

"I hate to be specific, Judge."

"Sit down, then."

"It was the officer's language, sir. *Malas palabras*. It might've made Saint Francis mad."

"Give me an example." The judge was leaning forward on his elbows.

" 'She's no woman, Corey. She's hung like a grandfather clock.' " García's brown eyes were unwavering. He held his brown hat in his hand.

"You mean to tell me Officer Britt said that in front of a woman?"

"In front of two of them, sir."

"Then what happened?"

"She hit him."

"Which one hit him?"

"The little one, sir," García said.

"He's lucky he ain't dead," the judge said.

García was tall, maybe six-three, and thin as Mister Gone. In profile his features were severe—straight nose of a decent size, a prominent chin, eyes set deeply under dark brows. Haughty and remote, he looked like pictures of old desperados. What did he have to be desperate about? Maybe not desperate but stiff, very stiff.

What would it take to make him smile?

In spite of García the fine was five hundred dollars apiece. They had exactly a hundred and thirteen for gas and food for the rest of the trip. When she heard the judge pronounce sentence and saw him rise, ready to leave the courtroom, she noticed another man out of the corner of her eye start up the center aisle toward the bench. His tanned forearms swung from blue workshirt sleeves as he took seven long strides to where the judge was still standing.

"May I speak, Your Honor?" he said.

"You just did, didn't you?" the judge said. "Well, since you're using up the air in here, spit it out." She liked this judge.

"The bishop sent me over here to tell you the diocese is willing to pay the fine for these two women."

The judge raised his thickety eyebrows. Wilma grabbed Oralee's arm, and did a little hop on the seat. What in hell did the bishop care about her?

"That's strange," the judge said, deliberately, "I didn't know the bishop had that kind of money to burn. What's he doing it for?"

When the young man answered, she could see his shoulders tense under his shirt. He had both long hands stuck into the hip pockets of his jeans. "The bishop works in mysterious ways, sir," he said. "He just told me to see if we could do anything for them."

Wilma's head was cattywampus. When they came in at nine last night there wasn't even an officer on duty at the desk in the jail lobby. Who could have told the young man they were there? Who was he, anyway? He was wonderful to look at, with large level gray eyes, and a thin face with too many deep lines in it for someone his age. Thirty-two, maybe thirty-five. Holding his hands together behind his back he rocked lightly on the balls of his feet as if waiting for a starting gun or a basketball to be tossed onto a court. While listening for the judge's answer, Wilma had time then to consider that today she was forty-two years old, probably as much a free woman as she'd ever be, and whatever she had the hots for, she'd better get on after it.

His name was Richard Standish, and he ran a sanctuary house near Harlingen where Central American refugees could rest a couple of weeks before going north. Sitting in the front seat of his battered VW bug, Wilma didn't have much time to make up her mind. It would take thirty minutes to reach her truck, and she had to let him know by then if she was interested.

He didn't care where she was headed as long as it was north. He had money from the bishop's fund to pay her to take up to ten people a load, whenever she could get a run from South Texas or the Valley.

"How'd the bishop know we were in jail?" Wilma asked. "He's a long way off."

"He didn't," Standish grinned. "I saw you rassling deputies at the checkpoint. Saw you around a couple times before that. I needed a driver, and you looked like you might be the one."

She was having trouble concentrating on what he was saying.

"We can only go as high as thirty-five a head. They've already spent most of what they had getting across the river." His eyelashes were tipped with gold, and his mouth was hard. He lived with his wife and three kids in a trailer house behind the house in San Benito, named after the murdered bishop of San Salvador. The church gave him the trailer and $300 a month to administer the sanctuary house. Before that he had taught in the San Antonio barrio for two years.

"Why are you doing this?" Wilma asked.

"It isn't simple," he said. "I'll tell you a story. The other day I went to talk to a church group in Kingsville, and a woman there asked some questions. The one that really got me thinking was 'Why don't you do something for your own kind? For white people? What you're doing is against the law.' The way I see it, there's assumptions behind the question that're completely alien to me. The first thing I'd say is my people are *all* people, and Our Lord's law overrides civil law every time."

He drove on for a few moments in silence, giving her time to wonder if she had any deep religious beliefs, or political ones, for that matter. It had been awhile since she was in church, since she took any interest in politics. Not since the Vietnam War, when she had signed petitions and written letters of recommendation for a few kids she knew who were conscientious objectors. She never stuck her neck out for any issue or profound belief; she just thought it wasn't fair for those kids to wreck their lives or end them in a war their country should have had nothing to do with in the first place. What did she have to do with anything going on in Central America? The ears and noses in sacks, hair hung in trees? She was too old to believe in justice.

"Where would I be dropping them off?" she asked. Her deadlines for delivery were tight. At any given stop she had to unload within a couple hours of the scheduled time or the dispatcher would raise sand.

"We'd arrange it. You'd tell us where you're due to drop a load, and when. We send you people headed the same way. Maybe they have farther to go, but if you can save them a two-hundred-mile walk, that's good. It's also good if they don't have to ride with forty-five others under a load of bricks or in a tank truck without any air. We lose too many." His voice was strong and deep, reassuring, like an airline pilot's. Wilma thought about Marta and the others, their narrow ankles. Then she thought about the family still in her truck and realized she'd already made a decision about saving them a walk. Like all of them she was in the moving business and had to believe in better times.

On the way from the courthouse to the Border Patrol checkpoint where the truck was parked, Wilma didn't stop grinning. Not even when Oralee told Standish she couldn't figure out what kind of a thrill people like him got out of keeping starving Ethiopian kids alive just so they could kick off later from dysentery or why he'd give a shack to a bunch of Mexicans who'd just raise more kids for the government to pay for.

Oralee leaned over the back of Standish's seat, her black hair hanging down around her face. "You got such a big heart why don't you go and marry one of those wetback women and adopt their kids, make 'em all citizens?"

"I already did," he said.

The minute they got into the truck, Oralee put Car into her pajamas, laid her on the bunk in the cubby and pulled down the dropcloth. As soon as Wilma had checked on the people in the van, saw they were alive and only pretty hungry after twelve hours, she started the truck and pulled out onto the highway headed south toward the sanctuary in San Benito. A few miles out of Van Horn Oralee was reaching under the seat, pulling out baby articles: a rubber teething ring, a plastic rattle, a plush cotton ball with easy fingerholds. Unzipping a blue duffel she began stuffing all these items in with unnecessary energy and speed.

"What's going on?" Wilma asked. Oralee's face was a mystery.

"When we get to Houston I'm checking out. Can't handle this new craziness of yours," she said. "Too dangerous and too stupid. I got enough problems without taking on Central America."

Wilma's stomach dropped into her toes with fearful abruptness. She had traveled with Oralee for three months, but even before she left the truck stop she had carried the girl's image in her mind. Oralee Sweet was the daughter she'd never been lucky enough to have, the sweet, skinny black-haired girl Wilma had wanted to be ever since her mother read her "Snow White." Without Oralee to laugh at them with her, the rude CB rap, the blowouts and other minor road disasters would grind her down.

Without the wets it was easy to predict what she'd be doing a week or a month or six months from now, as long as she kept making her payments. Racing over some four- or six-lane stretch of Super Highway America, stopping at some entirely imaginable truck stop on the interstate in Texas, New Mexico, Georgia, Virginia, North Dakota, Minnesota, Massachusetts. It all looked the same. When she'd begun driving she'd had a dream about discovering the U.S.A., finding out if cotton and corn looked different in different states, and how they built their bridges and cooked their chicken. After the first summer, when she took a run up the breadbasket midsection of the country, through Oklahoma, Kansas, Nebraska, and the Dakotas, she'd already figured it out. Wheat stalks bent in the fields exactly like rice, maybe a few inches taller. Corn was everywhere the same: green and still.

"What's the matter, Will? Are you bored?" Oralee leaned back against the window, propping her feet on the dash.

"You don't have to leave," she told Oralee. "We'll be careful. We'll only do a couple of runs, and if we decide it's too risky we'll quit." She knew good and well she was lying. She wouldn't be able to say no to Richard Standish if he sent her to the South Bronx with a load of cocaine. The minute she thought of him she felt a delicious pain somewhere under her right collar bone and knew she'd been hit. She was a hefty woman, five-eight, and, look at her, she was floating. Floating, hell, she soared and bobbed like a scrap of newspaper in a March wind. Oralee was leaving her. Texas was a dry hole. She had an inconvenient weakness for refugee mothers, five hundred to pay every month and a twenty-thousand insurance premium due in August. So far she wasn't off the shoulder, but the sand was slipping sideways under her wheels. Slipping fast, like miles and time. With all this reality glaring at her it was strange how she could float, how she could see in front of her nothing but big cauliflower clouds and a couple of golden eagles free-falling.

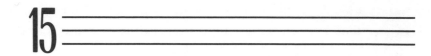

15

THEY ARGUED ALL THE WAY from Van Horn to Ozona. Ora-lee told her she was a fool and a runaround, taking up with any loony drifter as long as he'd tell her he liked her eyes.

"It's a tough world," she said, pulling the tab on Car's Pamper. "You got to take care of your own *mierda* and let the rest of the world hang out." Tossing the baby over her shoulder she stared at Wilma. "What's it with you anyway? You trying to win a Nobel Prize?"

Strays. They were irresistible. When she was seven it was a cardboard box full of young alligators somebody had dropped on the front steps. Her mama told her she could keep them if she could afford them, so to earn money she picked pecans or dewberries, whatever was in season, and weeded vegetable gardens, enough for fresh hamburger. When she was ten it was dogs, no matter what breed. Her papa let her keep the toy fox terrier she called Pete, for Peter Pan because he was so fast and smart he seemed to fly. Wilma wasn't particular about what she picked up; she brought home baby bluejays with mouths open so wide they looked jammed, and raccoons her papa's dogs had mauled but not quite killed, and six kittens someone had tied in a gunny sack and left on the shoulder.

On the way to San Benito Wilma stopped the truck near Marathon and let the refugees out of the truck to cool off. It was more bearable under the blue highway shelter, but at seven in the evening the wind was still blowing heat off the land. When it touched her skin, the breeze raised the hairs a little but did nothing to relieve the discomfort of her body or soothe her wind-roughened hands and arms or stop the thudding at the back of her head. Wilma leaned against the concrete picnic bench, watching sparrows peck at crumbs at the edge of the foundation. The goat sniffed the ground under the table, and the Mexican baby squatted in the dust and urinated. She wore no diapers, just a cotton shirt and gold studs in her ears. Miranda, the mother, spoke a quick-fire Spanish to her husband, something about the price of clothes for the little girl. Every two minutes she would look around, locate the child and start talking again. Wilma went over again in her mind all the risks in carrying refugees, how she would handle the Border Patrol if they stopped her, what she could lose.

So she wasn't expecting anything, wasn't wired for trouble, and when she observed the goat beginning to walk toward the pavement sixty feet away, none of her alarm signals went off. The goat took its time, not trotting, but picking its way over rocky ground, switching its rag tail and raising its head now and then to sniff the wind. It had its eye on something on the far side of the highway, and Wilma wondered idly what, out of strewn highway discards, could be attractive to a goat. She was too far away to see. It wasn't until the goat was well on its way to the center stripe that Wilma became alarmed, because the black-haired baby was following it toward the road, plump arms stretched in front of her. The child was making little shushing noises with her mouth as if to quiet her footsteps so the goat wouldn't notice she was tracking it. At the same time, Wilma heard a diesel engine approaching on the far side of the first hill to the west.

She didn't think or breathe again until she reached the girl at the near shoulder, came at her from the side, tackling her plump legs. The baby cried out, grabbed Wilma around the neck as she fell backward into a kind of seated sprawl, feeling the sucking backdraft of the truck as it roared past, the driver leaning on its horn as if Wilma and the baby were some scrubby cow wandering across the highway. He didn't even slow down.

"You little so-and-so," Wilma said.

The baby stretched out her stubby fingers toward Wilma. "Shh," she said.

"Shh, yourself," Wilma said. "I'm celebrating."

The sanctuary house was a white clapboard building flanked by a tall steel observation tower erected by local officials to monitor alien activities. A volleyball net was stretched between two poles in the yard, and a thirty-by-forty-foot garden had parched tomatoes and okra plants and twenty eggplants dangling from tall stems. Inside the kitchen thirty corn tortillas were laid down in blackened grease and browned. A hand-lettered sign was tacked on the wall behind the stove.

NO FUMAR EN CASA
NO PELEAR
NO SE PERMITE EN LA CALLE DESPUES 11:00

No smoking, no fighting, everybody indoors after eleven.

The kitchen was crowded. A group of young men who looked like members of a soccer team smoked and ate and spoke in Spanish so fast she couldn't understand. From the other room another man walked in. He stood at Standish's elbow, waited a few minutes, then spoke when it was clear he hadn't been noticed.

"*Señor, con permiso,*" he said.

"*Sí,* Enrique."

"*Tengo una carta,*" he said, blushing. He had a letter he couldn't read.

Standish told him he'd read the letter when he was finished cooking and suggested the man show it to Wilma. She couldn't get much out of it, though. Something about someone arriving on this side of the river.

"His sister," Standish told her, stirring chorizo and onions in a cast-iron skillet with one hand and another skillet of eggs with another. "She's coming soon from San Vicente, maybe the twentieth, and will cross alone. After that someone has to bring her to us here."

"But we're thirty miles from the river here," Wilma said.

"There are friends," Standish said.

She wasn't sure when she realized she was one of the friends. She let the refugees out of the van, but Oralee refused to leave the truck. "What do I want to get cozy with a bunch of revolutionaries for?" she said, combing Car's wispy black hair with a blue baby brush.

Wilma spoke with several people in the sanctuary living room, which was filled with cots and couches where people still slept wrapped in *rebozos* and army blankets. An old woman, Elvira, had brown skin so thin it showed the veins underneath and seemed near death except for her milky topaz eyes. This was not true, Wilma decided after watching her for a few moments. Though she spoke little and slowly, conserving strength, she was still burning with life. Some old people were kept alive by love and care, some by rage, others by a fierce humor. She wasn't sure about Elvira yet.

"De dónde es usted?" Wilma asked, her tongue blundering over the words.

She came from a mountain village, almost too high for coffee to grow, yet they farmed there. Everyone worked in the coffee plantation for a few *columbares* a day. When the war came, and the bombers, the village was *roto,* she said, broken, and the family, Elvira and her son and daughter and their five children, walked to San Salvador. They lived in a slum called La Fosa, the grave.

One night after a meeting Elvira's son disappeared. His wife and mother took pictures of him to the police. No news. They haunted the place called El Playón, waiting for a body to appear they might recognize. No news. As she told this story Elvira's expression showed only a terrible puzzlement. She did not know why he was gone, or why she had to leave her village and finally the capital city where the archbishop was dead of bullets at mass.

After helping Elvira to bandage her ankles Wilma followed Standish outside to the rusting three-room house trailer behind the Casa where he lived with his two young boys, his Mexican wife and her baby.

"How long do the refugees stay?" she asked him.

"Two or three years or until they get married," he joked. His long brown neck was stiff and his face deadpan.

"And how long will you?" she said. The Justice Department was starting to bring suits against sanctuary workers. Harboring and abetting.

"I'm on the books for three years," Standish told her. "Boys," he called to the kids wrestling on the orange shag rug, "lunch." He put a loaf of bread, a jar of peanut butter and some oranges on the table. The kids were eleven and six, Standish's from an earlier marriage that hadn't survived Vietnam. Thin blonds with tanned arms and lines at the neck and biceps where the T-shirts ended, they slid quietly into chairs and began eating.

"Well," he said, "what do you think?"

"I'm not political," she said.

"We need help."

She didn't know much about the Central American wars, only that the United States kept sending money to keep things heated up. It wasn't fair to do that, she thought, and not let the refugees cross the river to stay.

The oldest boy was reading a book at the table. He pointed to a photograph. "Look," he said to Wilma, "Ninja."

"What's a Ninja?" she asked. The photograph showed a tall, fierce-looking Japanese in a white robe and pointed fingernails.

"He's like a karate guy, only meaner. He turns his whole body into an arsenal."

"Are you interested in that stuff?" she asked.

"Sure," the kid said. "Yeah. That's what I want to do. Make an arsenal of my whole body."

She liked the curve of Standish's head bent to say grace; his neck didn't look anything like an arsenal. She wasn't sure why she had to do it. Something about the women's slender legs, their silent, frightened children, and not wanting him to do it alone.

When she got back to the truck Oralee had changed into a cotton flight jacket and camouflage army pants. For a long time she didn't speak, tucking a blanket around the baby, staring straight down the highway north to Houston.

"All you want is a chance to be Clint Eastwood, Wilma."

"I don't even like Clint Eastwood," Wilma said. "When you taking that baby back where she belongs?" she asked.

"I have some news for you, Will. It's Car," she said. "She's not mine." She let go of a long breath.

It had been obvious to Wilma from the start. From the girl's crazy delight in the baby. The way she'd flop her up on a shoulder, swing her over an arm like a waiter's towel, sometimes snatching her up out of the car seat and licking her face like a cherry popsicle.

"Whose is she then?" Wilma felt she ought to be stern.

"Papa married this woman." Oralee's voice was low. "Name's Colleen, and she had this baby. Her real name is Denise."

"Did you like her? Not the baby, your stepmother?"

"She's all right."

"Then why'd you leave?" Wilma said. "Looks like with Colleen to keep your daddy busy your troubles were over."

Oralee looked at Wilma like Jody did once when he heard Wilma admit she didn't know a touchback from a toothache.

"You think I coulda watched her grow till she had little angel-bite boobs and he could do her, too?"

The girl had the long strap of her duffel bag slung over one shoulder, the baby's diaper kit over the other. She stood in the empty street, swaying a little from fatigue, her face in the dim street lamp pale and full of shadows.

"I guess you can handle it all right alone, till you find someone else?" she whispered.

"I guess so," Wilma said. "I did it before." Maybe it was

better, nobody sharing the risk. But a big part of her nerve was leaving with Oralee.

"I hate losing you," she said. "Is it the principle of the thing?"

Oralee wasn't smiling, and she didn't answer. She took a couple of steps forward, resting her chin on Wilma's shoulder. Wilma put her arms around Oralee and held her for a long moment. "Be a good girl," Wilma said, and stepped back, giving her a slow, sad look.

Oralee turned around and walked through the little rusted wire gate across the walk leading to the house. At the gate she turned and said, "I got no principles except fear."

16

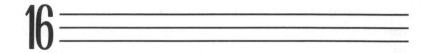

On the hottest day in August she went with Standish to the river. They stood on a little rise above the low-water bridge near Los Indios and looked at a small yellow bulldozer stuck in the mud.

"Somebody stole it in Harlingen and tried to cross it here. Couldn't drive it, maybe. Or got chased off by Federales because they hadn't paid the *mordida,*" he told her. Mexican national police took a bite of everything.

"Do you know who they are, the ones we're waiting for?" she asked him, and he said the person who called had said there was an old woman with two or three others, Salvadorans.

"Is she traveling alone?" Wilma said.

"There's a granddaughter." He frowned and looked at his watch. "We're worried about her. She's in her eighties, needs chemotherapy," Standish said. "She's supposed to be carrying money for treatment."

The south wind blew the short sunbleached hair back from his forehead. She wanted to press the deep wrinkle from between his eyebrows, reach out and take his hand.

"Shouldn't we hide?" she said. They were standing on

a hillock in sunlight so white and pure it cut the dry earth like a blade.

"They need to see us, to know where to cross," he said.

The sun hung heavy on their shoulders, as a soldier in black, a machine gun in his hand and a cartridge belt slung like a purse over one arm, came over the lip of the bank on the other side. He stood there for several minutes, legs spread wide, one hand on his hip. She got tired of watching and turned her eyes to the brown water, white butterflies dallying in clumps of flowering desert willow along the edge. When she looked again he was gone. A prickle ran up the back of her neck into her scalp.

"They should be here," Standish said.

She had picked up a load in Harlingen that morning and was waiting for her first refugees to cross four miles from San Benito. Now Wild Goose was sending her on more runs from South Texas, maybe because of the oil-price slide, maybe because everything in Texas seemed to be sliding including the banks. Families moving out of state were a bad sign—except they meant she had cupboards and chests to hide refugees headed for Chicago, Brooklyn and Philadelphia, the city of brotherly love.

When the eight-year-old boy peeped over the hill and started to slide down, he looked so much like Jody had at that age she caught her breath. A thatch of dark hair, long shanks and knees like a colt's. A young man in a Levi jacket, his hair caught back in a rubber band, hurried after him, then three young women, then the old one very slowly, a girl of fifteen holding one hand. The coyote followed, a fat man in a baby-blue cowboy shirt and a white straw hat. Wilma liked it that he held the old woman's other hand as she crawled down the steep bank, extending one foot carefully ahead of her like a blind man's cane. She wondered how she'd decided the fat man was the coyote.

Then she realized nobody who'd walked a lot of the way from El Salvador would be fat.

They paused at the water's edge, the man pulling his jeans up over his knees, removing his boots. The women tucked up their skirts and eyed the water with alarm. Already the boy was standing in the middle of the narrow stream, twenty feet from the rest, turning his face and waving at them to come on. The water flowed so slowly around his thin legs there wasn't a ripple on the surface. The women moved carefully toward the middle of the stream, their feet sliding across silt on the bottom, one of them holding the man's hand. Behind them on the top of the bank the black-uniformed soldier stood silhouetted against the sky, which was filling with baby-lamb clouds. At the edge of the water the coyote lifted the old woman onto his back, then started across after the others. The woman's granddaughter followed. Wilma looked up and down the bank as far as she could see but noticed nothing but a starved white-faced cow nosing along the weeds on the Texas side.

Halfway across the coyote stumbled and lost his balance. He tipped sharply to the right, and the old woman shrieked, "Ay," dropping one of her bundles. Wilma made an involuntary movement forward, but Standish put out his hand.

"Wait," he said, giving Wilma time to wonder how she happened to be standing in hundred-degree heat next to the Rio Grande.

It wasn't politics that got her into this, because she didn't think politics was real, and didn't care enough about it to try to understand. Vernon used to say politics was just money wearing big words, and she knew a lot of them were crooked, maybe some of the biggest ones, even the

President. Hell, maybe Duarte had paid the President a *mordida*. It didn't make much difference to her. But that baby she'd scooped up out of the highway and the old woman in the stream—they could get to her, and Standish with his dogged, dog-eared patience. Wilma looked around at acres of parched prickly pear and oajilla and ocotillo, at fields of sand and a trickle of muddy river at her feet, and couldn't hear anything but cowboy love songs on the radio.

When the refugees started up the bank on the other side, their faces sagged from relief and exhaustion. The young boy, a streak of clay across one cheek, looked on the edge of tears or sleep. The coyote set the old woman on the ground, then straightened himself with difficulty. The granddaughter was climbing the little incline toward Standish when the coyote saw the sun glinting on Wilma's hair, and took the old woman by the shoulders. *"Eres mía,"* he said.

"Déjame, cabrón," the old woman cried, beating him about the head with one of her string bags. From the bank, the granddaughter screamed. Once again the man hoisted the woman onto his back, his head seeming to sink between his shoulders away from the blows. His white hat fell into the stream and began drifting toward Dallas.

Wilma whispered, "What do we do now?"

"Sit tight. He's too greedy to turn her loose. Maybe he knows she's carrying more money than the rest. Or maybe he's bent out of shape about turning them over to a *gringo* coyote." He winked at her.

The coyote was trying to reason with the old woman, who was yelling in a high-pitched voice. Now and then she'd fall silent, exhausted, but after a minute or two she resumed her cries and took several more swings at him with the bag. *"Cabrón,"* she shrieked. Gangster. Her hair fell down her back in long gray strands, and one of her tennis shoes had fallen into the water, leaving her yellow ankle sock bare.

"He's trying to get her to pay him more," Wilma said. "Bastard."

There was nothing to do but try to keep the others calm. They watched while the coyote finally put the woman down in the stream, still keeping hold of her hand and pulling her back toward the other side. The old woman was crying. Her long blue skirt was wet almost to the waist, the air trapped underneath making little balloons around her. Wilma was afraid the coyote would decide to strip and search her right there. Standish pointed his finger at the bank on the opposite side. The national policeman was half-stepping, half-sliding down the bank through the sand until he reached the strip of beach and raised the gun, waved it at the coyote and said something in Spanish Wilma couldn't understand. The coyote released the woman's hand and walked back into Mexico. The old woman put her hands to her ears and sank into her skirts. She sat there waiting for the policeman to follow the coyote over the rim of the bank and disappear. Then she stood and called for the others waiting on the hill on the opposite side.

Walking through the cotton plants was like crossing a minefield between two armies. By now it was three in the afternoon. A hundred and ten degrees. The field and the sky above it were empty. On the paved road that ran around the edge of the field a white pickup headed in their direction. Standish kept walking, the refugees two hundred yards behind, a space he needed so it wouldn't look like he was leading. The white pickup hesitated opposite them on the highway a quarter of a mile away, the driver leaning one elbow out the window.

"Out here everybody's either smuggling something or trying to catch somebody," Standish said. "They're moving everything from TV sets and Contra generals to *candelilla* wax for chewing gum." She wanted him to stop being a hero long enough to smuggle her someplace pretty and quiet. She wobbled every time his shoulder brushed hers when they'd be reading a county map together across a kitchen table and their eyes would meet. They traced with their fingers the tiny blue dirt-road lines and she felt seventeen, with a flibbertigibbet heart.

His voice grew soft when he spoke of his wife. "She's fine-tuned," he said.

"What's that mean?" She had an image in her mind of a silver Ferrari with perfectly adjusted valves. She wished somebody thought she was fine-tuned.

"High-strung," he said, "intelligent. A lovely girl." She was afraid for him, for the work he was doing. She was born scared of La Migra. Wilma was scared she was too big and too old to be kissed.

There was a second truck on the road running north ahead of them, a milk delivery truck with RAYMONDVILLE DAIRY painted in red script on the side of the van. It turned the corner and started down the road west of the field.

"Billy Ray Ringo," Richard said. "He'll meet us by that windmill and tank north of the highway."

"Then why's he driving all the way around us?" she said.

"Taking a look. Testing the atmosphere. He wants to be sure La Migra won't bite us on the neck before we get loaded."

He was funny about never telling her ahead of time what was going to happen, no more than the skimpiest outline. It kept her from getting nervous. She was plenty nervous now, taking deep breaths and long, loping steps across the steep furrows. The milk truck pulled up along-side the white one. The two drivers were talking. Wilma held her breath and kept walking and sweating. What would two truckdrivers have to say to each other in this heat? The sky was full of buzzards circling. Zero breeze. Now the white truck was pulling ahead, raising a cloud of pale dust that hid the milk truck from view. What had been said? "I ain't got a clue about those people," Billy Ray might have said. "Never saw 'em before," or "That's the crew of wets works for Matt Gannow. I seen 'em out here yesterday." She could breathe again. Some days it was no more than a kind word that freed you. Sometimes even a blind pig will find an acorn.

They crossed the highway and opened an aluminum gate, entering a pasture where the windmill stood beside a cypress water tank in a little mesquite grove. There was no wind moving the blades, but the mossy sides of the tank were still damp, so she turned the spigot underneath, cupped her hands and drank. The water had a strong, clean taste of pennies. The old woman took a tin cup from a bag around her shoulder and filled it, walking a little way apart from the others to drink. Richard squatted down and stuck his head under the stream, letting the water run through his hair, and when he stood up the hair was shiny and black and his yellow shirt stuck to his chest. Billy Ray pulled the milk truck up the overgrown ruts and cut the motor. Leaning his chin on his sunburned arm, he squinted at the wets.

"I thought there was only three," he said.

"You got two bonuses," Richard said. "Who's in the truck?"

"Kinkaid. Maybe spying for García," Billy Ray said. "You give me an extra, you pay extra."

"Okay," Richard said. "You ready to go?"

"Well, run 'em in the back there," Billy Ray said. "I ain't driving no party bus."

The illegals stared into the van and the women started speaking in shrill voices. The old woman's granddaughter was missing.

"Tenía tanto miedo," the grandmother said. The girl was terrified.

For three hours they searched in the heat before Wilma lifted the lid of an underground silo. It was full of black water, and on its surface something was floating, dark hair swirling like a water plant. After they buried her the old woman refused to get back into the truck. Billy Ray was getting nervous.

"Leave her," Standish said.

"We can't," Wilma said. The old woman sat on the ground, her *rebozo* pulled over her face.

"You can't stay here, *abuelita*," Standish said, squatting down in front of her. The woman closed her eyes.

"Pick her up," Wilma said, staring at his tight mouth. But he wouldn't.

Reaching the Raymondville checkpoint they watched the back end of the truck growing small on the highway ahead of them, so she wasn't uptight when García stuck his head through the window and asked if they'd been stealing watermelons. García was everywhere she looked these days, and Wilma was glad she was the one driving the yellow VW bug, because by now she and the Border Patrol officer were into an almost easy relationship, halfway guarded, halfway flirtatious, and one hundred percent respectful. Over the last couple of months they had taken one another's measure. Because of her fight with the Sheriff's Department he knew she had some ginger in her and didn't mind a good brawl. He probably also had a hunch she was part of the underground railroad. But, as Standish assured her, he wouldn't waste his time picking on small fry like her.

"They don't want publicity. Especially about the U.S. and Duarte holding hands. So they try to leave sanctuary people alone as much as they can."

If García wasn't interested in small fry he was strangely curious about their feet.

"What's this about watermelons?" She punched him lightly on the shoulder.

"I see by the dirt on your shoes you were taking es-troll," he said.

She looked down at her waffle soles clogged with rich riverfront loam. "You don't miss much," she said, smiling at him.

His wide lips pulled back over flawless white teeth, but she could tell nothing about his eyes behind the sunglasses. "It's hot enough," he said, leaning his arm on the top of her window. For several minutes neither of them said anything. It must have looked crazy, her sunburned neck and arms. She was no Coppertone queen, not with this redhead's skin.

García could see through her. He knew Richard Standish's business, and she didn't think he was fooled by Billy Ray. Why was he letting them through? He took off his kidney-shaped glasses and bent his head so he looked directly into her eyes. He wasn't speaking to Richard Standish now, but only to her.

"I have been watching, *señora*. I am no fool. You have dangerous friends."

17

IN THE FALL OF '84 she made three runs to Philadelphia, New York and Burlington, and it hadn't taken García long to notice she was taking more than her share of trips north. When she passed through his checkpoint in Harlingen he stopped her to ask dumb questions: where she was born, where she was headed. He already knew the answers.

"Little Egypt's where I live, but I was born in Stonewall. Where you from?" He told her he was born of Mexican parents in San Antonio. She could tell from his voice he was touchy.

"Destination?"

"Chicago," she said. "So darned cold up there you got to have a heater goin' to keep the diesel from freezin' over."

She had seven Salvadorans in back, but she didn't mind leaving them and going into his office for the coffee he brewed as thick as molasses. He had a photograph on his desk of a young man. "My son," García said, "a Corps cadet at A & M."

"I can see you're real proud," she said.

Then he told her the boy had been killed in a waterskiing accident. As he related this, his face was an adobe wall. His control fascinated her, and his passion for work.

"How come you got into this business, Mario?" she asked.

"I was in the army," he told her. "Korea."

"Liked the uniform?"

"*Más o menos,*" he said. "I felt like something."

"A real man?"

He was almost blushing. Did real men cry when their sons were killed? She wanted to put her hand on his wrist where the dark hair bent like blown-over grass, wanted to bundle him in a hammock and help him swing.

In November he took her to a place near the river where the mesquite was a gray-green wall. Four wets had appeared on a radar screen, but the copters couldn't find them. They got out of the car where a caliche road intersected the highway near La Paloma and opened an iron gate marked with the Cattleman's Association NO TRES-PASSING sign. García squatted on his bootheels in the dust, studying a network of bird and snake tracks, then stood and walked into the brush. Thorns tore at her hair as she bent low to follow him. He must be smelling something, because she couldn't see how he could make out anything on the ground, which was littered with leaves and speckled with shadow web. She was reading sign so closely she nearly ran into him.

"There," he said, pointing down. At first she didn't see anything but a cow's pelvic bone, a gray forked branch, a clump of prickly pear.

"Don't you have eyes?" he said, taking her arm, directing it to the right and down where she finally saw the half-moon heelprint in the dust.

"But they're going *toward* the river," she said.

"A trick. He's walking backward." The others were spread out in a line, walking north parallel to this one, he said. He didn't need to check it out before calling the others to intercept.

"They round them up like cattle," Standish had told her. "Lock them in detention centers like prisons." *"El Corralón,"* they called one place. The corral.

Wilma was spending a lot of time with Standish and his girl helpers at the Casa, holding hands around the table, saying prayers, listening to the endless refugee talk. The girls were in their twenties, lay workers sent by their dioceses in Chicago or Detroit or Philadelphia to work with Catholic organizations that had their fingers in refugee business. There was a lot of refugee talk these days, about Asians and Central Americans and Ethiopians and Lord knew what else. She was beginning to be tired of the prayers and the politics; it was Marta and Micaela, their husbands and children who made something in her sing.

The girls at the Casa were young, hard-muscled as if they'd just arrived home from summer camp. They ran day-care centers and taught cooking and hygiene, raised consciousness in detention centers. To them South Texas was a foreign country, and Richard Standish a missionary saint. It took them only a few days to develop crushes and a firm conviction that Wilma was a homewrecker. Once they believed this, the girls' initial friendliness toward her cooled, and their worship of Standish became a possessive frenzy. Wilma wouldn't be in the trailer house ten minutes before five pairs of tanned, muscular legs in cutoffs lay stretched across the living-room floor. They came for briefings on immigration law, responses under interrogation, for spiritual advice, Diet Cokes and idle chatter. When they didn't come to see Standish, it was to play with the baby and talk with his wife about conditions in Mexican refugee camps. Their talk exhausted Wilma, made her head ache.

After making a dozen refugee runs for Standish in five months, she was less romantic about the illegals. Conditions in small villages in Guatemala and El Salvador were miserable, and American involvement in Central American wars cruel and pointless. She still wanted to wrap up the wanderers and take them home. But it was beginning to occur to Wilma that Texas couldn't absorb this wave of immigrants; there was no meat on the bone. The sanctuary girls were all right; they just hadn't developed humor. And she admired Standish, loved him, too, in a way, but finally couldn't like him. *He's all principle,* she thought, *and not enough gravel in his craw. He doesn't take it personally, the ears and tongues.*

"Don't they have to put them somewhere?" Wilma asked Standish, and immediately felt guilty. She said she guessed it must be awful for the INS people to do their dirty job.

"Most of them are racist," Standish said. "They feel okay."

"García's not," she said, with so much heat that he looked at her strangely.

"García's all right," Standish told her, and he sent her in his place to the Harlingen railyards to wait for the train from Matamoros. García was there watching for the same illegals, only he was in the green van, and she was high in a grain elevator a hundred yards away. The steering wheel of the van gleamed silver through the windshield, and behind it García sat in the shadow, still as a lizard, waiting.

Standish had sent her to the yards, not certain if two Guatemalans who had called from Mexico would be on it, but sure his own phone was tapped. He'd told her where to park and how to find the ladder inside the four-story elevator, where she could look down into the open cars. When the train blew its whistle a mile or so back toward Brownsville, she saw the green car door open and García get out. His movements were unhurried, as if he were leaving the car to go into a restaurant. He strolled to the center track, stood on a ladder on the outside of a boxcar and waited. The train came through a big clump of cottonwoods next to the bridge into the yard, the hard blue light bouncing off its blunt nose, brakes wheezing and shrieking. A slow hiss of steam from a valve, then the steady drip drip of water from refrigerated cars. Besides the six reefer cars there were mostly open boxcars filled with bricks or tiles, a brakeman with a flashlight walking alongside. From where she sat she couldn't see much of the man's face, only the top of his cap and a nose with wire-rim glasses. For several minutes nothing moved in the darkness, and cicadas in the cottonwoods started their static.

When a shadow appeared at the rim of one of the boxcars, then gathered itself into a tight bundle before dropping to the ground, she had to blink once to be sure. Where was the other one? She strained her eyes until they bulged, her gaze running the length of the train as far as she could see. But García seemed to know he was waiting for only one. She couldn't figure how he was certain of that or how he could tell when the man had landed, but he moved out of the shadow toward the place where the man's feet had hit the ground. She supposed García did this so often he was certain the man would continue along the tracks north, and all he had to do was quicken his own pace enough to get within sprinting distance in three minutes. From where she sat she could watch both dark silhouettes moving along the same set of tracks, García about fifty yards behind.

She knew the man had seen García when she began to hear the footfalls of his leather soles bouncing off the sides of the cars. García stood still and yelled, *"Alto,"* pulling out his pistol and firing it into the air. The sound made a sharp multiple echo that seemed to rush along between trains like water through a narrow tunnel. *"Alto,"* he yelled again, running toward the footsteps in the dark. Briefly Wilma wondered if there could be another one hiding somewhere in the cars, and then she thought to wonder if he was Central American or Mexican. No telling. He was thin and fast, that's all she knew, and beginning to lose García when a second car pulled in on the east side of the tracks with a searchlight and a bullhorn. When the two officers inside approached the fugitive he made a couple of quick angled rushes across the tracks, then finally leaned against a boxcar, head bent, hands spread out along his thighs. In the dark grain elevator she pounded her own leg with her fist, watched García walk up and speak to him. Then he put one hand lightly on the other's shoulder. The young man shrugged and laughed, walking beside García to the van.

"I had to turn one back for the third time," García told her later, as they were sitting in a coffeeshop in San Benito. "It gets to be a *tertulia,* a party, meeting old friends in the dark."

She liked García because he wasn't so noisy, because he told her his job was a *chiste,* a joke.

"U.S. immigration policy is a revolving door. They should call it Alien Travel. I pick them up, keep them a few months maybe, then send them home."

"To die," she said. *"Los Salvadoreños."*

"We have no figures on that."

Standish had told her maybe half, and she knew García had the same figures and wondered what he did with them.

When she had a rest day coming in mid-November and García asked her to go to San Antonio she wondered what he was up to. She liked his style but wasn't ready to get romantic. Hell, life was complicated enough. It was a relief to find out they were going to see his grandmother. The *abuelita* lived in a small room behind a candy shop in San Antonio's Westside neighborhood, where she had fifteen grandchildren and forty-six great-grandchildren close enough to run errands.

"*Mario de mi alma*," she cried, stretching her twiggy arms wide as they stepped into her tiny neat room.

"This lady is my friend," he said in Spanish, and Wilma extended her hand. The old woman's bones were light as a quail's but her grip was warm and firm. She was extremely shy, speaking always through García, asking how many children Wilma had, and if they were boys or girls.

"*Dos*," Wilma said, "two boys."

Wilma held her hand as she stepped gingerly into the front seat of the car. They drove through narrow streets, the grandmother pointing out landmarks.

"The old *teatro* was there—Cantinflas," she told them. A mural at one corner of Guadalupe Street, a painting of the Virgin flanked by prickly pear, a bakery where she bought *empanadas* and *pan dulces* before she lost her teeth. She was born in Matamoros, she told Wilma, and had worked in Brownsville as a maid. When it came time for her first child to be born, she rented a room on the U.S. side so the baby would be a citizen. They passed an old lowrider Chevy with two teenagers inside, radio blasting Latino rock. Wilma got a glimpse of leopard upholstery and a painting of the Mexican eagle on the trunk, holding a serpent in its jaws. On the way back to the grandmother's house they bought corn husks from a street vendor for the week's tamales. The old woman was gracious saying her goodbyes. She sat in the brightly lit room in a rocker covered with a piece of embroidered cotton, and she motioned for Wilma to come close enough for *un beso*. Kissing her on both cheeks, she held Wilma's shoulders and her old black eyes were crackling.

"You carry a thing very heavy in your arms." The word she used was *pesado*. "But all things *van mejorando,* improving. You will see."

In the evening they drank Mexican beer in a *conjunto* bar, where a small band played, and middle-aged couples did a dance that was a lively mix of cowboy two-step and polka. The men kept their hats on; their wives and girlfriends wore frilly blouses and tight pants and high heels. García was light on his feet, his hand pressing the small of her back steady but not insistent. His eyes were mild and sad.

"I'm happy you would come here."

"Why? You sound surprised."

"I have been curious about you a long time, *señora.*"

"Don't call me *señora:* it makes me feel old. What do you want to know?"

"What you're doing here?"

"Where, in the *barrio?*"

"In a truck. On the border. Why not home with your husband, your sons? You could tell me it was none of my business." How much did he already have on her?

"I'm running," she said, after a pause, "but not away."

"A truck is no place," he said. He was right. A truck was a time capsule that sealed her off from her big losses.

"What are you afraid of? It's only time, *comprende?*"

"I want some of my own," she said. Did he like her because she was a redhead and a *gringa?*

From a peddler's tray he bought her a silk rose, a wooden snake with a needle tongue and a four-inch tube of red and green braided straw.

"Here, put your finger in this end," he said and slipped his forefinger into one opening. Looking into her eyes he pulled on the straw. The braids tightened, holding her finger fast.

"Now you've got me," she said, laughing. It must have been on the little half-empty dance floor she got interested. Because he led her without pressure and seemed to know which way she wanted to be turned.

They walked by pale oleanders along the river, holding hands, and the skin of his palm was warm as a child's, and smooth.

"You left children at home?"

"One," she said, and felt for the first time the full weight of the thing she had done. "He's nearly grown."

"He still needs a mother."

She walked more quickly, pulling at his hand.

"*Lento, lento,*" he said. "Slow down."

As she stopped in her tracks he bumped into her chest, and it may have been to regain his balance that he put a hand on each of her shoulders, laughing.

"Excuse me."

Suddenly she was thirteen, all knees and elbows. "What is this?" she said.

"Very deep shit, *señora,*" he said, and kissed her on the cheek.

Two weeks later he took her to a friend's ranch near Uvalde. The owner showed her small shacks where wetback cowboys slept during spring roundup.

"They'll hang around a couple months, then head back home to mama or up north fruit picking. They'll keep coming as long as there's work," the man said.

"As long as *gringos* like you are willing to break the law," García said.

"Hell, Mario," the rancher said, "you know as well as I do the only way to stop illegal immigration is to shoot 'em as they come over the fence."

"In Waco a man sells *mojados* for two hundred fifty apiece," García said. "The farmer who buys them deducts that amount from their first wages, then sells them off to a neighbor. They might work for a year, two years, as indentured servants. We're looking at something pretty close to slavery, *hombre*." A muscle in his left cheek tensed.

At the riverbank in Brownsville they walked along the top of a steep embankment watching a Border Patrol helicopter hover overhead. Opposite them on the Mexican side people were hunkered down in clumps of sweet willow waiting for a break. Looking down the bank below her she saw sheets of black plastic, mismatched socks of many colors, jeans and T-shirts clinging to the grass.

"Why don't you pick them up here?" she asked.

"Too messy," he said, "with their families on the other side. But they think we will. We let them get into the center of town before we round them up."

"But they're your people," she said.

"My grandmother could never get a green card," he told her. "But she made sure her children were born here."

"So what?"

"If we can't enforce our immigration laws, citizenship means *nada*."

If she squinted she could make out a naked knee glowing in the weeds. The knee moved. Sun glinted on dark hair, and the Rio Grande inched along carrying flecks of soapsuds. The helicopter passed over, continuing toward downtown Brownsville. She heard a splash and turned her eyes back to the river but saw only a slight agitation on the surface. She wondered what she would do if she saw someone swimming, and knew García would do what he had to.

"They'll hide on this side until we leave."

"That bridge," she said, pointing. "The official bridge between the U.S. and Mexico?"

"Yes."

"Do they cross there at night?"

"*Claro*. They have many children. They'll cross whenever they can."

When they drove over this bridge into Matamoros at five in the afternoon she saw a young Mexican in a red nylon jacket crawling hand over hand along the scaffolding toward Texas.

Every chance they got they went dancing at the Andrew Jackson Hotel in San Benito, its lobby full of macaws and parrots and Midwestern snowbirds. It had a comfortble B-western look: cracked Naugahyde chairs, a tile floor, tall fishtail palms and a brass spittoon. In the dining room at eight a group of elderly couples did a polka to a three-piece combo, creaky but spirited. Wilma and García drank six Dos Equis apiece and danced nine out of eighteen numbers, most of them slow. García introduced her to the hotel proprietor, Luther Power, a well-built black man of seventy with two gold front teeth and a degree in engineering.

"What's a fine lady like you doin' in this godforsaken country?" he asked.

"I like the weather."

"The lady drives a semi," García told Power.

"I knew she was a humdinger," Luther said.

She was getting tired of this response. "Plenty of women are doing it," she said. "And then there's Sally Ride."

"All as good-lookin' as you?"

"Chill out," she said. She didn't trust him.

When García kissed her in the parking lot, she was so rattled she began to cry. Because he was a respectable kisser and because nobody but Oralee had kissed her for months. When he took his face from hers he sat quietly next to her in the front seat of the van watching the light breeze blow the *retama* branches into fantastic shapes. A hazy half-moon was rising over the town, and the combo was playing "Stranger in Paradise."

"Like to go for a drive?"

She shook her head. "I want to go swimming," she said.

It was a strange idea at midnight in South Texas, but there was still water in the cracked hotel pool behind a chainlink fence in back of the building. He sat in one of the medallion-backed iron chairs near the water and watched her remove her clothes.

"No fair," she called out, folding her skirt, laying it across her chair. "This is no strip show."

"I can't swim," he said.

She glowed in the fluorescent light, a cool Rubens.

"Bull," she said.

"They wouldn't let my parents into the country club."

"I'll teach you," she said. The night was warm and slightly damp, and she could feel the short hair around her face start to blow into curls. It wasn't her thing— wandering out under stars buck naked in front of a fully clothed man. She started putting on her clothes. What could she teach a Chicano who worked for La Migra, married, sitting on the other side of the fence? Buttoning up her shirt she started to walk past his chair to the car.

"Wait," he said, taking her hand. His face was in shadow, the outline of his thin shoulders sharp against Scorpio. "We could stay here."

While he checked in at the desk she crouched behind the palm nearest the stairway, clutching her duffel bag with the new toothbrush in it. The retirees had left, and the parrots were dozing. She had time to think that except for the nervous nights with Gary it was the first time she had checked into a hotel with a man who wasn't her husband, and to remember the awful embarrassment of running into Vernon on the way out of the shower the first week they were married. She locked herself in the closet and wouldn't come out for an hour.

"Name?" Luther asked, squinting up at García through the glaring desk lamp and pretending not to notice Wilma.

"Jones," García said. "John Jones."

"Right," Luther said. "Take fifteen. First floor."

The minute she put her foot on the first step a yellowhead parrot broke into a squeaky rendition of "El Paso":

"Dashing and daring a drink he was sharing with wicked Felina, the girl that I loved."

She carried her red face upstairs.

When García opened the heavy wooden door she got an impression of pink roses on a yellowish background, ancient wooden venetian blinds above the 1959 GE window unit with a front like the cockpit of a small private plane. The high ceiling had been beautified in the 1950s by square acoustical tile, now faintly green.

"Great bed," she said, sitting carefully on the patched quilt. The minute she got settled she heard a sharp report—an axe striking hardwood.

"I'll fix it," García said and knelt down to look under the bed. Replacing the board, he quickly withdrew.

"You could grow marijuana there," he said. "Would you like to try some?"

She didn't see why she shouldn't. Sitting on the bed next to her, he pulled out a clay cylinder an inch in diameter and started tamping green stuff down into it with his forefinger.

"Weren't you ever curious when your kids tried this?" García's eyebrows hooded his dark eyes so she couldn't be sure he was kidding her, and she did a lot of thinking about Jody in the several minutes it took for her to inhale too deeply and cough for several minutes. While coughing she leaned across the bed, squinting at a photograph of the 1907 University of Texas football team, the players' faces sun-blackened, shoulders ordinary without pads.

When she tired of the photograph she went into the bathroom and fiddled around in her cosmetic bag a while. She brushed her teeth for three minutes, lingering over the dental floss. Pulling the peasant blouse over her head and shimmying out of the skirt, she shook her thick hair and looked herself dead in the eye. Wilma didn't look a thing like Jamie Lee Curtis, but her cheek bones weren't bad. Standing on the wooden top of the toilet she looked herself up and down and decided to wrap up in a towel.

She had broad shoulders and arms that could carry something, breasts holding their own with gravity, a frank, high-colored face, healthy if not beautiful. Suddenly she wasn't scared or embarrassed. García had known enough to buy a bunch of small Tyler roses and stick them into a water glass. She had known enough to wear Joy. After all these years she was doing something for herself. And nobody had to know a thing.

When she opened the door he rose quickly from the bed and walked toward her, taking both her hands in his.

"You are *maravillosa*," he said, and kissed her, wrapping both their arms around her hips. His mouth was strong on hers, but there was no greed in him. Mario

García kissed her like a man who didn't want to turn loose of his hunger.

She was so excited she got the hiccoughs, but waited for him to unbutton his shirt before she touched him, bent her head toward his chest and brushed his nipple with her lips. He put one hand up and lifted her chin, admiring her. Her fingertips buzzed from the marijuana.

"You are strong, very beautiful," he told her. "I am not a man who has affairs."

"What are we doing here then?" she said. Did he think she was a woman who did?

His hands on her shoulders were pulling her closer.

"It's all right if we stay as we are," she said.

"What we are isn't all right, either." He kissed her on the neck.

She wished she could do something about her face, that highway in need of repairs, but she pulled on his hand, anyway, until he sat down with her on the bed and kissed his mouth and eyelids and nose and cheeks and ears.

He was whispering Spanish phrases.

"What?" she said.

"A song."

She laughed. "I thought they were cuss words."

"Tu eres tan libre," he whispered. "You are so free."

Her hiccoughs had left her. She bit his shoulder shyly and told him he was handsome, then lay on her side and touched his shoulder. At that moment she had an image of herself walking through knee-high Johnson grass. Ahead of her Vernon was taking such long steps she had to trot to keep up, and when she caught up with him she hooked one finger through a belt loop of his khakis and yelled at him to wait for her. Then he turned and knocked her hat off, and ran away while she bent to pick it up.

Mario spoke seldom, and that was okay. Communication wasn't the point. Their time in the little room canceled outside time and freeway space, the old AC drowned out the CB rap, and all she could hear was García singing sad border ballads called *corridas* about gunfights with Texas rangers and doomed, difficult loves. They made plans to go to Mexico City, Guanajuato, Baja California, trips they'd never take. Once Wilma asked why he'd never had another child. His look made her wish she'd kept her mouth shut, made her want to put her arms around his wind-burned neck. Instead she stood up, walked to the dresser, poured a shot of mescal and handed it to him.

"Sorry," she said.

He waved his hand and drank. "My wife never wished for more children," he said, and Wilma asked to see a picture. García's wife was smiling in the snapshot, holding a five-year-old boy by the hand. Her shoulders were bare, and she had pinned a ribbon in her dark hair.

When had she stopped smiling? How old was the little boy when she decided not to have more? Did she lie close against him with her hands curled inside his own? Wilma wanted to know everything about García but couldn't ask.

García was less shy about asking her personal questions. "Why did you leave your husband?"

She told him he was having an affair with a neighbor, had stolen her money.

"Why didn't you tell him how angry you were?"

"I didn't need to tell him," she said. "He's not stupid."

"I didn't think he was," García said. She got the feeling he considered her nuts, but admired her anyway. Sometimes, crossing a street or getting into the van, he put his hand on her elbow as lightly as if it were a bird.

While Wilma was falling in love with García she went with Standish on bus-station deliveries in Harlingen. He

236

was careful to go at night, without lights, park several blocks shy of the building. You didn't want to be caught with them in the car. After delivery they sometimes went to meetings in parish houses where short people who looked Mexican were introduced and told by the priest in Spanish they were safe in the church because it was *sanctuario*. The fourteen or fifteen members of the congregation sang a hymn after the introductions, or someone read from the Bible.

When a stranger sojourns with you in your land, you shall do him no wrong. The stranger who sojourns with you shall be to you as the native among you, and you shall love him as yourself; for you were strangers in the land of Egypt; I am the Lord your God.

She was a stranger in the land of Egypt.
Who was the stranger sojourning with her?

18

A WEEK BEFORE THANKSGIVING she left Harlingen, sneaked back to Little Egypt to check on Vernon and found a homemade poster tacked on a light post at the crossroads.

TOWN MEETING
SATURDAY. 6 P.M.
SUBJECT: CITY-WIDE EVICTIONS. HEALTH DEPARTMENT HASSLES.
HUMAN RIGHTS VIOLATIONS. WELFARE SPIES.

Wondering what kind of briar patch the town had gotten itself tangled in, she crept into the old store through a rear door and stood in a corner behind the turned backs. She hadn't been home in over a year, and didn't want to stir up a wasp nest so she made herself inconspicuous behind thirty people sitting in folding chairs pulled up near the open brick fireplace, where the wind was beginning to hum and hoot in the chimney. Staying out of sight, she watched her neighbors stroll up and down the center aisle between the rows, dressed as if it were a wedding or a christening. When Jeanette Edwards swept through the front door wearing a black robe and a purple satin turban

Wilma crouched a little lower behind the oak counter, where a couple of large round cheeses sat next to the cookie tin.

Coming home unannounced was Wilma's last wild scramble for the sugar tit. She missed Vernon, and what she was doing scared her. She was making fast south-north runs, picking up loadbacks in New York, Detroit, Chicago, making the circuit in a week. Running illegals was enough to make her grind her teeth in her sleep; dividing her loyalties between three men was worse.

When Vernon stood up from the three-legged book-keeper's stool and rapped on the front of the fireplace with a hammer, her motor got to racing a little. Waiting for the noise from the crowd to die down, he held his arms out wide, palms up, smiling, his eyes fixed on a point high on the back wall.

"Fellow travelers," he said, "you can chit-chat all the way to the nursing home if you want, but you're in a fix. And I'm in it with you."

"How's that, Vernon?" Ruby said. Wilma craned her neck to see more of Ruby than the frizzy orange perm and glasses in the middle of the crowd. If she backed all the way against the stocked shelves she could just make out a bandanna print shirt and a wide black belt below it. She started to do a slow burn behind the counter.

"Well, you might think what you're livin' in are houses you own free and clear in a town you were born in, and a democratic country. Maybe you think you're gonna get to decide what to do with your next twenty years. But that's pure D delusion, because you ain't walkin' on solid ground. No sir, you're forgetting something every last one of you learned in the ninth grade."

"What?" Jesse Mahalek said.

"This doggone planet's blasting so fast through the

dark it ain't even funny, and the world don't look anything the way it used to. People like us who can remember Korea and Vietnam, and Myrna Loy and Betty Grable, gravel roads and gar and catfish in the creeks before the 2-4-5-t got 'em, we're goin' out of style. They're fixing to take one of our John Deere combines and dip it in silver paint and put a historical marker on it."

Vernon didn't sound anything like himself, she decided, and must have been reading some scientific stuff. Probably Ruby was filling him full of new craziness. He even looked different, like a man who'd shed his skin and moved into a fresh one, like a man who'd been saved. Wilma could remember only one other time her husband had looked like this and that was the morning he came into the hospital room and found her with Jody in her arms. His face had a scrubbed shine; he was completely new.

Zeno Clayburg and his wife, Rosetta, had brought twin granddaughters, Jerrie and Jamie, who used to come to Wilma's for piano lessons once a week. The old couple were in their Sunday best, Rosetta with a shiny black suit and a high beaver hat pulled over her eyes. A haze of white goose down had settled over the fabric, and Zeno, too, was covered by the fine feather dust. He removed his felt hat, running a hand through his nappy gray hair before standing up.

"The gummints say we cain't pick our geese on the porch no more. Say we got to install a sink with runnin' water." The Clayburgs were stretching their Social Security checks by dressing wild ducks and geese for Houston hunters, who paid the elderly couple two dollars for each bird it took forty minutes to pick clean.

"We never had runnin' water in the house. Nothing but a spigot in the yard we run a hose from to fill the tub."

The old man waved his arms around, looking confused. "What I need running water for to clean them birds?"

Jay Bishop called out from a seat near the front door: "Listen to this. I got one of those letters, too. They told me I had to build a pen for my Angoras. Welfare woman came sniffing around one day and caught 'em up on the porch. I tell you what, people can't stand the sight of a little goat shit ought to stay home."

Everybody laughed as Vernon called for order and waited for the noise to die down. Hattie Mae and Edna Mae Madison raised their hands and stood up together. "We got a letter from the Health people saying we have to get a food license. We can't afford no license." The Madison twins were the only truly identical twins Wilma had ever known, and they accentuated the likeness by wearing the same hot pink jumpsuits and black workout shoes. What did they need a license for? All they sold in their roadside bar was a couple of cases of beer every week and a little nookie now and then.

"I don't like it when those pencil-pushing goat ropers sit up in Houston or Austin drawin' me diagrams on how to wipe my ass," Vernon said. "None of us like it, but we're gonna have to do what they say unless we can figure out a way around 'em. Well, I'm here to tell you people I been workin' on it for ten days now, and I think I'm onto something."

Vernon's face shone with a crazy religious light, and she knew she couldn't trust a word he said. The crowd were whispering and murmuring and turning around in their chairs. A tall kid toward the front eased out of his chair, stuck his long hands down in his back hip pockets and stood swaying from side to side before he worked up the nerve to speak.

"Whadayou gonna do, Vernon," he drawled, "pray?"

Everybody laughed again, but Vernon smiled patiently, like somebody'd just handed him a beer.

"Well, I been reading about Egypt, and I been reading about pyramids," he told the crowd, "and the one single thing that came out of ancient Egypt besides arithmetic was the pyramid. You remember what they used them for, don't you?" He waited, but nobody volunteered. "Well, they buried their kings in there, wrapped 'em up in sheets and stuck them in a room way down inside. And whenever it was those Englishmen busted in there about a million years later, there were those pharaohs with their same skin and whiskers still under the sheets and looking exactly like themselves, only a little dry."

At the back of the room Wilma felt her face grow hot. Thank God nobody had seen her yet. She wished she'd never laid eyes on Little Egypt again, or a single one of her neighbors. It was just too pitiful. The whole town was stuck somewhere between Dogpatch and God's Little Acre. She hated to think how she'd paid no attention while the world ran on, leaving her town in its backwater. Always she'd guessed people from big cities like Houston considered the place quaint and adorable, but it was home to her so it didn't matter that all the houses had paint peeling away, and the kids had to be bussed away to school. Now that Vernon had plunged into some nutty new project she was glad she didn't live here anymore.

Calvin Merriweather stood up in the fourth row.

"Vernon," he said, "you used to be a good, level-headed bohunk. What the hell happened?"

There was a buzz from the crowd.

"I can't blame you for thinking I'm losing my sawdust, Calvin. I guess my letter sounds funny to you, but lemme tell you something, baby. If they were moving you out of that mansion you'd be whistlin' another tune."

Vernon stopped talking abruptly, red in the face. Calvin was stunned. Nobody had ever called him "baby" before.

Vernon walked down the aisle between the rows and stood in the middle of the crowd, looking straight to the back of the room, so she thought he was bound to see her there next to the old metal cash register with the NO SALE sign permanently rung up. He pointed to the sign.

"You're losing it, people," he said. "Where we been while the whole world was blasting by at ninety miles an hour? We been sitting on our butts, letting this store die, letting the newspaper fizzle, and the softball games. We don't even have a schoolhouse now; the bus comes and hauls the kids to El Campo. It used to be we paid the teacher and she taught our kids what we wanted. Now what do we get? Vans of hophead weirdos driving out here from Houston every weekend, peddling coke and angel dust. Last thing I heard from Emmie Ferguson they were gonna take away the post office in the old store if we didn't build a modern sanitary bathroom in there, with a flush toilet; next thing they'll want a bidet."

"A hot tub?" Timmy Minos said.

"He's got it right about the post office," Emmie Ferguson said. For the last twenty years the postmistress had been sitting next to a wood stove in the lean-to room off Merriweather's General Store, sifting through the few letters and seed catalogues that came in every day. She read the catalogues, held up letters to the light, and examined the postcards. Then she'd sort the mail into small combination boxes opening onto the porch. Wilma loved walking up onto the porch in the mornings, dialing her combination, and pulling out her mail as if she were at a fancy hotel. She'd sit down on the long wooden bench beneath the boxes to visit with her neighbors or read her mail or the wanted posters, or she'd go inside for a cup of coffee and an oatmeal cookie, or a Big Red from the rusted cooler. She'd look around for some little thing to buy, because the store had a hard time competing with Safeway thirteen miles down the road.

"But we haven't got money for a john in the P.O.," Emmie said.

"We got to bring that money in," Vernon said, as if it were as simple as Santa Claus.

"What're we gonna use for bait?" Devel Edwards asked, and there was general snickering.

"Think about it. What was Egypt famous for?" Vernon repeated, crossing his arms and leaning back against the wall.

A couple of teenagers sat on the floor behind him, popping their gum, turning the pages of *Computer World.* One of them raised a hand.

"Are you talkin' this town, or the real Egypt?" she said.

"The real Egypt."

"They had a big river," the girl said, "a statue of a firecat that looked like a woman. And pyramids, like you said."

Vernon didn't say anything for a minute, then he launched into a staccato stream of big plans. They would build a pyramid, maybe a replica of the Sphinx. The buildings would rise from the Texas plain like a movie producer's dream, and tourists and travelers would detour miles down the farm-to-market road to see these relics from a forgotten past.

"We'll research it, put in all the hieroglyphics and murals, build copies of those tombs. It'll be historically accurate. But the best part'll be the people paying two dollars to get in the gate. For a while they'll walk around the damned thing, scratching their heads. Pretty soon they'll want to come on in that little square door painted with hen-scratch writing so they can climb three hundred stairs to the top. That'll be two dollars more. They'll get so high they can see the Dome, and the oxbow in the Colorado. On clear days they'll be able to make out the nuke plant at Matagorda that'll blow us all to smithereens. Maybe, when they see that, people won't worry so much about how we make our sausage."

Vernon was gone, wasted. She didn't know how it had happened, but he'd flat lost the rest of his stuffing. She'd rather see him drunk and crying into his vodka-and-Coke. She'd rather see him busted and laid flat than cuckoo. From her hiding place behind the cash register she looked at her neighbors as if for the first time. Maybe they were all crazy; they kept on listening to Vernon, and no one shouted him down. They really perked up when he tacked up a poster of fifty-seven old Cadillacs, their noses buried in sand. The poster was four feet long and in full color.

Vernon stood to the left of it, pointing to the cars with a long willow stick. "Practically nobody heard of Amarillo or T. Boone Pickens until Stanley Marsh commenced buyin' these old Cadillacs and plantin' 'em nose down in the sand out there. Hell, I bet you didn't know that old boy was ten years older'n I am right now when he got the idea. Hell, I bet you're wonderin' how come he did that and how he got his holes dug and all those old junked cars hauled out there in the first place." Vernon was waving the stick around like a wild band leader. His eyes were unnaturally bright, as he looked for volunteers.

Finally somebody spoke up.

"I ain't never heard of the Cadillac Ranch," Calvin

Merriweather said. "It sounds like a new kind of whore-house."

"You never heard of Amarillo's favorite son? Where you all been?"

"Living in the real world," Timmy Minos said. "Farming rice."

"Gettin' foreclosed," Calvin reminded him.

With his hands on his hips like a high school coach, Vernon told the crowd how Stanley Marsh had grown up in Amarillo during the Depression, but his family was in oil, which wasn't hit too hard back then. Sometime in the mid-nineteen-seventies when the oil business was still buttering just about everybody's white bread in Texas, Stanley bought those humongous tailfin Cadillacs and planted them in a row on his ranch.

"The whole damned town thought he'd gone loco," Vernon said, "but then Stanley Marsh made art history. They reviewed his show in New York, and Stanley commenced to get richer. Before he was through he owned three TV stations and a restaurant and washateria right there in Amarillo, Texas."

He paused to catch his breath and poked at the fire with his stick.

"Watchit, Vernon, don't burn the place down," somebody yelled.

"He's having an art event," Calvin said.

"That's real cute, Calvin, but you know, if they take away our post office we ain't even gonna be on the state highway maps anymore. One of these days you'll be sucking down too many beers and forget how to drive home, and then you'll look it up on your Triple A touring guide and Little Egypt flat won't be there. You'll spend the whole night wandering around in the dark."

"I don't get it, Vernon," Calvin said. "What do these Cadillacs have to do with your pyramid plan? And how much did Marsh make off 'em, anyhow?"

"I haven't got the bottom line on that, Calvin," Vernon said, grinning. "But I'll check on it right away. The main thing I want you to get from all this is folks will pay to look at anything, don't you see? Pyramids. Cadillacs. What's the difference? People, listen to me. You're livin' in a state where there ain't a lot to look at except sky and land. That is, if you don't live in Houston or Dallas–Fort Worth or San Antone or Austin. And there's a lot of us'll tell you there's not much to see there either when you get down to it."

She'd driven long enough; he didn't have to tell her about stretches of highway lined with barbed-wire fencing, beer cans and torn newsprint scattered along the grassy ditches, and just when she thought she'd drive off the shoulder from sleepiness or boredom a series of small hand-lettered signs caught her eye: HOMEMADE FUDGE. TAMALES. FRESH SHRIMP. BABY RABBITS. The rabbits made her think about times Vernon used to stop his tractor or combine in the middle of a field and jump down into the hip-high grass to snatch a nest of cottontails out of the way.

She'd be at home watching TV in the evenings when he'd drop them, four or five or eight, into the slack lap of her skirt and stand there grinning at her as if those rabbits were a basket of rubies or a new washing machine. Remembering these moments made Wilma wish she'd been more gracious.

"How we gonna pay for this pyramid?" Rosemary asked.

"How is it going to help?" That was Ruby.

"People will pay to see it. We'll give tours, sell souvenirs," Vernon told them.

"What're you going to build it out of? We got no timber around here," Devel Edwards said. *That was just like him*, she thought, *practical*.

"I'm not sure."

"How many rooms?"

"I want my own room," Velma Hairston said.

He didn't have it all nailed down yet, but he was working on it.

"But would you all walk outside with me a minute?" Vernon asked.

"Maybe he wants to tell us a bedtime story," Calvin said.

Everybody went out the double screen doors and down the porch steps till they were standing out in the gravel drive beside the highway. Wilma stepped out behind the others, keeping her face in shadow so she wouldn't turn the meeting upside down. She stood behind her neighbors, all thirty-eight of them, whispering and cracking jokes and looking up at the clear moonless sky. Vernon instructed them to hold their arms out sideways and face north.

"Listen, friends. Visualize the future. Shut your eyes tight till you can squeeze a picture out onto your eyelids of those pyramids we're gonna build in the pasture right in front of y'all and seventeen degrees to the east. They'll be eighty cubits tall and three hundred cubits around the base. Solid? I'll show you solid. Damned things'll last a thousand years."

Then he was quiet so they could close their eyes and see.

Wilma looked around at all the upturned faces with their eyes shut, as if waiting for bread from heaven. She wanted to put her arms around each one, whisper words of comfort and truth in their ears. But she didn't have any truth in her pocket, and nothing that she'd learned on the road was going to give any of them a place to lie down. Wilma felt a terrible sorrowful sadness for all of them, but especially for Vernon, who lost his farm, lost his wife, and now, his mind.

19

For NEARLY A YEAR Wilma and García made love whenever they got the chance, which wasn't often because South Texas furniture was heading north in a steady stream. From Harlingen, McAllen, Brownsville and Rio Grande City she carried Danish Modern chairs, Drexel bedroom suites, antique Spanish chests and Early Attic everything up the heart of the country to Kansas City, Springfield, Detroit, Cleveland, or east to Norfolk, D.C., Philadelphia, New York and Boston. Sometimes weeks went by when she saw García only at the cement-block building where he checked her papers.

"What's the load this trip?" he asked one October morning, his voice the slightest pressure.

"Sorry pale-wood Yankee trash."

Then he asked the question: "Ever hear of a lady trucker moving live freight?" She looked at him, raising her eyebrows. "I have been getting stories about a lady transporting *mojados* between here and the East Coast."

"Yeah? I hadn't heard." She hoped he hadn't heard her heart.

"She's supposed to work for Wild Goose," he said.

He'd started asking her about Standish, where he came from, his kids' names and ages, what work he did before the Casa.

"Why do you want to know?" she asked, and he said it was his job to know everything that went on in a 140-mile-wide strip between Harlingen and Laredo.

"You spend a lot of time with him. He must be a good man."

"He's all right," she said. From the first García had seen her with Standish, and he probably knew she was working for the movement, too.

In November she began to talk to Standish about quitting. She had been working for the Casa for over a year, and the tension was wearing on her because three or four refugees were hiding in half her loads from South Texas. The Justice Department was starting to hit the movement hard: sanctuary workers in Texas and Arizona had been given three to five years, one of them a Catholic lay worker pregnant with her first child.

"The odds are stacking up and I've had it with these *pobrecitos*," she told him. "Big eyes, grimy, grabby hands. Everybody needs too much." They sat alone at his dinner table.

"Maybe you should quit," he said. "I don't see you making this your life's work. Too risky. Besides, it must be awkward for you."

"What?"

"Working for us and getting into bed with La Migra." She could do without his sarcasm.

She hadn't dreamed he knew. It surprised her even more that he was jealous. She stood up and started taking plates out to the kitchen. Richard sat in his chair facing away from her, his forearms resting on the edge of the table, while she moved in and out of the room, picking up knives, forks, water glasses. She stood at the sink, rinsing the plates, stealing quick looks at the back of his neck. The hair on the right side grew in a little whorl, like an ear of wheat.

"Come back in here a minute, will you?" he said.

She walked slowly out of the kitchen, not wanting to meet his gaze. His eyes, the gray-blue of a faded shirt, didn't leave her anyplace to hide.

"I want you to understand what you've given us," he said.

"Us?"

"Me, then." He folded his arms across his chest and continued to watch her.

"Look," she said, spreading her hands on the table, "I had to do it." Because every damned thing she heard these days was lonesome as a boarded-up train station.

"No, you didn't," he said. "Shouldn't I thank you?" She shook her head. She didn't know. It wasn't thanks she was after, or praise.

"I guess I haven't given you much," he said. And she told him he'd given her plenty, just what she needed, a young man's hope and a young man's sharp shoulder to lean on for a while.

"There's no security," he said.

"There's the risk," she told him, and he couldn't see it was the gamble that gave her life and more life.

She'd had almost more than she could take by the first of December. It hadn't rained more than an inch anywhere in Texas since June, and the countryside looked as if somebody had been burning brush and cactus after root plowing. The heat and the miles were getting to her, but they didn't bother her as much as being in between. Every word she spoke to Standish or García sounded like a

made-up story. Everything she touched belonged to someone else. In strange houses she took inventory of other
people's furniture, turned the tables and chairs over and
attached small numbered yellow stickers underneath.
Handling other people's chairs and dishes and wine
glasses gave her an uneasy feeling.

At a Spanish house in San Antonio she had orders to
pack it all: china, glassware, towels, table linens, dresses.
The wife had made lists, then left for Cozumel. No one in
the house except the family wetback, no one in the shady
green yard but an arthritic retriever.

She decided to start in the bedroom and work her way
downstairs. The room was pale yellow with three sets of
French doors across one wall, king-sized bed on the opposite wall, fireplace at one end. It wasn't that any single
thing in the room was extravagant, but there were so
many cushions, couches, Indian rugs and love seats—
places to lie and sit and take it slow—that it made her
skin prickle with anger. She observed her wind-dried complexion in the gilt mirror, then telephoned García, using
the Princess phone on the night stand.

"Can you meet me?"

"Not tonight," he said. He never gave an excuse. There
was a pause in which she could hear his breathing. "I miss
you," he said.

And the pain in her chest was so heavy her voice was
tight and angry when she answered. "Yeah," she said.
"Sure."

"You want too much, *señora.*"

García had to make a trip to Laredo a week later,
asked her to go along.

"Take me to Boys' Town," she said. All her life she'd
heard about the whorehouses on the outskirts of Laredo.

"Why?"

She told him what she'd told her papa about wanting to drive a truck: "A woman needs experience."

Before going to Boys' Town they had made love all afternoon in the hotel. She opened the blinds so a column of sunlight fell over the bed, then lay back down with her hands stretched over her head. Sitting propped against the headboard, she tried to hold still while he placed a glass of José Cuervo on ice in the soft middle of her belly. Scarcely breathing, she waited for what seemed a week, picked up the glass and took a sip of the amber liquid that tasted like the codeine cough medicine her papa had used.

At the Cadillac Bar in Laredo, where the light was mellow, she slid into a seat next to his. He looked her over approvingly. "I like it when you dress," he said. She wore a full cotton skirt and a blouse cut low enough to be chilly.

"Thanks. What do your other girlfriends wear?" Was this a date they were on?

"You're the first woman I've brought here," he said.

After a couple of margaritas he drove her down the dark dirt road to Boys' Town. She imagined every man in a Mexican bordello would have a hard-on.

"Mario," she whispered in the dark, "what do they wear?" In the Pappagallo the whores had on everything from rhinestone peignoirs to satin ball dresses, and they looked nearly as spiffy as the Neo-Grecian white plaster statues lined up around the dance floor. Wilma hadn't seen so much exposed womanhood since skinny-dipping at camp. The girls sat at the bar swinging their legs, lounged in booths, rolled their haunches across the small dance floor, lazy as siestas. They were never alone for long. One sixteen-year-old in bikini pants cut high in the crotch squeezed in between Wilma and García. She was wearing a thin tank top that rippled over her nipples.

"Sucky-fucky?" she whispered.

254

"No, *chica*." He put his arm around Wilma.

A squat woman wrapped in silver lamé walked on-stage with a mike announcing *El Gran Concurso de Bikini* . . . Girls from all over Mexico would compete, *las mas bonita del país, mas chingada*. Wilma turned in her seat, trying to catch the filthy words.

"Where are they?"

"In the *Damas*. Putting makeup on their scars."

Wilma went to the *Damas*. Six girls were crowded around the mirror over a fake marble washstand. None looked older than eighteen, and most still had their baby fat. A chubby girl in a chair was wetting a finger in liquid foundation, touching it lightly to dark bruises on one contestant's cheek.

When the same slender barefoot girl began mincing around the edge of the dance floor, bumping her tiny hips, Wilma started getting mad.

"Seen enough?" García asked.

"Sure," she said, and they went out to the car.

"They were pieces of meat."

"What did you expect?" he said. "Don't let it get to you. The trouble with you, Wilma, you've led a sheltered life." He had a little smirk on his face like he knew where she lived and hurt and kept her party money.

"You don't know a damned thing about my life."

"Just a little," he said. "I know you like Almond Roca and used to have a boyfriend named Steve. I know the first song you learned as a kid was 'Don't Fence Me In.' "

She couldn't stay mad at García. He was too handsome, too romantic, and the first man besides Vernon who'd given her presents. He had brought her a red leather collar for Bear, a pair of blue *periquitos* in a bamboo cage she hung in the cubby, and a ruffly peasant blouse that made her look like a red-haired Dolly Parton. The blouse reminded her of Vernon and the dance halls when she was nineteen, though García was a much better dancer than Vernon and had flashier taste. He liked silver hoop earrings and silver-and-turquoise belt buckles, and each time they'd get to Nuevo Laredo or Matamoros or Ciudad Acuña he'd buy her something in the market. The jewelry did a lot for her morale. She used to laugh and make a face and say he'd better buy her lots of thingapretties because she only had about seven more good months left.

"Cheer up," he said, grinning at her. "While we're in the neighborhood I'll take you to a cockfight."

The *torneo de gallos* was well under way when he parked outside the fenced ring, which looked like a pen for goats. Inside was a grandstand with seats for eighty people and six mariachis.

From the first she knew that the black cock would win. Its tiny ferocious eyes blinked imperiously at the audience. This cock was king, anyone could see it. But she wanted the pretty one to win, the one with feathers all the colors of fire.

"The black one," García said, and she bet him five dollars. Two handlers squatted in the dust cradling their birds. The San Antonio cock was a dark maroon-black, heavier than the *gallo* from Reynosa, a wiry, reddish bird with blue and green tail feathers. When released, the smaller bird flared five feet into the air and began pecking the black bird on the neck. Soon the fight slowed, as the bright bird laid a wing across its opponent's face. The black bird seemed sleepy, its head drooping.

"Smothering him," García said. It was almost like an embrace.

Black's handler called for time out. After several minutes the fight went on, the black bird darting at the bright one, pecking furiously at its head and neck. Wilma turned her face toward the judge, the mayor of Matamoros, the city council. She didn't watch again until García shook her shoulder.

"The little cock has great spirit," he said.

When she looked back into the white square painted on the ground, the reddish bird was taking mincing steps. It looked exhausted. The larger bird circled warily, its head showing spots of blood. It seemed to Wilma the small bright bird was carrying its head lower, and in a minute the dark one made good use of the advantage, hammering at the small one's skull until it dropped to the ground, beak in the dust.

"That's it," García said, and started to stand.

Looking back at the ring, Wilma let out a little yelp. "My God." The fallen bird was standing unsteadily on its legs, holding a black feather in its beak, and now the black bird was on the ground.

For twenty more minutes the fight continued, the darker, larger bird seeming many times at the point of defeating his weaker opponent, but each time the scrawny, plucky cock righted himself and retaliated. The crowd was screaming, the handlers in tears. The ground was a mass of blood and feathers when the two birds finally lay still. Neither could rise. Both handlers walked over to pick up their birds, and the judge declared the contest a draw.

"Those birds sure had each other," Wilma said.

Driving back through Nuevo Laredo she let him see her cry. They were talking about her boys, the noise and mess they'd made, never letting her sit down with a magazine.

"You spoiled them," he said. Then he grinned. "You look like you're ready to start your next family, Wilma."

Her hands were splashed with big sloppy tears. One more thing they couldn't do together. Reality. She needed either more of it or less. More might kill her. Less would let her greed machine rev up to ten thousand and go spinning off the shoulder. García never gave her a chance to get greedy. In the beginning she hoped he would change, open his life, but he'd stayed to himself, keeping her hungry, angry, and, finally, alone.

They drove for a while without speaking. The clock on the dash said 2:00. Three hours to Harlingen.

"We could stop somewhere." He looked at her inquiringly.

"I don't care," she said. "I'll sleep." She had a low fever from these nights and days with him. Each time they met her senses were so clear for a week afterwards she could count the individual oak leaves blowing their pale undersides out, hear every note in the mockingbird's song.

It startled her when, a few minutes later, he turned to her out of the blue and said, "You should stop doing this kind of work, Wilma. It's too dangerous."

She breathed several times before answering. "I have lots of friends on the road, Mario. They look out for me."

"And you have enemies you don't know about," he said.

"I wouldn't be so sure." She wasn't afraid of him.

Passing over the bridge, they left the city. Stars were huge and furry in the black leather sky, center stripes rushing beneath the van. For a hundred miles they scarcely spoke. She was exhausted when they walked into the empty hotel lobby at three, waked Luther, climbed the narrow stairs with the key to their room. As soon as she started the water in the tub García said he needed a beer and went out into the hall. She peeled off her clothes, stepped carefully over the high sides, let herself down slow. When he came back thirty minutes later she was still lying there. The sight of her water-whitened toes on the faucet handle depressed her, but not nearly as much as his face staring past her into the mirror.

"Come on," he said, "let's go to bed."

"What's your hurry?" She turned the HOT handle with her toes and started a trickle, turned around so she faced him. It was still her favorite face.

"There's a deportation hearing tomorrow at ten."

"Oh boy. You get to send a few more back home to get fragged." He had taught her the word.

"*Cállate, mujer,*" he said through his teeth, shut up, woman, and left the room.

"You make me feel like hell," she told him in bed.

"I don't mean to make you feel bad," he said. "I just wanted a drink."

"You know what I mean. You make me feel like a slut." What she wanted to say was *puta,* the word for whore.

"You want to talk?"

What would she say that she hadn't already told him? That the old couples in the lobby looked at her funny? That they had too much on each other, and, politics or no politics, could never be on the same side?

"There's nothing to say."

Their lovemaking was a mean scrimmage. She hung on to the bars of the iron bedstead and fought him with her hips and legs, holding her eyes wide open in the half light from the open bathroom door, fixing in her memory the way he looked. Stubborn, defiant, too proud to know how to tell her what his losses were. His eyes were flat and shallow, the lights gone out of them, and his grin expressed only tension.

"What's wrong?" he said. "You're not with me."

"You were never with me," she said through her teeth.

Tonight it was his turn to knock and be turned away,

and she took a beating resisting him. He didn't abuse her, only gazed down at her with the look of a lone hitchhiker, while he asked her for everything she had.

The next morning they kept bumping into each other while they packed, excusing themselves when they touched, avoiding direct glances. Walking downstairs to the lobby, he followed behind her out of habit, carrying his bag, letting her sling her own over her shoulder. At the desk she left a sealed note to Luther along with the room key, not looking at García until she reached the front door, where she hesitated a moment. The green-and-yellow parrot on the nearest iron stand shrieked. "Wanna buy a bird?" it said.

She loved everything about that lobby, the red square tiles on the floor, the four-foot-by-six-foot portrait of Andrew Jackson hanging behind the desk, brass spittoons as big as elephants' feet next to both doors—everything had character. They stood together next to the truck, the sun hot and white, bouncing off the chrome.

"Don't get too serious," she said, standing back to admire his strong, thin face and stern mouth, his eyes glassy with tears.

"Don't hurry, *señora*," he said. "You'll have time for everything."

She doubted it. Leaving him in front of the hotel door, she climbed into the driver's seat and turned the key in the ignition, letting the big engine run for a minute. Then she leaned out the window and grinned, waving a red bandanna at him as if from the deck of a ship. Pulling out of the parking lot, she turned once to see if he was still standing there, but the doorway to the hotel was empty, so she shifted into second and whispered, "I love you, I love you."

20

SHE WAS LISTENING to Gabby's *Cowboy Corral* on a Houston station, ripping through Splendora, Cleveland, New Caney. On the Eastex Freeway heading north across the Trinity River, she wondered at ten on a sunny morning if she had stayed too long. Too long in Texas, too long with Vernon, with Standish and the wets, too long with García. She was nobody's baby now.

On the way to Shreveport road signs and billboards took on a new strangeness.

FOR SALE
FIVE ACRES AND INDEPENDENCE

That was in Cleveland. Outside Lufkin another billboard:

RAYMOND HARVARD
QUARTER HORSES
USED CARS
CHRISTMAS TREES

And in the heart of metropolitan Corinth a Primitive Baptist church held Saturday-night bingo.

This morning she had to whip up on herself so she could leave her apartment, leave Houston skyscrapers rising in apricot haze. Along Allen Parkway newly planted oak trees showered sparks in the morning dew, and Vietnamese children from doomed city housing projects crossed with the light at Dallas. *I have hope, I have a big heart, I can do this,* she thought. What Wilma was doing was leaving home one more time, everyone she knew. A week past her forty-fourth birthday with a lot of highway behind her, she was more lonesome than she'd ever been in her life.

Loading the truck for Boston the night before, she couldn't help crying when Standish took her hand.

"When are you going to quit being Wonder Woman?" he said. She couldn't remember what Wonder Woman looked like.

The Salvadorans who'd be leaving with her in the morning were listening to instructions. No smoking in the truck, no noise. There'd be a walkie-talkie between the cab and the van they could use if they got into trouble. She'd drop them at a Catholic church in Boston's North End. Make it home before Christmas, whenever that was. When she said goodbye to Standish he looked young and sad.

"You're the blade of my shovel," he said, and she had to blink rapidly and laugh and punch him lightly on the shoulder because she always was half in love with him.

Between Jackson and Meridian at four in the afternoon IH 20 was a birth canal between walls of black pines narrowing the passage, and there was no turning back from this new world. Calling ahead to westbound drivers, she asked for leads on county mounties and other cops. Lord knows she didn't need them nosing around with three women in back and a couple of babies, all without papers. Funny thing, she found herself thinking not so much about the law but about Vernon and Gary, Blaise Broussard, Standish and García, and what did any of them have to do with her now?

In Uniontown, Alabama, the land looked like the country around Little Egypt, the radio playing a cowboy ballad.

Wouldn't you give your hand to a friend?
I think we can make it
One more time
If we try,
One more time for all the old times.

Wilma loved every last one of them, and she had a big heart. Her heart had its limits was all. She stayed with Vernon till he stole from her, till Ruby put something on him he couldn't wash off, Gary till he got too crazy and mean, Standish till she couldn't live with his cool politics any longer. Though she left him when he knew too much about her to remember to forget his job, she could love García and the rest, and the feeling could be sweet and sad and calm like the slow Gulfstream rollers that never crest, never break.

For a while Wilma kept the walkie-talkie tuned in to the women in back, straining to catch the fast Spanish. Carmela, the old woman, was well enough to travel, the local doctor had told Standish. The other two, in their thirties, carried infants in slings. The father of the three-year-old girl with a head wound had disappeared into the jungle near La Libertad, the mother said.

In Boston there would be plenty to eat, the women were saying. They'd read in the *Ladies' Home Journal* about fat pills. In America were two-story mansions, flowers on window curtains, toilets where water would flow fresh every time. It was a place *de milagros,* of miracles. The hands didn't dry or crack from the dishes. The face didn't wrinkle, either, for there were no more griefs and worries. Babies did not weaken and die. And there would be a microwave oven to cook a whole meal in thirty seconds and a *máquina* in the kitchen to chew garbage for the whole family, if the family had garbage at all, if they did not themselves eat the rinds of the oranges and lemons and the cool pulp and even the seeds. And the clothes they would wear in America—ay, Chula, ay, Lupita—the pushup bras, the nylons, the blouses of white lace, the high needle heels!

Their hopes made Wilma sad. She knew what it meant to cross a river, looking for someplace. What she found was Jessie Louise, and not such a large space, after all, filled, at times, with every man, woman and kid she had ever made grits for, parents, friends, horses, bird dogs, all of them yelling at once. Thinking of bird dogs, Wilma reached down in front of the driver's seat to scratch Bear behind the ear. A puppy no longer, the Labrador was huge, spreading across the floorboards like a black lake. She'd have to admit she'd have gone nuts without the dog these last months. What she'd never admit was that they slept together in the bunk behind the seat.

Standish had told her there had been another murder of a U.S. narcotics agent, and the Border Patrol was stopping everything coming over, nearly sifting it by hand. She had to watch herself, because anytime something unusual was up García was likely to come sniffing around. She hated the idea of García leaning on her now; he'd be

264

impossible to shake. Wilma remembered hearing Gary say that everything living in South Texas had thorns or horns or fangs. She didn't see any of these on García, but he was armed.

When he came out of the Harlingen office wearing the .357 magnum on his hip like a scalp, she whistled low under her breath.

He didn't bother to joke with her the way he usually did, just asked right away for her license and Bingo Card and wanted to take a look at her log book.

"What's up?" she asked, speaking more quickly than usual from the shock of seeing him after three weeks.

"You hear about Alegría?"

She shook her head.

"Narcotics. They shot him someplace near Guadalajara. We've got orders to run everybody through a hopper. Sorry for the hassle."

She didn't know what to say so she stared at the hair on the back of his left hand gripping the windowsill.

"Go ahead," he said. "I don't want to hold you up."

"Thanks," she said, but she didn't shove off. He kept holding on to the grab rail looking in at her through the window.

"What's on your mind?" she said. A part of her wanted him to ask her to stay.

"Please don't do anything noble," he said. Some careful coolness slipped behind his eyes.

"I wouldn't do anything that'd embarrass either one of us, Mario," she said. "Want to look in back?" She didn't know why she was acting so cocky.

He shook his head, irritated by her challenge. The wets were in big boxes marked "Linens."

"I'll just check the seal," he said, and walked to the back of the trailer.

"I'll just stretch my legs," she said, and climbed out.

The seal was a small tag embossed with numbers connecting two ends of a thin wire cable fastened around the door latch. It was easily cut with wire cutters. Behind her seat Wilma had a sack that held a hundred of these disks exactly like the one on the van door. She also had the electric tool for stamping the numbers on. It was a breeze, making the seal look like the original Wild Goose job, and though every driver on the road knew how it was done, few ever bothered. Most of the furniture she unloaded from people's homes she wouldn't want to sit down in or lie down on or eat off of. A lot of it smelled bad. Besides, what would she do with anybody else's icebox or couch, anybody's king-sized mattress with the important brown stains? All she owned now was a statue of St. Francis, a book of photographs and a few old needlepoint pillows and a gun.

The gun was an old .38 Vernon had made her take with her the last time she had left home.

"I don't need this," she'd told him, "but thanks anyway."

"It's crazy out there," he said.

Then he reached into his pocket and pulled out a blue plastic statue of St. Francis. "If he can take care of my coyotes and ferrets, he'll look out after you, too."

"I'll keep it on the dash," she said. From two feet away his skin had a healthy shine, and his blue eyes were clear ice. He had remembered to shave. Vernon was a strong man, steady on his feet in his middle fifties with plenty to offer a woman, and what was it with her that she couldn't stay? She took the St. Francis, the gun because he needed her to, the photographs of him and the kids because they were the only real protection and her needlepoint pillows for comfort.

García held the seal in his hands, turning it over, examining the edges. Wilma watched his face for giveaway tics. The skin along his cheek was fawn-colored, as smooth as a twenty-year-old's, the only sign of wear a few gray strands in his sideburns. His eyes were the warm, rich brown of expensive leather upholstery. When she got back into the truck, he stood at the window again, so close she could see the whiskers on his cheeks, the flecks of reddish gold in his dark hair. It was the first time in months she'd forgotten to bring him the little sack of peppermint *dulces* she always bought at the drugstore in San Benito.

"The snow is bad in Boston," he said. "Safe trip." Then he bowed to her. "You should stay out of the Northeast," he told her. "Remember the Alamo."

All these months García had been holding back, Standish had told her, waiting until he had the two of them and the illegals in one place. He could have had them a dozen different times, but waited. Now that they'd turned each other loose he was giving her warning. She pumped the engine more than she needed to before heading down the ramp and out into the traffic. It was good that he hadn't seen the gun. Wilma recalled another battle of the Texas revolution in which the Mexican general was decisively defeated.

"Remember San Jacinto," she said, and waved.

Five hours after leaving García, the coffee high ran down and she pulled off and called Oralee, who was living in Houston. It had been months since they'd talked.

"Hey, girl, you still got your wandering boots on?" She couldn't tell Oralee how scared she was.

The voice on the other end was bouncy and aggressive. It was three in the afternoon. "Who the hell's this?"

"It ain't your dear old dad," Wilma said. It took another two hours to get to Houston, but the highway was empty, and the thought of seeing Oralee gave her the first little lift she'd had in months. Swinging the screen door wide, with her hair cut punk style but still shiny, Oralee in the flesh was a Christmas blessing. The two women danced around her tiny living room, hugging each other and hooting, before Wilma asked her if she wanted to make a trip. Oralee never asked why Wilma needed her just then or where she'd been or where she was going. She just packed a duffel in five minutes, fed the parakeet and climbed into the passenger seat.

They spent the night at Wilma's apartment. Oralee was so full of talk Wilma thought she'd split her sides. When Wilma told her they'd be carrying refugees, Oralee said she'd heard plenty about refugees in a year and a half. Her opinions hadn't changed much, except now she'd found Jesus, who gave them a tighter grip. She had things figured.

"Jesus didn't mean for us to try to change things around from the way he made 'em to start with. And Mexicans or Salvadorans or whoever else comes from down there, he made 'em poor so he could keep the rest of us grateful."

"Try explaining that to those people in back," Wilma said.

In a book at the Casa Wilma had read about the Salvadoran custom of making tiny scenes of weddings, painting the lives of the bride and groom, the marimba bands and the lovers on seeds of the *copinal* called "the seeds of God." Since the civil war began, the book said, the villages were periodically emptied by fighting, .the people returning when it was over to gather the dead. When they had written down all the names they knew they poured lime over the bodies until they looked frozen in sudden snow.

When Oralee had found Jesus, she phoned Car's mother, hopped a bus to Lone Star and handed the baby over.

"He says, 'Suffer the little children,' but he didn't say the kids had to suffer. So I says to myself, When she grows up will she be bitchin' if she knows I kept her from her real mama? and I got to admit she would. Plus, I was seein' all these ads everywhere about stolen kids, their mothers and dads with eyes all swole up from cryin'."

They were in a truck stop near Chattanooga when she spotted the tail. Carmela was having trouble breathing, so she'd stopped for a Coke with ice, and saw the two men in plainclothes sitting in a booth, watching her. As soon as she left the checkout line the same two made tracks for a blue unmarked van out front. García wasn't with them.

"I couldn't tell if they were plainclothes border inspectors or some other kind of cop," she told Oralee. "But I'm sure it's the law." She picked up the walkie-talkie, told them to keep quiet in the back, and started earning her keep. After she was safely on the highway, she picked up the Cobra receiver and called for help.

"This is Prairie Fire eastbound at 578. I got some kind of goofy four-wheeler tailin' me with federal plates. Can somebody give me shelter, come on?"

"You ever try this before?" Oralee said.

"You ever been this scared?"

Within two minutes a man's voice came on. "Got you in the scope, Prairie Fire. There's four of us comin' up behind."

She looked in the side mirror and there he was, a shiny blue Kenworth piled high with stacked logs leading three others. It took them five minutes to build a wall around her, filling both lanes, cutting off the van.

She left the big slab at the next exit, then backroaded

it to Morehead City, North Carolina, where she planned to take the ferry to the Outer Banks. By now she was getting a very bad feeling about the trip and wanted to get as far out on the edge of things as she could. On the road map the long barrier islands of the Carolinas looked like two diagonals of a pulled bowstring. Nobody would think of looking for her there. But when she called to make a reservation they told her the ferry from Cedar Island didn't run on a regular basis in winter.

"I got six kids in back and an old lady," she told the man. "We gotta get 'em to a hospital for treatment." Lord, how she'd learned to lie.

The road from Morehead City to Cedar Island was a two-lane crossing small arched drawbridges between swampy islands, the water black in roadside ditches, the grass silver gray and green. Sky like coastal Texas, high and blue, wash on a line. The ferry attendant was twenty-four, tanned and blond. He wore a patch on his khaki shirt that said CEDAR ISLAND FERRY. When he saw Jessie Louise his jaw lost altitude and he nearly dropped his gum.

"Now wait a minute. You didn't say a thing about no eighteen-wheeler." He put his hand up in front of her face. "We got weight regulations."

"And I got real live people in trouble, son. Are you gonna be responsible for these people not gettin' medical attention? Maybe dyin'?"

Oralee leaned forward and turned her exquisite tragic face on the attendant. "There's a two-month-old baby back there, hon," she said. "Terrible case of appendicitis." The young man got a good look at Oralee's black eyes. Then he caught sight of the Lab.

"Looks like you got your hands full, sure enough," he said. He never asked why they thought their passengers would get medical help on the National Seashore, but it wouldn't have mattered. It might have been easier turning Mother Teresa down.

They didn't run into any traffic along Okracoke Island, where the breakers were splashing on the tops of the dunes to her right, the gulls blowing like scraps of newsprint overhead. She kept looking over her shoulder for the blue van, but the road was clear behind her. Once she stopped to talk to the old woman in back, give her a local root beer in a paper cup. Carmela took the cup in her skinny yellow hands and drank while Wilma supported her head, but she was shaking so hard most of the drink spilled.

"Shock," Wilma told Oralee. "She's catching up with those memories, or they're catching up with her." She felt sorriest for the old ones, who had already endured so much, and the youngest, who'd have to dream about these things for the next forty or fifty years.

"Don't I remember something about 'Come unto me all ye that travail?' Didn't Jesus say something like that?" she asked Oralee.

"He did. So what?"

"Wake up," Wilma said. "If this old lady isn't worn out and travailed all to pieces my name is Madonna. Ain't it my Christian duty?"

"Nope," Oralee said, holding up a small mirror and tweezers, plucking a stray hair between her eyebrows. She laid the mirror down in her lap and grinned. "Pray for 'em," she said. "That's the way to get His attention."

Raining in Kitty Hawk, late afternoon. Hiss of tires on the wet road. Oralee asleep against the far window, Wilma lulled into some kind of poem. Was it like this at Kitty Hawk for the brothers, she wondered? Did the clouds fall over the dune like a sunk tent? Did water turn sapphire and blow into ridges? Over the Oregon Inlet the tires spit and thunked over tar mendings and raindrops exploded and smeared under wipers. Orville, Wilbur, did your wings get wet and lift you still?

Average speed for the last twenty minutes was fifteen miles an hour, slowing to ten when they hit the Kennedy Expressway into Boston. The snow was three inches thick and rutted across six lanes approaching Boston from the south.

"I don't much care for these places," Oralee told Wilma. "Roll up your windows, lock your doors, and watch your mirrors at intersections. These punks'll jump on your grab rail or climb up top, anything for a kick. They'll be so wigged-out crazy with crack, angel dust, whatever, you can't ever tell if they know what they're doing enough not to fall under your wheels."

It was eight on a Friday evening when they hit the city limits, streets gleaming like licorice and a fine spitting sleet bouncing off the shiny black surface. Wilma exited on State Street, and in minutes she was winding through Boston's downtown canyons, walls rising seventy-five stories on either side of narrow streets with damnyankee names: Tremont, Chatham, Clinton, Franklin. Signs along the way indicated Revolutionary landmarks. Faneuil Hall, Old North Church, Paul Revere's house. Too bad not to see more of the city of the founding fathers than a truck terminal and the North End church, the house on Beacon Hill where they were scheduled to unload tomorrow. If she ever found her way out of this maze.

Making a left on Clinton she ran the van up over the sidewalk. Pedestrians kept plowing through the muck— wealthy women in furs and high boots, shopworn secretaries and shopgirls in polo coats or trenchcoats with collars turned up. By the time they reached the Combat Zone, Wilma hadn't seen a Boston punk yet, or any kids, for that matter. In the dark rain the city seemed a place no children could live. Too many brick walls, not enough sun. These people on the way home would be too chilled when they got there to embrace, though a good many must be doing something like it in the Combat Zone. She'd heard this neighborhood was a raunchy place, and she was prepared to be shocked, but wasn't. The neighborhood was sleazy enough, streets lined with old tenements converted to sex joints with the usual signs: Totally Nude Girls, Completely Nude Girls, and One Hundred Percent Nude Girls. Topless, Bottomless, Nudie Cuties, Pussies Galore, and Steam Heat, Discreet Escort Services, Passion Flower and Flower Drum Song massage parlors. A dive called Boobie Ruby's and one named Bodacious Ta-tas, with the phone number emblazoned in red. Doors to adult bookstores and sex shows stood open and inviting, and in spite of the wind leggy girls in net stockings and cutaway coats and top hats lolled outside, grinding their hips, waving the customers in. These skinny, sexy girls were pathetic-cute.

At the corner of LaGrange and Washington Wilma stopped at a light. The intersection was crowded with Chinese and Vietnamese women in black slacks and satin kimonos, sleek black girls with Medusa braids and high leather boots, blondes with crew cuts, dresses slit to mid-thigh. The women walked against the light, as if they owned the street, ignoring the squad car pulled up next to the truck headed north on Washington. A cop in the passenger seat rolled down his window and yelled at Oralee.

"Hit 'em, hit 'em. They deserve to be hit!" A tall Chinese girl with hair to her waist put her arms around a lamp post, leaned over and flipped her skirt up over her hips. Her white buttocks gleamed under the hazy light. Oralee clapped and whistled.

"Run over the bitches," the cop yelled. "Whose side you on?"

Oralee came back too fast, as usual. "The bitches, for sure, babycakes."

"Jaywalkin'," the cop said. "They're makin' it a varsity sport. Gowan up to Harvard Square any tima day or night and there's three hundred people crossin' against the light."

"But it's the Combat Zone," Wilma grinned.

"And you tell me what ain't," the cop said, and turned the corner, tires squealing.

"Try to keep your lip in line, girl," Wilma said. "All we need is for one of these Yankees to run us in now."

Oralee watched a couple of transvestites swivel their narrow hips across the street. Their legs looked okay.

"I'll be good if you'll just get me outa this town and back to where the whores don't dress up like men or men like whores, and there's not a bunch of in-between people you can't tell what they are."

She took the next right into the North End and saw the blue van fifty yards behind, the same two guys in the front seat. No way to lose them in the maze of narrow streets lined with bakeries and cafés and meat markets. Though the windows were dark she could see by street lamps long fingers of bread pointing and the peeled, plucked carcasses of small animals and birds hung by their necks and legs. Ducks with big webbed feet and yellow bills dangled in the windows as naked as nudie dancers.

She stopped the truck on Prince Street under an expressway half a block from St. Stephen's Church. At one A.M. nobody moved except an orange cat cruising the gutters. Beneath the single old-fashioned iron lamp the pavement was slate blue and wet under her feet as she walked past concrete pillars toward the gray stone building. She lifted the heavy pewter knocker and let it fall against the door, which had a tiny window covered with a metal grate she could peek through. While she waited for somebody to answer she shot a look back over her shoulder at the blue van pulling to a stop sixty yards behind the trailer. The dim light didn't show the faces inside.

She wanted to put two fingers to her lips and whistle to Oralee to be on guard. But it was too late to do much of anything now that the Yankee border investigators knew they'd been seen. Why did they bother stationing Border Patrol people way up here, anyway? She'd been amazed when a priest from Corpus Christi wrote down the address in Boston's North End and told her Father Grapelli had been taking in refugees for over a year now.

Grapelli. Would an Italian understand Spanish? The priest who opened the door wore a salt-and-pepper beard and a black turtleneck and looked like Jerry Lewis. He took her hand and pulled her in out of the chill.

"Cuppa coffee?"

"No thanks, Reverend—I mean Father. I've got eight people outside. Immigration is sitting on our tail out there ready to bite."

She dropped into a cracked leather chair and rubbed her hands together. The rectory office was a handsome room, warm with flowered wallpaper and cherry bookshelves, photos of black kids and Italian kids in softball uniforms, some of the players holding up trophies.

"Nice going," she said, setting down one of the pictures. "Did I blow your cover stopping here?"

"City champs," the priest said. "Two years running. Don't give it a second thought. Six months we've been under surveillance. Sometimes we got twelve in the base-

ment watching Johnny Carson. By the way, name's Leo."
He held out a hairy hand.

"Pleased to meet you," she said, but she didn't have
time for Emily Post. "I don't know what to do now. I can
take them to the house on Beacon Hill, maybe slip them in
with the furniture . . ."

She didn't sound convincing.

He told her to head for Cambridge; the whole town was
a sanctuary. Handing her a scribbled address of a safe
house there, he pumped her hand like a mayor and shooed
her out the door.

"Thanks," she said, stepping out into the night.

"You're the one with thanks coming," the priest said.
"Y'know, this thing has given my parish a kick in the
butt. Most of my people are out of work. Plenty over sixty-
five, on welfare. This thing has them steaming, gives them
something to get out of the rack for. Last week we had
forty-eight people in the parish house writing Tip O'Neill
about it."

"How many Central Americans you got here?" she
asked.

"Over fifty thousand," he told her. "Crazy. A lot of
them in the North End."

Her mama thought all Italians were Mafia. "Stay away
from wetbacks and Italians. You're nice people."

"I'm sick of being nice," she told her mother.

Wilma walked across the street, hands jammed deep
into her pockets, the address in Cambridge crumpled into
her right fist. Opening the door of the cab, she slid onto the
seat, watching the van in the rear view.

"What took so long?" Oralee said, rubbing her eyes.
"Was he giving you the last rites?"

"Bigger news," Wilma said. "The whole damned town
of Cambridge, Massachusetts, just voted itself safe for

Central Americans. Now if we can get across the river before these drugstore cowboys behind us get us roped and tied we'll be okay."

Oralee whistled through her teeth. "Where's the bus station?" she said.

Wilma was quiet for several minutes, turning a corner and handing Oralee a Boston street map. Illegal transport wasn't what Oralee needed right now; she was starting junior college after the Christmas break.

"We're a few minutes from South Station. I think some kind of buses leave from there. Might take you to New York or Provincetown. At least you'd be free of this business."

Oralee threw a fit.

"You think my mama never taught me manners? You think I got no pride? I signed up for this party knowing what they might be servin' for dessert. Forget it. What're we gonna do now?"

Wilma switched on the overhead lamp, pointed at the map spread out on Oralee's knees. "Look at the map," she said. "Find me the nearest bridge across that river."

"Longfellow all right?"

"Anything close crossing the Charles," Wilma said. The address the priest had given her was on Berkeley Street. She decided to take Hampshire Street west, drive down Cambridge Avenue past the Harvard Co-op and turn on St. Johns. By then it would be getting light. She wasn't sure they let big rigs in there, but this was no time for detours. She looked at her watch. Five forty-five. Too early for nasty traffic. She had no idea what might happen when she started to unload the refugees.

It was nearly six when she swung the truck onto the expressway running beside the river. The four lanes were filling up with the earliest risers, commuters from Medford and Arlington and Bedford and Watertown making it in early to get an hour's paperwork done before the secretaries came in with their distracting hair. Big refrigerated food trucks and silver tank trucks homed in on Safeway and A&P warehouses, milk trucks gleaming, EDIBLES ONLY written on their sleek fuselages, Sunbeam bread trucks with the blue gingham girl spreading her chubby arms across the side of the van, sweet enough to feed the world. Oil trucks hauling heating fuel passed—Texaco, Amoco, Gulf, Amergas, Mobil, Tenneco, Exxon—and moving trucks—Rodeway, World Wide, Red Ball, Allied, the Careful Movers. All the way downriver they ran, provisioners converging on Boston and Cambridge, running lights ablaze like tiaras, the line of brake lights glowing on and off, and the whole train of vehicles slowing as the expressways started to clog. A long semi pulled up beside her. The driver was saying something. The truck's logo read HEARTLAND EXPRESS. Wilma rolled down her window, and the man in a wool cap grinned and said, "Happy Valentine's Day."

"I thought it was two days before Christmas," she said, grinning at him because he looked nice, his graying hair poking out around the edges of his red cap.

"Yeah, sweetheart, so it is," he said, "but every day I get a look at a doll like you it's bluebirds and roses. Beats Father Christmas all to hell." He blew her a kiss.

"Same to you, handsome," she yelled and waved her hand.

She was nearing the end of the Longfellow bridge. Traffic slowed to a crawl. She didn't want to be in the wrong lane with the van still trailing her, and what looked like a dense thicket of winding streets on the map of the city ahead. What did it mean that Cambridge was a sanctuary? She was sure it didn't mean the feds would throw roses, that they couldn't come into town and do what they had to. The lights on the bridge railing went out as she was halfway across, and her vision blurred a little, the brake lights ahead of her running together in a pink stream.

"Breaker 19, Breaker 19 for the Braintree Bomber." The voice was young, pretty.

"I hear you, hon. Where you headed?"

"Plymouth, Provincetown, back home and on up to Montreal, sweets. Wish you 'uz here."

The voices bled into one another like the lights, rose and fell in waves, the waves crackling with static, stinging the ears.

"Everybody hustling to get someplace else," Oralee said, her voice sounding tired and strained, her face white as a peeled onion.

"I 'uz hearin' on Sunday it's supposed to be a terrific day," one of the voices was saying. "How 'bout us rentin' one a them little dinghies and sailin' in the Charles?"

"Cheez, Sunday I'll be out in Arizona, California maybe."

"Ten-four, Nomad, catcha later."

"Ten-four, tell 'em old Rattlesnake's in town."

A high little-girl voice came on through the static.

"Iceman, this is Twister, come back?" Then a pause of thirty seconds before somebody answered, maybe Iceman.

"Oh, little ladayuh," he said.

García was waiting for her at the end of the bridge, standing next to a second unmarked van, wearing the same dark greenish-brown uniform he wore in Harlingen, carrying the same pistol on his hip. Another officer with a bullhorn was yelling something at her. Before pulling over, Wilma only had time to whisper, "Sit tight, kid," and to give Oralee's hand a squeeze.

When she climbed down from the truck, her legs cramping from sitting so long and her left ankle swollen, García's face was gray. She had to lean against the front fender.

"How are you, *señora?*" he said. He looked steadily at her, sorry to be where he was.

She held out her hand, palm flat over the ground, rolling it a little like a boat tossing in a chop. She didn't say anything.

"I'm here on business," he said.

"You've never had any business with me, Mario," she said, softly.

"*Con permiso,* I believe I do now. This has been a long time coming."

"You mean you ran all the way up country after me?" she said. "Makes me feel like somebody."

"I always knew you were somebody, *señora,*" García said.

21

WAKING IN THE BUS outside the Houston Greyhound Terminal, she knew right away Vernon wouldn't be there to meet her. Outside on the greasy pavement a couple of drunks hunkered down against the wall next to a young Latino with a guitar case and a blind man with a shepherd dog. It was funny how she always knew when Vernon was lying and when she should call him on it. She suspected he wouldn't make it when she called him from Boston two days earlier, suspected it from the false, hearty note in his voice, maybe, but let it go. Sure, he said, he'd be there. Glad to. She looked at her watch; they were an hour into the new year. If he wasn't here now he'd never be, and she'd have to hitch.

He must be wasted somewhere, and she only hoped it wasn't on the road. They used to throw a New Year's Day party. She'd mix a batch of her mother's eggnog: one dozen eggs, a pound of sugar, a quart of whipping cream and a pint of red whiskey. The neighbors would come around eleven, some of them still shaky from the night before, and they'd start drinking eggnog and eating blackeyed peas, and pretty soon the Cotton Bowl would come on and everybody'd be yelling and cheering, making bets. When the game was over and Texas had won, the women retired to the kitchen to fix fried oysters and hush puppies. Sometimes in the middle of the afternoon three or four men would rip off their ties, put on waders and go out on the winter prairie after geese. Wilma loved the sight of those men with their arms around each other, wobbling down the porch steps, going home to get their guns. By now the eggnog had run out, and somebody went for beer, which took a lot of legwork on New Year's Day. It always turned out to be a good party. Nobody went home until midnight.

She'd hoped Vernon would meet her, so she'd have time in the car to tell him how she'd lost the truck. Only it was going to take more than an hour to get all that out, how she started with the Central Americans in the first place and why she had decided finally that Oralee was right, and the risk wasn't worth what you paid. After working a year in the sanctuary movement Wilma had to admit she and the others weren't doing much to straighten out the refugee snarl, and anyhow, there were limits to hospitality.

There was a lot to hash out with Vernon. Still, they might have had a quiet visit together for the first time in a couple of years. She could open the window somewhere around Hungerford and smell the nice winter wet-earth smells, hear the geese honking overhead, count the stars in Orion's belt. Wilma might have had a chance to get used to the idea that Jessie Louise was gone, that she'd have to use every dime she'd saved to pay her defense lawyer, that she'd probably have to borrow some money from Vernon. If he had any.

When she stepped out of the bus the driver was already down on the sidewalk opening the luggage compartment, and sleepwalking passengers stood in front of the gaping hold as if waiting for someone to hand them a bowl of oatmeal. The Boston lay worker held on to the Guatemalan string bag she'd bought at the Harvard Coop, clutched it with both hands like a bridal bouquet. The Bostonians she'd met always treated Wilma as if they thought she ate rattlesnake for breakfast.

"Thanks for talking to me," the girl said, showing her fillings. "You've done a terrific job. I hope I can do as well."

Wilma looked at her, remembering what it felt like to begin. Behind the girl an Italian woman stood patient as a plaster saint, a little boy asleep on her shoulder. Two seventeen-year-olds kept the caps pulled down over their eyes and leaned against the wall facing the bus, not caring if any of their luggage had arrived because everything that mattered was in the pockets of their jeans. They had the soft, pale faces of night prowlers.

The girl still looked at her expectantly. Wilma ransacked her heart for an appropriate feeling. She didn't have it in her.

"Work on your Spanish," she said. "Good luck." She dodged past the girl and pushed through a heavy glass door into the waiting room, where 150 plastic seats offered TVs you could slip a quarter into for fifteen minutes, enough for half a soap and three commercials. She walked past these comforts to the opposite end of the nearly empty room and put a nickel in the wall phone. After a few tries she reached Blaise up in East Texas with one of his families.

"What you doin' home on New Year's Eve?" she said.

"Who's this chile?" His voice made her feel warm.

"It's Wilma, Blaise. How are you?"

"Holdin' on, lost a few teeth since I saw you," he said. "Where you at?"

She told him Houston, and he said he'd pick her up. Only it'd take him a while to get to her. He'd see her at ten.

"Ten when?" she said, a little groggy from sixteen hundred miles.

"Ten this mornin'," he said. *"Au 'voir."*

When the Coca-Cola bottling truck she was riding in made the last wide turn around the caved-in cotton gin three miles her side of town, Wilma already understood things were different at home. The bottles in back leaned over and smacked and rattled against each other, and Blaise asked her again for directions. At the crossroads Wilma had to blink a couple of times before she got her bearings. The abandoned general store where Ruby had her lending library was transformed by a coat of white paint. Somebody had done the trim around the four front windows in Mediterranean blue. The benches in front of the combination-lock mailboxes were painted blue to match, and there was a sign next to the mailboxes that read LITTLE EGYPT COMMUNITY CENTER.

"This it, down here to the right?" Blaise asked, and Wilma nodded. The truck rattled and squealed to a stop in front of her house. She recognized the small wooden bridge first, then the two pear trees stretching wintry limbs to the flat blue sky. Seeing those trees for the first time in months Wilma sent a confused message to the Lord. It had something to do with Vernon's being sober enough to understand what Wilma was up to and sweet enough to forgive her for it. She wasn't dead sure herself what she was up to, but she wasn't asking to be let back in under Vernon's big arm. Just because she had lost the truck and would probably have to let go of her license, too, and pay a whopping fine on top of that, she wasn't about to snuggle up to Vernon and beg him to take her back. He might not be interested, anyway. *Grow up,* she told herself sternly. *You left that man years ago.*

She sat daydreaming for a minute or two before she noticed the giant crawfish sign rising above the pear trees. The crawfish was painted a deep Chinese red. Its two-foot feelers were pointing at the grain elevators, whose white tops rose over the oak grove west of the house. It had small beady eyes that stuck out from its head, and, despite the tiny gold crown it wore, its attitude was hostile, the pincers wide open, fully extended, menacing. A sign beneath the crawfish read:

CRAWFISH KINGDOM.
BEST DAMNED CRAWFISH
THIS SIDE OF
THE ATCHAFALAYA

Wilma wondered where the Atchafalaya was, and whether Vernon had learned to cook or found somebody to do it for him.

"This all right for you, *chère?*" Blaise asked. "I got to make it to Lake Charles 'fore night."

"Sure, Blaise. Can't thank you enough." If anybody could make her feel she fit into the world someplace it was Blaise. He hadn't asked her any questions on the way, and Wilma was thankful. Now she leaned over and gave him a smart little pucker on the cheek.

He put his two hands on her cheeks. "Go see how your old man makin' it, girl. Give him some of that good lazy love."

As she walked up the path to her house Wilma saw a small line forming at the front door. Most of the men were dressed in new jeans, the women in jeans and sweaters and three or four gold chain necklaces. What were all these Republicans doing at Vernon's party?

" 'Scuse me," she said, brushing past a woman with blue hair and a mink jacket.

"Hey, just a second," the woman said. "You got to wait your turn."

"It *is* my turn," Wilma said. She walked up the concrete steps onto the screened porch that ran the length of the house. Eight round tables were set up there, and groups of four and six people were throwing off their jackets and rolling up their sleeves to get at the five-pound baskets of boiled crawfish set in the middle of the tables. Red sauce was flying through the air, and people were laughing and carrying on. Someone yelled at Vernon to come on out of the kitchen and bring him a bib. She stepped into the living room, pressing through the wall of backs turned her way. Inside it was close and hot. The floor wasn't strong enough to support the weight of all these strangers.

Wilma didn't recognize a single stick of furniture, a single pillow thrown at that certain angle on a chair that would have suggested she'd lived here. A photograph of Vernon and the boys on a John Deere combine was missing from the corner where the piano used to be. Vernon's diploma from Texas A & M was gone, and the Ducks Unlimited plaque honoring his twenty-five years as a member. In the spot where Wilma's set of souvenir spoons once hung was a three-by-five-foot Pearl Beer sign, depicting a moving waterfall on the Guadalupe River, the water an unnatural electric blue, foaming over large rocks.

She started breaking out in cool perspiration. The overstuffed armchairs with the floral chintz covers. Her needlepoint footstool. Gone. Her grandmother's mahogany Victorian desk. Her legs were shaky and she needed to sit down, but couldn't find an empty chair because her living room was crammed with ten round tables full of laughing fools licking their fingers and pinching the heads off smaller versions of the King Crawfish on the front lawn. Most of the men were middle-aged, might have been

286

land men or Yankees, and some of the women were second wives. A few were girlfriends. Wilma could tell a girl-friend by her makeup, and by the way her eyes kept roaming around the room while she pretended to be listening to what her boyfriend was saying.

She missed Cornelia and Zeno and Rosetta Clayburg, all the gang she used to see around. Devel Edwards and Jeanette, who cooked up a lavish jambalaya dinner on June Teenth and invited the whole town. Timmy Minos and his snakes and Calvin Merriweather, who could always be counted on to come up with a derogatory remark about somebody, not just an ordinary slur, but a fine, full-bodied insult. She missed Vernon and didn't know what she'd say to him. Probably she ought to ask him for a divorce.

She and Oralee had thrashed it out about divorce before they hit Boston, Oralee taking the hard-line funda-mentalist view of marriage, and Wilma trying to argue for something looser.

"Did you have a church wedding?" Oralee wanted to know.

"Sure. Everybody did in those days."

"Well, then you must've used words pretty close to 'till death do us part.'"

"Sure. What about it?"

"Well, don't you know God wrote those words? Don't you know he meant every last word he said?" Oralee was leaning back against the passenger window. Her face had that mother-of-pearl shine it always took on when she shifted into preaching.

"I was too young to know if He meant them or not, and besides, how was I to know God wrote the prayer book?"

Wilma was pretty certain she hadn't thought too hard about the words twenty years ago. Since then Vernon had been an okay father and a good husband, and, Wilma figured, looking back over the years of her marriage, she hadn't done such a bad job herself. She had loved, honored and obeyed, all right. Cooked and cleaned and pressed and baked and doctored until she wore out and sat down. When she sat down she had time to think about what else love might mean besides those acts of care and duty and what "honor" and "obey" meant when applied to the husband. She guessed they meant he shouldn't mess around, and she had to admit Vernon had been pretty good about that as far as she knew. Until Ruby. A couple of times Wilma had intercepted glances between Vernon and Kelly Burkhalter, the wife of the town veterinarian, and she supposed they might've met one another a few times, but it didn't last long. Kelly caught hepatitis from a bad oyster, turned a brilliant saffron yellow and had to go to bed for three months. Vernon moped around the house for a week, saying little. Wilma made three pies that week and washed her hair four times.

She thought now that she might have a handle on love. It wasn't roses and bluebirds and Whitman Samplers, hardly ever a black satin nightgown. What it was, she realized, was being ready to make repairs. But there was a difference between a minor collision and a wreck. In all the years she had been married to Vernon he had never given her reason to think it occurred to him that she might have something to do besides keeping his house and fixing the okra and tomatoes the way he liked and wearing Chanel No. 5 to bed. Love, honor and obey. Now that she considered it, Wilma decided that if they wanted marriage to hold up they'd have to change the language.

When she finally shouldered her way into her kitchen Wilma was so glad to see Devel Edwards standing in front of a restaurant stove she nearly grabbed him around the neck and kissed him. She didn't, because his wife Jeanette was at another stove next to his and wouldn't have liked it. Fifteen people crowded into the kitchen, half of them pulling lettuce, chopping onions, slicing chili *petíns* into small murderous pieces. This was more like it. Wilma took a couple of steps toward Devel, pausing as he turned and faced her and blinked a couple of times before his face crinkled up like wadded paper, and he showed all the teeth he owned.

"Hidy, Wilma," he said, dropping the towel he was holding and grabbing her hand. Devel's hand felt good in hers, strong and dry, the calluses hard like field-dried corn against her palm. He handed her a long wooden spoon.

"Would you mind takin' a turn here while I go find me some more filé gumbo?" Wilma took the spoon and looked into the kettle. Everything in there looked like it belonged.

"That's some of my crawfish gumbo. Take a taste," he said.

Wilma took a sip from the spoon. The gumbo had just the right balance of bay leaf and cayenne and filé gumbo. It had okra and tomatoes in it, and rice and a mixture of seafood impossible to identify. But there were plenty of crawfish in it, all right.

"Hi, Jeanette," Wilma said, turning to her right. Jeanette kept right on chopping okra with an eight-inch butcher knife.

"How you doin'?" Jeanette looked at Wilma, cocking her head to one side. "Seems t'me you've been getting a new kind of exercise. Yes ma'am, sneakin' into one of those spas." Jeanette was still as wide as a barge.

"Trimming down, Jeanette," Wilma confessed. "Traveling lighter."

"Where you been? Looks like we've all been so busy down here we ain't had time to miss you."

"I don't believe Vernon knows I left yet." Wilma grinned. The mention of Vernon's name produced a vague expression on Jeanette's face, like that of an Alzheimer's patient.

"Look here, ever'body," Jeanette called out in a voice a hair too hearty, "Wilma's back."

If Wilma had thought it strange that in the last five minutes no one had noticed her, she was now suddenly in the center of the kitchen with fifteen pairs of eyes riveted on her. She wiped the hair off her forehead and blushed and smiled shyly, having no idea where to begin.

"Hi," she said, tentatively. "Is this my welcome-home party?" They looked at her blankly. Several people giggled.

"Whose party is this?" she asked. There was a fairly long pause before Devel said in a false jocular tone. "It's yours, honey."

"Why, Wilma, you look like you could use a glass of lemonade." Ruby was suddenly at her side, clutching her around the waist. "Somebody bring poor Wilma a chair. She looks like she's about to faint." Behind her thick lenses Ruby's eyes swam with sympathy. She fanned Wilma with an old issue of *Texas Highways*.

"Look at my precious baby, Will. Just take a look at this sweet face." It was old Miss Cornelia with a baby in her arms. She still looked like a mummy somebody'd just unwrapped, only tonight she was out of her wheelchair and up on her feet, standing on those toothpick legs, and pretty steady at that.

"I'm glad you're better, Miss Cornelia," Wilma said. "Did you find a Fountain of Youth somewhere or a new doctor?"

"It's this baby. Her mama had to go to work in town, and you can't take care of a baby in no wheelchair." The baby was two, on her feet and on the move. She'd slip

290

down to all fours now and then to make her way through the forest of legs in the kitchen. The cooks stepped carefully, as if the baby were a litter of kittens.

Wilma wanted to ask Devel where Vernon was, but it seemed a question only a tourist would ask.

Eight-year-old Rosie LaBelle walked up to her chair and picked up Wilma's hand.

" 'Scuse me Miz Hemshoff," she said, "but Momma says would you like a little spot of elderberry wine?"

When Wilma started checking things out around the kitchen she had a hard time keeping herself nailed down. A great many improvements had taken place in her absence. There were tiny blue flowered valances on the windows, some small glass shelves with potted violets growing on them, and some cutesy plaster decorations hanging on the walls: a pair of Dutch children with white caps and wooden shoes; Wynken, Blynken and Nod in a boat. Above the sink hung a stainless-steel rack holding cooking pots and implements, large aluminum kettles and heavy metal spoons with black handles, and one copper frying pan. Wilma wondered where all her cast-iron skillets had gone that heated up so nice and even, and the big earthenware bowls she used for mixing bread.

Next to the sink a tall woman stood with her back to Wilma, one hand on her hip, the other chopping tomatoes with a long knife. She wore a white peasant blouse falling off one shoulder, and a pair of purple satin Jordache jeans. Every now and then she would barely turn her head in Wilma's direction, never looking directly at her but sideways through long black lashes. Wilma wondered why the woman would get all made up like she was just to come over to the house to cook. She tugged at Jeanette's sleeve and whispered.

"Who's that?"

Jeanette's big beacon eyes swept the room.

"Who's that you mean?"

"You know good and well who I mean. Who's that chippie in the satin pants?"

"Her? Oh, that's Ruby's cousin, Marie. She ran fresh out of husbands and rent money sometime last winter so she left N'awlins and moved in with Ruby. Marie," she called out. "Honey. Come ovah heah, will you please?" Wilma thought Jeanette's voice unnecessarily loud. Approaching the two women, Marie put one foot in front of the other as if she were stepping across a river stone by stone, and held out a cool, smooth hand.

"It's a pleasure," she said to Wilma in a voice like grass in the wind. She might as well have been wearing a sandwich board with GIRLFRIEND written on it.

"How do you do," Wilma said, taking in the big black eyes heavily outlined in ochre, the eyelids a blue never seen in the sky. She had rubbed spots of red into her cheekbones and pinned a black braid into a complicated figure-eight knot at the back of her sleek head. The rest of her was sleek and complicated, too.

"Welcome home, Wilma. You been travelin'?" Marie's smile showed teeth that had never required a dentist.

"No," Wilma said. "Working. I drive a truck."

"Is that right? Where's the truck at? I always was crazy to sit up in one of those big rigs and see how it feels."

Wilma snorted.

"What's that?" Marie asked, cocking her head.

Wilma coughed deeply for as long as she was able.

"Vernon's told me enough about you so I feel like we've met before," Marie said, looking even more like a girlfriend. Wilma couldn't bear the weight of those eyes, boring in, trying to get under her skin. She turned her eyes away, looking everywhere but into Marie's unlined face, a face that her husband might have held between both his hands and kissed. Who could blame him?

"Where is Vernon?" Wilma called out in a clear, loud voice.

"Don't he be out back watching that boilin' pot, mixing up that crawfish boil?" Jeanette said, in the voice doctors use speaking to children before their shots. "He's right out that back door, honey. I bet he be tickled to see you."

Wilma laughed shortly. "Sure he's crazy to see me. Me and the IRS."

Jeanette wiped her hands on her apron. "I'll go get 'im right this minute, Will," she said, and, trimming her sails, tacked out the door.

Wilma leaned against the sink. What she had been missing, what she hadn't been able to put her finger on, were Vernon's pets. The hawk on his homemade stand, the ferrets in their cages—where had they gone? She longed for the musky ferret odor and the crinkly, rusty sound of the hawk's feathers shuffling like a deck of cards. She let her eyes wander out the kitchen door and into the dining room, lit with imitation ships' lanterns, its white walls hung with framed posters of Greek ports and French fishing villages.

"For God's sake," Wilma said out loud, "he's turned my home into a San Francisco fern bar."

"I liked it better with the ferrets," Wilma said, once she was finally face-to-face with Vernon. He had his long white apron rolled up and flipped over his arm, and as he bent to kiss Wilma on the cheek the tall, starched chef's hat tipped over and fell into her face.

Wilma wiped the tears out of her eyes.

"What in the name of sky-blue heaven are you doing here, Vernon?" she asked. He was wearing a red T-shirt with a four-line message printed on the front:

PINCH ME
PEEL ME
FEEL ME
EAT ME

And below these words in larger letters:

VERNON HEMSHOFF'S CRAWFISH KINGDOM

"It's my new business, honey," Vernon told her. "Soon as I got the farm goin' good I started a restaurant. You know, there's not an awful lot of people that'll eat crawfish, that knows you can eat 'em. A crawfish is just another lowdown varmint as far as the grassroots majority is concerned."

"That's all he is as far as I'm concerned," Wilma said shortly. He didn't even let this slow him down.

"Then you're in real good company, sugar," he said. "Most people figure a crawfish is just an oversized roach. But these fish we're raisin' out here is as good as anything out of the Atchafalaya, I guarantee." He paused for breath. He must have gotten hot under that hat. Wilma held back an impulse to reach up and wipe the moisture from his forehead.

"How are you, sugar?" Vernon said finally, his round blue eyes looking into her face as if he really wanted an answer.

"I guess I've been better, Vernon," Wilma said. She didn't know how to begin her story, or how to continue it or end it, either. All she knew was that he looked like a patch of crimson clover, and she wanted more than anything to lie down in his arms.

"Can we talk someplace?" Wilma said. Vernon looked at his watch. Then he turned and looked over his shoulder at Devel and Jeanette and Marie, who were staring into the kettles of gumbo like professors looking at archaeological fill.

He led the way upstairs and down the long hall to the bedroom. While she lived at home Wilma had kept this room clean and uncluttered so it could be a hideout for her once the kids left for school. When she'd left Little Egypt, the bedroom had held just the queen-sized bed and cane-seat rocking chair, and a sewing table with a hidden lever that pushed to open a secret well where she kept her embroidery needles and small spools of thread. Wilma would sew or read travel magazines for hours there.

When Vernon opened the door and set her grip down, Wilma drew back at the sight of the junk. The bed was covered with stacks of bills and letters and postcards she had mailed from places like Pennybacker's Pig Farm in Oneonta, New York, and Boot Hill in North Dakota. A homemade bookshelf along the east wall held scientific books and pamphlets with titles like *Fish Farming for Fun and Profit,* and *Aquaculture, Feeding the Future.* Vernon had certainly become a reader. On the table next to the bed was a copy of *The Ancient Art of Falconry.* A wig stand on top of the bookcase was covered by a brown leather hood with eye pieces sewn into it.

She bent over and started throwing things off the bed. A Sears catalogue, a letter from the Houston Lighting and Power Company, and another from the County Welfare Department, several from the Texas Raptor Society and the Restaurant Association. Wilma had a powerful urge to open all this mail and had to remind herself it was not addressed to her.

"Here, just stack that stuff on the floor," Vernon said.

Wilma sat down on the edge of the bed, suddenly bone-tired. "Vernon," she said, "where do you sleep?"

He paused a second too long. When he spoke his voice was rough.

"Hell, Wilma, where do you think I sleep?" he said. "I sleep right here."

She resisted the impulse to slap him.

He finished cleaning off the bed, pulled back the white spread on one side, and plumped the pillows.

"There you go," he said. "Why don't you take you a nice long soak in the tub and crawl in and call it a day?"

"But what is going on, Vernon? I don't know who all those people are downstairs." Her voice shook, and there was an awful sinking in her stomach.

"No time to talk now, sugar. I got to go back and keep an eye on the pot. We'll have lots of time for talking." He patted her on the head and left the room.

Wilma had plenty of time to think about Vernon's lying to her as she unpacked the dirty clothes in her duffel. Well, what did she expect him to reply to a question like that? From the bottom of the bag she pulled out a small package, untied the blue ribbon around it and spread the contents on the bed. Strange how she'd never had fancy underwear until she hit her forties, and never anything like this fine peach silk from the Philippines embroidered in tiny gray stitches. She had bought the panties and bra and camisole top on Newbury Street in Boston. There had been a couple of days before the hearing when she and Oralee had time to sightsee and shop and visit museums. Wilma felt fine walking past cafés and shops, looking at women dressed in leather and lace, with spiky orange and yellow hair and long Oriental eyes. Lots of the men looked like exotic birds, with shaved heads topped by brilliant cockades. Cockatoos. Birds of Paradise. On Newbury Street nobody had anything important to do except eat frozen Italian ices and swish around.

On one of their outings Oralee hung back in front of a store named Frills.

"Nothing in here I want," she said, eying the antique lace bloomers in the window. "No fancy feathers for me." For somebody good-looking Oralee sure had something against fixing herself up. From her earlier days of low-cut T-shirts and cut-off jeans she'd taken to wearing boys' Levi's, rugby shirts and no makeup. She sat in a chair next to the door of the shop and scowled while Wilma went into the dressing room with the camisole and boxer shorts in the palest shade of apricot. When she stepped out again to admire herself in the skinny mirror, she didn't look like Katharine Hepburn, but fell purely in love with her own reflection anyway. The line of the little shorts just grazed the bottom of her butt, and the color set off Wilma's white skin and the russet of her hair. She stood in front of the mirror doing slow pirouettes for at least seven minutes before Oralee stuck her head around the corner and made a face at her.

"Consider the lilies of the field," she said.

"Those lilies are young," Wilma retorted.

"I thought you were getting a divorce," Oralee said.

"Is there a better time to buy underwear?"

The sound of laughter came into the room through the open door to the hall, and the smell of crawfish and red pepper rose up the stairwell. Wilma bent over and unlaced her Nikes, lining them up just under the dust ruffle on her side of the bed. Then she removed her windbreaker and shirt and laid them in a pile on the bed. Standing up, she unzipped her jeans and pulled them down her hips. It felt like peeling away old skin. She was stiff in every joint. Her eyes burned, and her skin was wind-whipped and dry from the speed she'd been holding, from sleepless nights on the road and roaring grinding gears and goddamn gut-wrench braking behind jerkoff four-wheelers cutting her off at the exits. And that wasn't the half of it. Her ears hurt from the whine and crackle of CB voices, raucous laughter, the mean remarks and propositions that were nothing but raw assaults. Wilma reached back to pull the hair up off her neck, wrapped it into a coil, and pinned it up. She liked the look—firm and round and romantic, like old-timey paintings.

As the water rushed into the tub she paced her old bedroom looking for clues. The big surprise was a large picture book about bird and animal behavior. Into the pages of this five-pound book someone, presumably Vernon, had stuck strips of notebook paper on which messages were written. "Peregrines," "Redtails," "Buteos." There was a red line drawn under everything in the section on falcons. Wilma picked up a reprint of a medieval treatise on hood design dating back to twelfth-century France. Falcons were obviously his major passion. In addition Vernon had developed several significant new hobbies in Wilma's absence. He had books on herb gardening, Cajun cookery, Japanese flower arranging, Hatha Yoga, and Swedish massage. There were also some mysterious pieces of gear: fifteen wire cylinders stacked like logs under a window in the corner of the bedroom. Wilma imagined they were somehow related to falconry and Louisiana cooking, though the connection was hazy.

She lay down on the bed nude, her hands propping her chin, and stared at the stacked rolls for a good while.

After a few minutes she opened her eyes and rattled around in a stack of magazines on a wicker hamper next to the tub. A plastic photo album lay underneath issues of *Texas Parks and Wildlife* and *Audubon*. Another surprise. Wilma didn't know Vernon had a camera. Opening the album, she had to giggle. The first few pages were filled with snapshots of Vernon in a pair of hip boots, wading in a rice field. Then there were snapshots of Vernon sitting in a flat-bottomed skiff with Devel Edwards sitting in the bow and Vernon with his arm around Devel and Jeanette in front of their house. Marie must have taken that one because on the next page she was holding up a long string of sausage links from Devel's hogs. There were a lot more pictures of Marie in the album, sitting in the skiff, dressed up in a pair of red jeans and a peasant blouse, and on a horse behind Vernon with her arms around his waist.

"Why are you going home?" Oralee had asked before they left Boston. They were standing outside the old South Station, which looked like a cross between the capitol building in Austin and a federal penitentiary. Wilma sat down on the top step and watched the passing traffic, feeling like an amputee at a track meet.

"Because it's home, I guess, and I've lost everything else in the world. Except my friends." Wilma threw her arms wide. "I need a hug," she said, and Oralee came over and kneeled down on the step in front of her. The two women embraced.

"But I thought you left Vernon because he was a loser, a do-nothing dreamer, a sleaze bag who stole your money when you needed it. I thought you were running the road in the other direction. What happened to freedom?"

Wilma put her hands on Oralee's shoulders and smiled a peaked little smile.

"La Migra got it," she said.

22

HER FREEDOM WAS LOCKED UP with Jessie Louise behind a seven-foot chainlink fence in Boston. It hadn't taken twenty minutes for the federal judge to reach a decision. The hearing had been set for ten. At nine-thirty Wilma, Oralee, and the two lawyers were shivering in a small, dim room in the John F. Kennedy Federal Building downtown. They sat in the last row back so Wilma's lawyer and the United States attorney could work out a deal.

Chip Elkins, the *pro bono* lawyer assigned to her case, wore a brown tweed jacket and a blue shirt with a shredded collar. The prosecutor, Pimenta, was natty in a brown pinstripe. The two men leaned against the wall, talking fast and earnestly.

"For God's sake, Pete, she didn't make a dime," Elkins said. "She was driving for the Catholics."

"I don't care if she was a fuckin' nun. She was transporting aliens, and that, in case you've lost your marbles, Chipper boy, is still a felony." Pimenta combed his fingers through thick gray and black curls.

Chip shot a quick look at Wilma and Oralee, mouthing the words "We're okay." He put an arm around Pimenta's shoulder. "Why not let her plead guilty, go for a cease and desist? You can tell she's had it. She can hardly wait to get back home and get into her soaps."

"You do and I'll enroll you in Christian Couples," Oralee whispered. They'd been assured the judge would go easy on Oralee because she was young and new at smuggling.

When the judge bounced into the room everybody moved up closer to the bench. Everything went as expected. Pete and Chip huddled with the judge, a blue-eyed man with a white pompadour. Once Wilma heard him say, "Now, I don't want to be a shithead about this," and she thought they were in the clear until an officer walked in from a side door and said another witness was waiting outside.

When the judge gave his assent a short man in a navy-blue suit trotted into the room. Pete and the prosecuting attorney looked at each other and shrugged. Chip swung around, faced Wilma, held his hands palms down, and moved them through the air as if smoothing troubled water.

"Not to worry," he had told her. "Judges don't like convicting nice ladies of federal crimes. It makes them look bad." If she kept quiet and let him do most of the talking she'd probably get off with probation, maybe even a cease and desist.

She didn't know why García couldn't cease and desist. Even with his back to her, even knowing she'd lost him, Wilma felt her heart rev up to three thousand. They hadn't spoken since the bridge.

"Get on with it," the judge said.

The man in blue was representing Wild Goose, he said. "James Peterkin, Your Honor. The Houston office flew me up here to clear the record. Wild Goose has nothing to do with this alien traffic. Mrs. Hemshoff was carrying on her operation under our noses and behind our backs."

"Neat trick," the judge said, raising an eyebrow. He could have done without the news.

García sat in the front row, shoulders rigid, face front. He never even looked at Wilma.

The judge had to hit her with everything. Instead of cease and desist she got a $2,000 fine. The truck was impounded. She'd have to make it home hammer-down and lonely without her wheels.

When voices downstairs woke her at ten, Wilma stretched her arm to Vernon's side of the bed. Finding only pillows, she opened her eyes. She could hear him roaring at someone below.

"I told you those traps had to be checked and baited ever' day. And you had to take the weekend off. The redfish were running off Matagorda so you don't say a whisper to nobody, just light out on your own leaving a thousand pounds of live fish in the traps we coulda shipped to San Antonio yesterday if we'da had 'em. Hell and damn."

Whoever it was made some response she couldn't hear.

"I don't give a good lead sinker how many days straight you been workin'. You're either workin' for me or you ain't. Get it?"

"What do you want me to do?" she asked him after he'd made her coffee, Louisiana chicory. It tasted like the inside of a horse's hoof. Vernon was sitting on the back porch in a folding lawn chair with a fifty-gallon Coleman cooler full of crabs. Every five minutes he reached in and pulled another pair of claws out of the packed ice and started working on it with a metal cracker.

302

He looked at her with guileless blue eyes. "How do you mean, sugar?"

"There's been some changes around here. I mean I feel like a fifth wheel, and I'm wondering if you want me to stay."

"Well, sugar, I sure don't want you to feel uncomfortable. What can I do for you?" He tossed a nice hunk of white crabmeat into a bowl next to his foot.

"Well, you could give me something to do, so I don't feel like I'm in your way. You could ask me about my life. You could sleep in the same bed with me." Wilma stopped because she could hear a whine creep into her words.

Vernon's voice was gentle. "Like you just said, there's been some changes."

"Funny," Wilma said. "I always thought it was Ruby."

"I know," Vernon said. "I tried to tell you it was nothing serious."

Wilma had a sense of unreality about the conversation. It sounded like *As the World Turns.* "What do you want me to do, Vernon?" she asked again. She was hearing a sound like the wind rushing by outside the truck window, only this time it was the sound of García leaving her, and Vernon. She stood there leaning against one of the posts supporting the roof, and the roaring was like the sound a conch shell makes held against an ear. It occurred to Wilma that what she was hearing was the sound of her own speedy departures. It was a hard habit to break.

She was way out on an empty prairie, with nothing but this roaring in her head. She wished she had Oralee's faith, a fine and hopeful stuff that could sparkle on life like April rain.

"There's nothing that gets me down for long," Oralee had told her over and over. "See, he's on my side. He's at my right hand. I can tell you're searching, Wilma," she said.

"Yeah, I may be searching, and I may be tired, but I know it isn't Jesus," Wilma said.

A coyote made five hundred a head moving live freight. At that rate, Wilma could've made $60,000 if she'd done it for hire, but she'd refused what Standish offered. Out of her thirty-odd runs she hadn't made a thin dime. Now she didn't feel so strong. She was forty-four. She had traveled maybe 250,000 miles in two years. That was the same as going around the world ten times. It was the distance between Little Egypt and the moon.

Vernon stood up, holding the bowl of crabmeat.

"You can come with me out to the field to pick up the traps, if you want," he said. Wilma followed him into the kitchen, where he opened the refrigerator and slid the crabmeat in next to a couple of five-gallon kettles of gumbo. He grabbed his red billed cap from the kitchen table and pulled it low over his eyes. The cap had KING HEMSHOFF'S CRAWFISH KINGDOM printed on its front.

"How does it feel to be king?" Wilma said.

"Tired," Vernon said. "Worried. Not enough hours in the day." He held the door of the pickup open for Wilma. It was a new one-ton GMC.

"Nice four-wheeler," Wilma said. "Where's the field where the crawfish live?"

"Lissie, remember? It's rice land, sixty acres with a graveyard on it."

She had known this once and forgotten it. "And now you've flooded that little cemetery and those graves have crawfish crawling all over 'em. Ugh," Wilma said. "You look out. Somebody'll come around to haunt you one of these nights."

Vernon's smile was a little dog-eared. "I turned that little patch of land into a hundred-and-seventy-five-thousand-dollar investment. You don't think anybody'd hold it against me, do you?" He told her how it had started from the first flooding after the harvest, when he'd seeded the land with a thousand dollars' worth of baby crawfish and begun a regular program of experimenting with different kinds of food. He swung the truck off the paved highway and onto a gravel road with rice fields on either side. The fields were empty now, but there were signs somebody had been out there with a harrow preparing the land for spring planting.

Wilma wondered if Vernon were as tough-minded and rational as he sounded about losing the farm. She remembered his face, sun-reddened, the fine dust from the combine clinging to his skin, softening his features like the gentlest fur. Sometimes at the end of the day she'd drive out with one of the kids in the car, and run out into the middle of the rice, which was up to her waist and brassy gold, so dry as her skirt brushed it that it crackled as if it were on fire. She'd wait as he spun the wheel in the turn row and headed in her direction, his head and shoulders backlit by the lowering sun.

Vernon stopped the truck on a culvert across an irrigation ditch, where the road took a sharp right and ended at a barbed-wire fence.

"This is it?" She could see way off in the distance the half-acre patch with a wire fence around it where the graves were. Beyond the barbed wire were soggy rice stubble and a lot of muddy water with a few levees snaking through it like giant mole tunnels. Vernon reached into the back of the pickup and took out a pair of green hip boots, sat down again in the truck, and started pulling them on over his khaki pants. He huffed and puffed a little over his belly.

"What are you going to do?" Wilma asked. "Are we going to slosh around in all that water?"

Vernon shook his head. "Don't you see that Go-Devil over there?"

"What in the world is a Go-Devil?"

It was a flat-bottomed skiff, like a bass boat, only the motor had a long drive shaft and a propeller that pushed along through the mud on the bottom. It was obviously built for very shallow water, and pulled up on the bank it looked like nobody in all its history had ever taken soap and water to it. Wilma glanced down at her white pointy-toed tennis shoes and her aquamarine Bermuda shorts.

"I guess I didn't wear the right stuff," she said. Vernon reached into the pickup and handed her his wire-mesh folding seat. She could see him observing her calves.

"That'll keep your bottom clean," he said. He pulled out an Igloo cooler and placed it in the bottom of the skiff along with a twenty-gallon washtub. Pushing the skiff out into the water, he held it for Wilma to step in.

"I haven't been in a boat for years," she said, stepping gingerly over the side so her white shoes wouldn't get messed. She sat on one of the thwart seats in the middle of the boat. Vernon waded out until the water was up to his knees.

"Get way over on the other side so I won't sink us," he said. Wilma moved, but Vernon's weight as he clambered over the other side made the skiff rock alarmingly. She gave a little yelp of fear and gripped the gunwale till her knuckles whitened.

"Relax, woman, we're all right," Vernon said, a little breathless from the effort. He settled himself on the seat in the stern, turned and pulled on the starter string several times. The five-horsepower motor roared its tinny roar, and the boat backed further out into the pond. It was high noon. A brisk wind blew out of the north, rippling the muddy water, and a few geese passed a half mile high overhead.

"You ever go hunting anymore, Vernon?" Wilma asked.

"I got a blind on the north end, sunk down in the mud," he said, "but I hardly ever shoot it. Hunting's for kids." He reached under his seat and took out a fishing rod. "There's some good-sized bass out here. I always bring a nice mess home when I clean out the traps."

They moved along slowly until Wilma saw a row of white Styrofoam squares bobbing in the water. Vernon cut the motor until they were almost drifting past the floats, and he could reach over the side, pull out the wire cylinders and shake the contents into the washtub. The first time he dumped a half-dozen crawfish at Wilma's feet she shrieked as if he'd poured a bucketful of rattlesnakes into her lap. The crawfish, a dark greenish black, gleamed mysteriously, as if they had climbed out of the earth's original ooze. Some were lying on their backs, their legs waving fruitlessly, pincers thrashing from side to side. Others were crawling over the backs of their companions. If they hadn't looked so ugly Wilma might have been able to work up some compassion.

"I know they're an important food source, Vernon," she said, "but can't you do something about the way they look?"

"I guarantee, after a dinner at my place you'll be tearing off those heads and laying in five pounds an hour. Just you wait." Wilma's stomach turned over at the idea. The crawfish had a powerful fishy smell. It was going to be a long afternoon.

They didn't talk much. Vernon baited his hook with a lure and trolled lackadaisically behind the boat, casting out and reeling in about once every half hour and each time pulling a long strip of bright green weed off the silver spoon. Once or twice he got a bite, but it was too sunny, even starting to get hot by four, and the bass were hiding in the deep shade alongside the levees. Several times Wilma lifted a trap into the boat and emptied the crawfish into the galvanized tub. The trap, filled with water, weighed eight or ten pounds, not including the crawfish. In two hours they must have pulled in a hundred, so the washtub was filled with a shiny green mass of waving legs and feelers and pincers.

"I'm gonna have nightmares about giant crawfish mothers." Wilma wiped a strand of her hair away from her eyes, using her damp forearm. By now she'd gotten so she could stand up in the bottom of the skiff without rocking it or losing her balance.

"Vernon, what's that wig stand in the bedroom?" she asked.

"That's for Sweet Crystal Marie."

"Well, I met Marie, and I think she's too big for it," Wilma said.

"Sweet Baby Crystal Marie is my hunting hawk. Prettiest peregrine falcon you ever laid eyes on. She wears the hood when I take her out. I pull it off when I let her fly off my arm after some poor unsuspecting owl. I been reading about these birds in an old, old book by someone named Frederick of Hohenstaufer. This fellow lived in the middle ages, Will, and he liked these falcons so much he built a lot of small castles for them. He'd bring all his friends out and hunt a few times a year so he could show his birds off and his velvet hunting suit with a codpiece. I'll show you the book when I get home."

"How often's the restaurant open, Vernon?" Wilma asked. Five nights a week, he told her, and six days for lunch.

"Who's doing all that work?" As it turned out, he told her, it was the whole community. Everybody pitched in, because it was the restaurant that was keeping a lot of them out of trouble. He reminded her about the meddling Health Department and County Welfare people, Lydia and the others who'd threatened him and half the neighbors with citations and who told Miss Cornelia she was too old to live alone.

"We had us a time," Vernon said. "Once or twice I nearly gave up and moved into an old folks' home myself, just to get rid of those Welfare pigs."

The washtub was full. By the looks of the sun it was around five, but Vernon didn't seem in any hurry to go back to the truck. He cast a few times, reeled in, cast again. Wilma sat with her elbows propped on her knees, chin in her hands, staring at the water. A couple of swallows swooped low over the pond, doing barrel rolls for fun. On the surface of the water some big diamond-shaped water bugs snapped their legs together and scooted across like jet boats. Wilma wondered how long it had been since she had time to stare into pond water and watch the bugs fool around in there.

"Want a beer?" Vernon asked. "I got sandwiches, too." Wilma nodded, and he fished in the cooler and handed her a little package in waxed paper. She unwrapped the peanut-butter-and-honey sandwich and sipped on the beer. Now there were a good many swallows skimming the water, catching mosquitoes.

"Shouldn't we get these babies into some ice?" Wilma asked.

"No rush," Vernon said. "Tell me what happened to the truck."

"Jessie Louise is in jail," Wilma said. "Busted."

"What for?"

"I was transporting illegal aliens, Vernon," she said. She waited for him to explode, but he just made another cast over the port side. He reeled in his line.

"What'd you get out of it?"

"Good question," Wilma said. "For a while I think it gave me a reason to keep on driving the truck. It felt good having people depending on me."

"You didn't make anything from it?"

She shook her head.

"There were these people, Vernon, traveling all the way from jungle towns, trying to get someplace where their kids didn't find bodies on the way to school."

"I didn't know you cared about politics, Wilma," Vernon said. "I thought you were just interested in your sewing and the soaps." He looked at her under the cap and grinned. "Guess that just goes to show."

"But it wasn't politics," Wilma said. Then she told him the story about the first wetbacks she hadn't even meant to pick up, about the baby wandering out into the highway and her running after it, and how the baby felt.

"The thing is," Vernon said, "you can't hang on to those babies. I was counting on you, Wilma, and you took off."

"I know it," she said, and it wasn't an apology.

"There's a lot in this world to keep you interested," he said. Vernon reeled in the line. She could hear the little drippy sound of the lure splashing through water.

She wasn't sure what it meant, anymore, having a mate, being married. The children weren't there to hold you together, and sex wasn't enough glue.

When the moon rose over the pond there was still plenty of pink in the sky. Vernon handed Wilma his Levi jacket, and she put it on and huddled on the hard pine seat with her knees starting to knock together a little from the chill. But she wouldn't have moved, wouldn't have wanted to be anywhere else in the world but in the Go-Devil with Vernon at the dead middle of that pond, watching the moon climb the January sky.

"It's almost full," Vernon said, pointing to the three-quarter moon that looked a little like a football at this stage, its sides coming together into points.

Wilma liked this moon better than the full. There was something satisfying about its asymmetry, the smudges on its face that seemed to shift each time she looked. The moon hung in the sky not far from Orion and the Bear, and it seemed to her she could see the stars pass behind it in a steady slide from the earth's rotation.

"The world's rolling," she told Vernon. "I can see it."

"Nobody can. The earth's too big," he said. "You're crazy, Wilma."

"I may be crazy," she told him, "but I'm buyin' a new truck."

He cast again. "Yeah? And use what for money?"

Her elbows on her knees, she looked at him mildly. "I'm countin' on you," she said, "payin' back the money you stole."

He let this stand a few moments. "Shoot. Why can't you relax awhile, Wilma, live a regular life?"

"But this *is* my regular life, Vernon," Wilma said.

He didn't respond, but cast once more into the pond, the pink reflection fading now to a cool blue mauve as the bright bars in the sky fell apart. Something on the bank rustled its wings.

Wilma wanted something to happen just then, she wasn't sure what. She didn't know what Vernon expected. She expected she'd have to keep moving, taking the long step out the door, reaching for the grab rail. Maybe she'd gotten used to leaving and could never stop for more than a month or two because she couldn't stand the house filled with strangers. There wasn't enough air.

As the light went, the frogs grew shrill, intense, like the sound of metal clickers on Halloween.

"You stayin' long this time?" Vernon said.

"Long enough to do gumbo," she said, grinning in the dark.

"It's not enough," Vernon said.

"Enough what?"

"Hugging. Cooking."

"Want to take a run to Alaska when the permafrost melts?" she said.